Praise for
DANGEROUS ALLIANCE

"Charming and fun. Replete with intrigue, grand parties, and romantic entanglements, fans of Jane Austen will positively devour this book."
—Jessica Cluess, author of *A Shadow Bright and Burning*

"Romance fans and Jane Austen devotees will devour this delicious Regency romp."
—Alexa Donne, author of *Brightly Burning* and *The Stars We Steal*

"Bathed in Cohen's richly textured language, *Dangerous Alliance* is a tale that boldly shines a light on issues women struggled with historically: abuse, obstruction, and dominance. The hunger to overcome these plights is what makes the story timeless."
—Shelley Sackier, author of *The Antidote* and *The Freemason's Daughter*

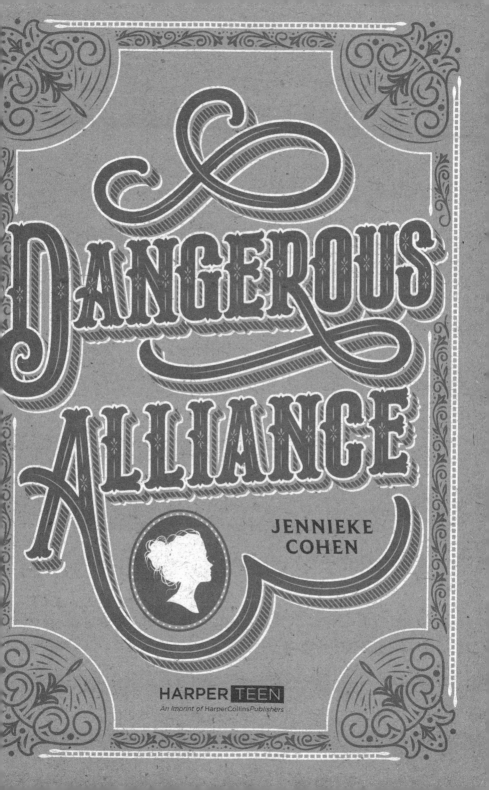

DANGEROUS ALLIANCE

JENNIEKE COHEN

HARPER TEEN
An Imprint of HarperCollinsPublishers

HarperTeen is an imprint of HarperCollins Publishers.
Dangerous Alliance
Copyright © 2019 by Jennieke Cohen

Library of Congress Cataloging-in-Publication Data

Names: Cohen, Jennieke, author.
Title: Dangerous alliance / Jennieke Cohen.
Description: First edition. | New York, NY : HarperTeen, [2019] | Summary: Lady
    Victoria Aston, obsessed with Jane Austen and content to stay home, is suddenly
    expected to enter society and find a husband, preferably one who cares for her more
    than her dowry.
Identifiers: LCCN 2019021104 | ISBN 978-0-06-285730-9 (hardback)
Subjects: | CYAC: Aristocracy (Social class)—Fiction. | Marriage—Fiction. | Great
    Britain—History—George III, 1760-1820—Fiction.
Classification: LCC PZ7.1.C6396 Dan 2019 | DDC [Fic]—dc23 LC record available
    at https://lccn.loc.gov/2019021104

Typography by Jessie Gang
19 20 21 22 23 PC/LSCH 10 9 8 7 6 5 4 3 2 1
❖
First Edition

For Jonathan Cohen and Nasson,
who both always knew this day would come.
Here's to the next adventure!

DANGEROUS ALLIANCE

CHAPTER THE FIRST

The danger, however, was at present so unperceived, that
they did not by any means rank as misfortunes with her.
—Jane Austen, *Emma*

April 1817

Oakbridge Estate, Hampshire, England

The lichen-kissed stone dropped onto the rock pile with a hollow clack. Lady Victoria Aston rested her aching hands on the rough stone. She wiped her muddy palms down the front of her thighs, smearing muck onto her father's old tan breeches. When attempting to save the lives of a particularly bothersome flock of sheep, one had to make sacrifices.

With two more sizable stones, she would close the gap in the wall. Then she could scour Oakbridge's 6,562 acres for the estate shepherd. Vicky narrowed her eyes at a shaggy old ewe: one of many she'd found out-of-bounds in the neighboring pasture. They'd jumped over the crumbling gap and gobbled a patch of indigestible clover. Soon, their bellies would bloat, and without the shepherd's aid, they would certainly perish.

Inhaling the clean morning air, redolent with the perfume of freshly drying grass, Vicky bent for another rock. This would never have happened to Emma Woodhouse. Or rather, Emma Woodhouse would never have *let* it happen to her.

Having just finished reading *Emma* for the third time since its publication, Vicky had lately found herself comparing her own country existence to the heroine of said novel. Not that Emma was her favorite heroine from the four novels written by the author known only to the public as "a lady" (but whom most of the local Hampshire society knew to be one Miss Jane Austen). No, Vicky reserved that honor for Miss Elizabeth Bennet of *Pride and Prejudice*.

A clear picture of Elizabeth Bennet muddying her gown to fix a stone wall darted into Vicky's mind—after all, Elizabeth had walked miles unaccompanied to see her sister, Jane, when she was ill and staying at Netherfield. Vicky's lips curved into a smile at the idea that her favorite heroine would approve of her behavior.

As Vicky straightened, movement far in the distance caught her eye. She squinted. Amid the emerald-green fields on the other side of the wall, a rider in a russet coat and dark hat cantered adjacent to a short hedgerow. She couldn't see his face, but his bearing looked familiar. She blinked.

Surely, it wasn't the *one* person she had no wish to see on such a morning. Fate wouldn't be so cruel.

She glanced down at her father's muddy breeches. They didn't exactly outline her legs, but they weren't particularly loose either. They hugged her hips just tightly enough to allow her to tuck a muslin shirt into them and actually stay up without other assistance. She'd buttoned the top half of her olive-green riding habit almost up to her neck for a semblance of decency, but by any stranger's standard, she was courting scandal.

She peered at the rider again. His attire proclaimed him a gentleman, and although she still couldn't make out his features, he rode a peculiar chestnut of medium height that looked something like a working horse. She had never seen the breed before.

Well, if he—whoever he was—felt scandalized by her appearance, that was his affair. Breeches afforded more comfort on her post-dawn inspections across the estate and allowed her to ride astride. That meant she could be more efficient helping her father, especially when something went wrong, like today. Their management strategies shouldered the livelihoods of more than a hundred individuals; if her father or his steward couldn't allocate funds or attention to one small piece of the puzzle making up the estate, someone less fortunate would suffer. Vicky helped wherever and whenever she could.

She hauled the stone up and set it on the pile with an involuntary squeak before glancing back at the rider.

He had jumped the hedgerow. Now he rode toward her, picking up speed. *What was he—*

Vicky's stomach tensed as his face came into focus. It was just as she'd feared: the rider was Tom Sherborne. Blast! She looked at her breeches again and winced.

Still some fifty feet away, Tom raised his hand and something fluttered in her chest. But he wasn't greeting her as she'd thought. With his whole arm, he pointed at something behind her.

She frowned. As she turned, something hard collided with the side of her head. White-hot pain burst through her skull. Her vision pitched sideways and her neck whipped to the right. As her knees smacked into the soggy turf, everything went black.

A rhythmic thudding invaded Vicky's head. Was it her heart? The rumble grew louder with each thump. She inhaled, and the smell of wet grass, mud, and sheep droppings flooded her nostrils. She groaned and forced her eyes open.

Her head sat askew on the ground, though it seemed she'd fallen face-first. A tender spot on the side of her head made her wince. She traced it with careful fingers, but that only intensified the pounding in her ears.

What had struck her? Through the blades of grass, a blurred movement caught her eye. Each motion was an agony, but Vicky pushed herself off the soggy ground with both hands until she sat upright. Blinking to clear her vision, she concentrated on the moving shape coming toward her.

Her cheeks blanched. The horse and rider she'd seen earlier—correction, Tom Sherborne and his horse—effortlessly jumped the stone wall. Her stomach dropped.

She'd never seen Tom riding at such an early hour—not a single time since he'd returned to England. Although his own estate bordered Oakbridge, she'd only glimpsed him twice in the last year: once in the village from opposite ends of the high street where he'd promptly disappeared into a tavern, and once at the village fair where he'd bought a gingerbread square and promptly ridden away.

Anyone else might have considered these circumstances coincidental, but Vicky knew better. She *knew* Tom Sherborne was avoiding her. *Unjustly* in point of fact, and he had been doing so for the last five years. Yet there he sat, reining in his odd-looking chestnut a mere two and a half feet away.

"Are you all right?" he bellowed from the saddle.

Her head whirled as she stared up at the face she'd known so well as a child. His hair fell in the same mahogany-brown waves around his forehead and ears, contrasting slightly with his light brown eyes. He was clean-shaven just as he'd been at fourteen, but his jaw and cheeks now had the angular sharpness of a man. His nose and forehead could have been copied from a marble bust of some Roman emperor.

Her pulse thrummed in her ears, so she pulled in a breath. "Er..."

His lips compressed into a frown, and his dark brows knit together.

How she'd missed that serious countenance. Yet that boy she'd known had thrown away their friendship and never given her a reason.

"My head," she muttered. She touched the lump materializing on her skull. "What happened?" She swallowed several times and wished for a glass of water.

"A man attacked you. I tried to warn you."

"What do you mean, 'attacked'? Who would possibly attack me?" She touched her head again.

Tom caught her eye for a brief moment before looking off into the distance behind her. "Whoever he was, he had a horse tethered at the edge of the trees."

Vicky shook her head. "But why—I don't understand—"

"I can still catch him," Tom interrupted. "Are you well enough to stay here?"

She inhaled and tilted her head gingerly. The pain had dulled a bit. "I think so." She looked up at him. "What do you mean stay—"

"*Stay* here," he repeated, kicking his boots into his horse's flanks. Clods of grass and mud flew into the air as they raced away.

"Wait!" But his horse had already carried him out of earshot.

Vicky clenched her jaw as she watched horse and rider disappear into a nearby copse of trees. How dare Tom hurry off and leave her sitting in a field? Especially if someone had attacked her! Well, if he thought she'd allow him to fight her battles for her, he was very much mistaken. She bent her knees and pushed herself off the ground. Stars reeled before her eyes. She swallowed an unladylike curse as she drew in a deep breath. Then she glanced in the direction Tom had disappeared.

If Tom had ridden that way, her attacker must have fled toward the road to London. If that were his goal, then the fastest way to head him off would be to ride across the field *around* the trees and intercept him. Tom should know as well as she did that he would never overtake the man by following him through the dense forest.

But she still could. Moreover, she was not about to sit here like an invalid just because her head hurt. Who did Tom think he was, trying to act the hero now? He'd been the one playing the coward these last five years.

Vicky stumbled to the tree where she'd tied her horse, Jilly. She unwound the reins, led her to an undamaged stretch of wall, and used it to jump into the saddle. A wave of dizziness washed through her head down into her stomach. She stilled and breathed, fully aware she was losing time.

Just get moving. Vicky gritted her teeth, pulled the reins to the right, kicked Jilly's flanks, and urged her to gallop across the field toward the attacker.

Jilly's ears pricked up, almost as though she sensed the urgency of the situation. They crossed the field in record time. The wind whipped Vicky's loose hair back as she steered Jilly around the edge of the trees. Her heart hammered in her chest. Would she catch the villain before he reached the road to London?

Vicky scanned ahead, her gaze narrowing in on the country lane that fed into the London post road. She glanced to the left, where Tom and the attacker should emerge. She couldn't see them yet, but they would soon arrive.

The thundering of hooves reached her ears.

With a satisfied breath, Vicky urged Jilly forward until they reached the edge of the road. But what could she do now that she had positioned herself in front of the chase? She looked around for something to give her an advantage. Just a smattering of broken twigs and dead leaves lay scattered on the road; she couldn't see one fallen branch or throwable rock—nothing she could use to slow the assailant.

Several yards farther down, trees lined her side of the road. Opposite those trees, a tall, overgrown hedgerow began. If she could maneuver Jilly to stand across the road in that narrow space, the man would have to stop. She guided her horse to the spot and made her stand so her head was near the hedgerow. The gap wasn't as narrow as it had looked. Just enough space for the man to maneuver around them remained, although there certainly wasn't enough width for a horse galloping at full speed.

Pummeling horse hooves resounded up through the earth as a man with a handkerchief tied around his nose and mouth charged down the road toward her, his black greatcoat flapping in the wind like the cape of a demonic villain straight from the pages of one of Mrs. Radcliffe's preposterous romances. Vicky's stomach quavered. It was too late to question her plan. Tom and his stocky horse followed close at the man's back.

Vicky swallowed hard. The man wasn't slowing.

She tightened her grip on the reins, causing Jilly to totter beneath her. She pressed her knees into Jilly's flanks, trying to steady her, but Jilly only jittered more. The horse sensed her fear.

Vicky closed her eyes and breathed. "Stand, Jilly. Stand and stay." Beneath her, the horse stilled. Vicky's eyes flew open in triumph, but as she looked to the side, the man still barreled down the road.

Only a few yards separated them now; they were so close she could see white foam outlining the horse's mouth. The man's eyes narrowed. He was not going to stop.

"Move," Tom shouted. "Move!"

In that moment, time slowed to a crawl. She wanted to listen, but she could no longer feel her legs. All she felt was her pounding heart and the leather of the reins cutting into her palms. The man would hit her!

Vicky closed her eyes, waiting for the impact. Then Jilly reared up on her hind legs, and the back of her head slammed into Vicky's face. Sparks clouded her vision as the weightlessness disappeared and a wave of dizziness took its place. A rush of air blew past her as the assailant and his horse careened in front of them. Then she was falling, falling until she landed with a bone-jarring thud onto a muddy patch of ground.

Vicky blinked. Once. Twice.

She vaguely knew Jilly hadn't yet trampled her, and through the pain and nausea, she forced herself to look to ensure she was in no more danger.

To her left, Tom pulled back hard on his reins to keep from colliding with Jilly. For a terrifying moment, Vicky thought he wouldn't be able to stop his horse. The muscles in the horse's legs bulged and its shoulders strained until it skidded to a halt merely feet away.

Vicky slumped back onto the ground in relief, not remembering the road's damp condition until her hair squished in the mud. Ugh.

Of the countless embarrassing moments in all her seventeen years, this one secured the prize for most ghastly.

Tom's mount pawed the ground with its front hooves. The horse's hind legs clenched in anticipation, intent on continuing the chase. Evidently considering it, Tom pulled the reins sideways to make his horse go around her.

Hope surged through her. Falling off her horse in such a useless fashion had dealt her dignity a serious blow, but if he continued on, at least she'd be spared the humiliation of conversing with him while caked in mud. To encourage him to leave, she pushed herself to sit upright, but an involuntary hiss of pain escaped her.

Tom cursed and jumped to the ground. "I cannot believe your

recklessness! Are you incapable of doing as you're told?"

Anger bloomed in her cheeks as she gaped up at him. He hadn't said one word to her in five years, and now he was berating her?

She squelched back the urge to lie down and cry. This wasn't supposed to happen. During the last fourteen months since Tom had returned to England and settled in at Halworth Hall, Vicky had prepared herself for their first meeting. She'd known it would happen eventually, with him living only miles away, and the prospect of speaking with him again had actually kept her in alternating states of excitement and nervous anticipation for weeks. Yet despite her nerves she had wisely planned for their meeting. As her sister, Althea, often said: planning was the mark of an evolved individual.

So Vicky had intended to be perfectly composed when she met Tom again—absolutely radiant in her favorite pale pink, satin ball gown—and graciously allow him to take her hand as he bowed in greeting. He would see she was no longer the improper little girl he'd deemed unworthy to be his friend.

She bit her lip until it throbbed. At the moment, she certainly wasn't doing a brilliant job of showing him how grown-up she was. The backs of her eyes started to prickle. No. She absolutely would not cry.

She lifted her chin and tried to look regal despite her pathetic, muddied position. "I do not take orders, Lord Halworth. Despite what you may recall, I am not a child."

"And I suppose many ladies lie down in puddles and dart about the countryside after they've been attacked by a madman."

She looked around her as though she'd only now realized where she sat. "Oh! Well, I may spend every pleasant spring day in mud puddles from now on! Doing so might be good for one's constitution, I daresay."

He blinked in surprise or annoyance, she couldn't decide which. Then his frown deepened. "How can you be so indifferent? You were knocked unconscious, fell off your bloody horse, were nearly trampled by mine—"

"There's no need to rehash it." She straightened to her full height, or as full as she could manage while seated. "My memory was not damaged in the fall."

He scowled. Then he looked away and looped his horse's reins through a branch in the hedgerow.

She sighed. He was right, after all. She'd been foolish. "I thought I could head the ruffian off. Which I succeeded in, by the way! I didn't bargain on him refusing to stop."

"How likely was it he'd stop to avoid harming you when that was clearly his original purpose?"

She exhaled. Blast him for his indisputable logic! She'd acted rashly and now fate was punishing her with this humiliating confrontation. If experience had taught her anything, it was that an apology went a long way. Nevertheless, her eyes narrowed when her mind tried to formulate the words.

"I am just as capable a rider as you are. As I recall, I bested you many times in the past and—"

"You. Fell. Off," he interrupted, "not I."

She wrinkled her nose but held his gaze. He was so insufferably . . . correct. Yet she absolutely refused to be cowed by his reasoning. If he thought she was about to apologize for something so inconsequential as this when he hadn't apologized for the past, he was sorely mistaken. She raised her chin even higher.

"I should go. I must tell my father about the brute who assaulted me. Not to mention tell our shepherd the sheep have gotten into the clover in your field *and* inform the steward about the wall." She slowly put one foot on the ground to stand up. "So, if you and my friend the puddle will excuse me . . ."

He seized her arms and leaned back until she stood. But when she was steady, he didn't release her. She couldn't bring herself to look into his eyes again, but as she stood there, the heat of his hands seeped through the leather of his riding gloves into her forearms. Warmth spread across her neck despite the chill leaching into her legs and shoulders from the mud. She stared into his white cravat, which was nothing more than the simplest knot, and realized he stood half a head taller than she remembered.

He pulled at her left arm, and her body pivoted to the side. The scent of toast, newspaper ink, and something else—cinnamon?— wafted toward her as he stepped closer. She craned her neck up in confusion and realized he'd turned her to inspect her from behind. His eyes traveled down her mud-caked, respectably clad back to her mud-coated breeches now adhering to her thighs. Blood rushed to her cheeks.

"What are you—"

"You need a physician. Where do you hurt the most?" he asked, turning her forward to catch her attention.

She cleared her throat. He'd been inspecting her for injuries.

What else would he be doing, you ninny?

His brows were pinched in the middle, his brown eyes serious. She could almost swear he looked concerned. For *her*.

Then his gaze shot away, and she remembered he'd been the one to toss her aside as though nearly thirteen years of friendship had meant nothing.

She tugged her arms away from him, but his grip did not loosen. "I am quite well. You needn't trouble yourself."

His eyes bored into hers. "If you think I'll let you gallop all over creation alone after you . . ." He looked away and released her. Her arms fell to her sides. "After you made me lose that criminal, then you are mistaken."

She felt her ears burning now. He may be right about her getting in his way, but it wasn't very gentlemanly of him to keep reiterating it. "You wouldn't have caught him anyway. He was lengths ahead."

He glared at her again, his eyes hard. "I was close enough to almost run you over. I *would* have caught him, Victoria." His cold stare made her want to squirm.

"We could debate this matter for the rest of the day, to be sure. If you wish to inform the magistrate of this incident, please do so. I shall tell my father, but I must go now and attend to my responsibilities. Kindly step aside," she stated with a scowl she knew barely rivaled his for intensity.

Tom's jaw hardened. "Whether you care for my company or not, I *will* accompany you home."

She bit her lip. "That is . . . kind of you."

"As a gentleman I can do no less."

She bristled and turned away with an irritated huff. Of course. No real gentleman would leave an injured lady on a muddied stretch of road without ensuring her safety. But the way he'd phrased it implied she was no more than some stranger he'd encountered whom he felt duty-bound to assist.

In some ways, she supposed she was.

Ever since Tom had stopped responding to her letters in what would otherwise have been a lovely summer in the year '12, Vicky had wondered what she could have done to drive him away. She'd moped around the house for weeks and neither her parents nor her sister had been able to cheer her. Then Tom's father had banished him to the Continent. Vicky had no way to contact him, no way to fix things.

She'd gone about her life at Oakbridge and tried, rather unsuccessfully, to forget him. But when his father died last year and Tom returned home as the new Earl of Halworth, he'd taken every possible measure to avoid her—no small feat since their estates shared a mile-long border.

Fine. It was all perfectly agreeable to her. He'd cut *her* off, after all. If he didn't care for her company, then so be it.

She pressed her lips together. Who needed him anyway?

She moved toward Jilly and took her reins in hand. As she searched for a stump or rock to use as a mounting block, Tom walked behind her and offered his hands as a step. She sighed. She couldn't see another way to mount the horse. With a reluctant murmur of thanks, she jumped into the saddle, wincing at the pain in her backside.

Too mortified to do anything but look at the reins in her hands, she slumped in relief as he turned away.

She could pout at the unfairness of it all. She'd missed him so much during those years he'd been away; she'd missed their talks, their ill-advised adventures, and even their arguments. And now he was here, escorting her home—indeed, offering to help her—and all she wanted was for him to leave her alone.

She tried to imagine what her sister, who always knew just how to behave, would do in such a situation as this. Then she realized Althea would never find herself in such a situation. Vicky bit her lip, wondering what Elizabeth Bennet might do. But not one incident in *Pride and Prejudice* coincided to any degree with being knocked over the head by a masked man in a black greatcoat.

Vicky forced her spine straight. Surely any lady of society would be cordial and gracious if she found herself being escorted home by a gentleman who had tried to capture such a ruffian. So despite looking very little like a lady at the moment, and *despite* their past history, Vicky would act the same as any other lady. She absolutely would not broach the subject of him apologizing for forsaking her all those years ago. No, indeed. No matter how much she wanted to. No mature, evolved lady would do *that*.

Vicky raised her chin. In fact, she'd sooner ride her father's ox backward through the village on market day.

Peeking at Tom through her lashes, she noted the firm set of his jaw as he strode to his horse.

Her lips thinned to a tight line. She'd gotten along without him for years and would doubtless continue to do so for years to come.

Which was just as well; she suspected she'd be hopping onto that ox long before Tom apologized for anything.

Tom inhaled slowly as he walked to his horse, attempting to calm the thundering in his chest. He cursed under his breath and jumped astride Horatio.

The image of that masked man bludgeoning Vicky with a tree branch replayed in his mind, doing little to slow his pulse. The villain would have done it a second time if Tom hadn't yelled across the field and kicked his horse into action. The second blow surely would have done permanent harm.

No matter his intentions, the stranger had felt no compunction hurting Vicky to achieve them; a fact he'd doubly proven when he'd ridden straight toward her and *not* toward the gap between her horse and the trees. What the devil could it mean?

Tom ran his hand through his hair. He nudged Horatio forward and looked back. Vicky and her horse moved up beside him. Her hazel eyes focused straight ahead, refusing to meet his gaze. He assessed her horse. It walked along without any ill effects. Well . . . at least none that were visible. Unlike Vicky. She was almost certainly concussed after the blow to the head and the fall from her horse. By tomorrow she would likely be bruised all over.

He huffed out a breath and faced forward. He'd been a bloody idiot to imagine she'd stay where he'd told her. Maybe some part of him thought she would have grown up in the last five years—that she'd be able to listen to reason—but it seemed she'd changed little.

He glanced at her again. The cupid's bow of her lips was pursed, accentuating the chin that formed the point of her heart-shaped face. His eyes traveled to her chestnut-and-copper-brown hair. The waves that had escaped her pins fell to the middle of her back, but the majority of them were caked in mud, punctuated by the occasional leaf. Her clothes had fared no better. She'd often worn boys' clothing as a child when they went fishing or tree climbing, so he wouldn't have given her attire a second thought if not for the fact that in his absence she had gained curves in certain . . . areas. And the spencer and breeches, currently earthen brown from all that mud, hugged those areas in such a way that any fellow in possession of his faculties could not ignore.

He forced his gaze away from her legs and back up to her face. Despite her efforts to remain expressionless, she couldn't hide the occasional crinkling around her lips and at the bridge of her nose. Her attempt to mask her aches and pains didn't really surprise him. She was as headstrong as ever.

Those first years of his exile, thoughts of Vicky, his mother, and his brother had caused him nothing but pain. So he'd learned to lock all those memories away and had rarely given himself the liberty of using the key. He'd long since stopped imagining what Vicky had been doing back home. Her carefree smile and fits of giggles had been the final pieces he'd banished to oblivion.

Without warning, she raised her head and caught him staring. He looked away.

"You needn't gawk. I feel ridiculous enough as it is." She sounded angry, but her words said otherwise.

"I was contemplating why that man wished to harm you." Not an utter lie.

She frowned. Whether it was because she regretted her comment or because she wondered the same, he could not tell. "He must have been some sort of thief," she pronounced.

"Why was he out on the edge of the estate where there's nothing of value but sheep?"

"A sheep thief, then. Or maybe he was taking a circuitous route to the house?" Even she didn't seem to believe that conclusion.

"He would have hit you again if I hadn't alerted him to my presence."

Her brows knit. "It makes no sense for this to have happened here—we've never had any crimes of violence in the area." She shook her head as though it were too strange to contemplate.

How little she knew. Tom swallowed.

"Did you see where he came from?" she asked. "He wasn't there when I arrived."

"I saw you down in that valley. Then I looked away, and when I looked back, that man stood a few feet from you with a branch. He must have been hiding on my side of the wall, but I didn't see him until that moment."

"Perhaps he'd been where the wall curves."

That would explain why Tom hadn't seen him. Still, if the sight of her hadn't surprised him, he might have noticed the fellow—in what should have been a conspicuous black greatcoat—crouching behind the wall.

Tom had failed to protect her. Just as he'd almost failed on that appalling day five years ago.

He shook his head. To be fair, he was almost certain Vicky hadn't understood all she'd witnessed then. Yet she'd suspected enough to ask for answers Tom couldn't give. So he'd driven her away. Then his father had banished him from the house.

"For that matter, what were *you* doing out there?" she asked, turning her face his way.

"I have a perfect right to inspect my land."

She made a frustrated noise. "I meant, what were you doing out so early? In the whole year you've been home, not once have I so much as *glimpsed* you at such an hour."

She was right. He generally avoided venturing too close to Oakbridge in the early morning. Whether he did so because his mother had mentioned Vicky's habit of riding early, or because he preferred to tackle other business at that hour, he could not say. Since his return, he'd attempted to repair his relationships with his mother and brother—to fix his fractured family—but he still found himself turning the other way when he saw Victoria.

In addition to depriving him of his home and his family, Tom's father had cost him his closest friendship. Now the old man was gone, and Tom should be happy. He could regain what he'd lost. Tell Vicky the truth about the past. But as he looked out over the green fields and hills of the country they'd ridden roughshod over as children, he felt nothing.

He didn't realize he'd been clenching his fists until the reins bit through his gloves into the flesh of his palms. Vicky murmured something, but he couldn't make it out.

She'd ridden closer so only a foot stood between them. In his peripheral vision, he saw her peering at him with concern.

"What's the matter?"

He shook his head and relaxed his grip on the reins. "Nothing at all." Then he said the first evasion that came to mind. "I have matters at home to attend to."

Her jaw tensed. "I told you you needn't accompany me. Especially if you have such pressing matters desirous of your attention."

He'd wounded her pride. "My affairs can wait. I said I would see you home and I shall. I must speak with your father."

"There is no need to speak with Papa," she said with a petulant shake of her head.

"We must both tell him what we saw so he may take appropriate precautions for your safety."

She huffed as they reached the ancient oak bridge from which the estate derived its name.

They had ridden around the west side of the property through the fields, and now Tom saw the cream-colored stone manor for the first time in five years. Oakbridge House's two-story Palladian facade of impeccably white Ionic columns and high-arched windows stood like a sentinel in the countryside. Sculpted gardens and an expanse of lawn framed the mansion on either side. Mature trees peered down at the house and gardens from atop a gentle hill. It all looked just as he remembered.

At least *something* did. His family home had not fared so well. Though in his opinion, Halworth Hall had never looked attractive when compared to Oakbridge. Sixty years ago, his grandfather had used his wife's dowry to convert the house's outdated Tudor architecture into an imposing and formidable gray monstrosity that was now in need of repairs.

Their horses' shoes clacked on the wood of the bridge as they crossed. Tom glanced beyond the house and caught sight of the colossal oak tree still standing patiently up beyond the water garden. A small part of him itched to ride there now. To climb those sturdy branches with Vicky at his heels. But he was no longer a child. He steered Horatio toward the stables.

Vicky pulled her horse to a halt as a groom emerged. At least the fellow had the good grace not to make a face at Vicky's disheveled appearance.

Tom dismounted and gave Horatio's reins to the man. Without waiting for anyone's assistance, Vicky hopped to the ground with a grunt.

Tom winced. "Your pride is one thing, Victoria, but when you give it more weight than your health, you do yourself no favors." He reached her side and offered his arm for her to lean on.

She turned on her heel and marched toward the house. He watched her take two purposeful strides, which then transformed into a series of limps.

He ran his hand through his hair and let out a breath. He caught up to her and grasped her upper arm. "I beg your pardon."

She half turned. "Do you mind—"

"Not at all." He bent, put one arm under her legs, his other around her waist, and lifted her. She was remarkably light in his arms.

"Wh-what are you doing?" she sputtered.

"If you won't have a care for your person, you leave me no choice but to carry you to the house." He strode forward.

"I am perfectly capable of walking. Put me down this instant!"

He glanced down at her but continued on. Her hazel eyes met his with defiance as she raised her chin.

"Will you take more care?" he asked.

She looked away. "I'm under no obligation to answer to you."

He frowned at the words, but he knew she was correct. He caught her gaze once more, inclined his head, and gingerly lowered her feet to the ground. Pieces of dried mud flaked off onto the sleeves of his coat. He exhaled. It was one of his few newer coats, but the damage was done. He had only himself to blame.

Vicky cast her head about, and Tom realized how scandalous this might appear to an onlooker. Victoria was a beautiful young lady in breeches. Whom he'd been cradling in his arms. An unscrupulous fellow wouldn't have hesitated to use such a situation to his advantage. But *he* was a gentleman. And she was . . . well, *Vicky*.

Still, as she was injured, he had done no wrong.

Vicky started toward the path that led to the main door of the house without sparing Tom a glance. He followed a short length behind her. Despite her protestations, he did think she walked with slightly more attention than before.

She was limping again when they reached the massive iron door. It was nearly as tall as a man standing on another's shoulders and just as thick. Tom remembered it well.

Vicky faced him with a glare. "You needn't feel obligated to help me just because you happened to be there."

Her eyes were hard, but something in the tremor of her voice blew a pin-sized hole through the cold fog surrounding him. The old Tom—the Tom he'd been before his exile—would have told her he would always come to her aid if she needed him. But the words stuck fast in his throat. Instead, he said, "Anyone would have done the same."

She pivoted away and opened the door.

As he followed her into the marble-floored grand entryway, he knew he couldn't fault her.

CHAPTER THE SECOND

Happiness in marriage is entirely a matter of chance.
—Jane Austen, *Pride and Prejudice*

As Vicky trudged through the front door of Oakbridge House in her mud-caked hair and clothes, clumps of dirt fell from her boots, besmirching the gleaming ivory marble entryway. Her whole head pounded and her left hip throbbed with every step she took. She winced as her mother turned the corner into the foyer.

Her mother always dressed impeccably, as befitted her status as the Countess of Oakbridge, and today, as usual, she had not a pin out of place. Her indigo-blue morning dress fell in perfectly straight lines down her perfectly svelte hips; her coffee-brown curls sat in an elegant coif on the crown of her head. Vicky grimaced as her mother's green eyes narrowed on her disheveled state, flitted over to Tom, and settled back on Vicky with dissatisfaction.

She graced Tom with a quick and rather cold greeting before asking, "Will one of you please tell me why my daughter appears to have emerged from a pond?"

Vicky inhaled. She related the events of the morning, ending miserably with the information that Tom wanted to speak with her father about the incident.

Any traces of disapproval in her mother's eyes disappeared as she embraced Vicky. "Oh, my poor, dear girl! How could this have happened? I must tell your father at once. How dreadful for this to occur on the same day . . ." Instead of finishing the thought, she held Vicky at arm's length to inspect her from head to toe. Her light brown brows wove together.

Vicky frowned. "The same day as what, Mama?"

Her mother's green eyes darted to Tom. "This is no small matter."

Vicky bit her lip. Her mama was always so composed, always ready to handle any family crisis or household trifle. Perhaps she was just concerned, but her distraction seemed to point to some other emotion. Could it be fear? "Do not worry, Mama. The man must be halfway to London by now. A day of rest and I'll be back to rights."

Her mother didn't smile. "Go and change, dear. I'll ring for your maid to draw you a bath. Come to your father's study as soon as you're ready. We have much to discuss. I will take Tom there presently."

Vicky couldn't shake the feeling that something was dreadfully wrong. Something her mother couldn't speak of with Tom in attendance. The tiny hairs on the back of Vicky's neck stood on end. "Mama?"

Her mother looked at Tom, and her face became impassive. "Just hurry, my dear."

"Forgive me, Lady Oakbridge, but I'd hoped Victoria could tell the earl her version of events," Tom interjected.

Her mother nodded. "She shall, of course, but all that can wait until she's more comfortable." She looked at Vicky and lifted her chin toward the stairs.

Vicky took the hint and moved away, but again Tom spoke.

"Surely it would be easier for the earl to act quickly with all information at his disposal. We must at least inform the magistrate of this outrage. There is a bandit at large, Lady Oakbridge—"

"And from what Victoria says, he will be miles away by now," her mother interrupted, giving Tom a quelling look.

"Perhaps, but for Vicky's safety, I believe—"

"If you imagine I would put anything above my daughter's safety, Lord Halworth, you are very much mistaken. Now, if you wish to speak with Lord Oakbridge, I suggest you follow me and allow *Lady* Victoria her privacy."

Vicky felt her ears burning. Why was her mother acting so rudely? Her emphasis on Tom's lack of formality was surely unwarranted. Yes, Tom had embarrassed her and frustrated her and acted infuriatingly high-handed, but they'd known each other their whole lives. And he had *tried* to help today.

Tom frowned. He glanced her way, but Vicky couldn't meet his gaze. "As you wish, Lady Oakbridge," he said to her mother. He bowed in Vicky's direction. "Good day, Lady Victoria."

Vicky curtsied, which felt silly when wearing breeches, and forced herself to look into his eyes. "Good morning, Tom. Thank you." There. She refused to be browbeaten by either one of them.

Elizabeth Bennet would have said what she deemed correct in such a situation—and so had Vicky.

Half an hour later, clean but still sore, Vicky knocked on the door to her father's study. As Vicky had changed, her maid had shocked her with the news that her sister, Althea, had arrived without notice. Althea should be at her London town house preparing for the start of the social season with her husband, so this unexpected visit was more than a little strange.

As Vicky stepped inside the study, the usual scent of leather and paper surrounded her. Her father, the Earl of Oakbridge, sat in a leather chair behind his medieval oak desk where countless generations of Astons had conducted estate business. His fastidious valet had pressed his brown coat and green embroidered waistcoat without fault and tied his cravat to sit crisply at the precise folds. His freshly combed hair was still in perfect order, which struck her as out of place. Here in the country, her father was far less careful with his appearance, and by this time of the morning, his brown waves—just a shade lighter than hers and touched by gray—were usually mussed enough to vex his valet. But not today.

He gestured for her to come in, but his jaw remained stiff and his thick brows furrowed. It was a look she remembered well from childhood—one he usually reserved for a lecture about the danger of jumping in the river from the top of a tree or what a serious infraction it was to ride a cow.

Vicky's mother sat perched upon a wing chair opposite the desk. Next to her, in a matching chair, sat Althea. Her sister turned her head toward the doorway, and Vicky crossed the room to embrace her.

"Thea! It's *so* good to see you." With arms outstretched, Vicky stopped beside her chair. Her sister did not rise. Vicky frowned. "Althea?" she asked, bewildered. She touched her sister's arm. Her skin felt cold and slightly rough from gooseflesh, despite the fire roaring in the corner. Then Althea looked into her eyes.

Vicky's throat tightened. Althea's big, brown eyes stared back, hollow and haunted. Her previously lustrous chocolate-brown hair, which usually framed her face in effortless tendrils, now hung in limp, dull strands. Her formerly slender figure now looked painfully thin, and the delicate oval of her face was paler than Vicky had ever seen it.

Though Vicky's head had still ached when she'd entered the study, the pounding had decreased. Now the hammering returned as Vicky's mouth went dry. "What's wrong?"

For a moment, the look of despair in Althea's eyes disappeared, replaced by a diamond-hard edge Vicky had never seen before. A second later, Althea concealed it with a blank expression. Her back stiffened to a straight line, and she clasped her hands in her lap. It was the manner she put on for society, minus a smile: the demeanor proclaiming her the perfect, dutiful daughter of the Earl and Countess of Oakbridge and the perfect, dutiful wife of the Viscount Dain. Vicky had always admired Althea's ability to present herself so well, and even more so since Vicky's first season last year, when she realized that society's prying eyes constantly gave her the sensation a hare must feel when evading a hawk.

Her shoulders tensed. Yes, she knew that look well, but Thea hadn't used it with her for many years—not since Tom had left and Vicky had started confiding in her sister. She would wager ten guineas it meant Althea didn't want Vicky to know what she was thinking.

Vicky looked to her parents. Her mother also sat with her hands folded in her lap, by all appearances her usual, calm self. Yet Vicky saw the lines between her eyebrows that only appeared when she was troubled. Vicky's father made no such attempt to hide his frown. His right thumb rubbed the pad of his forefinger in agitation. The back of Vicky's neck tingled again, and her concern for Althea transformed into dreadful apprehension. Her sister's head turned toward their father, still showing no inclination to speak.

Vicky's question hung in the air.

Finally, their father broke the silence. "Althea has fled her London house. She left late last night on horseback and then caught the mail coach, which dropped her at the village."

Vicky's terrible sense of foreboding compounded. Something truly frightful must have occurred for Althea to do such a thing. Again she noted her sister's haggard appearance.

"Why?"

Althea still said nothing. This time she didn't even acknowledge Vicky's question with a glance.

"Papa?" Vicky pressed.

Her father motioned for her to sit and cleared his throat. His thumbnail continued to slide under his index finger. "It appears Lord Dain has been mistreating your sister." He paused, taking a deep breath. "Violently."

Vicky collapsed into her seat, forgetting until too late what the force would do to her aches and pains. She flinched, but turned so she could see Althea's face.

"Oh, Thea." Despite her sister's bent head, Vicky saw her large brown eyes swimming with tears. Althea raised her head, and the blood rushed from Vicky's cheeks at the bleakness of her stare. Her sister opened her mouth as if to speak, but in the next moment, she clamped her jaw shut.

Vicky shook her head. Althea and Dain had seemed so in love. Althea had always been the ideal older sister: patient, kind, an excellent judge of character, and understanding of Vicky's flaws. If she had any fault, it was perhaps that she was *too* kind on occasion, very much like Elizabeth Bennet's sister Jane.

Viscount Dain had set eyes on Althea three years ago in London, two years before Vicky's own society debut. After a month of courting, he'd proposed, and Althea had accepted. Dain's charm easily won over her parents, and he'd always acted very courteously to Vicky. She'd imagined that, like Jane Bennet, Althea had found her own Mr. Bingley, and that Althea and Dain were living ever so happily in London.

The couple spent Christmases with Vicky and her parents at Oakbridge, and they'd all seen each other often at events during last year's season in London, but those were the extent of Vicky's dealings with her brother-in-law. She'd never seen him act oddly.

But then, she'd never felt completely at ease with the man either. She hadn't known why, so she'd never said anything. On no occasion had Althea hinted her marriage suffered any problems, and Vicky had thought she didn't know Dain as her sister did.

Perhaps none of them had known him.

Vicky clenched her fist. "What did he do to you?"

Instead of answering, Althea squeezed her eyes shut and lifted a hand to her forehead, as though she could keep the memories at bay through sheer force of will. Althea's hand shifted the hair framing her face, and for the first time, Vicky saw the puffy red-and-blue bruise the strands had so cleverly hidden. The bruise started at her sister's left temple and disappeared beneath her hairline. A shallow cut also marked the skin above it.

The angry pounding trebled in Vicky's head. Her hands gripped the wooden armrests. Shock and disgust coursed through her, settling in the pit of her stomach. What kind of fiend would do such a thing?

"I can scarce believe it, but for . . ." Vicky gestured at her own forehead and sprang to her feet. "That abominable louse! I'd like to throw him to a dozen mad dogs! Papa, what is to be done?" she demanded.

"Victoria." Her mother's voice was reproving.

Vicky turned to her. "Look at her face! How does he *dare*? We cannot let this go unanswered." Her father's social standing equaled Dain's—surpassed his, even, for his title was older and ranked higher than Dain's viscountcy. Vicky leaned over her father's desk. "Papa, you should accuse him in the House of Lords!"

"Victoria, calm yourself," her mother snapped.

Stunned by her mother's tone, Vicky looked back and forth between her parents. In her eyes, they were ever the embodiment of the perfect earl and countess, but the situation had clearly shaken them. Her father's mouth set into a grim line as he watched her mother observe Althea with glassy eyes.

Then her mother inhaled. "You are upsetting your sister."

Vicky turned. Tears spilled down Althea's cheeks.

Vicky's chest shrank. How could she be so thoughtless? "I'm sorry, Mama." She moved to Althea's chair and bent over. She pulled her into a hug, no longer caring if her sister resisted. "I'm so sorry, Thea." Althea sniffled and tears leaked onto Vicky's shoulder. Vicky held her sister tighter. When Althea sat back in her chair, Vicky relaxed her hold. But as her gaze focused on the swollen, red skin on Althea's forehead, a dark fury pooled within her. That loathsome, horrible whoreson of a—

"My dear," her father said, interrupting her thoughts, "you cannot fault Vicky for saying what we all feel. We shall ask her to conduct herself with decorum on a more ordinary day." He turned to Vicky. "As to your question, that would be impractical. If I accused him in the Lords, the scandal would be inescapable. He is not friendless, and his supporters in the House could contend I was trying to tarnish his reputation out of malice. We'd grace the pages of every newspaper and gossip rag from London to York."

Vicky winced. Althea blanched.

Their father shook his head. "No, I dare not attempt it, lest I cause more harm than good."

Vicky angled her body to face him, but kept one hand on Althea's arm. "Then what can we do?" she asked, although she was already devising foul punishments in her head, the majority of which she'd read about in a long, didactic volume on English history she'd once found in their library. The first that came to mind was something barbaric they'd done to a medieval monarch with a red-hot poker.

"Clearly, Thea must stay with us, but will Dain allow it?" Vicky knew little of the law, but she knew a man's wife was essentially his property. She couldn't count the number of novels she'd read where an injured lady had no recourse against her faithless husband.

"I will ride to London without delay and confront Dain," her father stated.

Vicky frowned.

He continued, "I must hear his side of the story"—he gestured for silence as Vicky opened her mouth to protest and Althea's head jerked upward—"to determine what we must face. I suspect he shall deny everything, but perhaps I can persuade him to consent to a separation. For this cannot and shall not continue." He looked over them all with a decisive air.

Vicky nodded her assent, and her mother did the same. She ventured a glance at her sister. Althea's face remained blank. Vicky rubbed her sister's arm gently. It felt like an empty gesture, but she didn't know what else to do. She wished she knew how to help.

"Very well," their father said. "I will leave this morning, and send for you all after I have met with him."

"What about the man who attacked Vicky?" Althea said.

Vicky blinked. It was the first sentence her sister had uttered. Her voice sounded reed-like, thin, and terribly quiet. Vicky had completely forgotten about her own unpleasant incident. "Were you here when Tom spoke to Papa?"

"I spoke to Halworth alone," her father answered, calling Tom by his new title. It seemed neither of her parents had forgiven Tom for hurting her all those years ago. Or at the very least, they wished to maintain a formal distance with him. "Your sister was in no state to see anyone."

"No, of course not," Vicky murmured.

Her father continued, "Halworth volunteered to find our shepherd and direct him to the affected sheep. I trust they will soon have the situation well in hand. And, as Halworth was in possession of all the particulars, I also asked him to notify the local magistrate of the incident. Though I doubt Sir Aylward will do more than take down Halworth's account."

"Should we not take precautions in case he returns?" Althea asked.

"Precautions from Tom?" Vicky asked, incredulous.

"From the bandit, Victoria," her mother said.

Vicky felt her cheeks redden. "Oh."

Her father nodded. "I will send for men from the village to watch the house and grounds. I would take you all with me to London, but you girls both need at least one night's rest after today."

Althea looked at Vicky. "You weren't injured?"

Vicky tried to smile and squeezed her sister's arm. "My head hurts and I'll be achy for a few days, but 'tis nothing serious." Nothing compared to what her sister must have gone through.

"'Nothing serious' means you likely need a doctor's care," her mother interjected. "I have already sent for him."

"Yes, I want you both examined," their father said in a tone that brooked no argument. He stood and started for the door.

As he skirted the desk, Vicky's mother rose as well. She

intercepted him before he reached the door handle and took his arm. "Promise you will not challenge him, James," she said in a firm tone. "No matter what happens."

Vicky's eyes widened. It hadn't yet occurred to her that gentlemen often did duel over such matters.

Her father smiled and took her mother's hand. "Nothing could induce me to do so."

Despite his words, her mother stared at him with pursed lips.

"Perhaps I might have in my youth, Felicia, but I am too old to point a pistol. Besides," he continued with another smile in Vicky and Althea's direction, "I wouldn't dream of leaving you all just yet."

Vicky's mother dropped his hand. "I will tell Baden to pack what you'll need." She left the room, calling for the earl's valet.

Vicky's father sighed and moved to follow her. "My dear, I didn't mean to be flippant . . ." His voice trailed off as he stepped out of earshot.

Vicky exhaled. Her poor mother must be worried to react so to her father's attempt to lighten the mood. She only hoped her father's powers of diplomacy would prove more successful with Lord Dain than they had with her mother. Vicky looked at Althea.

"Thea, may we speak? We could go to your bedchamber or take a walk in the gardens if you like."

Althea refused to meet her gaze. "I've rather had my fill of talking."

Vicky wanted to kick herself. Of course she couldn't expect her sister to be anything but exhausted after her ordeal.

"I'm sorry. You need your rest. Shall I help you upstairs?"

Her sister shook her head and rose from her chair. "You needn't bother."

"It's no bother. I know this must be dreadful for you, but at least you're home now. Papa will take care of everything."

Althea glared at her with cold eyes. "Are you truly so naive? Sooner or later, you must discover there are some nightmares that do not disappear on waking."

Vicky grimaced. "I'm sorry, but I cannot believe that. I know everything will turn out for the best. We will *make* it so." She took Althea's hand, but her sister snatched it away and hurried out of the study, leaving Vicky wide-eyed and worried.

Later that day, after Vicky's father had left for London, she ventured into the garden. She had made sure to tell him her version of what had occurred on the estate grounds early that morning. He had said little, other than echoing her own thoughts that Tom's arrival had been fortuitous. Thankfully, he'd spared her a lecture on the stupidity of chasing after masked men, but she supposed that due more to distraction on his part than oversight. Or perhaps he'd thought she'd endured enough for one day.

Vicky's father had ridden off on his gray Thoroughbred with determination etched on his brow. Things looked bleak now, but Vicky knew they had nothing to worry about. Her papa could fix almost every problem—it was a trait on which he took great pride.

The village doctor had come and gone, proclaiming Vicky well enough for a slow walk if she wished, but had cautioned her against riding or other exertion for at least a week.

The estate shepherd had reported that six sheep had died before he could reverse the bloat. At least they'd saved most of the flock. The shepherd said they would have lost far more if not for her efforts to rebuild the wall, but Vicky couldn't celebrate. The events of the day and the idea of those dead sheep offset whatever sense of accomplishment she usually felt after doing good for the estate.

Usually Vicky collected her thoughts while strolling the boxwood-lined, pebbled paths of the kitchen garden, but today she paced without seeing any of it. She collapsed onto an iron bench and rubbed at her eyes. But they flew open as her mind flashed to the image of Althea's face crumpling when she'd broken into tears this morning.

Althea had retired to her bedroom after the meeting in the study, and thus far, she had seen no one besides their mother and the doctor. Vicky's maid had told her Althea had taken breakfast, and later some broth, alone in her room. Vicky hadn't spoken to her since their earlier exchange.

Vicky's gaze focused out into the distance, beyond the edge of the gardens, to the stream and the old wooden bridge that gave the estate its name. It was an eccentric family tradition that every Aston bride travel underneath the bridge in a flower-filled boat punted by her bridegroom. Only two years ago, Dain had punted Althea down the river with a self-satisfied smile. Vicky, her parents, and a gaggle of Aston relations who'd traveled from every corner of England to witness the event had stood on the bridge waving as Althea and Dain floated beneath them amid bunches of fragrant wildflowers.

Akin to a princess in a fairy tale, Althea had glowed with

contentment that day, the light strands in her brown hair glinting in the sun beneath a crown of purple and white flowers. Vicky's chest had ached as she'd realized her sister was leaving their home for good—that their lives would never be the same—but she'd found comfort in the idea that her sister was happy. For how could Althea do anything but live happily ever after now that she'd found her own amiable prince?

But she hadn't. Althea had been close-lipped about her marriage from the beginning. When Vicky asked her questions, either in person, or by post, Althea always spoke in generalities, leaving the specifics of her day-to-day life to Vicky's imagination. Had Althea glossed over the subject of her marriage because she was hiding the truth?

Vicky closed her eyes and inhaled the fresh scent of the hedges drying after months of rain. She had to discover exactly what had occurred between Althea and Dain.

She rose from the bench and strode back toward the house, clenching her fists at her sides at the memory of Dain whipping his horses when he'd brought them to Oakbridge. She knew that was a flaw many men shared, but perhaps it also explained why Vicky had never truly trusted him. She'd even mentioned it to Althea once, but her sister had shrugged it off.

Vicky swallowed hard, trying to ignore the churning in her stomach. She racked her brain for other instances of Dain displaying strange behavior, but very little came to mind.

After speaking to two footmen and an undergardener, Vicky found her sister wandering through the glass conservatory amidst the small selection of tropical flowers. Althea wore a walking dress Vicky remembered from before her marriage: a pale yellow, long-sleeved muslin printed with tiny pink flowers. In days gone by, the material had emphasized the roses in her cheeks and the burnished highlights in her hair, but today, the print could not conceal Althea's pallor. The dress hung loosely on her shoulders. Vicky called her name from the doorway.

Althea flinched, a look of panic crossing her face. As she recognized Vicky, the fear melted from her expression. Yet her awkward stance called to mind the image of a doe about to bolt. Whether Althea was angry or simply uncomfortable, Vicky couldn't guess.

Vicky took a deep breath to shore up her courage. The air within the glass walls of the conservatory always stayed humid, but today it felt oppressively so. She glanced up at the sun shining through the ceiling. She stepped down the path until she hovered a few feet from her sister and motioned to the flowers basking in the humidity.

"Aren't they beautiful?" she asked. Perhaps idle chitchat would restore a measure of normalcy to the day.

Althea nodded.

"These ones are from seeds Papa bought years ago from that trader who had just returned from the West Indies. It took the gardener all this time to get them to bloom," she said, bending down to touch the silky petals of a bright red saucer-shaped flower with a yellow stamen. "They're so—so un-English, I suppose," she said with a laugh. She looked up at Althea with a smile as the flower's tropical perfume filled her nostrils.

Althea turned from the blossoms and looked outside.

Vicky rose, feeling like a little girl again. One trying to play with an older sister who claimed to be thoroughly grown-up. Evidently, polite conversation had been the wrong tack to take. Very well, how would Elizabeth Bennet handle this? *She'd* speak her mind to her sister Jane.

"Thea, if I've angered you, I'm very sorry." She paused. "The last thing I wish to do is quarrel."

Althea turned her head and gave a small nod. Vicky supposed that meant she'd accepted her apology.

"How are you feeling? What did the doctor say?" Vicky asked.

"That I am well enough."

Vicky furrowed her brow. "And your head?" she asked, sidestepping so she was facing her.

"'Tis nothing," Althea said, avoiding Vicky's gaze. "He left a salve."

"How can it be nothing?" Vicky reached up to move her sister's hair away from where it shielded the bruise.

Althea twisted away and started down the path toward the small group of orange trees that provided the luxury of fruit during the winter months.

Vicky swallowed down the lump in her throat. She wanted to let the matter lie—to leave her sister to the privacy she so clearly craved, but Vicky needed to know more.

"Did it only begin recently? When you married him, and even at Christmas, you seemed happy. When did he change?"

Althea didn't acknowledge her. She stared through the glass walls of the conservatory at some fixed point in the garden.

"Thea, please. I only want to help. But how can I if you won't speak to me?" She stepped forward and rested her hand on her sister's shoulder.

Althea spun, and the force knocked Vicky's hand away.

Althea faced her with resentment in her eyes. In a stony voice she whispered, "Do not ask me to explain what you cannot understand. How could you possibly help?"

Vicky's mouth opened and closed. Then she shook her head. "I don't know. But if you do, you have only to ask and I'll do it."

"There is nothing. Even Papa will not be able to help me."

Vicky frowned at her sister's lack of faith in their father. "He will, Thea. And if for some unforeseeable reason he cannot, then *I* will."

Althea glared at her.

Vicky stepped forward. "I promise I will do anything I can to keep you safe."

Her sister looked down. "You know nothing of suffering—or of sacrifice. I am sick to my very soul of empty promises."

Vicky's chest constricted. She'd never once made her sister a false promise. But she knew who must have done. Althea may have escaped her husband, but Dain's actions haunted her.

In that moment, Vicky swore she would not rest until Althea's future was secure. She took her sister's cold hand in hers and gripped it. "Thea, I give my word. I will not fail you."

Althea caught her gaze.

Vicky stared back, unblinking. Then, for the smallest instant, Vicky thought she saw a glimmer of hope in her sister's eyes.

CHAPTER THE THIRD

*I cannot see that London has any great advantage over
the country for my part, except the shops and public places.
The country is a vast deal pleasanter . . .*
—Jane Austen, *Pride and Prejudice*

Vicky breathed a sigh of relief as the carriage slowed. Although the journey to London from Oakbridge took less than a day, Vicky always dreaded the tedium of sitting for so long. She couldn't read in carriages without growing ill, which left her at the mercy of her jumbled thoughts. Too many of those thoughts had centered on Tom's reasons for not calling at Oakbridge House to see if she was recovering. At the very least, he could have sent a note to tell her what the magistrate had said. Yet judging by their history, she should have expected his silence.

She hadn't truly believed she and Tom would pick up where they'd left off, but she *had* imagined that one day they could meet and converse as cordial adults. But if that wasn't what he wanted, so be it! She had far more important considerations to contend with.

She shook her head as she stared out the carriage window at the four-story structure where the vehicle would soon stop. Aston House was one of the widest on Kingsford Square and was constructed almost entirely of cream-colored stone. A pair of fluted columns supporting a stone balcony flanked a tall, rectangular door. The balcony, in turn, supported four massive Corinthian columns that spanned the height of the second and third floors, drawing the eye up toward ornate cornicing set below the top floor. Though Aston House had always been their London home, Vicky had never felt wholly comfortable here. In her mind, the house had never acquired the coziness of Oakbridge.

She sighed inwardly. Perhaps it was because at Oakbridge she had the freedom to do as she pleased, whereas in London she had to conform to the rules of society. Although London boasted numerous diversions, within a week of arriving, Vicky always itched to ride over the green pastures of home and inhale the fresh country air.

Vicky sneaked a glance at her sister. Althea had grown more ashen and subdued the closer they'd come to London. Vicky, Althea, and their mother had left Oakbridge early that morning after receiving a letter from their father the night before. Throughout the day, Althea had shown little inclination to speak. Now she gazed out the carriage window facing the grass and bench-lined walkways of the square with an unreadable expression. Vicky wondered if she was looking for her husband.

The carriage stopped, and liveried footmen opened the doors. Vicky's father met them in the foyer and embraced them one by one. Vicky asked what had passed between him and Lord Dain, but he would say nothing except that the family solicitor would call at the house in two hours. Vicky and the others hurried upstairs to bathe away the dust from the journey and ready themselves.

Two hours later, Vicky, her family, and their solicitor, Mr. Barnes, seated themselves within the dark paneled walls of the earl's study. The room was smaller than her father's study at Oakbridge House, but his desk was equally large, though less ornate. Her father's leather upholstered chair sat behind the desk, and a footman had placed four cushioned chairs with spindly arms in front of the desk to accommodate everyone.

Althea quickly took the seat nearest the fireplace. Vicky's mother sat beside her, and Vicky perched on the front of the chair nearest the window, waiting for her father and Mr. Barnes to sit so they could begin. The stocky, bespectacled Mr. Barnes took the chair nearest the door.

"I am sure you all wish to hear what happened with Dain, so I will keep you in suspense no longer," her father began. "Mr. Barnes has heard the particulars, but I hope he will forgive me repeating the story," he said, inclining his head toward the solicitor.

"Of course, my lord."

The earl nodded. "I called on Dain the day after I arrived in London. I told him without prevarication that Althea had appeared at Oakbridge days before without informing anyone of her imminent arrival. He expressed surprise. When I asked if he knew why Althea had left for Hampshire without telling him, he replied, contrary to his initial reaction, that he *had* known of her plans to leave."

Althea spoke in quiet tones. "That is a blatant falsehood, Papa. I left in the night. He was"—she paused—"not in the house. And not expected home for hours."

"But you told him nothing of your plans?" their mother asked.

"If I had, I would not be with you now."

Vicky's eyes widened. She looked at her father. He had raised an eyebrow at the statement.

Their father spoke. "I told him you would not be returning to his London home in the foreseeable future. He seemed astonished by the notion. When I asked if he would willingly admit he was completely at fault for Althea's departure, he denied any wrongdoing on his part. I saw fit to tell him exactly what he'd done to her, and to us all, by painting himself as a man of honor and proving himself the complete opposite."

Vicky nodded.

Her father paused.

"What did he say?" Vicky asked.

"He laughed in my face."

Vicky's eyebrows shot up. Her mother gasped.

"He said whatever Althea had told us were the ramblings of a jealous spouse. He claimed, Althea, that you were angry with him for acquiring a mistress and had returned to Oakbridge telling stories of abuse to punish him."

Vicky turned to her sister. Althea would never fabricate such a story. And although Vicky hadn't any concrete reason to distrust Dain before now, she had no trouble believing him to be more adept at lying than her sister.

Althea stared into her lap with her hands clasped together so tightly, her knuckles were turning white.

Their father continued, "He said you would undoubtedly change your story if I questioned you, and in a few weeks, everything would blow over, and you would forgive him and return to your London house. When I asked if he would consent to a private separation agreement, he refused."

Countless moments passed, but Althea said nothing.

Vicky could stay silent no longer. "But did you ask him about her bruises, Papa? What brilliant answer had he for those?"

"He said she fell and bumped her head. He ordered a physician to dress the wound."

"Does he think us fools?" their mother scoffed.

After what seemed an eternity, Althea spoke. She was shaking, but whether it was from anger or fear, Vicky could not discern. Now her delicate hands gripped the arms of her chair, almost as though she was forcing herself to stay seated.

"You do not know him. Even *I* do not know him. I realized he was lying about everything—where he went, whom he met, what he was doing. Several weeks ago, when I confronted him about his dishonesty, he"—she paused and swallowed—"he took his anger out on me. Then he locked me in my room and instructed the servants to watch my every move. They lost all respect for me as mistress. Indeed, they took delight in humbling me." She closed her eyes.

Vicky exhaled through her nose and held her breath to keep her tears at bay.

Althea seemed to force her eyes open. "They all followed Dain's lead . . ." She hid her face in her hands. "There was nothing I could do to stop it. Only the stable master showed me any pity by allowing me to take my horse to flee and promising to say he had no knowledge of the incident."

Vicky looked at the floor and clenched her fists, wanting desperately to comfort Althea, but not knowing how.

"Do you wish to start proceedings for a legal separation?" their father asked.

Althea raised her head from her hands and nodded. "I shall never return to his house."

"Despite the social scandal it will inevitably bring? Your reputation in society will never be the same, regardless of his guilt."

Her gaze dropped. "I must find the strength to bear it."

"We'll help you, Thea," Vicky said firmly. Her sister glanced her way, but Vicky could not interpret her look.

Althea lifted her chin. "I will be free of him, Papa."

Vicky smiled at her sister's proclamation. She would support Althea in any capacity she could. Just as she'd promised.

"Very well." Their father nodded. He made eye contact with their mother. "Mr. Barnes, will you be so good as to explain the procedure."

Mr. Barnes cleared his throat. "Indeed, my lord. The primary course of action would be for Lady Dain to apply to the Court of Chancery for a writ of *supplicavit*. If granted, this will protect her from her husband for a year. Legally he will be unable to force her to return to his home or control her in any way. That is the most immediate and practical solution."

"But that only protects her for *a year*?" Vicky asked with a frown.

Mr. Barnes nodded. "However, your sister can also sue Lord Dain for a separation on the grounds of cruelty in the ecclesiastical court. Cases of excessive marital abuse are not uncommon, and when there is proof, many judges rule in favor of the wife. If we are successful, Lady Dain would be free of the viscount, and the court could order him to pay her alimony."

Vicky's eyebrows rose. It sounded so simple.

"Yet, I must stress, Lady Dain," Mr. Barnes continued, "that you would not be able to remarry."

Vicky's eyes widened. She looked at Althea.

Her sister blanched, but nodded slowly. "What about him?"

"If the suit is successful, Lord Dain will not be permitted to remarry either. Judging by his recent declarations, it seems certain he will contest the suit. If so, the proceedings could take as long as two years."

Vicky exhaled. Two years sounded like an awfully long time for poor Althea to wait for her separation, and she wouldn't even be able to find another husband when it was over. "Is there no way for Althea to remarry?" Vicky said.

"The only way would be to obtain a Parliamentary divorce, but Lord Dain would have to bring a petition to the House of Lords on the grounds that Lady Dain had committed adultery."

Which her sister clearly hadn't done. "But can't Althea petition Parliament on those grounds?" Dain had already admitted to having a mistress. Vicky looked at her father. "Or you on her behalf, Papa?"

Her father shook his head.

"It would not be successful," Mr. Barnes said. "Suits brought by wives against adulterous husbands rarely succeed even in the ecclesiastical courts, let alone Parliament."

Vicky's blood boiled at the injustice of it all. Why shouldn't

Parliament allow a wife the same recourse as a husband? Her sister had done nothing save try to be a good wife, and now her life would never be the same.

Their father nodded. "Go on, Barnes."

Mr. Barnes eyed Althea. "Lady Dain, are you still determined?"

Althea gave a short nod. "I am."

Mr. Barnes inclined his head. "Our difficulties in the case would lie chiefly in the evidence. The viscount has already claimed he never touched Lady Dain and the bruises on her person were the result of a fall. It would seem his servants are loyal to him, save for, perhaps, the stable master," he said with a nod to Althea. "I am afraid, due to the lack of reliable witnesses, the suit might be hard to prove."

"But surely if we all swear to seeing her injuries, our reputations will be enough to convince a judge we are in earnest," Vicky said.

"Perhaps," her father agreed. "But all testimony is reviewed in writing. A witness's character can be more difficult to determine in written statements."

"That is correct," Mr. Barnes said. He lifted one side of his spectacles with his thumb and forefinger, repositioning them slightly. "We can assume the majority of Lord Dain's servants will not speak in Lady Dain's favor in their statements. However, if we can secure an excellent proctor to argue on Lady Dain's behalf, as well as persuade Lord Dain's stable master to attest to what he saw, I could foresee the court ruling in Lady Dain's favor."

Vicky's heart lightened at his words. She peered around the room. Her mother and father exchanged glances, and her father nodded. Althea's eyelids sagged, but her jaw remained set.

Vicky smiled. Soon everything would be well again. Her papa could fix any problem.

"You must be exhausted," she said to her sister. Althea was staring into the middle distance, but at Vicky's words, her gaze flicked sideways to the door. Vicky stood and turned to her parents. "I will take Thea to her room."

"Victoria," her mother said with a strange, unreadable expression, "there is still more to discuss."

Vicky tilted her head to the side. "Mama, Thea needs to rest."

Her parents exchanged glances again.

"Victoria," her father began, "you must marry. By the end of the season."

Vicky's breath seized in her throat. Silence permeated the room, interrupted only by the crackling of the fire. He could not be in earnest.

She inhaled deeply to compose herself. "What have *I* to do with any of this?"

Her father stood and motioned for her to sit again. He nodded at the solicitor. "Mr. Barnes, please begin the proceedings to appeal to the Court of Chancery. I trust you will apprise me of the proctors you intend to approach about the suit for the ecclesiastical court?"

The man stood. "Of course, my lord. Lady Dain must be in residence in London for a short period before a proctor can register a citation to summon Lord Dain to the court. However, I shall find the best proctor possible in the interim."

"Thank you, Mr. Barnes," Althea said.

Mr. Barnes smiled at Althea with a slightly melancholy air. Then he bowed and left the study.

Vicky's father returned to his chair, turning his attention to her.

Vicky's heart drummed in her ears. "Why did you not wish Mr. Barnes to stay?"

"We thought it would be more comfortable for you," her mother replied.

Vicky swallowed. *Comfortable.* How considerate they were. At the moment, she felt about as comfortable as a rabbit in a snare.

"As you are aware," her father began, "you and Althea are my heirs. Because you have no brother, one of you will inherit my title, the Oakbridge estate, and all its holdings. Under common law, I must petition the crown to choose one of you to inherit the title. If I were to petition the king now—or rather the prince regent—he would choose Althea, as she is our eldest daughter and married to a peer of the realm. Your mother and I had intended to allow you the time you needed to choose a husband. We had thought to wait until then to decide which of you girls would be best equipped to maintain Oakbridge after I am gone. Unfortunately, circumstances now require us to act."

He paused, and Vicky coughed, her throat suddenly dry.

"If something should happen to me, and we do not win the suit for Althea's separation, the estate will fall into Dain's hands. Now that we know Dain for what he is, we cannot allow him to gain control of Oakbridge if you remain unmarried."

Vicky inhaled to calm her racing pulse. In the last year since her debut into society, she had not met a man who had so much as tempted her to give up her freedom. She'd decided that if she could manage it, she would remain at Oakbridge permanently. However, she hadn't told her parents that. She'd rather thought they'd figure it out eventually. But now what could she do? Well, to begin with, she could not let Dain ruin her life as well.

"But Papa," Vicky said, hating the lilt of frustration—or was it desperation?—in her voice, "Mr. Barnes seemed confident we would win the suit."

Her father shook his head. "We must not rely on possibilities. Certainties must be the order of the day. And it is an utter certainty the regent will choose whom he thinks worthy to inherit Oakbridge by virtue of her husband. If we do secure Althea a separation from Lord Dain, the scandal attached to her name will make the regent disinclined to give her the title and lands, but if you are still unmarried, he could let the petition languish unanswered at *his* leisure."

Vicky dragged in another deep breath. She knew what her father had not voiced: if the regent refused to decide who would inherit Oakbridge, the estate, the tenants, and everyone who depended on the Astons would suffer. Without a known heir, their tenants wouldn't know who to pay rent to. Without rents, repairs and improvements couldn't be made. The longer uncertainty reigned, the faster their well-functioning estate would devolve into chaos.

Vicky shut her eyes tight. She felt as though a dense fog had enveloped the room and now pressed in on her from all sides. Her pulse thrummed in her ears as she pictured herself shackled to someone like Dain: someone who wouldn't want her recommendations, someone who'd lock her in a room if she disobeyed him. Most of the gentlemen she'd met were decidedly narrow-minded when it came to females interfering in what they considered the male sphere. One of their neighbors had actually choked on his wine when she'd mentioned an essay on animal husbandry she'd recently read.

She ventured a glance at her father, but she couldn't read his expression. Her gaze shot to her mother; regret shrouded her regal features. Her parents' marriage—an actual love match that still flourished—constituted the exception, rather than the rule. Most men didn't care to give their wives the intellectual and physical freedom Vicky's mother had grown so accustomed to over the years. Vicky's father had never subscribed to the philosophy that women were inferior, feebleminded beings.

Vicky thought he had always treated her much as he would have treated a son. Until now.

She raised her chin. "Do you imagine to sell me to the highest bidder like some broodmare at auction?" she bit off.

"Of course not, Victoria," her mother said at the precise moment her father said, "Do you wish to lose Oakbridge to Dain?"

Vicky looked down at her hands, pressing her lips together. She couldn't allow Dain to gain control of her home and everything she'd helped her parents build there. The people, the land, the traditions: their preservation was far more important than her happiness. For that matter, if she kept her freedom, how could she possibly be happy knowing she'd sacrificed everything she held dear?

She glanced at Althea out of the corner of her eye. Her sister's head was bowed, her face a blank. She was pale. Too pale. Vicky knew it was selfish, but she wondered if Thea felt any remorse over the situation Vicky now found herself in.

Heavens, she was a *despicable* person to think such thoughts!

Her stomach roiled. Vicky looked down into her hands again,

wanting desperately to return to her idyllic life of a week prior. Then again, if she were wishing for impossibilities, she'd rather return to the days of her childhood when nothing had been so complex.

"You said you would help." Althea's airy voice echoed through the room.

Vicky turned to her sister. Althea caught her gaze and held it, daring her—or perhaps expecting her—to break her promise. Vicky swallowed back her qualms. She sat up straight in her chair. "And so I shall."

CHAPTER THE FOURTH

Matrimony, as the origin of change,
was always disagreeable...
—Jane Austen, *Emma*

As Vicky and her mother stood at the top of the Duchess of Rutherfurd's grand staircase, Vicky held her breath as she peered down at the ballroom. The room twinkled with hundreds of beeswax candles, illuminating the duchess's Indian theme. Great bolts of richly colored silks draped from the ceiling, swathing the room in a brilliant red hue. Exotic orange flowers imported from the West Indies overflowed from massive urns and vases while East Indian delicacies, artfully arranged on gold platters, waited to be nibbled. One could not help but feel as though a Raj's palace had been constructed in the heart of Mayfair.

However, Vicky's admiration melted with the sound of the murmuring crowd. She would have been more than happy to observe the ball from this very spot rather than become part of the display, but she had promised Althea.

Dear Althea should have been here, smiling and composed, not at home frightened to venture out because of her fiend of a husband. Vicky's sole consolation was that all the fiends she'd ever read about did get their punishment in the end, even if it was only the general disapprobation of society like the silver-tongued Henry Crawford in *Mansfield Park*.

Vicky bit her lower lip as she surveyed the people in the ballroom below. In Miss Austen's novels, girls with country manners and little dowry attended balls and captured every worthy gentleman's eye. *She* at least had a respectable dowry. She should win *someone's* favor. Shouldn't she?

She tilted her head. She really had no reason to suppose she'd have as little success finding a nice gentleman as she'd had last season. In truth, she hadn't really looked, and her parents had generally let her alone to do as she pleased, which had entailed dancing whenever possible and avoiding the girls who acted cattish or rude. Though this was not her debut, she had more to recommend her than Fanny Price, whose first ball in *Mansfield Park* had eventually led to an offer of marriage (from Henry Crawford, but an offer nonetheless).

Vicky's mother gave her a tiny nod, and they descended the staircase.

Vicky's pulse quickened as the beady, hawkish eyes of society assessed her from every angle. She wet her lips. The Duchess of Rutherfurd's ball was the first ostentatious event of the social season, and many considered it the unofficial opening of the marriage mart. Vicky wrinkled her nose, then remembered herself and forced a smile. She would simply have to act as Fanny Price for the evening;

she'd nod and smile and keep her opinions to herself. It wouldn't be easy, but she would keep her promise to Althea, cost what it may.

Exhaling, she glanced down at her gown, thankful her mother had insisted on having new dresses made. According to her mama, one couldn't actively hunt for a husband without a new wardrobe. Whether that was true or not, neither the stuffiest matrons nor the fiercely fashionable could find fault with her lilac gown tonight. The bodice was modestly cut, but the cap sleeves had been trimmed with expensive blond lace and the hem adorned with festoons of the same delicate material. The waist sat fashionably high, and the skirt, ornamented with small pearls, contrasted with the dress's hue and gave it a flirtatious yet elegant appearance.

Vicky's maid had swept her waves into an intricate twist and curled wisps at her hairline to frame her face. The entire process had taken hours. Yet, as much as she appreciated her appearance at this moment, she would much rather be in her favorite breeches or the serviceable frocks she wore to amble about the countryside. Come to that, she'd also rather be curled up in a corner of the library at Oakbridge.

When Vicky and her mother reached the receiving line at the bottom of the staircase, the Duchess of Rutherfurd stared down her beaky nose at them. "Why, Lady Oakbridge, Lady Victoria, what a surprise to see you in Town this early in the season. I had heard the Astons would not be coming up to London until June at the earliest. Yet here you are."

The duchess was a rather large woman with graying hair and a propensity for cutting comments. Unfortunately, as Vicky's mother had reminded her before the ball, the duchess's social position was such that only the prince regent—and sometimes not even he—could make her hold her tongue.

"Duchess," Vicky's mother said, "we would not miss your annual ball for anything. You always host *the* social event of the season."

Vicky smiled politely at the duchess. Her mother had always been a master of social niceties. Vicky's tendency to speak her mind meant the elder members of the *haut ton* had relegated her to the rank of mediocre conversationalist. But in cases such as these, with a disgruntled hostess, Vicky's strategy was to keep her mouth firmly shut and smile. She suppressed the urge to tell the woman there were far more important things happening in the world than her silly ball.

The duchess eyed them both. "That is a verity, to be sure. My balls are rarely surpassed."

Vicky pressed her lips together to suppress a giggle.

"And where is the earl tonight?" the duchess continued.

"He is unwell, I'm afraid," her mother replied. "He sends his apologies."

Ah, her father's well-worn excuse for bowing out of any social function he had no wish to attend. Tonight, however, Althea had refused to venture beyond the confines of Aston House. Their father had stayed to watch over her, lest Dain take the opportunity to steal her back. Until her father had voiced his concerns on the subject, Vicky hadn't imagined Dain might be so desperate as to resort to kidnapping. Yet she had to admit she still knew very little about what the man was capable of.

Althea continued to evade Vicky's attempts to talk about him.

Each day her sister kept her silence increased Vicky's worry for her. And when Vicky wasn't fretting about her sister, her own circumstances troubled her.

The duchess sniffed, clearly displeased. "And where is your other daughter, Lady Oakbridge? She and Lord Dain confirmed they would attend as usual."

Startled, Vicky opened her mouth to inquire further about Dain, but her mother answered quickly.

"Unfortunately, my daughter has also taken ill. Nothing serious. I am certain she must have told Lord Dain to go on without her. No doubt he will arrive later."

The duchess stepped backward. "Two illnesses! I do hope it's nothing catching. It would hardly do for the Aston family to die out."

Vicky's gaze narrowed. The terrible old harpy!

"Indeed," her mother said coldly.

The duchess dismissed them both, with the rejoinder that they simply must enjoy themselves and tell the earl everything he'd missed by not attending.

"Mama, are you not worried about Dain?" Vicky whispered as they crossed the room side by side.

"Not precisely worried. And nor should you be. Althea must have accepted the invitation weeks ago."

"Do you think she feared seeing him here tonight?"

Her mother nodded.

Vicky asked in a whisper, "Has Althea told you anything more of what happened between them?"

"Victoria, this is hardly the place." Her mother looked around her as though someone might have heard them. Guests continued to descend the staircase. Clusters of gentlemen and ladies peppered the room, but few stood within earshot.

"Please, Mama." Dain showing his face tonight was now a very real possibility. It would be prudent to know more of his true character.

Her mother hesitated, but then paced to an empty pocket on the side of the ballroom. She whispered, "I know very little. Althea showed me more of her bruises, but she would not speak further of what had happened. Your father said he would try to draw her out tonight. Perhaps she will have told him more by now. I pray being home under your father's protection and away from Dain for almost a fortnight has put her more at ease."

Vicky sighed and added her own prayers to her mother's. "But what are we to do if Dain comes tonight? He will undoubtedly speak with us. And I cannot fathom his behavior. I know if he comes near me, I'll give that villain a piece of my mind. I'll—"

"No." Her mother narrowed her gaze. "Vicky, you must control yourself. You must act as though nothing has happened."

Vicky gaped at her. "After what he did to Thea! Mama, you cannot be serious."

"I am quite serious," she said, smiling and inclining her head to a small group of middle-aged ladies walking past them toward the refreshment table.

Noting her mother's behavior, Vicky managed a half smile.

"If you make a scene, it will only hurt your chances with the gentlemen," her mother continued. "Simply avoid Dain if you can. If you cannot, come find me or stay in the crowd. Do not give him any opportunity to get you alone."

Vicky bristled. For her sister's sake, she wanted nothing more than to tell Dain how despicable he was, preferably before a crowd of witnesses. But now, thanks to her mother's orders, she wouldn't even be able to berate him in private. She pressed her lips together, remembering her resolve to act as Fanny Price and keep her opinions to herself.

Taking Vicky's silence as acquiescence, her mother changed the subject and pointed out a young gentleman Vicky had met during last year's season, one Lord Waring who would one day inherit a marquisate. Last season, he'd been very much in demand amongst the ladies by sheer virtue of his future title. Vicky had only spoken to him once or twice. But as she followed her mother toward him, Vicky pictured him asking her for the first two dances and finding her company utterly charming.

"How do you do, Lord Waring?" Vicky's mother said.

"Well, Lady Oakbridge, and yourself?" he replied with a bow.

"Very well, indeed. You remember my daughter, Lady Victoria?"

"Of course. How do you find the evening, Lady Victoria?"

"Well, it's barely begun," Vicky said with a smile.

"Indeed," he replied. For a moment he said no more.

"The duchess has outdone herself," Vicky's mother said.

Lord Waring nodded, glancing around him.

Vicky spoke to fill the silence. "I wonder if the food will be brimming with chili peppers. I've read that the food in India is filled with spices and chilies, though I've never sampled the cuisine myself. Have you, Lord Waring?"

"I'm afraid not."

Vicky nodded. "Which would make it all the more interesting if we had the opportunity to sample some this evening, don't you think?"

"Yes, quite. Perhaps I shall see you ladies at dinner." He bowed to them both and walked away.

Vicky blinked. She'd thought their exchange had been going well. Apparently, Lord Waring hadn't thought the same. She made a passable imitation of one of her mother's elegant shrugs.

Her mother nodded. "Don't worry, dear, his looks are slightly less than average anyway."

Vicky wouldn't have gone that far, though he was certainly no Mr. Darcy. Then she realized she hadn't acted like Fanny Price at all. "I should have spoken less, I suppose."

"His father isn't much for conversation either."

Still, if she wished this evening to progress like Fanny Price's triumphant first ball in *Mansfield Park*, then she shouldn't back down from her plan now.

Her mother directed Vicky's attention to one of their acquaintances, Mr. Carmichael. Mr. Carmichael was an attractive gentleman of twenty-five or so, whose fortune was as vast as his holdings. Last summer, he and Vicky's father had bought land adjoining the Kennet and Avon Canal. Primarily a boggy marsh, the land could not be farmed, but if the canal company decided to expand, they'd need to drain water from the property.

Two months ago, Mr. Carmichael had come down to Oakbridge with news that the canal company was expanding; he'd negotiated a lucrative deal for their property's water rights. In addition, they could use the property, once drained, as farmland. Her father had put their success down to Carmichael's business acumen and had nothing but admiration for him. Vicky had thought Mr. Carmichael very agreeable at Oakbridge, and they had even flirted a little, but it had gone no further.

At this moment, Mr. Carmichael stood by the refreshment table speaking with a gentleman Vicky didn't know. The man looked slightly younger than Carmichael and had rather average good looks.

"Stand up straight, dear," her mother said, signaling for Vicky to follow.

Thinking of Fanny Price, Vicky pasted on a demure smile. She intended to be very much a success tonight.

Before they reached the gentlemen, the unknown man departed in the direction of the card room. At least she wouldn't have to worry about assessing someone new just yet. And she knew Mr. Carmichael considerably better than Lord Waring.

Vicky's mother extended her hand as they approached. "Mr. Carmichael, what a pleasure. We have not seen you since the winter."

Mr. Carmichael took her hand in his. "Lady Oakbridge, the pleasure is mine entirely."

Vicky watched as Carmichael's dark head bent over her mother's hand. The man was more attractive than she remembered. Black hair waved about his ears in an unaffected style. His expensive black coat and trousers had been tailored to show off his broad chest and muscular frame to their best advantage. His facial features, if considered separately, were rather sharp, but as Vicky gazed at him, she mused that his aquiline nose, cleft chin, and square jaw and forehead rendered him strikingly handsome when taken together.

"And how is your lovely mother? Is she in Town?" Vicky's mother asked.

Carmichael nodded. "I'm certain you will see her shortly." He looked around. "She is about somewhere."

Vicky's mother gestured to her. "Of course you remember my daughter?"

"Impossible that I should forget such beauty." Carmichael turned to smile at Vicky. "Lady Victoria, are you not taller than when last I saw you?"

Vicky gave him an arch look. One thing she hadn't forgotten about him was his height. At just an inch over five feet tall, Vicky was accustomed to looking up at men's faces, but the contrast between her and Mr. Carmichael was somewhat absurd. If they stood closely together, she had to crane her neck upward at an uncomfortable angle to avoid holding a conversation with his chest.

Speaking to him now was equally as uncomfortable as it had been two months ago, of which he was no doubt completely aware. How typical of him to follow a compliment with a jibe. At Oakbridge, he'd made a habit of trying to catch her off-guard.

"Not unless you have shrunk by some mysterious method, Mr. Carmichael."

Inwardly, she winced. She must remember her aim. *Fanny Price, Mansfield Park.* She repeated the words like a mantra in her head. *Be delicate, restrained . . .*

But Carmichael laughed, and she held out her hand to him with a smile. He bowed over it slightly, gazing down into her eyes as he brushed the back of her glove with his lips. The action was rather scandalous, and he watched for her reaction. But if he wanted her to blush or simper, Vicky wouldn't give him the satisfaction.

"I don't believe this roguish demeanor quite becomes you," she said.

His brows shot upward.

"Victoria," her mother hissed.

"I had no notion I was affecting one, Lady Victoria," Carmichael said, though his lips quirked up at one side.

"Or perhaps you have different manners in Town than you had in the country."

"*Victoria*," her mother said in a warning tone.

"Lady Victoria is quite right, Lady Oakbridge," Mr. Carmichael said. "I shall endeavor to better behave myself." He nodded at her, but Vicky bit her lip. She hadn't meant to tell him how to behave— he was a capable, grown gentleman.

Fanny Price would never have been so forward. "No, I should apologize. I did not mean to imply—that is, I hope I have not . . ." She trailed off, unsure what to say next. This was why she hated society. At Oakbridge, he might have tried to tease her, but she never would have worried over her conduct and made such a blunder. Well, she might have spoken her mind and floundered in the process, but it would have been far less embarrassing in the comfort of home.

He shook his head. "There is no need for apologies. You have done me a favor, Lady Victoria. I should hate to appear insincere." He said it with a smile, but mortification still clawed at her.

"You are too kind, Mr. Carmichael," her mother said.

"Not at all," he said.

Vicky smiled at him, but resolved to keep her lips firmly pressed together from this moment on.

"Oh, there is your charming mother, Mr. Carmichael," Vicky's mother said, gesturing across the room at a group of ladies. "Do excuse me a moment."

Mr. Carmichael gave a shallow bow. Vicky widened her eyes to signal her mama to stay, but her mother simply smiled at them both before sweeping herself away.

Vicky let out a slow breath. Her mother was only slightly less subtle than Mrs. Bennet in *Pride and Prejudice*. If not for Vicky's dowry, she shuddered to think what blunt tactics her mama might employ to gain her a husband.

Vicky gave Mr. Carmichael an awkward smile. Carmichael smiled back at her. She couldn't very well *not* speak to him now.

"How have you been since we saw you last, Mr. Carmichael?" she asked, thinking that would be a safe, proper subject.

"Oh, pray, let us speak of the fascinating state of each other's health—I am quite well, by the by, as indeed you seem to be. Or perhaps we could discuss the even more enthralling topic of the weather." He clasped his hands behind his back.

She laughed, then pressed her lips together. Leave it to him to come to the point and avoid idle chitchat. "What do you wish to speak of?"

He frowned, considering. "Have you been in London long?"

"That is hardly a scintillating topic," she replied with a smile.

He nodded. "True, but I ask so I may discern whether you've had sufficient opportunity to see the sapient pig yet?"

She tilted her chin down. "The 'sapient' pig?"

He inclined his head solemnly. "The most intelligent performing pig in all England. His name is Toby. He and his owner appeared at Vauxhall Gardens this past week."

"I had not heard." She raised her brows. "What does a sapient pig do?"

He shrugged. "I could not say what all sapient pigs do, but Toby spells, figures sums, reads the time, and finds points on the globe."

Her lip twitched. "Remarkable. If only he could read thoughts as well." Her eyes widened. "*Or* tell fortunes. I have always thought the world needed more oracular pigs."

"Then he will not disappoint."

"Really? How do you know?"

"Well, Lady Victoria, for one indisputable reason." He leaned in and down so his face was only marginally higher than hers. "The advertisement said so."

She blinked. Then she laughed. Louder than she'd meant to.

Mr. Carmichael straightened with a grin.

"I see," she said, not daring to look around to see if anyone was currently watching them. "Then you did not actually experience the wonder that is Toby firsthand."

As he laughed—a rich, warm resonance emanating from deep in his throat—Vicky's lips curved into a smile. She hoped he laughed often, because it would be a shame to deprive the world of that sound.

"Regrettably, no," he said.

"A great loss, I am certain," she pronounced, still smiling.

He grinned back at her, and her stomach did a little flip. He *was* quite handsome. Especially when his sable eyes fixed on hers.

"I didn't know you possessed such talent for levity, Carmichael," said a familiar, unwelcome voice. Vicky slowly turned.

"You know me, Dain," Mr. Carmichael said. "I am a veritable fount of frivolity."

"Hardly how I would describe you."

Carmichael shrugged. "Perhaps I find myself in the right company," he said, inclining his head in Vicky's direction.

"Quite so," Dain replied, turning to face her.

Vicky shuddered. She wasn't sure what she'd expected, but Dain had not grown fangs, or attained a ghastly green pallor. He appeared to be his usual, composed self. Though he was of medium height and build, Dain carried himself with the self-assured confidence of a man who believed himself the superior of everyone else in the room. His light brown hair curled around his forehead in the popular Greek fashion he favored. His mouth curved in a smug smile.

Vicky struggled not to sneer at him.

"My dear sister. How are you on this fine evening?" he said without a trace of sarcasm.

Vicky thought of Althea. She thought of all the days her poor, lovely sister must have spent trying not to anger this man, all the times she must have cowered away from him. He'd fooled her whole family with his charm.

Outwardly, Dain hadn't changed since Vicky had last seen him, but now the sight of him made her sick to her stomach.

"I am well. Thank you." She kept her tone curt, her answer concise. She had no wish to speak to him, but if she made a scene, everyone would know Dain and the Astons were on unfavorable terms. For Althea's sake, they all had to minimize the scandal.

Vicky tried to catch Carmichael's eye, but he'd focused his gaze on Lord Dain. She racked her brain for a new subject—anything to get the conversation going again or induce Dain to leave. "Have you attended the new opera, Mr. Carmichael?"

Carmichael shook his head and started to respond, but Dain cut him off.

"Sister, I was wondering if we could take a turn around the room?"

She stared at him. This was exactly what her mother had warned her of. And exactly what she shouldn't allow to happen.

"I'm afraid I am engaged at present." Vicky smiled at Mr. Carmichael, hoping he'd catch the hint. Maybe he would ask her to dance. But no, the music hadn't started yet.

"So I see, but it concerns your sister," Dain continued. His countenance betrayed nothing of his thoughts. "She has a request—one she would rather I apprise you of privately."

Vicky suppressed a scowl. She couldn't very well refuse without Mr. Carmichael wondering why. She scanned the room for her mother as subtly as she could, but she was hidden amongst the masses.

To Vicky's amazement, Carmichael seemed to sense something amiss. "Lord Dain," Carmichael began, "could I trouble you with something before I forget? It's a business matter."

Vicky sighed inwardly. He'd saved her, if only for a moment. She looked around the room again.

Meanwhile, Dain turned to respond to Mr. Carmichael.

"Surely it can wait," he said, sounding irritated. "We can discuss business at a more appropriate occasion."

Vicky frowned. Did Mr. Carmichael and Dain actually have business dealings?

Lord Dain offered her his arm. Gooseflesh rose on the back of her neck. What more could Mr. Carmichael do? Vicky swallowed hard. What could *she* do?

At that precise moment, a booming voice announced, "Lord Thomas Sherborne, the Earl of Halworth."

CHAPTER THE FIFTH

I cannot forget the follies and vices of others so soon as I ought, nor their offences against myself.
—Jane Austen, *Pride and Prejudice*

As countless feet pivoted and scores of heads craned to focus on him, Tom forced himself to look past the sea of scrutinizing eyes and make his way down the staircase with a modicum of dignity—no easy task since every giggle and whisper made him want to do something unspeakable to his brother. This night—the night Tom had anticipated for weeks—could make or break their family. He had thought he'd made Charles acutely aware of that fact.

Charles had even sworn to stand by him, all in the name of family honor, brotherly love, and other such gibberish. But tonight at eleven, when Tom had sent his butler to track his brother's progress, the man had returned with an apologetic frown, saying, "Mr. Sherborne says he shall be another quarter of an hour." When, sometime past midnight, the butler's response devolved into "Mr. Sherborne says he can meet you there if you're impatient, my lord," Tom had been too offended to do anything but leave for the ball.

He took a deep breath and tried to shake off his annoyance. He should be accustomed to people disappointing him by now.

Tom scanned the room for anyone he knew but only saw curious, unfamiliar eyes. It was no surprise. His father had cut him off without so much as a shilling when he was still in his early years at Eton. He'd lost contact with all his school friends; as a result, he knew nobody in society other than a few acquaintances of his parents. The Duchess of Rutherfurd was one such connection and the reason he'd received an invitation.

Tom's mother felt it high time he take his place in the social order. She wanted him to reclaim all his father had denied him five years ago. But Tom's ambitions for this evening had little to do with regaining his social position.

If not for his mother's family, Tom would have been the only fourteen-year-old lord living on the London streets. The price of survival came complete with room, board, and permanent employment in his uncle's hotel in the Swiss city of Solothurn. Eventually he'd worked his way into the position of assistant manager of the Bodmerhaus am Fluss.

His experience helping his uncle had given him the idea to open London's very first European-inspired luxury hotel. With Napoleon Bonaparte now safely exiled to St. Helena, travel was safer, and it was considerably simpler for people from the Continent to journey to England. If a city as small as Solothurn could accommodate more than one successful hotel, a city of London's magnitude could certainly benefit from such a place as Tom envisioned.

Unfortunately, the brother who had promised to help him in this undertaking by introducing him to potential backers had proved unreliable. Leaving the town house without him may not have been the wisest course.

No, he should have dragged Charles down the stairs, into the carriage . . .

But Tom didn't finish the thought. The duchess's grand staircase ended, and as he reached the bottom, he smiled as though he were greeting the wealthiest patron of his uncle's hotel and bowed over the duchess's extended hand. He could bloody well do this on his own.

"Lord Halworth, I am honored to be the first in London to have you as a guest," the duchess said grandly.

"Duchess, it is I who am honored by your invitation."

"Come now, your mother and I have been friends since her first season out in society. The Sherbornes have a standing invitation to my annual ball," she said.

Tom inclined his head in thanks.

"Where is your charming mother?"

"I'm afraid she elected to remain in the country. She is still in mourning."

"But surely she is now in half mourning. It has been more than a year since the earl's passing."

Tom could only nod. His mother *was* in half mourning, and she could attend balls and social gatherings if it pleased her. Yet she had told her sons to say she was still grieving.

"You will tell her I asked after her?" the duchess asked.

"Of course."

As she nodded and moved to dismiss him, Tom realized the answer to his problem stood before him.

"Duchess, would you be so kind as to introduce me to some of your guests? I admit I have no acquaintance here."

The duchess raised a single eyebrow at his question.

"My dear boy, you surprise me."

Tom couldn't fathom why. He *had* been abroad for nearly four years. "Do I?"

"I know for a certainty there are *two* ladies of your acquaintance here tonight."

Tom nearly groaned aloud. Was the duchess referring to whom he thought she was? "Indeed?"

"Lady Oakbridge and her daughter."

"Ah, certainly. And which daughter, pray?" *Let it be Althea.*

"Lady Victoria."

Of course it was.

"I'm sure they would be happy to introduce you to some of my guests as I am still rather busy."

She surveyed the room, and Tom tried to think of a way out of the blasted situation. The last thing he wanted to do was impose on Victoria and the countess. During their encounter last week, Vicky's mother had been short with him, and the earl had been polite in an aloof sort of way. Tom had gone away with the distinct impression they'd both be glad to see the back of him.

When Tom was a boy, the Earl of Oakbridge had taken more interest in his endeavors than his own father had. The thought that more had changed in Tom's absence than he'd realized had kept Tom from returning to Oakbridge to inquire after Victoria's health. Within days of the incident with the bandit, Tom's mother had told him the Astons had removed to London. Tom had departed for Town soon after. Yet for some foolish reason, it had not occurred to him that the Astons might be present this evening.

The duchess pointed across the room. "Ah, there is Lady Victoria! Near the refreshment table."

Tom's eyes followed her bejeweled hand to rest upon Vicky. She wore a flattering, pale purple gown and stood between two men, one of whom towered over her. Obviously, Victoria had recovered from the other day without any lasting effects.

"Go over there," the duchess commanded. "I shall find you later when I have some time."

Tom swallowed hard. He really *should* tell the duchess no. This was bound to be terribly awkward. Instead, he bowed and hoped he'd disguised his grimace.

Tom moved farther into the ballroom. He couldn't walk directly toward Victoria as the musicians had finished tuning their instruments, and many of the guests were making their way to the center of the room, taking their places in the line of dancers in order of precedence.

The violinist began to play, the flautists joined him, and couples bowed and curtsied to each other.

Skirting a golden urn overflowing with red and orange flowers and a knee-high, papier-mâché figurine that appeared to be an elephant with the shaggy tail of a deerhound, Tom started around the perimeter of the ballroom. He searched the crowd thoroughly, hoping for salvation in the form of an old school friend or someone similar, but no one materialized.

He would simply have to ask for Vicky's help in a civilized fashion. Surely she wouldn't refuse to perform a few introductions.

He cleared his throat. He didn't like asking her for a favor. Tom maneuvered around a group of giggling girls who frantically fanned themselves as he passed.

If he couldn't make his hotel work . . . well, he couldn't consider that possibility now. And if swallowing his pride by asking for Vicky's help with something trivial was the only way, then so be it.

All around Vicky, heads turned curiously toward the staircase.

Any thoughts of Dain and Mr. Carmichael disappeared as the air fled her body and her left hand flew to the base of her throat. Tom couldn't be *here*. She wanted to look, but her neck felt frozen. What was he doing in London? He hadn't mentioned he'd be taking part in the season.

She frowned. Then again, they hadn't really spoken of anything commonplace that day at Oakbridge.

Hoping it wasn't true, she craned her neck toward the grand staircase. Tom walked down the stairs and into the ballroom.

His face was somber, but he held his head high. He wore a black coat and trousers that contrasted perfectly with his cream-colored waistcoat. A closer examination proved impossible, for when the staircase ended, Tom disappeared behind the crowd. Vicky forced herself to lower her hand to the side of her body.

Thanks to Tom's mother, Vicky's family knew the old Lord Halworth had banished Tom and prevented him from returning to Halworth Hall, but Tom's exile was not common knowledge. Society knew the heir to the Earl of Halworth had been abroad for many years, but nothing more.

Unfortunately for Tom, that made him a social oddity. Eldest sons of the peerage were kept close to home where their fathers could monitor their behavior—not sent to live on the Continent in a time of war before they'd even finished school. Many in society likely thought Tom had been at fault.

From what Vicky had seen the last day they'd spoken in 1812, Tom's father had certainly thought so. She'd known Tom too well to think the worst of him, but the fact that he'd refused to see or speak with her afterward had shaken some of her confidence in him. Now she didn't know what she thought.

Many young ladies tittered behind their hands; Vicky could hear some of them murmuring Tom's name. Meanwhile, the matrons bent their heads to gossip and throw predatory looks in Tom's direction. Vicky pursed her lips. It was fitting that Tom, who had made no forays into society in the entire year since he'd returned home, should get more attention tonight than he probably had in his whole life.

Encountering Tom unprepared twice in the course of a fortnight seemed the height of injustice. She took a deep breath. At least she was suitably attired this time.

As she turned back to face the gentlemen, she remembered she had been about to tell Dain to go to the devil. That or run for her mother's skirts like a frightened child. If only she could use Tom's entrance as an excuse to leave, but a young lady could not leave her companions to greet a gentleman without the company of a chaperone. Mr. Carmichael would think her forward or ill-mannered. Or both.

She raised her chin. She would handle this situation as Elizabeth Bennet would. After Mr. Wickham had run off to London with Elizabeth's sister Lydia, the couple returned to Longbourn. Elizabeth had been polite to Wickham but had also made it clear she knew what kind of scoundrel he was.

Vicky could do the same to Dain. As she stretched to her full height, she realized Mr. Carmichael's blackish-brown gaze centered on her. She could not guess his thoughts, but unfortunately, there would be no further help from that quarter. Mr. Carmichael had no claim on her that could keep her from a family member.

Mr. Carmichael locked eyes with her just as Dain pulled her arm into the crook of his. Vicky's lips tightened into a line. *Blasted, beastly brother-in-law . . .*

Dain nodded to Carmichael and led her away.

She glanced back at Mr. Carmichael. He watched her, a small crease forming between his brows. Vicky searched for her mother once again, but she had disappeared.

"Well, my dear, dear sister," said Dain. "You look stunning this evening. A new gown, I take it?" His amber eyes traveled up and down her body.

Vicky's stomach lurched. "You swine," she spat. "How dare you look at me in such a fashion?" So much for being polite.

"Why, Lady Victoria, such language," he mocked.

She narrowed her eyes. "But then, I suppose I've answered my own question," she continued. "Swine are too bestial to have a conscience. Indeed, they enjoy wallowing in the mud." Elizabeth Bennet's subtlety had deserted her, but blast it. Dain deserved to know what he was!

He put his free hand on her arm and squeezed. The motion would look like fraternal devotion to any onlooker, but it was becoming more and more painful by the second.

Vicky gasped.

He chuckled deep in his throat.

How had he hidden his cruelty all these years? She tried to move away, but his grip tightened. She suppressed her grimace.

She spoke through clenched teeth. "Take your hand off me."

"Or what, dear sister? What can you possibly do?" He smiled again.

Bile rose in her throat. So *this* was the monster Thea had lived with for two years. But his question remained: What could she do? What if he took her out of the ballroom? Who knew what he might do to her if they were beyond the gaze of prying eyes?

Vicky's heart drummed in her chest. Maybe she could knock him in the face with her reticule, or if worse came to worse, somewhere more painful, but she couldn't do *that* in the ballroom without appearing mad. If she waited until he took her somewhere private, there was no guarantee she'd be able to break free of him.

Suddenly, an answer came to her. She spoke loudly so the guests nearby would overhear. "Oh, Lord Dain, the ribbon on my slipper has snapped. Pray excuse me. I am certain someone in the retiring room will be able to assist me."

He tutted with false concern, then gestured to the side of the ballroom. "There is a chair. I shall fix it for you."

She raised her voice again. "No, no. I'd much rather retire for a moment." If she said much more, the entire ballroom would think she needed the privy.

He pulled her to the edge of the ballroom. "My dear sister, I could not possibly part with your company." His hand gripped her arm like a vise.

Vicky narrowed her eyes. She wouldn't give him the satisfaction of thinking he could do this to her. "Take your hand off me, or I swear to scream the truth to the entire ballroom," she whispered.

"What truth would that be?" he drawled.

"That you've been beating my sister to within an inch of her life and you're taking me outside to do the same to me."

He laughed. "I'm afraid, dear sister, no one would believe you." His lips curved into a sneer.

His repeated use of "sister" made her itch to slap him. "Perhaps not now. Not yet."

He gripped her arm even tighter and angled his body to face her. "Just what does that mean?"

Her stomach dropped. She'd said too much. Althea had only been in London a week and the lawyers couldn't start the proceedings for her legal separation yet. Her mind raced for an answer to distract Dain. "That you will reveal your own character. Just as you have tonight." She glared at him, refusing to blink.

His lips twisted in a snarl. "Do not try my patience," he said, anger infused into every syllable.

Before she could say another word, Dain abruptly released her arm and stepped back.

"Lady Victoria. How lovely to see you again."

Vicky's throat went dry. She turned and saw that, to her simultaneous joy and dismay, Tom stood beside her.

Tom smiled and took Vicky's hand.

She could hardly believe it. He'd sought her out amongst the hordes of people here? She blinked several times, trying to guess his reasoning. A short stillness ensued until Vicky realized she'd left her hand in his grip a hair longer than was proper. She pulled her hand back and cast her eyes down, hoping her heated cheeks weren't noticeable.

"L-Lord Halworth, what a surprise." Unsure of what to do, Vicky forced a polite smile.

"I suppose it must be. No doubt you thought me still in Hampshire."

Vicky frowned. Was he implying her family should have called at Halworth Hall to say goodbye when they'd left for London? Perhaps they should have done, but they'd all been so rattled about Althea's situation and their impending removal to London, it hadn't occurred to them. At least, it hadn't crossed *her* mind. She couldn't speak for her mother. And it wasn't as though *he* had called to see after her health.

"And Murton," he addressed Dain, "it *has* been a long while. Not since Eton."

Vicky raised her brows. She hadn't been aware they knew each other.

"It's Lord Dain now, Halworth," Dain answered smoothly. "I'll admit I never thought to see *you* at an assembly such as this."

"No more did I," Tom replied with an agreeable smile.

Vicky frowned. Had Tom thought he wouldn't return? His father couldn't have lived forever.

"The fellows laid odds as to the mystery of your disappearance for months," Dain continued.

"My uncle fell ill abroad. I was the only one who could be of use to him," Tom rattled off easily.

"I have no doubt," Dain said, his tone dripping with sarcasm. "What a prolonged illness it must have been."

"*The war* made my immediate return rather difficult."

Dain seemed to have no reply. Vicky bit her lip to hide her smile.

"But I am here now and, to celebrate my return, I am of a mind to dance."

Vicky tipped her chin to the side. This new amiability was so at odds with his stiff demeanor the other day.

He inclined his head toward her. "Would you do me the honor of partnering me for the next set, Lady Victoria? I believe it is about to begin."

Her eyes widened as her lips formed an "Oh." Had he really sought her out before any other lady in the room for a dance? "I would be delighted, Lord Halworth." Not that she'd forgiven him for, well . . . anything. But what cared she for his motives when he'd given her an escape from Dain?

Tom offered his arm. She put her gloved hand on his forearm and stepped away from Dain. The contours of Dain's face hardened, and then he wiped clean any expression. She silently thanked Tom for rescuing her.

"Dain," Tom said by way of farewell.

Dain did not return the nicety.

Tom steered them away. Vicky threw Dain a nasty look over her shoulder. His face did not alter. He continued to stand there as Tom led her to the center of the room.

Vicky peeked up at Tom's profile. "I must thank you."

He raised an eyebrow. "For?"

She paused. *Saving me from a horrible brute.* "You are the first gentleman to ask me to dance."

His lips twitched as he set her on the ladies' side of the line of couples. He leaned in and murmured, "You are the first lady to dance with me at a ball."

"Am I?"

His smile came on by degrees, each increment lightening the serious set of his jaw and brow. For the life of her, she couldn't drag her eye away from her first glimpse of that boyish grin she remembered so well. "You didn't attend balls abroad?"

He shook his head, then turned to stand across from her, next to the other gentlemen. When he looked at her again, he'd erased all remnants of the smile from his face. How very reserved and changeable he was. Almost like Edward Ferrars at the beginning of *Sense and Sensibility*. Perhaps he too had a secret engagement? A commitment to someone on the Continent? She raised her glove to her lips to disguise a giggle. It would serve him right if he'd made an imprudent attachment to a girl who'd only chased him for his title—not that it would be any of Vicky's business, of course.

The dance announced was to be a quick country dance where partners changed frequently. There'd be little time for conversation. The music began and they stepped together. She clasped Tom's gloved hand with her own across their bodies, and they switched positions. Holding his gaze unnerved her, and she was glad as they turned away from each other and weaved through the other dancers.

How strange it felt to be near him in this way—to be dancing in a ballroom like proper adults—not fishing or riding or climbing a haystack. She bit her lip, dearly wishing she didn't miss those days as much as she did.

They met again down the line of couples. "I did care to ask you something," Tom said as they joined hands. "But if you'd rather not—" He broke off as two other couples danced between them.

She tilted her head. What could he need?

They turned and cast down the line. When they met once more, Vicky prompted him. "Yes?"

But more couples danced between them through the line. Tom looked around and didn't seem to care to say more. Vicky stayed silent and enjoyed the energetic movements.

As the dance continued at a lively pace, Tom's restraint drained away until he seemed to have forgotten whatever force made him so distant. On each occasion when he took her hand and caught her eye, she saw another glimmer of the boy she remembered: the boy who'd smiled easily and raced with her around the rose garden, in good spirits whether he won or lost.

As the musicians struck the last chords and Vicky curtsied to Tom, she couldn't stop herself from smiling. Her cheeks were pink with joy, her spirit brighter. The candlelight flickered, casting an inviting glow over Tom's brow and cheekbones as he offered her his arm with a smile.

She placed her hand on his coat. "You dance rather well for one who doesn't attend balls."

He issued a strangled laugh. "I never said I didn't dance."

She wondered when he could have learned, but she didn't dare ask in case it made his good humor disappear. "True. Perhaps we could again?" She didn't care how bold she sounded. The dance had been so pleasant. He'd actually looked *happy.* Then she remembered she wasn't there to have fun; she was there to find a husband.

It was just as well, for his smile faded. She looked forward. Fanny Price *never* would have asked a gentleman for a dance. Vicky pressed her lips together. Not even Emma Woodhouse would have exhibited such foolish disregard for the rules of society. Vicky glanced at Tom out of the corner of her eye, almost fancying he'd say, "It was badly done, indeed!" as Mr. Knightley said to Emma at Box Hill.

Instead, he simply said, "Of course."

But he did have a very Mr. Knightley demeanor when he said it.

"First there was something I wished to ask."

She nodded. "Yes, indeed. I had forgotten."

Tom cleared his throat. "Victoria, do you think, that is, would you . . ."

She looked up to catch his eye.

"Would you be so kind as to introduce me to some of your acquaintances?"

She laughed. "Oh, Tom! Is that all? You made me think you needed something quite impossible. Of course I shall."

"Thank you. Having been away so long—" He exhaled and nodded at her. "Thank you." His light brown gaze captured hers with its sincerity.

She looked away. His variability puzzled her.

Then it struck her. *This* must be why he'd sought her out. "Don't you have any acquaintances present?"

He led her around the edge of the ballroom. "You, Lady Oakbridge, Lord Dain, and our hostess are the only people here with whom I am acquainted."

"I see." Vicky frowned. But why had he come to the ball alone? Charles or his mother should have accompanied him, especially if he needed to make new acquaintances.

"Did the countess and Charles accompany you to Town?"

He cleared his throat. "My mother stayed in the country. Charles was unexpectedly . . . detained this evening."

Vicky nodded, biting her lower lip. "Clearly, you didn't care to ask Dain or my mother, but what of the duchess?"

"She was"—he paused—"busy." He stared straight ahead as he said it. He couldn't even be bothered to look at her.

She straightened to her full height. "So you needed not a dance, but my help."

He caught her eye. "Yes. Very much. If you'd be so kind." The authenticity in his voice partially melted through her anger.

Very well, perhaps a dash more than *partially*. "Of course." She cleared her throat, telling herself Althea would have done the same had she been here.

"Again, I thank you," he said, inclining his head with a smile that would have charmed her if it reached his eyes.

She furrowed her brow, not at all certain she liked this new Tom. He was guarded, cautious, and it seemed not altogether *honest*.

"Are you quite recovered after last week's events?" he asked.

She blinked, at first mistaking him to mean Althea. "Me? Ah. Yes, my head is much better."

"I'm pleased to hear it. I wrote your father a note, but I don't believe he received it. Sir Aylward sent men and dogs to track the man, but they found no trace of him."

Vicky sighed, remembering the determination in the man's eyes as he galloped straight toward her. "He didn't seem likely to stay in the neighborhood."

Tom made a noise in his throat. "True." Then he asked abruptly, "How do you know Dain?"

She frowned at the question. "He is my brother-in-law."

Tom stopped midstride. He turned to face her. "*He* is Althea's husband?"

"Didn't you know?"

"My mother told me of her marriage, but I don't recall her mentioning Dain's name. When did they marry?"

"Almost two years past."

Tom nodded with a creased brow. "Letters from England were scarce those years. The French intercepted a great deal."

Vicky shook her head. "It must have been so strange. I cannot imagine how you must have lived—"

"Yes. Well, there's no need to dwell on those old griefs now. We survived."

Vicky grimaced and didn't press him further. There'd been no question of survival at Oakbridge. They'd grown extra crops to sell to the government for the soldiers abroad and been paid handsomely for their efforts. Life had continued much as it always had. Except Tom had been absent.

"Well," she said, trying to sound cheerful, "shall we introduce you to someone or do you plan to walk the fringes of the ballroom with me all evening?"

"Lead the way, Lady Victoria."

She espied Mr. Carmichael speaking with two men. One of them, she recognized as the Viscount Axley. He was another friend of her parents. She steered Tom toward the group.

She begged their pardon for interrupting their discourse, then proceeded to perform the proper introductions. Lord Axley greeted Tom warmly. Mr. Carmichael acknowledged Tom with a short nod. The third gentleman was the same man she'd seen speaking to Mr. Carmichael earlier. He had straight, dark hair and looked to be slightly younger than Mr. Carmichael.

Mr. Carmichael spoke. "Lady Victoria, may I present the Honorable Rupert Silby, son of the Baron Scarborough?"

She nodded and smiled.

"Silby, this is Lady Victoria Aston."

"Lady Victoria," Mr. Silby said, taking her hand and bowing

over it, "it is a pleasure to meet you. I had the honor of making your mother's acquaintance while you were dancing."

He must have asked her mother's permission for the introduction. "Ah yes. How pleasant." She introduced Mr. Silby to Tom.

Both men inclined their heads. "I hear you were abroad for several years," Silby said to Tom. "Where did you frequent?"

"I was in the Swiss Confederation primarily. Solothurn. I returned to England last year."

"Ah, I was there on my grand tour," Lord Axley said. "Though I must say I preferred Lucerne. By the time I crossed the Channel in the spring of '98, I learned I'd just narrowly missed the French invasion."

"You were fortunate, sir," Tom said with a serious nod.

Silby and Axley plied Tom with more questions about his time abroad, seemingly fascinated by how the Swiss had lived with the French, and how anyone could stand being without steady English fare for so long. Tom weathered their questions with ease, though he spoke only in generalities. Vicky looked away, irritated he could speak of his life abroad with men he'd just met, yet not at all with her.

She set her jaw. His behavior all led to one inexorable conclusion: he no longer wished to be anything other than acquaintances.

Which was all the better for her. After tonight, she would think of him as a full-blown character from her past—one she'd remember with occasional fondness, but no regret. The way Emma Woodhouse thought of Frank Churchill.

When Vicky looked up, she discovered that in contrast to

everyone else, Mr. Carmichael's dark eyes—just a shade or two lighter than black—focused not on Tom, but on her. She swallowed. The same crease she'd noticed earlier appeared between his brows. He broke eye contact and scanned the area behind her.

She followed his gaze. Was he looking for Dain? A moment later, he caught her eye and smiled. Was he trying to tell her Dain had gone? If so, she liked him all the more. She smiled back and realized he had a small, thin scar above his left eyebrow.

Worried she'd been staring, she looked away, turning her attention back to Tom and the tide of conversation. She peeked at Mr. Carmichael through her eyelashes. He watched her still. Her pulse quickened.

"Have you been reading lately, Lady Victoria?" Mr. Carmichael said, changing the subject so abruptly, the other men glanced at him.

"Er, yes," she said as the focus shifted to her.

"Lady Victoria is a great reader, I believe," Mr. Carmichael said to the group. She wondered if Mr. Carmichael was teasing her again, but she detected no mirth in his face.

"Really?" Lord Axley said.

"Not a *great* reader," Vicky said, remembering the few times she'd attempted to speak to gentlemen of books last season and the glazed expressions she'd always elicited. But her father had actually boasted of her knowledge of estate workings to Mr. Carmichael when he'd visited Oakbridge, and he hadn't seemed at all disapproving. "I try to keep abreast of the latest tracts on animal husbandry, crop yields, and the most beneficial management strategies." As she spoke, Lord Axley and Mr. Carmichael nodded and smiled. Tom remained still, and Mr. Silby's eyes widened with what she took for disbelief. "But beyond that I mostly read novels."

"Ah, which are your favorites?" Lord Axley asked.

"*Pride and Prejudice, Emma*, and *Sense and Sensibility*," Vicky pronounced without hesitation.

"Ah, those of Miss Jane Austen, I believe," Lord Axley said. "I quite liked *Emma*, myself."

Vicky hadn't understood Miss Austen's identity to be public knowledge, yet she *had* dedicated *Emma* to the prince regent, so perhaps certain members of London society knew more of her than Vicky had realized.

Vicky smiled at Lord Axley. It felt like her first genuine one of the evening. "Did you, Lord Axley?"

"Very much, though I did think *Mansfield Park* a better novel," he replied.

Vicky nodded. Althea felt much the same as Lord Axley, and she and Althea had often debated the point.

"Perhaps, but Elizabeth Bennet is surely the most delightful of Miss Austen's heroines," said Carmichael.

Vicky's eyes widened as she caught Mr. Carmichael's gaze. "That is precisely what *I* believe."

He nodded as if that were obvious. "What say you, Silby?"

"I'm not one for novels," Mr. Silby replied, looking like he'd attended little to the conversation since it began.

"Have you read them, Lord Halworth?" Lord Axley asked.

Tom shook his head. "I'm afraid I haven't yet had the opportunity. Are they at all like Mrs. Radcliffe's novels?"

Vicky shook her head. "Not at all." Ann Radcliffe wrote sensational romances where the women were often the victims of terrible villains and rogues. "Mrs. Radcliffe's novels are an exaggerated version of life—dark abbeys with skeletons in chests, trapdoors, abductions, assassins—those sorts of things don't happen to real people. Miss Austen's novels are much more analogous to life."

"Really?" Tom said.

Vicky nodded. "Ladies with no dowries find wealthy husbands who cherish them. Worthy men act honorably. Life *should* be so tidy and end so happily."

Tom frowned slightly. Then he looked away, saying nothing.

Vicky pressed her lips together and tried not to let his judgment anger her. What did he know? He hadn't even read any of Miss Austen's books!

"And how do you know Lady Victoria, Lord Halworth?" Mr. Silby asked.

Vicky glanced at Tom. He smiled as he pushed his right hand through his hair. The waves of his hair had been brushed sometime earlier in the evening, but now the brown locks fell over his forehead in disarray. In that at least, he had not changed.

"Would you believe we grew up together, on neighboring estates?" Tom replied.

"Indeed?" Silby said.

"Indeed," Tom affirmed. "We were inseparable even into our adolescence."

Vicky's chest constricted. Everything was so different now.

"*That*, I do not believe," Silby pronounced. "When I was younger, I would have been ashamed to associate with a girl. Even one so lovely as Lady Victoria," he added, almost as an afterthought.

Carmichael clapped him on the arm. "Your loss, I am certain, Silby."

Axley laughed. "Quite right!"

Silby shot Carmichael an annoyed look. Mr. Carmichael ignored him. Tom's expression stayed neutral.

Vicky pasted a tolerant smile on her face, even as the irony of Mr. Silby's comment brought roses to her cheeks. That was precisely what *had* happened. Tom had turned his back on their friendship without a second thought, without even giving her an opportunity to fix it.

She took a fortifying breath. Tom could go to the devil. She wasn't here to think about him. She was here for Althea.

"Gentlemen, if you will excuse me, I believe I see my friend. I really must say hello before she is claimed for every dance." It was a feeble excuse. She had no friend in this room. Oh, she could speak to some of the young ladies who'd made their debut with her the previous year, but no one would be genuinely happy to see her. Perhaps if she spoke only of the newest fashions in gloves and refrained from offering opinions about whether feeding dairy cows turnips or swede yielded the best milk as she had at Lady Grembly's ball last season, then—

"You mustn't run off just yet, Lady Victoria. Not before you agree to dance the next with me," Lord Axley said with a smile. He was being kind. Lord Axley was a confirmed bachelor in his late thirties who rarely danced, so he must have seen her distress. How very Mr. Knightley of him.

She smiled. "Of course, Lord Axley. I would be delighted." Up on the balcony, musicians began the opening chords of a minuet. Lord Axley offered her his arm. She took it. This wasn't turning out to be quite the successful evening she'd envisioned, but at least someone other than Tom had asked her for a dance, even if Lord Axley had only done so to be benevolent.

As Lord Axley led her away from the group, she stole a brief glance at Tom out of the corner of her eye. He was speaking to Mr. Silby, asking whether he had attended Eton.

Vicky shook her head. No, she didn't think she liked this new Tom at all.

But truly, that mattered little; she was here to keep her promise to Althea. She raised her chin and took her place across from Lord Axley in the line of dancers. She wouldn't allow Tom or Dain or anyone else to get in her way.

CHAPTER THE SIXTH

Can such abominable pride as his, have ever done him good?
—Jane Austen, *Pride and Prejudice*

In his peripheral vision, Tom watched Victoria stroll away on Lord Axley's arm. He thanked his occasionally lucky stars that their encounter was over. Tom took a deep breath. He'd truly thought she would have grown up a little more by now. She was still very much like the girl he remembered who'd believed in fairy stories, except now she believed in the novels of some Miss Austen.

He exhaled. But then, why would she have changed? Her idyllic life had not altered. The only transformation was that she was now of marriageable age.

Of course, he was grateful to her for performing introductions and wished her well, but she belonged in his past along with the bad memories of his childhood; he could not allow history to distract him from his present purpose.

Tom turned his attention back to Mr. Silby. Apparently, the

fellow had gone to Harrow; they had no mutual friends Tom could discover. He struggled for a new topic. He had to convince Silby or Mr. Carmichael to introduce him to more people, but he didn't feel right asking either of them after such a short acquaintance. Simultaneously pompous and awkward, Silby was proving difficult to converse with. And Carmichael had said no more than two sentences to Tom since Vicky had introduced them.

Tom needed to speak with as many people as he could if he wanted to discover prospective financial backers for his hotel. But how was he to achieve that with these two?

Then it came to him. "Would either of you care to repair to the card room?"

"Better than dancing with debutantes, eh, Halworth?" Silby said.

Tom wouldn't have said so, but he smiled to be agreeable.

"I'm surprised you do not wish to capitalize on your fame, Halworth," Carmichael said without inflection. "The whole room was agog when you were announced."

"I am simply here attending to familial duty."

"And is performing introductions Lady Victoria's duty?"

"Not at all. She did me a kindness." Not that it was any of his business.

"Oh, of course. Because you were inseparable," Carmichael continued.

"As I said, Lady Victoria and I grew up together." What was the fellow driving at?

"And you now presume to use that connection to your advantage."

Tom started. He had every intention of leaving Vicky to her own devices, but he also had a perfect right to speak with her if he wished. For that matter, even if he wanted to revive their friendship, it wouldn't be any of Carmichael's affair.

"Presume? If I'm not mistaken, it is no crime to converse with one's neighbors, even if one has been abroad for an extended time."

Carmichael's expression remained unyielding. "No one spoke of crimes. Yet some might consider taking advantage of a lady's kind nature to be a breach of manly conduct."

Tom threw Silby a look, waiting for him to comment on Carmichael's behavior, but Silby, it seemed, was content to watch the exchange. His eyes widened with interest.

Tom looked back at Carmichael. His emotionless stare did not waver. The man comported himself with the hauteur of a royal duke. Unusual for an untitled gentleman.

"One might place discourtesy in the same class," Tom said evenly.

Carmichael's eyes narrowed.

Tom set his jaw. Clearly he could expect no help for his hotel from either Carmichael or Silby. He'd repair to the card room alone and insinuate himself into a game. Men were always eager to meet someone ready to lose money. It would be a small price to pay.

He favored Carmichael and Silby with a condescending nod worthy of his father and strode away without a backward glance.

CHAPTER THE SEVENTH

There was no possibility of rest.
—Jane Austen, *Mansfield Park*

Late that night, Tom dragged himself up the steps of his town house and stumbled through the door with an exhausted sigh. He locked the front door, turned, and picked up the candlestick the butler had left for him on an entry table. Earlier that evening, he'd told the servants not to wait up for him.

Shielding the candle from drafts, Tom stalked through the hall toward the library—the closest room that might not be ice-cold. The furniture, shrouded in white-and-gray dust sheets, stood like stationary specters, watching him from the fringes of the candlelight.

God, how he hated this house. At least he had few childhood memories of the place. Only now that he knew how his father had used it for so many years did he find the house repulsive.

He didn't give a damn that it had been in the family for fifty years. In the morning, he would look for somewhere cheap to rent for the season and get an estimate on what this pile of bricks could bring.

He shivered. It was colder in here than it was outdoors. He moved faster.

When he finally reached the library, a light shone underneath the door. He yanked it open.

Charles lay sprawled out in an armchair, his head lolling to one side as he snored, a book splayed open on his lap. He still wore his black evening clothes.

Under normal circumstances, Tom would have left Charles to enjoy his dreams. These were not normal circumstances.

The good-for-nothing had fallen *asleep*, never materialized at the ball, and left Tom to face the wolves alone.

Charles emitted a guttural snore.

Tom clenched his jaw. He was in no mood to be generous. Setting down his candle, he picked up the book Charles had been reading. He felt a nasty sort of pleasure in slamming it shut as loudly as he could.

His brother started and shook his head about, looking for the cause of the noise. He blinked before his gaze centered on Tom.

"Good morning. What time is it?"

"It's three."

"In the morning? What am I doing in here?"

"That's a very good question. Especially since you were supposed to meet me at the duchess's ball."

Charles sat up and rubbed his brow with one hand. "Oh, the ball. Damn. Sorry about that."

"Yes, the ball you are still dressed for. The ball we were supposed to use to introduce me to potential backers. Any of that sound familiar?" Tom walked over to the fireplace and banked the fire. He stood for a moment relishing the warmth before dropping into the leather armchair across from Charles.

"So how did you get on?" Charles stifled a yawn.

Before Tom could respond, a floorboard creaked behind him.

"Tom?"

A girl stood in the doorway, covered only in her shift and a thin night-rail. Susan had to be freezing, but her strawberry-blond curls bounced with excitement. "How was it?"

Tom exhaled. "Didn't I tell you not to wait for me?"

"I heard you come through the front door. I couldn't very well go to sleep without hearing what happened on your first night out in society."

He sighed, but he wouldn't have curbed one of her diversions in any case. "Come in. And close the door behind you. The hall is glacial."

Susie did so and settled herself on a small gilded chair next to the fire. She tucked her bare feet up under her and rubbed her hands together close to the flames.

"If you become fatigued during your lessons tomorrow, you'll have only yourself to blame." Though they constituted the smallest portion of what he wished to do for Susie, Tom had arranged weekly dance and elocution lessons to prepare her for society.

"You've no need to worry, Tom," she said with a wide grin that brought out the dimples in her cheeks.

Charles cleared his throat. "May we get on with it?"

Tom sent him a frosty glare. "Every woman in the room eyed me like a rib roast. Which might not have been disagreeable except I had no one to perform introductions," he said with another pointed look.

His brother didn't even bother to look sheepish. "What of the Duchess of Rutherfurd? She claims to be a great friend of Mama's."

"So she told me. But she fobbed me off on the Astons."

Charles let out an undignified hoot of laughter.

Tom scowled. "Charles——"

"I beg your pardon," Charles said. He cleared his throat, but his eyes betrayed his mirth.

"How did that go?" Susie asked, glancing back and forth between them.

Tom swallowed, uncomfortable. "She—Victoria—was cordial about it."

Charles chuckled.

Tom took a deep breath. Charles knew just how to get under his skin. His younger brother had enough good sense not to emulate their father's dissolute conduct, but he'd still become the idle second son of a lord. In the country, he hunted and rode, and in London, he spent his days at his club and his evenings dining at his friends' expense. "Charles, our situation will soon make our social position precarious. We cannot afford to slight someone as socially powerful as the duchess. Or the Astons, for that matter."

"I quite agree," Charles said. "But asking Victoria for introductions? You avoided her society for a year, only to be forced to speak with her twice in the space of a fortnight." He scratched his chin. "The irony is palpable."

Tom wiped his features clean of any expression, trying to forget the way her face had fallen when she'd realized why he'd asked her to dance.

"Ignore him, Tom," Susie interjected. "Whom did you meet?"

"She introduced me to three gentlemen. Lord Axley was the only one of any help." In the card room, Tom had been searching for the game with the lowest stakes when Lord Axley had appeared. Tom had asked him where else he had traveled on his grand tour and had found Axley agreeable and very sensible. Axley had introduced him to more of his acquaintances. As the evening progressed, they'd spoken of Lord Axley's interests in the funds and general investments. He'd even introduced Tom to a handful of men who might prove to be potential hotel backers.

Tom turned to Charles. "Do you know a Mr. Carmichael?"

"Everyone knows Carmichael. Why?"

Tom nodded, unsurprised. Charles's favorite topics boiled down to society gossip, horse racing, and women, in that precise order. "He accused me of taking advantage of Victoria's good nature."

Charles sniffed. "Sounds just like the man. From what I hear, he has quarreled with half the gentlemen in London. I have it on the best authority that the Duke of Devonshire cannot stand the sight of him."

Tom could well believe it, but he asked, "For what reason?"

Charles waggled his head, a look of disgust curving his lip. "The size of his fortune. I've heard his annual income measures in excess of seventy-five thousand pounds."

Susie let out a breath.

Tom tilted his head and frowned. "You exaggerate."

"Regrettably, I do not. His income is greater than the prince regent's and rivals the duke's."

Tom's frown deepened. "Where does his money come from?"

"Gentlemen of our station do not engage in trade. It's all very well for Carmichael to be rich as Croesus and for you to sully the family name by partaking in business, but do not ask *me* about the source of other men's finances."

Bloody hell. Tom pressed his temples with one hand. He was too exhausted to cope with Charles's classist prejudices.

"And," Charles continued with uncharacteristic gravity, "he has many friends in the Lords and the Commons—powerful allies. Supposedly, he pays well for their cooperation. I wouldn't care to be on the wrong side of a legal argument with him. You, on the other hand, have a seat in the Lords you've ignored, and you've severed all friendships with Father's old supporters."

"That was necessary—" Tom began.

"I do not fault you for that," Charles interrupted with a wave of his hand. "However, Carmichael is not to be trifled with."

Susie shifted in her seat.

"Actually," Charles continued with an arch look at Susie, "my friend Kirkham challenged Carmichael to a bout over some inconsequential matter. It's due to take place on the morrow at Gentleman Jackson's Boxing Saloon." He looked at Tom. "Would you care to see Carmichael get a good trouncing?"

Tom shook his head. On his scale of enjoyable ways to pass the time, pugilism sat damned close to the bottom.

"A boxing match is the perfect venue to meet other backers for your scheme, I daresay. No ladies present to distract," Charles said, raising his brows.

Susie let out a breath. "No one present but men who wish to beat each other senseless."

"Yes, won't they be rather more interested in the sport?" Tom asked with a smile at Susie.

Charles rolled his eyes. "Far be it from me to tell you both about the ways of society. I'd forgotten the sheer breadth of your collective experience," he replied, sarcasm dripping from every syllable.

Tom's jaw clenched and unclenched. "Susie's a member of this family now." He shot a glance at her. She met his gaze with a small smile.

Charles's eyes narrowed. His fingers smoothed a wrinkle out of the left sleeve of his black evening coat. "As you say. At any rate, we can arrive at the club early and I'll make introductions." He caught Tom's eye. "It will give me a chance to make amends for this evening."

Tom sighed. "Very well. When you put it that way, how can I refuse?"

CHAPTER THE EIGHTH

I believe he is one of the very best
tempered men that ever existed.
—Jane Austen, *Emma*

Vicky spread a dollop of dark bramble preserves on her toast and took a dainty bite off the corner. She closed her eyes as the sweet tartness of the berries bloomed in her mouth. With any luck, the good weather would hold, and they'd have fresh berries before long. Vicky sent her mama a furtive glance, and as the countess sprinkled salt over her egg, Vicky licked a rather large bead of jam off the edge of her bread. She smiled to herself.

Only a few months more and she'd be relocating fresh, sun-warmed berries from their bushes to her mouth.

Of course, if she found a husband before the summer, she might be living on *his* estate by then. What if his estate didn't have bramble bushes or a strawberry garden like Oakbridge? She put down her toast with a pout and sipped her tea.

She glanced at Althea. Her sister sat across from her, staring into her porridge bowl and lifting the occasional spoonful to her mouth. Vicky swallowed as her hatred for Dain washed over her. She couldn't allow that disgusting brute to ruin their lives. She'd find a husband. Her pulse quickened unpleasantly, and she dragged in a breath to tamp down the panic.

She'd find someone kind who cared what she thought. Then they could secure Oakbridge and Althea's separation, and all would be well.

From the head of the table, Vicky's father speared a kipper with his fork. "Did you enjoy the ball, Victoria?"

She'd failed rather miserably at acting as Fanny Price would have, but it had been a moderate success overall. Vicky nodded.

"Your mother told me you danced with Mr. Carmichael twice."

At least Mr. Carmichael hadn't seemed to mind her dearth of Fanny Price–like qualities. "Yes, Papa."

"And he asked to take you to Gunter's this afternoon?"

Gunter's Tea Shop in Berkeley Square was famous for its frozen confections. Vicky never missed an opportunity to indulge in a cream ice. Though Vicky adored their French chef at Oakbridge, the prickly fellow refused to make ices more than three times a year. However, in peculiar French fashion, he baked pastries—no matter how complex—with utter abandon.

"He arrives at two," she said, imagining what flavors Gunter's would have. The image of a luscious chocolate cream came to mind, and her spirits brightened.

"You'll need a chaperone," Vicky's mother said over the rim of her teacup.

Vicky looked at her sister. "I wish you'd come, Thea."

Althea raised her head from her barely touched porridge. Her shoulders lifted and fell as she took a deep breath. "I don't—"

"That is out of the question," Vicky's father interrupted.

"Yes, I don't think it advisable," her mother agreed.

Althea dropped her gaze.

Vicky bit the inside of her cheek. "I know. I just . . . wish she could," she murmured.

Althea caught her eye and offered a tiny, sad smile before looking away.

"Sarah can accompany you," her mother said.

Vicky frowned. The rules of propriety allowed her maid to accompany her, but only if no other more appropriate chaperone was available. "Why not you, Mama?"

"Your father must go to Mr. Barnes's office, so I must stay with your sister."

Vicky nodded.

"And there is another reason," her mother said, dabbing the corners of her lips with her napkin. She shared a glance with Vicky's father. "Your father and I are pleased you and Mr. Carmichael seem to be getting on so well."

"He's an excellent fellow," her father said, pausing in the midst of buttering a piece of toast.

Vicky raised her brows at him. "He's very pleasant, Papa."

Her father nodded. "And to that end, your mother and I feel he is the best candidate for your hand."

Vicky's mouth fell open. "I beg your pardon?"

Her father arched a brow and crunched into his toast.

"See what you think of him today, Victoria," her mother said.

Vicky tapped her fingers on the table. She had liked Mr. Carmichael the best of all the gentlemen she'd met last night, but the fact that her parents were making their preference for him known so quickly unnerved her.

"But . . . he is untitled. Would that not be a factor for the prince regent when you ask him to choose the heir to Oakbridge?"

"Mr. Carmichael's mother is the daughter of a baron in the north," Vicky's mother said.

"With Carmichael's fortune he could buy a title if he wished," said Vicky's father, "however, that may not be necessary. I happen to know he did the prince a good turn that he is eager to repay. And, in addition, Carmichael has connections in the House of Lords and the Commons."

Vicky sighed. "Papa, I know you think him brilliant because he thought to buy that land near the canal, but—"

"I've never met a man of his years with such a head for property and finance. But that aside, he is by far the best choice. The most logical choice," her father pronounced, giving Vicky a pointed look. "I know we can trust Carmichael. Based on that factor alone, I would be happy to have him join the family. I would prefer not to be encumbered with another son-in-law like Dain." He glanced at Althea and frowned with what seemed to be remorse.

Althea put down her spoon, refusing to meet anyone's eye.

Vicky pursed her lips and exhaled. She tried to imagine herself married to Mr. Carmichael, yet she could not picture it. Admittedly, that might be because she didn't know enough about him to guess what a life with him would be like. Oh, she could not deny his good looks and clever mind; he'd even made her laugh, which must be a good sign. Still, a part of her had no desire to know. "If you'll excuse me," she said rising from her chair, "I believe I need more rest before my outing." She hurried from the dining room, fleeing the disappointment clouding her parents' faces.

Vicky adjusted her bonnet and turned her head to the left, then to the right, to ascertain that it sat at the perfect angle. She practiced a smile in the mirror, assessing the overall effect. Not too shabby, if she did say so herself. But a moment later, her face fell. She turned from her reflection and collapsed into a nearby chair.

Just because Mr. Carmichael would be calling within the hour was no reason to behave like a preening goose. If only her parents hadn't told her how much they wished her to marry Mr. Carmichael. If she'd thought this nothing but a social outing with an agreeable gentleman, she could have enjoyed herself.

Vicky turned to her maid, Sarah.

"Perhaps I should change? This yellow muslin makes me look like I'm trying to catch Mr. Carmichael's eye."

The girl shook her head. "Oh no, my lady. The dress suits you."

"But I look *too* fashionable for such a short outing. What will he think?"

"Begging your pardon, my lady," Sarah said, in a tone Vicky knew meant she was doing no such thing, "but a lady of your station can never look too fashionable. I suspect Mr. Carmichael will think you almost as handsome as you were last night."

Vicky sighed, uneasy. Why was this so difficult? She was going on a civilized outing with a charming gentleman to safeguard the home and family she loved, not walking into a den of robbers.

What she really needed was her sister's advice. After Tom's exile, she and Althea had become closer than they'd ever been as children. Whenever Vicky had confided her fears about leaving Oakbridge and entering society, Althea always calmed her. She'd tried to teach Vicky the art of projecting a dignified, confident air at any event. Vicky had always admired Althea's ability to navigate society's treacherous waters without fear, and although Vicky hadn't completely absorbed the finer points of her sister's lessons, Vicky had loved her for the effort.

Vicky hurried down the hall to Althea's room and knocked. Ever since that day in the conservatory at Oakbridge, Althea had avoided spending time alone with her. They'd barely spoken outside of their daily meals, which Althea did not always attend. Whenever Vicky thought of the silence between them, she had to swallow against an inexplicable pain in the back of her throat.

She couldn't predict how Althea would react to her asking about men, especially now, but she had to try.

After hearing her sister's acknowledgment, Vicky entered.

Althea sat near the fire in an upholstered armchair, reading a book. She glanced up from the pages. "Don't you have an excursion?"

Vicky nodded. "Does it look like I'm trying too hard?"

"Not to my eye."

"Thea—" Vicky began. She wanted to say she didn't wish to marry anyone. That the thought of being trapped in a marriage of convenience terrified her. That she wished none of this was necessary, but she voiced none of it. It was the truth, but what good could it do? She'd made her sister a promise, and she would keep it.

Vicky walked to the window. Like her own room, Althea's bedroom sat on the front side of the town house; it boasted a large window overlooking the square. Gentlemen on horseback nodded to women trundling along in open carriages, while nursemaids looked on as their young charges played on the grass.

"I wish Mama and Papa had waited to tell me." She turned to face her sister. "What if Mr. Carmichael and I have nothing to say to one another?"

A line appeared between Althea's brows. "Had you anything to say last night?"

Vicky looked down at her fingernails. "Yes. He was very pleasant."

"But you worry he will not be today?"

Vicky bit her lip. What could she say that wouldn't sound like she wished to break her promise?

Althea closed her book on her finger. "Do you like Mr. Carmichael less because our parents sanction him?"

Vicky frowned. "Of course not, that would be foolish." She'd known how highly they'd thought of him. She just hadn't known they wished her to *marry* him.

"Then pretend they said nothing."

She inhaled. Despite her parents' wishes, she was not bound to Mr. Carmichael. "You're right, Thea. If I don't care for him today, I shall find someone else to marry."

"Someone else with a large fortune, whom the prince regent approves of, with unimpeachable moral conduct," Althea muttered.

Vicky turned to face the window with a tiny pout. When Althea put it that way, the whole endeavor sounded quite impossible. "I did fancy I would have done better than I did last night. I danced a respectable number of times, but the only new gentleman I met was Mr. Silby, and I don't think he cared for me overmuch, even if he did ask me to accompany him on an outing." After they'd danced a set last night, Mr. Silby had asked her to accompany him to Hyde Park later in the week.

"I don't know that he's much of a catch anyway," Althea said.

"Thea . . ." Vicky turned to look at her. "You always say one should have a plan, so I rather thought"—she hesitated, feeling silly—"that if I acted as Fanny Price did at her first ball, all the gentlemen in the room would find me irresistible."

Althea's eyes widened. "This is no novel, Vicky. This is our lives!"

Vicky exhaled. "I'm well aware of that, but there are lessons to be learned from books too."

Althea threw her gaze to the ceiling. "You've never agreed with Fanny Price's actions, anyway. Why would you adopt her manners now?"

"I wanted the evening to be a success."

"With two outings with two separate gentlemen, you cannot call it a failure."

Vicky blinked. "I suppose not. Though I *was* dreadful at acting like Fanny Price."

"I cannot say I'm surprised. If you must adopt a pretense, you'd be far better off imitating someone you actually admire."

Vicky chewed the inside of her cheek. Althea was right. By attempting to act like Fanny Price, she'd been trying to be something she wasn't. Little wonder events hadn't progressed as she'd imagined.

"Mr. Carmichael actually said Elizabeth Bennet was his favorite of Miss Austen's heroines."

"Did he indeed? There you are—you have much in common. You can spend the afternoon speaking of *Pride and Prejudice*."

Vicky nodded, her heart lightening. She grinned at her sister.

"Just don't expect him to be Mr. Darcy," Althea said, looking down at her book.

She was dismissing her, but Vicky turned back to the window. "I don't imagine I shall find a Mr. Darcy." Although she certainly wouldn't object. "But I do wish to avoid someone like Dain. How can I?"

"I'm hardly the one to ask," Althea replied without inflection.

Vicky clasped her hands together and grimaced at the window. Why could she never say anything right? As Vicky observed the activity of Mayfair, an elegant black barouche pulled by a pair of matching red chestnuts separated itself from the stream of traffic, and the driver stopped the horses in front of their house. Mr. Carmichael disembarked the vehicle wearing a charcoal coat and black hat.

She took three deep breaths, but the knot in her stomach remained. "I'm sorry, Thea. I will not fail us."

With one last glance at Althea's eyes, so large in her delicate face, Vicky straightened her spine and marched from the bedroom.

Vicky reached the bottom of the stairs with what she hoped was a composed air. Mr. Carmichael stood at the foot of the staircase looking tall and broad-shouldered in his charcoal coat and blue waistcoat. He held his hat under his arm. One side of his mouth curved up in a slow grin at the sight of her, and despite her earlier worries, Vicky blushed. Her stomach gave a tiny flip as she held out her gloved hand.

"Mr. Carmichael." She inclined her head, feeling the epitome of prim elegance.

Carmichael took her hand in his, bowing low over it as he looked into her eyes. "Lady Victoria."

She smiled, and he released her hand.

Vicky introduced Sarah, who had materialized from the hall to her left.

Carmichael nodded and smiled at Sarah. He offered Vicky his arm. "Shall we?"

Mr. Carmichael's barouche boasted neither crest nor symbols, but the black wood inlaid with gold trim carried an understated sophistication that suited him. His driver had lowered the carriage's top so they could take advantage of the fine day.

Vicky admired the red chestnuts pulling the carriage as Mr. Carmichael opened the door. He assisted both Vicky and Sarah inside before joining them. Happy she'd secured the forward-facing seat, Vicky smiled at Carmichael, who sat across from her and Sarah.

When they'd all settled comfortably, Mr. Carmichael motioned to the driver. With a snap of the reins, the horses took off at a steady pace. The barouche commenced a gentle rocking as it traversed the cobbled street.

As the sights of Mayfair passed by, Vicky recalled the incident in *Sense and Sensibility* when Mr. Willoughby took Marianne Dashwood for a drive to see the house he was meant to inherit, and they'd returned hours later. Of course, *they'd* been unchaperoned, but Vicky wondered how long Mr. Carmichael meant their outing to last. Would they have enough conversation to sustain such a duration? Would he even wish to speak about *Pride and Prejudice* again? Well, it was worth trying.

"I do not believe I've ever met a gentleman who cared for *Pride and Prejudice* as much as I, Mr. Carmichael," she said with a smile at him.

"Most gentlemen cannot tell what is good for them."

She raised an eyebrow. "But you can?"

He shrugged slightly. "I have little time for the Edmund Bertrams of this world. A gentleman should not be taken in by flattery or fripperies." He inclined his head as a smile played upon his lips. "If he can help it."

He referred, of course, to Edmund Bertram's ill-fated regard for the flawed Mary Crawford in *Mansfield Park*, despite the constant, unselfish love Fanny Price carried for him. "You prefer Mr. Darcy, then?" she asked.

"At least he knows his own mind," Mr. Carmichael said. "Though he is laughably stiff-mannered."

Vicky frowned. "Why *laughably*?"

He seemed to consider the point. "Perhaps I simply find him lacking."

"But of course he is lacking in the beginning," she said, trying to understand his reasoning.

He nodded. "Objectively, there is nothing wrong with him that he himself does not mention by the end of the novel, but one wonders what kind of life he and Elizabeth Bennet would have. I imagine she would grow quite bored with his stony manner."

Vicky raised her brows. Althea had been correct as usual. *He* was no Mr. Darcy. But perhaps that was not necessarily a detraction. "I suppose that could be possible," she admitted, though she'd never thought of Elizabeth and Mr. Darcy living any way except happily ever after. But how delightful to find a gentleman with so many complex opinions about her favorite books! "I admit, I'm amazed at your knowledge of Miss Austen's novels. I had no notion you had time for reading. Especially fiction."

"The mind cannot thrive on documents and ledgers alone. Or *tracts on animal husbandry*," he said with a smile at her. "I must travel often, and I find novels the best diversion when one is stopping at a coaching inn."

She grinned at him. "That is admirable, I must say." The image of them sitting side by side in a sunny conservatory reading the same book and smiling at each other flashed through her mind.

He shrugged. "How did you find the ball last evening?"

"I would have enjoyed it far more with the addition of an oracular pig."

Carmichael smirked. His eyes had appeared almost black the night before, but in the sunlight, they were closer to dark rosewood with medium brown flecks. "And what fortune would you have it tell?"

Vicky looked away and considered her answer. "Good health and happiness for my family."

He nodded. Then, when she said no more: "Nothing else?"

Vicky tilted her head. "Prosperity for Oakbridge."

Carmichael's smile widened. "And for yourself?"

Vicky raised her brows. "What more could I want?"

For a moment, Carmichael only looked at her, his smile unwavering. "Well said."

Vicky blushed. "And you?" she asked. "What fortune do you wish for?"

Still smiling, he shook his head. "Ah. A gentleman must have some secrets."

She frowned. The last thing she wanted was a husband with secrets. "Must he?"

He eyed her. "Only those he cannot honorably disclose."

Vicky bit her inner cheek. "I see."

Carmichael opened his mouth to say something else, but the barouche came to a stop.

"Oh!" Vicky exclaimed, looking to her left. "We're here."

A little farther up the street from Mr. Carmichael's barouche, various landaus and phaetons sat idly beside the lawn in the center of Berkeley Square. Elegantly dressed ladies, perched on the edge of their carriage seats, enjoyed their ices with delicate spoons, while the men accompanying them leaned against the railings surrounding the grass, paying more attention to the women than their own confections.

Mr. Carmichael motioned to a waiter taking the order of a couple who had brought their children. The waiter scurried over, and as Vicky, Mr. Carmichael, and Sarah sat in the barouche, he told them the day's ice flavors. After they'd ordered, and the waiter left to procure their ices, Mr. Carmichael sat back in his seat.

"May I ask how you found Lord Halworth after so many years?"

Vicky started at the mention of Tom's name. She'd barely thought of him at all since this morning. "I found him . . . older," she said.

Carmichael chuckled. "As one would expect."

Vicky smiled and shrugged, hoping he'd grasp her wish to change the subject.

But instead, he raised his brows. "Was that all?"

"That was all," she replied lightly.

Mr. Carmichael brushed an invisible speck of dust from his knee. "Silby and I thought it rather shabby of him to ask you to perform introductions."

Vicky frowned. She'd felt the same way, but she wasn't about to admit it. "It was no bother."

"Where was his family?"

Vicky shifted in her seat. "I'm sure I don't know." It wasn't a lie even if it was an evasion—all she knew was what Tom had told her.

"I know for a fact that Charles Sherborne is in Town," Carmichael persisted.

Vicky pasted on a false smile. "If he is, he was certainly absent last night. Or did you see him at the ball?"

Carmichael shook his head.

"Then it is of no consequence. I take it you would not ask an old friend to perform introductions for you, Mr. Carmichael?"

He considered the question. "Only if I were certain of my reception—certain I would not be causing inconvenience or pain."

She started. *Pain*. How had he known? Had her feelings been so obviously written on her face? If so, she must be more careful. What could she say now? Should she lie and act as though Tom's behavior had no effect on her? Or admit the truth?

Carmichael's astute understanding of last night's situation made her want to confide in him. Surely that was a desirable trait in a prospective husband.

Thankfully, at that moment, the waiter returned, carrying their ices on a tray, and she didn't have to think of a reply.

Vicky sighed at the sight of her chocolate cream ice. Sarah had ordered a barberry water ice, and as soon as the waiter passed her the dish, she eyed it with glee. Vicky caught Sarah's attention, smiled, and took a spoonful of her own. She closed her eyes in bliss as the frozen cream melted on her tongue.

She ventured a glance at Mr. Carmichael's dish. He'd ordered a light green pistachio cream ice. Vicky wrinkled her nose. It certainly wouldn't be *her* first choice.

He must have seen her expression, because he said, "Is it not to your liking?"

"No. Oh, er, mine?" she sputtered. "No, it's delightful. Exactly what I wanted."

Carmichael smirked at her muddled answer. "So, I believe you have an outing with Silby on Thursday?"

Vicky nodded. "Are you well acquainted with Mr. Silby?" she asked, licking chocolate from the corner of her mouth.

Carmichael inclined his head. "Tolerably so. He was a particular friend of my cousin Gerard Rackham."

"Was?"

Carmichael nodded. "Gerard fell at Waterloo."

Vicky looked up from her dish. "I'm so sorry."

Carmichael nodded and thanked her. "I hadn't seen him since we were boys. But Silby took it rather hard. He had planned to accompany Gerard to Belgium, but at the last moment, Silby's father discovered the plan and forced him to stay. Silby is the heir, you know."

Vicky frowned and brought another spoonful of ice into her mouth. Poor Mr. Silby. Vicky certainly understood the pain of losing a cherished friend. Though Tom, thank goodness, had not *died* abroad. She could not imagine the pain of losing someone in that way.

Vicky glanced up and saw Mr. Carmichael observing her with a bemused expression.

"I believe I can perceive your thoughts."

Vicky arched her brows. "Indeed?"

"Could it be my tale has endeared your tender heart to Silby?"

Vicky smiled at his teasing tone. "I would rather have a tender disposition than eat that pea-green concoction you just devoured."

Carmichael looked at his dish. He laughed slightly before raising his head. "Pity him if you must, but I do not believe you will be so enamored after your outing."

Vicky was hardly enamored with Silby now, but she asked, "And why should that be?"

"I would explain further, but I doubt you would believe me."

"Mr. Carmichael," Vicky said, "you are being infuriatingly vague. Is there something I should know before my outing with Mr. Silby?"

"Simply that he is not a man who deserves you."

Vicky pursed her lips and looked at him skeptically. "And who, if I may ask, is worthy in your opinion?"

"Perhaps no one," he said with a smile, "but those of us who endeavor to become so—those are the gentlemen with whom you should be spending your precious time."

He looked at her with those dark eyes, and Vicky's breath caught. How did he have the ability to do that? He spoke so well, as though he were indeed a character from Miss Austen's novels. Did he practice such pleasantries on all the ladies of his acquaintance?

She broke the connection between them by looking down into her now-empty dish. Out of the corner of her eye, she watched as Carmichael dropped his gaze from her face and took out his pocket watch.

"Now, if you will permit me, Lady Victoria," he said, "I shall signal the waiter to take our dishes."

Vicky blinked. "Shall we drive home through the park?"

Carmichael frowned. "I'm afraid not. Unfortunately, my mother engaged my services this afternoon."

Vicky's brow furrowed. "Your mother?"

"Indeed. She entreated me to accompany her to the shops before they close. I'm afraid I could not refuse her. Please forgive me for cutting our outing short, but I must join her by four o'clock."

"Of course," Vicky said, but she frowned inwardly. How odd of him to invite her on an outing when he was engaged to go shopping with his mother.

At Carmichael's behest, the waiter returned and collected their dishes.

Vicky's mind revolved around the strange turn of events. Could it be he was not enjoying her company? She wrung her hands in her lap, feeling both foolish and irritated that she'd pictured him wishing to spend hours in her company like Willoughby had with Marianne.

Vicky had never thought Mr. Carmichael the sort of man who would escort his mother to the shops. Nor, for that matter, had she thought of Mrs. Carmichael as a mother who needed her son for such an idle task.

After Mr. Carmichael seated himself across from her in the barouche again and told the driver to go back to Aston House, she said, "Mrs. Carmichael is fortunate to have such an agreeable son."

"'Tis no more than her due."

"Not at all, Mr. Carmichael," she said in a teasing tone. "Such maternal devotion is rare and definitely to be commended."

He watched her, as though uncertain if she were speaking in earnest.

She blinked. His eagerness to end their outing *had* actually disappointed her.

She still didn't wish to rush into marriage, but he *was* very agreeable. And he cared for his mother, which should be a good indicator of his character. She peered at him through her lashes, wondering what he thought of her.

"Your father's last letter intimated your family would not come up to London for at least another month. To what bit of fortune do I owe the pleasure of your company now?"

"Er . . . yes." Vicky arranged her features into what she hoped was a neutral expression. "As to that, Mr. Carmichael, I think it would be more prudent for you to speak with my father."

He frowned. "Is something wrong?"

"Yes." At the look of concern on his face, Vicky amended her statement. "That is to say, no."

This time his expression turned to one of confusion.

What was she supposed to say? That life as she knew it would never be the same? That instead of being home where she belonged, selecting the very brightest rhubarb stalks, or watching the cherry trees blossom, or assisting with the lambing, she was here, desperate to find someone to marry her because her life was no longer hers to control?

No. She couldn't say any of those things.

Vicky sighed. "Mr. Carmichael, I'm afraid it's not my tale to tell." She attempted to rescue the moment with a well-timed joke like Elizabeth Bennet might. "A lady must have some secrets, after all—just as men do."

His brow creased, and he settled back against the cushion. He did not speak again.

Vicky exhaled and turned her head to the side. Courtship was pointless. And exhausting! It was just as well they were returning now. After all, Marianne and Willoughby's unchaperoned outing had only led to unhappiness.

Town houses passed by, and Vicky wished for the verdant hills and valleys of home. She closed her eyes at the sight of a dustman shoveling a new specimen into his wagon full of dung. How had her life transformed into such a fetid heap? Tom, Althea, Dain, and her parents had reordered the pattern of her life, leaving her helpless. Now all she could do was push ahead until her noisome existence returned to normal.

Perhaps she should apologize to Mr. Carmichael. She opened her eyes to gauge his expression, but as she did, a man on the street caught her eye. He wore a black greatcoat and trousers, had black hair, and was staring straight at her. She couldn't remember ever seeing him before, but something about him looked familiar. He stood on a corner with one arm bent behind him and continued to stare until the back of her neck prickled.

She frowned to discourage him, but instead of looking away, he inclined his head a fraction of an inch. Vicky screwed up her face at his audacity and deliberately turned away. She should alert Mr. Carmichael. She ventured another glance with her peripheral vision, but the man—whoever he was—had disappeared.

CHAPTER THE NINTH

It is very difficult for the prosperous to be humble.
—Jane Austen, *Emma*

As Tom entered number 13 Bond Street at nearly four o'clock that afternoon, the smell of stale sweat assaulted his nostrils. Gentleman Jackson's Boxing Saloon was a modest set of rooms where, most days, Jackson trained young gentlemen in the science of pugilism. Today gentlemen filled the large rectangular room near to bursting as they jockeyed for the best viewing position for the impending fight.

Tom followed as Charles led the way through clusters of gentlemen discussing their predictions of how many rounds the fight would last, and the even larger groups of men placing last-minute bets. Nearly all in attendance were well-dressed men of station. In the center of the room, someone had drawn a three-foot square inside a larger circle.

"It's not yet four," Charles stated. "We have a few minutes before the fight starts."

Tom started. "A few minutes? I thought you said it began at half past."

Charles tapped his chin. "Did I?"

"You also said we'd arrive early."

Charles's eyes widened innocently. "How odd. Well, I'll make introductions after the bout."

Tom glared at Charles and rolled his shoulders back to relieve the tension.

Ignoring him, Charles surveyed the room. Then he looked at Tom with a gleam in his eye. "Care to make a wager?"

Tom decided not to dignify his brother's question with a response.

"What does the square inside the ring signify?" This would be the first fight Tom had witnessed in a saloon, and he didn't know the official rules.

Charles grunted, no doubt annoyed Tom hadn't risen to his bait. "The square is where the men face off before beginning each round. The fight can take place anywhere in the ring once they have both stepped to the square. If a man goes to his knees, he has half a minute to get up and return to the square, or he loses the fight."

"How long do the bouts last?"

"I've heard of them lasting some sixty rounds, but that is certainly not the average. Fights continue until one man is knocked out or someone resigns," Charles said.

It sounded so crude. Before Tom could ask another question, the din around them grew louder.

Mr. Carmichael, Mr. Silby, Charles's friend Kirkham, and

another man walked through the crowd to the ring in the center of the room. Both Carmichael and Kirkham wore breeches and tan-colored coats without tails that Tom assumed must be the uniform they trained in since a handful of other gentlemen were dressed the same. With Carmichael's stature and muscled biceps that were obvious even through the fabric of his coat, he resembled a well-dressed dockworker who pounded men into the ground for entertainment.

Kirkham was a light-haired young man of eighteen or so who had a vaguely distracted air about him. He was a good half foot shorter than Carmichael, and quite a bit slimmer, but he looked agile. Perhaps Kirkham could evade Carmichael's blows. The man walking next to Kirkham seemed to be supporting him with one hand. Tom assumed he was Kirkham's second. Silby must be acting as Carmichael's second.

The few men standing in the ring moved to the sides as Kirkham and Carmichael took their places. The two seconds stepped to the edge.

Without his second's support, Kirkham wobbled.

Charles spoke in Tom's ear. "Kirkham's drunk, the fool. This shouldn't last long."

After both Carmichael and Kirkham had chosen an umpire from the men in the crowd, the combatants lined up at the center square, and the fight began.

The men around the two fighters shouted encouragement.

Carmichael backed up and circled Kirkham. He must have noticed Kirkham's condition, because he appeared to be biding his time.

Kirkham, on the other hand, charged Carmichael at every opportunity—he'd step forward and throw a punch, hit nothing, and step clumsily back.

A few times, the men surrounding the ring stepped inside it, and the seconds and umpires forced them back.

At one point, Kirkham stumbled and seemed about to fall. The crowd took a collective breath.

Yet he regained his balance and continued his pursuit of Carmichael.

Tom looked around at the gentlemen who all seemed so engrossed in the bout. He didn't understand what was so fascinating about two grown men trying, however unsuccessfully, to pummel the life out of each other. Tom glanced at the door and calculated how long it would take to navigate the crowd. He had just delineated his escape route when Charles and the crowd roared.

Kirkham lobbed his right fist wildly at Carmichael's face.

Carmichael ducked the blow with ease and then, while Kirkham's side was momentarily unguarded, Carmichael stood, grabbed Kirkham by the hair, and punched him in the face.

Some men cheered, while others, presumably Kirkham's supporters, yelled. The umpires did nothing. Carmichael pummeled Kirkham's face again and again until his body went limp and Carmichael could no longer hold up his weight by his hair alone.

Carmichael released him, and Kirkham collapsed to the floor with a thud, covered in blood.

Kirkham's second rushed in to tend him.

Carmichael turned and raised his hands to the men in the room.

Silby clapped him on the shoulder. Tom's gaze dropped to Kirkham. He was out cold.

Carmichael had won.

"Despicable," Charles mumbled, turning away from Kirkham's prostrate body.

Tom had to agree. "Why didn't they stop him?"

"There is nothing in the rules to prevent it; in fact, I believe Gentleman Jackson himself used the same tactic against Daniel Mendoza to win his championship title. Still, it seems rather uncouth."

Tom shook his head. "Uncouth" was hardly the word. Carmichael was a brute in the truest sense. A brute, he had no doubt, who'd stop at nothing to get his own way.

"Should you attend to Kirkham?" Tom asked.

Charles shook his head and started to push his way through the crowd. "His second is taking care of him," he said over his shoulder. "Besides, he was the one who decided to get drunk before the bout. He should never have challenged Carmichael in the first place."

"Kirkham challenged Carmichael?"

Charles stopped as three men crossed in front of him. Tom pushed his way forward until he and Charles stood shoulder to shoulder.

"Carmichael bumped into him at the theater, but he wouldn't apologize because Kirkham had spilled some of his drink on him," Charles said as they started toward the door. "Carmichael then insisted Kirkham apologize, but of course he refused since Carmichael had been the one to jostle him in the first place. So Kirkham challenged him—it was all rather foolish. Still, Carmichael didn't need to bludgeon him. Anyone could see how foxed Kirkham was." He paused. "Someone should put the bloody giant in his place."

Tom was about to remark that Carmichael wasn't *that* tall when boisterous laughter erupted from a group of gentlemen idling near the door.

"Capital bout, Carmichael."

"He shan't be leaving his bed for a good few days."

"Poor fool didn't know what hit him, he was so soused."

Carmichael stood in the middle of the commotion, laughing heartily at all the comments.

Grinning, he said, "He was already an unattractive fellow. I was merely improving the shape of his jaw."

The men in the circle roared with laughter.

Charles's hands tightened into fists, and he mumbled something unintelligible under his breath. Tom glanced at the men. Heads turned toward him and Charles.

Carmichael smirked at them both. "Have you something to say, Sherborne?" he addressed Charles.

Charles made no answer, but his jaw shifted.

Carmichael continued, "Care for a lesson of your own? Or have you not the stomach for it?"

His companions burst into raucous guffaws.

Charles launched himself at Carmichael.

Tom grabbed Charles's arm. He struggled to get free, but Tom stepped in front of him and took hold of his opposite shoulder. Tom glared over his shoulder at Carmichael, whose grin only widened. "Since you are a self-proclaimed arbiter of gentlemanly conduct,

Carmichael, I wonder at your unscrupulous tactics," Tom said.

"Wonder all you wish, Halworth. No one has ever accused me of taking advantage of a lady."

Tom's narrowed gaze met Carmichael's mocking stare. Tom would give the man one thing: he was remarkably arrogant.

Tom's back teeth clenched. He had never taken advantage of anyone, let alone a lady. But he'd be damned before he'd explain a thing to Carmichael or his cronies.

"When I saw her last, Lady Victoria was less than complimentary of your behavior," Carmichael continued, raising an eyebrow.

The men around Carmichael bombarded Tom with black scowls.

"Forgive me if I do not take your word on the matter," Tom replied, although part of him wondered if she had confided in Carmichael last night. As Tom had spent the rest of the ball in the card room, he had no way of knowing.

Tom pushed Charles's shoulder and began to force him away, but before he had taken two steps, Carmichael reached out and grabbed Tom's arm.

Tom gaped at Carmichael. A quick-tempered man would have challenged him to a duel by now. Fortunately, keeping his emotions hidden was one of many things Tom had learned living with a father like Henry Halworth. It would be so satisfying to stop Carmichael's overconfident tongue from wagging, but Tom wouldn't risk his life simply because a bully had insulted him.

He fixed Carmichael with an icy glare. "You would be well-advised to remove your hand."

Carmichael dropped Tom's arm, but not before adding with a

chuckle, "Leave the fisticuffs to the men, Halworth. I would expect nothing less."

Charles bucked against Tom's grip again. Tom shook his head and forced Charles from the club.

"The man's unbalanced," Tom said as they turned onto Albemarle Street.

"If you hadn't dragged me away—"

"Charles, Carmichael outweighs us both."

"But that he would dare lay a hand on a peer of the realm," Charles said with a sneer.

"Are you suggesting *peers of the realm* should engage in street brawls when they disagree?" Tom asked, attempting to lighten the mood.

Charles looked sideways at Tom and sniffed disdainfully. "He had the gall to do it before witnesses. He must think himself above the law."

Tom frowned. "I think you may be overstating—"

"Are you aware that by not challenging him, you might as well have confirmed his accusations?"

"His accusations are baseless."

"Which matters not one whit! He has besmirched your reputation."

Tom exhaled. Society was proving more tiresome than he'd anticipated.

They turned the corner onto Palmer Street, and the town house's gray stone facade came into view. A hackney cab sat in front of the steps. "What's that doing there?"

Susan never left the house unaccompanied. Tom acted as her escort if she needed to go out.

"I haven't the foggiest," said Charles.

Which left only one possibility. They had an unexpected visitor. Tom quickened his pace.

As they strode through the front door, two men Tom had never seen before loitered in the entryway. In the corner behind the door, a burly, bald man flanked a short, dark-whiskered fellow rising from a chair. They were both professionally dressed in gray trousers and coats. Their attire and Charles's hasty excuses led Tom to deduce they weren't his brother's acquaintances. Charles disappeared down the hall toward the kitchen.

The shorter man addressed Tom with a bow. "Lord Halworth?"

Tom nodded warily. "And you are?"

"My name is Nathaniel Clarkson, Lord Halworth, and this is my associate Mr. Talbot. We are here on the matter of some three hundred twenty-seven pounds, six shillings, and tuppence owed to a Mr. Smithfield of Smithfield's Food Purveyors in Broughton Street."

Tom swallowed hard at the number and nearly choked in the process. "Gentlemen, I assure you I have never entered that establishment."

Mr. Clarkson pulled a piece of paper from inside his coat and handed it to Tom. "As you can see, the Earl of Halworth's account at Smithfield's has been in existence since 1799. Invoices have not been paid in a number of years. It is commonly known that you inherited the earldom only a year ago, but regular purchases have continued since the late earl's death."

Tom's gaze slid down the paper, registering the accounting for the many crates of foodstuffs ordered in the last year. "I have not authorized these purchases," he ground out.

A rhythmic pounding began between his ears. He could easily surmise who had added to this specific debt of their father's. And if he knew his brother, Charles was probably eating contraband caviar at this very moment.

"Perhaps not, my lord, but Mr. Smithfield has brought suit against you. You must pay the debt or my colleague and I will be forced to take up residence in your town house."

"Move in *here*?" Tom sputtered. The pounding multiplied tenfold. "You cannot be serious, sir."

"Unfortunately, I am in earnest. We will move in and watch your spending until we find a way for you to pay your debts."

Tom scrubbed his face with one hand. He could wring Charles's neck. Luckily for him, a lord couldn't be detained in debtors' prison. However, Clarkson was correct. Creditors could collect their money by installing bailiffs in the peer's home. The bailiff would then take any money he saw coming into the household and return it to the creditor.

Tom couldn't contend with this today. "Look here, Mr. Clarkson," Tom began, advancing toward the man.

Mr. Talbot stepped in front of Clarkson, his bulk practically shielding the shorter man from view.

"Tom!"

Tom turned toward the voice. Susie hurried down the staircase, her strawberry-blond curls bouncing with every step.

"Hello, Miss Naseby," Mr. Clarkson said from behind Talbot. Tom watched as Talbot's gaze shifted to Susie. The man bowed politely.

Susie smiled at the men. When Talbot the brute started to blush, Tom nearly snorted. Susie's kindness, coupled with her sweet face, made it hard for any man to dislike her. Even now, her smile and dimpled cheeks drew one's eye away from her shabby, mulberry-colored dress.

Tom's pulse slowed, and he marveled that her presence never failed to lighten his spirits. But as she came closer, his calm faded. Susie's sad dress only reminded him of their situation. He couldn't pay these men, let alone buy Susie some much-needed new clothes. Tom had promised himself her life would be so much improved by returning to England, but at best, she looked like a poor relation and, at worst, like a servant. Meanwhile, she was the one member of the household who actually knew the value of money.

"Susan," Tom asked, "do you know these men?"

Mr. Clarkson stepped around Mr. Talbot to face Tom again. "Miss Naseby was kind enough to greet us when we arrived, Lord Halworth."

Tom gave her a questioning look. Instead of offering an explanation, she smiled. "Gentlemen, would you excuse us a moment?"

"Susan—" Tom said, but he quieted when she gave him a meaningful look.

The men nodded, and Susie headed down the hall. Tom

followed. They entered the library, and Tom closed the door behind him.

"I'm sorry I didn't speak with you before you encountered those two," Susie said.

"Maybe you can charm them into leaving. I want them gone."

"They have every intention of moving in if you do not pay them."

In theory, a bailiff living with you wasn't quite the epitome of shame; apparently, Lord Byron had endured their presence in his home two years ago. But they'd be yet another reminder of how Tom had failed his family. It didn't matter that the debts weren't his own. As the Earl of Halworth, they were his responsibility.

"I have some ideas about how to pacify them," Susie continued.

"Really? Have you also found a way to rid us of our infernal father's debts?" he asked.

"I have some thoughts on the matter."

Tom moved to the fire, motioning for her to go on.

"I believe I've persuaded them to take something other than cash." At Tom's silence, she continued. "Your horse, Tom."

Instantly, new pain materialized at the base of his neck. He raised his hand to knead it away. "You must be jesting. How am I supposed to get around?"

"We'll still have the carriage horses. And you can walk. Besides, can *you* think of anything else to give them?"

Tom sighed. Unfortunately, there was nothing else. All the family treasures, including paintings by Titian and Brueghel, were protected by a trust ensuring none of the Sherbornes or their descendants could sell them—another legacy from Tom's grandfather, the seventh Earl of Halworth. The guest room furniture in both houses had gone a month ago, which had left them with almost enough to pay everyone's wages on the estate. The only rooms Tom had approved for heating in the town house were their three bedchambers, the servants' rooms, the kitchen, and the library. Heating those rooms alone sat on the edge of imprudence, but the house would be unlivable with anything less.

Tom's mother had remained at Halworth Hall because they simply couldn't afford for her to take part in the season. Susie wasn't out in society yet, and therefore couldn't attend events, but since it would cost just as much to house her here as it would at Halworth Hall, she had come to London.

All other expenses, including food, were being bought on credit. Tom would much rather sell the carriage horses than his own, but that would be impractical. For one thing, he, Susie, and Charles would have a difficult time returning to Hampshire when the season ended.

Still, Tom couldn't imagine giving up Horatio. His uncle had traveled to Prussia to purchase the gentle, sturdy Trakehner for Tom's seventeenth birthday. It was the first time any male figure in Tom's life had given him something other than their own cast-off possessions, and Tom had always taken the greatest care with his new friend. On the trip back to England, through the Swiss Confederacy and France, they'd stopped frequently and Tom had always attended to Horatio himself. The horse had even weathered the Channel crossing without incident. Tom couldn't sell him.

"Didn't you say you had more than one idea?" he asked, rubbing the nape of his neck.

Susie nodded. "We must cease my lessons."

He grimaced, but said nothing. He couldn't deny that her lessons were becoming a frivolous expense. If he hadn't the money for a new wardrobe for her, he couldn't afford to bring her out in society. At least, not yet. Her debut would have to wait until he had the funds to bring her out in the style she deserved.

"And . . ." She hesitated, before continuing, "I need to take up some employment."

Tom groaned. "No. The debt isn't yours."

"Nor is it yours. It is our father's. But unfortunately, it has fallen on your shoulders, and I want to help. I owe it to you."

Tom walked to an armchair and dropped into it. "You owe me nothing."

"I owe you my life, Tom."

Tom shifted in the chair. This conversation wasn't one he cared to relive.

"What happened then is in the past. I'll consent to postponing your lessons for a time, but there is no reason to take up employment again. And you have done more than enough for me over the years."

Susie shook her head. "I could go back to being a maid, but I think I would make more money as a governess."

He exhaled. "English ladies do not take employment. And you of all people should know what unspeakable things can happen to pretty, young girls of six and ten—governesses and maids alike. I will not have your reputation ruined."

Susie tilted her head to the side. "Need I remind you I am the bastard daughter of an earl and a parlor maid? I have no reputation. Besides, we both worked in Solothurn. It wasn't improper for me to sweep floors in your uncle's hotel. Nor did you mind managing it when he let you."

The throbbing pain that had materialized earlier pulsed in his forehead, and Tom ran his hand across it. Susie was partly correct— the times his uncle had entrusted him to manage the hotel had been exhilarating. Bodmerhaus am Fluss was one of the few hotels in Solothurn catering to wealthy travelers; it boasted some of the largest rooms in the city or the canton. Tom hadn't always enjoyed pandering to the customers' whims or taking care of menial tasks, but he still remembered the way his chest swelled with pride after helping his uncle appease a particularly difficult guest. Once they were alone, his uncle's whiskers would quiver into a crooked smile as he gave Tom a clap on the back.

His aunt and uncle had no son—only three daughters who were already married by the time Tom and Susie came to Solothurn—so his uncle had taken Tom under his wing. His aunt, a kind, plump woman, spent her days at her daughters' homes supervising the raising of her grandchildren. She had a fondness for pastries and a habit of buying *läckerli* or *magenbrot*—the Swiss versions of gingerbread Tom could never choose between.

Tom fiddled with the leg of his trousers. He often missed his uncle's family and the cobbled streets of Solothurn. Even now, he could picture the cozy interior of his uncle's home with its carved wooden furniture and massive ceramic fireplace that heated the main sitting room so quickly. He pictured his uncle and aunt sitting to take their afternoon meal before a platter of cured ham, grassy Emmentaler cheese, sauerkraut, and brown bread, and his stomach growled.

Unfortunately, he was here—in the dull, gray town house that chilled the bones and the spirit almost as much as Halworth Hall did, eating food bland enough to make him lose half a stone, and worrying over how to keep the estate alive and running.

For the first time in his life, he was the sole manager of an enterprise. Only now, he was the manager of an ancient, thankless estate instead of a bustling hotel. He should be as energetic about running Halworth as he had been those times he'd managed the Bodmerhaus am Fluss, but the Halworth estate, unlike his uncle's hotel, was tainted—tainted by debt, tainted by indifference, and most of all, tainted by agonizing memories.

Tom cleared his throat. "Our lives are different now. I promised myself when we returned that at least *your* life would be better."

Susan opened her mouth.

He held up a hand. "I may have inherited an estate and a title I don't want, but you have no such obligations. I won't see you working again. You are the daughter of an earl, and I intend you to be treated as such. Once I've cleared some of this debt, you *will* have the season you deserve. I know you wish to help, but recall that as a peer, I can't be hauled to debtors' prison. I'm safe for the time being."

His empty stomach dropped like a stone as he realized what he'd have to do. "Horatio will go. But I want Charles's horse included in this. He was the one adding to the food merchant's bill this past year, and his Thoroughbred will fetch a higher price than Horatio. I'll sell them at auction myself and give the bailiffs the proceeds. I'll tell them now."

He started to push himself up from the chair.

"No, Tom. Let me," Susie said.

He nodded his thanks and let himself collapse back down, stretching his neck back. The pounding in his forehead had spread to the top of his skull.

Susie went to the door, but then turned back, her palm still on the handle. "You returned earlier than expected. Did you enjoy your afternoon of barbaric male ritual?" she asked.

Tom grimaced.

She raised her delicate brows. "What happened?"

Tom explained what they'd witnessed at the boxing club.

With each detail, Susie's eyes widened. "Tom, you must be careful."

"Have no fear." He smiled to reassure her. "I have no intention of going near the fellow again."

Her forehead creased, but she opened the door. "I'd better see to the bailiffs. You will sell the horses, won't you, Tom? I know how much Horatio means to you, but the situation is getting out of hand. If we cannot conjure some money, the bailiffs truly *will* take up residence with us."

"Let's hope it won't come to that. I'll sell the horses. I promise."

She nodded and turned to go.

"The next step is to curb Charles's spending," he muttered.

"Perhaps *he* can find some occupation. What say you to Charles as a dung-shoveler?"

Susie snorted with laughter. "He'd think twice about nagging you for 'sullying the family name by partaking in business.'"

Tom wished he could laugh, but her jest only reminded him that Charles had failed to introduce him to potential backers after the match. Again. Though to be fair, Carmichael had interfered with that plan.

Tom gave Susie another half smile. Some days the urge to board the first ship out of England with Susie and Horatio was so strong, Tom could smell the crisp scent of cut grass from the pastures beyond the Solothurn city walls floating across the river Aare to meet him. Life would be so pleasant without debts and endless responsibilities. But then the image of his father laughing from beyond the grave rooted him in place. He couldn't walk away from his family. Tom would *not* let the old tyrant win.

CHAPTER THE TENTH

She was willing to allow he might have more good qualities
than she had been wont to suppose.
—Jane Austen, *Mansfield Park*

Vicky nodded at the butler, Sheldon, as she stepped into the foyer of the Aston House with Sarah at her heels. Her escort for the afternoon, the Honorable Bartholomew Shore, trudged in after them. Sarah took Vicky's shawl and disappeared down the hall.

Vicky turned to Mr. Shore. "Thank you for the walk. It was most . . . pleasant."

Mr. Shore waggled his eyebrows. He must have thought the gesture projected a rakish charm because he'd done it no less than ten times—Vicky had counted—in the space of the last hour. Unfortunately, the waggling only made him look silly or, if she were to be uncharitable, slightly deranged at worst. The art at the Royal Academy Exhibition had proved both a blessing and a curse, as it had kept Vicky from noticing how often he did it for the entire first room of paintings. When she finally did notice, they were too far into the inner room to do anything but continue on—albeit at a quicker pace.

"The pleasure was all mine, Lady Victoria." Mr. Shore stepped toward the entry table in the center of the foyer and brushed an imaginary speck of dirt from the table onto the floor.

Vicky glanced at Sheldon, who stood stock-still next to the door, but he was too well-versed in his duty to make any outward show of his thoughts. Vicky barely suppressed a grimace, irked as she was at Mr. Shore's implication that the Aston House staff was remiss in their housekeeping.

Still, he'd been kind enough to ask her for an outing without so much as meeting her first, so she would remain polite.

In the interest of giving Vicky choices beyond Mr. Carmichael, her mother had written missives to some of her friends who currently resided in Town. A good number of them had responded favorably, including her former schoolmate Lady Allenby. As her second son, Mr. Shore would never inherit his father's earldom, but his parents planned to grant him a sizable estate in Berkshire once he came into his majority.

He waggled his brows again, nearly winking at her in the process. "So much art does put one in a mind for refreshment."

She pressed her lips together. He wanted her to offer him a drink. She supposed she could invite him to stay for tea, but as he took a step closer to her and raised his thick, reddish brown brows at her—for the twelfth time—she knew tea was out of the question, let alone the disturbing notion of having to watch his eyebrow maneuvers for decades to come if she married him.

"Perhaps you might find one at your club," Vicky said, gracing him with a smile.

He took another step toward her. "Ah, but I had thought . . ." He trailed off but met her gaze, and this time the red-brown caterpillars danced up and down as if fighting for supremacy.

Thirteen. "I'm afraid I have another engagement this afternoon, but thank you again for the outing." She turned to the butler. "Sheldon, would you be so good as to show Mr. Shore out?"

Sheldon nodded. "Of course, my lady." He opened the door. "Mr. Shore," he intoned.

Realizing he was being dismissed, Shore inclined his head to her. "Another time then, Lady Victoria."

Vicky kept her smile but said nothing.

He walked to the door and looked back at her with what looked like a genuine smile. "I bid you good day."

Vicky smiled back. He really wasn't *so* bad. Maybe his company improved on closer acquaintance. She really shouldn't be so judgmental. He started down the steps to the street.

"Good day, Mr. Shore," she called to him.

He turned back, his eyebrows dancing another absurd jig.

Vicky pressed her lips together and gave Sheldon a meaningful look.

Sheldon shut the door.

"Thank you for the outing, Mr. Fothergill, it was . . . most pleasant," Vicky said. Swinging his walking stick, Mr. Fothergill thwacked it on the doorjamb as he followed Sarah through the threshold into the Aston House foyer.

"I say," he exclaimed, looking between his stick and the door, "that came out of nowhere."

Just as the railing on the great staircase at the British Museum had come out of nowhere. She tried not to roll her eyes as Sarah caught her gaze. Vicky glanced at Mr. Fothergill's battered, ebony stick, then back at Sarah, who was suppressing a laugh as she took Vicky's bonnet and gloves and hurried down the hall. Vicky wished she could follow.

One might think she would have learned her lesson about planning long afternoons after her outing with Mr. Shore, but Mr. Fothergill was the eldest son of the Viscount Lindsley, and they'd actually met as children at one of the gatherings at Oakbridge. She recalled him being a small ruddy-faced boy who'd been happy to join her, Tom, Charles, and Althea in racing paper boats down the stream. She'd thought an afternoon at the British Museum would lend them time to reacquaint themselves with each other and see some interesting artifacts in the process.

Yet Mr. Fothergill had grown into a lanky, thin fellow who still seemed to be gaining control of his frame. He'd almost tripped over her twice. And she'd nearly squealed aloud when his stick had knocked the base of the display holding up the Rosetta Stone. All that, she could overlook.

What she could *not* was that he'd insisted on stopping to take pinches out of his jewel-inlaid snuff box no less than four times while they were inside the museum, and in his clumsiness, he'd nearly spilled it each time. The first time, he'd almost dropped it on an

Etruscan vase, and the second he'd almost fumbled the box and its contents onto her new blue day dress. She'd hopped backward, and the box had fallen to the floor beside the Parthenon sculptures. He'd lost half his snuff, and received many a cold glare, but that hadn't stopped him from pausing to take another sniff a few minutes later.

"It was a good day for it," Mr. Fothergill said as he nodded at her. "Not too fine out, you know. Waste of the air to be inside looking at dusty coins and urns when the weather's fine."

Vicky offered a half smile. They weren't *dusty* objects so much as fascinating pieces of the past, but she did agree that a fine day should not be wasted.

He rubbed the silver handle of his walking stick against his trouser leg, and Vicky held her breath as the end flailed in the air. "Perhaps when the weather improves, we could take a drive."

Vicky's eyes widened involuntarily as she imagined him trying to juggle the reins of a vehicle as he took a pinch of snuff. She smiled wider so she wouldn't have to answer.

Mr. Fothergill nodded and pulled out his snuff box. He grasped it in one hand while holding his walking stick with his last three fingers as he tried to take a pinch of the powder with his forefinger and thumb. Vicky glanced at Sheldon as Mr. Fothergill snorted the tobacco up his nose. Truly, was it so much to ask that a potential suitor be more interested in her than his snuff? Or, at the very least, contain his vices to an appropriate place and time? Sheldon caught her eye, but as usual his expression did not waver.

She glanced back at Mr. Fothergill, who had somehow pulled out a dark handkerchief. He was wiping his nose when his grip on the stick loosened and it crashed to the floor. He crouched to retrieve it and nearly dropped his snuff box again; he grabbed for it with his other hand, sending the handkerchief winging to the floor, where it landed with a slight *squash*.

Vicky grimaced at Sheldon.

"Allow me, sir," Sheldon said and moved from his post by the door at his usual sedate pace.

Mr. Fothergill looked at Sheldon. "No need, my good man. I need only secure my snuff back into my pocket . . ."

Before he had done so, Sheldon had retrieved the wayward stick and handkerchief. He plodded back to the door with the items and Vicky followed, hoping Mr. Fothergill would take the hint.

After he returned his precious snuff to its protective pocket, he saw them standing at the door and moved there himself.

"Thank you for the delightful afternoon, Mr. Fothergill," Vicky said with a smile.

"A great pleasure, Lady Victoria," he replied.

"Your stick, Mr. Fothergill," intoned Sheldon, holding it out.

Fothergill took it and started through the door.

"And your handkerchief, sir," Sheldon said, holding it delicately aloft with two fingers.

Fothergill snatched it from Sheldon, nodded at Vicky, and stepped outside. Vicky winced as his stick slapped the doorjamb again.

Sheldon swung the door shut.

Vicky paused at the front door of Aston House and turned to Lord Blankenship, who stood two steps below her. Behind her, Sarah opened the door and hastened through.

"Thank you for the outing, Lord Blankenship. It was . . . most pleasant." And thankfully *brief.* Vicky had learned her lesson this time and only allowed Lord Blankenship to take her for a walk to Hyde Park and back.

"Quite so, Lady Victoria. Most pleasant," said the young viscount, spittle flying from his lips as he said the "p" in "pleasant." He climbed another step closer to her.

Vicky stepped back until she was standing in the door's frame. It hadn't been *so* bad conversing with Lord Blankenship in the park, where they were walking side by side and she needn't face him— although watching his saliva reflect in the sun's rays as it showered to the ground had certainly not been pleasant—but how was she to avoid being spit upon when he insisted on speaking face-to-face?

"The park always makes for such a diverting outing."

Vicky winced as spittle flew closer to her with each "t" sound. She didn't care if his mother and hers thought him a good marital prospect. Nothing was worth dodging dribble for the rest of her life. She inched backward and saw Sheldon holding the door, standing straight and serious as ever.

"Perhaps I shall see you at Lady Tefft's garden party."

Saliva flew toward her, and Vicky shrank back until she stood inside the door. Of all the people to be having a garden party and to have invited *him*, it had to be Lady *Tefft*! "Possibly, Lord Blankenship," Vicky replied, giving Sheldon a meaningful look.

Lord Blankenship stepped to the threshold. "Capital, capital—"

His final assault of spittle hit the door as Sheldon swung it shut.

As Mr. Silby turned his yellow-lacquered curricle onto the long, straight stretch of track in Hyde Park known as "Rotten Row," Vicky schooled her features into what she hoped was a sympathetic smile.

"So I told the impudent fellow I would not buy one of his toothpick cases if the king himself were in the habit of singing their praises," Mr. Silby said.

Thinking his smirk detracted from his classical good looks, Vicky nodded. Mr. Carmichael had proven quite right. Despite Mr. Silby's recent hardships, he was distinctly unlikable. Which was a shame, really. Mr. Silby was only twenty or so. Vicky liked his features and his straight, dark hair, but he was also an utter dolt. Although after enduring men with obnoxious eyebrows, clumsy snuff obsessions, and projectile saliva, she supposed she should be grateful he wasn't picking his teeth with one of the toothpicks he hadn't bought a case for.

She'd just endured a twenty-minute story about Silby's encounter with a shopkeeper. The merchant had had the effrontery to tell Mr. Silby pure gold was far too malleable a metal to make into an effective toothpick case. Silby had harangued the man, saying the son of a baron would have nothing but the best.

Vicky looked out at the trees of the park so he couldn't gauge her disinterest. His quip to the shopkeeper about the king hardly proved his point since King George had been mad for some years. Her lips curved in a tiny smile as she pictured the shopkeeper sniggering at Silby's snobbery.

Then she sobered, remembering why she was here today. Silby

was certainly not the kind of man Vicky wanted to live with for the next forty years. She almost shuddered as she imagined such a fate. Her mind turned to Mr. Carmichael again. How had he known she would dislike Mr. Silby by the end of their outing? Did he understand her so well already? Or was this simply every lady's reaction to Silby? She decided to believe it the latter.

After her experiences of the last few days, she couldn't deny that Mr. Carmichael stood head and shoulders above everyone else she'd met—though that wasn't difficult given the pool.

As Mr. Silby continued to prattle on about the incompetence of shopkeepers in general, Vicky gazed at the greenery of the park. It was a lovely day. A bit chilly perhaps, but the sun shone through the trees. Ducks waddled on the grass, idling the day away until the next pair of children with a nursemaid in tow came to feed them. A few gentlemen cantered around the track on horseback. The hour wasn't quite fashionable enough for society to be out on parade, so Rotten Row was not yet crowded.

At the last minute, Silby had proposed they take his new curricle—a chariot-like vehicle only wide enough for a driver and passenger seated side by side and one groom sitting on the small back seat—instead of riding to the park as they'd originally arranged. Since her walk to the park with Lord Blankenship had been the briefest of her outings thus far, Vicky had thought a ride through the park would be even better. Driving through the park *should* be equally short, but she wouldn't be able to set the pace, so Vicky had initially resisted, but when Mr. Silby had remained adamant, she hadn't pressed the point.

However, as the narrow curricle seat forced her to sit closer to Mr. Silby than she would have liked, and to inhale his potent frankincense cologne, Vicky wished she'd insisted on taking her horse.

Beside her, Silby cleared his throat. Vicky flicked a glance at him. Two young men on horseback touched the brims of their hats as they passed the curricle. One of them wore a dark orange coat, the other a red waistcoat. Their ostentatious style of dress amused her. Vicky smiled politely.

"I never saw such a pair of posturing puppies," Mr. Silby remarked after they'd passed.

Thinking Silby dressed in similarly bad taste, Vicky rolled her eyes. "Why do you say so, Mr. Silby?" she asked with an innocent smile.

"Didn't you see that fellow's bloodred waistcoat? Where does he think he is, the Continent?"

Vicky looked at Silby's bisque-colored waistcoat and purple tailcoat and wrinkled her nose at the combination. The strange colors made his skin look unappealingly pale. He looked just as much a fop as the two riders. If it hadn't been for his clothes, Silby might have cut a fine figure, for he'd looked perfectly presentable in his black evening clothes at the ball.

Silby went on to enumerate all the other fashion *faux pas* the two riders had committed. Vicky tried to ignore him and still nod at the appropriate moments.

"Did you notice that?" Silby asked.

"Pardon?" Confused, Vicky shook her head.

"I felt a jolt, and the horses are pulling unevenly now."

"Oh." Vicky glanced at the matched pair of grays. To her, they seemed to be moving at a steady trot. "I didn't detect any jolt, but I'm sure you know your curricle better than I."

"I'd best get out and inspect the vehicle."

Silby stopped the horses and gave Vicky the reins. He dismounted and bent to look at the left side of the curricle.

Vicky twisted in her seat to look back at Sarah, who sat in the tiny seat on the back of the vehicle where a groom, or *tiger*, usually sat. Poor Sarah gripped the back of Vicky's seat so tightly, her knuckles were white. How horrid it must've been for Sarah bouncing around on the cramped seat listening to Silby drone on, but Vicky's mother had decided yet again to assign Sarah as chaperone, thereby giving Vicky some measure of privacy to assess Mr. Silby.

Vicky understood her mother's reasoning, but she couldn't help feeling guilty having subjected Sarah to the agonizing outings of this week. Vicky would do something especially nice for Sarah when they got home.

"Lady Victoria," Sarah began, "would you mind if I got down?"

"No, of course not." Vicky glanced at Silby, and after ascertaining he was still busy, she whispered, "I'm sorry about the seat. I didn't think we would be taking this contraption."

Sarah shrugged. She pointed at Silby discreetly and wrinkled her nose. Vicky hid her giggle with a small cough. Sarah jumped off her perch and onto the sandy track. Vicky started to turn forward when the horse nearest Silby whinnied. It reared up, causing the entire curricle to tilt backward.

Vicky's torso slammed against the back of the seat. For a moment, she thought she might topple out and onto the hard ground. Instead, the vehicle leveled with a great THUURRUMP.

The horses jolted forward.

Vicky steadied herself with her right hand. Too late, she realized she'd let go of the reins in the confusion. She looked for the ends. They were slipping over the front edge of the curricle. With each shudder of the carriage, the reins slipped farther out of her reach. In a matter of moments, they'd be lost.

Vicky's heart pounded in her ears. She had to do something, but she couldn't make herself let go of the seat.

The reins were almost gone.

She forced herself to stretch and make a grab for them. As her fingers brushed the stiff leather, the carriage bounced, and the reins slipped over the edge.

Tom pulled Horatio to a stop as they reached the entrance to the park. Two dandies on horseback wearing orange and red trotted by. Even though they posted up and down in the saddle, they took the time to touch the brims of their hats. Tom nodded and sat back.

He patted Horatio's neck. They'd ridden through a good portion of the city today, and Tom could tell the old boy was ready for a long rubdown. He pulled out his pocket watch. They'd left the town house three hours ago. Tom smoothed some of Horatio's chestnut mane by way of apology.

Trakehners were sturdy horses bred either for farm work or for the Prussian cavalry, and able to endure rigorous exercise, but Tom always took care not to overtax Horatio. To own the truth, he'd spoiled the animal. Tom never went to the stables without a treat in his pocket, and he allowed Horatio far more carrots and apples than he ought. As it happened, Horatio had already gobbled the three carrots Tom had brought with him today.

Tom sighed. He couldn't bear to part with the big greedy beast, but tomorrow he'd have to. He and Charles were taking the horses to Tattersall's Auction House in the morning. It was all so damnably unfair.

He patted the horse's neck. Under his breath, he promised he would find a way to buy Horatio back. He could hardly believe this was his and Horatio's last ride together. Still, he started to worry he'd ridden him too long today.

Tom stood in the stirrups and looked down the path. Cutting through Hyde Park would be the shortest route home. Unfortunately, all of society's highfliers came to Rotten Row to see and be seen, and Tom was in no mood for socializing. Yet it wasn't quite five o'clock. With any luck, the gossiping ladies of the *ton* wouldn't yet be out in droves.

Tom took a deep breath and looked down at Horatio. For *his* sake, the risk was worth it. Tom patted the horse's neck again before nudging him into a walk.

After they turned onto the Row, Tom scanned the track. It stood relatively clear. Only a handful of gentlemen on horseback and a few open carriages ambled along. Perhaps the journey wouldn't be too trying.

He kicked Horatio into a trot and admired the landscape. Of course, it was nothing compared to the abundant grass fields and hills of Hampshire, or to the gentle green pastures outside Solothurn, but at least it served as an oasis in the center of the dirty, bustling city.

Down the track, a yellow-lacquered curricle some three hundred feet away had stopped. The driver, in an unsightly purple coat, descended. One of the two female passengers sat on the small back seat usually reserved for the driver's footman. She wore the plain attire of a servant. The other passenger, judging by her bright yellow bonnet, was a lady. She turned in her seat to face the other woman, and Tom swallowed as he registered Victoria's features.

The muscles in his shoulders tensed. He hadn't seen her since the ball, but Charles had told him Carmichael's accusations at the boxing match were now circulating through society's gossip mill.

But no matter what the gossips thought, Tom would have to stop and offer help. Horatio nickered and Tom forced himself to relax. The last thing he needed was for Horatio to grow skittish. The sooner Tom discharged his duty, the sooner he'd get Horatio home. Tom urged the horse to move faster.

Vicky's maid, as he assumed her to be, jumped off the back seat. The curricle didn't appear to be going anywhere soon.

Then, one of the matching horses reared up.

The curricle tilted backward before the horse's feet touched down again. Both horses took off at a breakneck pace with the curricle still attached. For a moment, Tom gaped. What the hell had happened? But he didn't have time to think. The curricle was picking up speed.

He spurred Horatio forward.

☙❧

Vicky collapsed on the floor of the curricle, cursing herself for not moving sooner. What was she to do? Without reins, she couldn't stop a pair of team horses. Her only option was to jump. She looked down at the sandy track rushing past her, and her stomach lurched.

She changed her mind. No. There had to be a way to get the reins.

Grasping the front of the curricle, she raised herself up to her knees to look for them. They swung from the crossbar that connected the vehicle to the pole running between the two horses. She squinted as something caught her eye. The pole connected to the crossbar looked cracked, probably from when the horse had reared. If it broke, she'd certainly go toppling out of the two-wheeled body of the carriage. She'd be fortunate if the vehicle didn't crush her in the process.

She swallowed and tried to reach the reins, but they dangled a good arm's length farther away than she could reach. In order to get close, she'd have to stand and lean out over the lip of the curricle, which would hardly be safe. The curved wood at the curricle's front appeared too thin to support much weight. She looked for anything that could help her reach the reins. There was nothing.

She had to risk it. Gritting her teeth, she stood, leaned forward, and stretched toward the reins.

Beneath her, the wood cracked.

Tom had never ridden Horatio so hard, but the horse didn't seem to mind. Horatio sprinted toward the runaway carriage like a racehorse. As they drew near, Tom saw Vicky's torso folded over the front of the curricle. *What was she—*

Her hand flailed in front of her, reaching for something. She must have lost the reins. That had to be why she hadn't stopped the horses by now.

When he'd reached the horses, Tom slowed Horatio to match their stride. He maneuvered Horatio to the left, as near to the grays as he could. He stretched his arm out for the closest horse's bridle, near the bit.

His hand was a foot away, then inches away. Finally, his fingers closed around the leather. He sat back on Horatio and pulled backward on the bridle. The horses ignored him.

He tried again, this time pulling harder. As he did, he noticed two large, open carriages ambling down the path toward him. Moving parallel to each other, one trundled down the right-hand side of the road while the other took up the center. At their current speed, it wouldn't be long before he and Horatio collided with the center carriage.

Tom released the gray's bridle and spurred Horatio. Little by little, they pulled ahead of the curricle horses. But they weren't moving fast enough, and for a hair-raising moment, he thought Horatio wouldn't make it.

The opposing carriages drew closer.

Tom didn't have much time. He dug his heels into Horatio's flanks. With a burst of speed, Horatio overtook the curricle horses. Tom pulled the reins to the left, and they veered away from the oncoming carriages just in time.

The air whipped at Tom's hat. He threw a glance over his right shoulder to see how close the curricle horses were.

But they weren't behind him.

He turned over his left shoulder. The curricle had left the track. It now sped across the grass toward the Serpentine.

If he didn't act quickly, the horses—and Victoria—would careen into the lake.

Vicky looked back, trying to see what had happened to Tom. He'd appeared out of nowhere just as the front of the curricle began cracking under her weight. Then relief took over. He'd rescue her and they'd laugh about how close she'd come to disaster. That was before he'd lurched in front of Silby's horses, causing them to turn off the road.

The Serpentine loomed before her. She turned one last time to look for Tom. He'd almost reached the curricle's right wheel, but he didn't seem to be gaining much ground. Vicky glanced at the water.

She edged herself to the left side of the curricle and peered over the edge. The grass blurred past.

She took a deep breath, closed her eyes, and jumped.

Her knees hit the ground first. The momentum forced her torso to flop to the right, causing her to land on her arms. She slid on her side for a few yards before coming to a stop.

For countless moments, Vicky lay there on the ground, trying to sense if she'd broken anything. Eventually, she propped herself on her elbow and pushed herself up to sit. Her knees throbbed, but she could move them. No doubt they'd be bruised and sore for a few days, but she thought she could walk. She turned toward the Serpentine to look for the curricle. But the water remained undisturbed. On the bank, Tom was pulling the bridle of one of the horses and slowly directing them both to back away from the lake.

Vicky sighed. At least he'd saved the horses. She set one foot on the grass, but as she put pressure on her knee to stand, pain shot through it. She sat back with a grimace and cut a glance at Tom. He certainly had impeccable timing.

Inching the horses away from the bank of the Serpentine, Tom exhaled, quite pleased with himself. Victoria was unscathed, the horses safe, and the curricle undamaged.

Horatio had done marvelously and had caught up with the horses in what must be record time. As Tom turned to Vicky, his brows knit together.

He couldn't see her.

He stood up in his stirrups to see if she was crouching on the floor of the curricle. His breath seized in his windpipe. She wasn't there.

A throat cleared behind him.

His head whipped around.

Vicky limped toward him. Mud splattered the skirt of her dark blue riding habit. One sleeve gaped open at the elbow, and the other had ripped where her arm met her torso. Her yellow bonnet appeared to be the only unscathed part of her, though a few blades of grass had attached themselves to the ribbons at one side.

"Good God," he breathed. She'd *jumped*.

Though he couldn't guess how the curricle horses would react, he dropped their reins and dismounted, pulling Horatio behind him so he could approach Vicky. "Take my arm."

She placed her hand on his arm without argument, but put no pressure on it.

He frowned. "Are you quite all right?"

Her brows knit together. "Not really."

He splayed open his hand, palm up. "Press down on my hand instead."

She glanced up at him, but she put her gloved hand on his and pushed down.

"Now try walking."

She took a tentative step and made a noise in her throat.

"It will be easier if you hold my hand while you press down."

She shot him a look, her hazel eyes widening slightly. "Er . . . of course." She dropped her gaze, and her small hand closed over his. "I don't wish to hurt you."

A smile pulled at his lips. "I appreciate your concern, but your welfare is of more import at the moment."

"Very well, if you're certain," she murmured. She gripped his hand, pushed down, and took a few steps.

"Any better?" he asked.

Her brows lifted. "Yes, a little. And your hand?"

He couldn't stop the smile this time. "Perfectly sound."

She nodded. "Good." She paused. "And thank you."

He shook his head. "Not at all."

She angled her head to catch his eye. "Thank you for trying to save me."

His stomach twisted. "I should have been faster."

Her hazel gaze pierced through him. "You couldn't have antici-pated those other carriages."

As he started to reply, Mr. Silby ran up with Vicky's maid not far behind.

"Are you hurt?" Silby said, panting from exertion as he looked Vicky up and down. His vision rested briefly where Vicky's hand held Tom's. "I tried to keep up after the horses bolted, but I saw Lord Hal-worth in pursuit." His brow furrowed as he caught Tom's eye. "I don't know what could have happened to cause them to shy like that."

Tom clenched his jaw, trying to stay silent. After his two previ-ous encounters with Silby, he had no great opinion of the man, but now he was certain Silby was a blockhead. The urge to yell at him for putting Vicky in danger clawed at him, but he held his tongue. It was none of his affair.

Vicky's maid rushed to her side, fussing over her mistress's appearance.

Victoria smiled coolly at Silby. "Despite what my appearance might suggest, I will soon be well. I do, however, wish to go home."

While Tom had attended to Victoria, Silby's horses had wan-dered several yards away. Silby moved to fetch them. Once he took the reins, he examined his horses and vehicle. "Notwithstanding the scare, everything seems to be in order," he said as he returned. "I can drive you home immediately, Lady Victoria."

Tom grimaced, wondering if he should protest, but Vicky spoke first.

"I thank you again, Mr. Silby, but I do believe you'll find the pole is cracked where it meets the crossbar."

Silby blinked twice.

Still supporting herself on Tom's hand, Vicky walked to the vehicle, stopping behind the grays. She leaned forward and released his hand to point at the black-lacquered wooden pole. Just as she'd said, the wood had splintered on one side.

Tom lowered himself onto his haunches to inspect it. The cracking should have been obvious to anyone who knew what to look for.

"You cannot possibly drive home in this," Tom stated. He looked to Silby. "Not only for your own safety, but for your horses' as well."

Silby approached from the other side. He frowned down at the crack. "That wasn't there before."

Tom stood. "Of course it was *there*. Lady Victoria saw it." Tom looked at her, and she bit her lip. "The question is why you *didn't* see it, Silby."

Silby's eyes narrowed. "See here, Halworth—"

"I'm certain it was an honest mistake," Vicky interjected.

Tom gaped at her. Her lips were set in a determined line. He looked away. He shouldn't have interfered.

"Of course it was," Silby said, still staring at Tom.

Tom clenched his jaw. Silby then broke eye contact and nodded at Vicky. "I shall walk you home now, Lady Victoria."

"That won't be necessary. Lord Halworth can accompany me," she said, her eyes darting in his direction.

Tom's gaze snapped to her face.

She shifted her weight. "I'm sure you'll wish to give your full attention to your horses and curricle, Mr. Silby, and it would be far better to walk them directly home rather than stop at Aston House first," she continued. Then she looked at Tom with wide, pleading eyes.

He raised an eyebrow, but said nothing.

Silby shook his head. "Lady Victoria, I really must insist—"

"Mr. Silby," she said, "truly, your grays need your care more than I. They are such a beautifully matched pair, and I can well imagine the time and effort it must have cost to breed them."

Silby's jaw dropped, his mouth forming a little O. Tom didn't know if his surprise stemmed from Vicky's reference to horse husbandry or her dismissal of him.

Vicky angled her head. "I have Sarah and Lord Halworth to attend me, whereas they have only you. Please understand my distress."

Silby blinked at Tom. Then his blue eyes narrowed and he took a step forward. "Halworth," he said, the pitch of his voice moving up the scale, "I will not allow you to—"

"To what, Mr. Silby? To honor my request?" Vicky stepped toward Silby and met his glare. "Please be so good as to excuse us."

Vicky's voice was losing its steadiness, but her resolve was unmistakable.

A strange feeling bloomed in Tom's chest. Was it amusement at Silby's inability to match his unshakable friend, stubborn as when she was six? Or was it something more?

Silby must have realized he was on shaky ground because he stepped back. His mouth opened and closed like a hooked trout.

The side of Tom's mouth quirked upward as he inclined his head at Silby's fishy expression. He looked down at Vicky. "Shall we?"

Vicky ventured a glance at Tom's profile as they left the park.

Tom flanked her right side, holding his left arm rigid to support her weight as he held his horse's reins with his right.

Sarah walked on Vicky's left. She'd wanted to help support Vicky on the way home, but Tom had insisted on tending to her. He'd also proposed Vicky ride his horse home to ease her aches and pains, but she'd decided to walk. Normally, she would have jumped at the chance to ride such a beautiful and unusual mount, but after today's incident, she didn't think she'd trust anything other than her own two legs for a while.

After they'd set off toward Mayfair, Vicky's throbbing knees had made her regret her decision, but before long the pain subsided, and now she could almost stroll without limping—especially if she kept pressure on Tom's hand. A breeze picked up loose tendrils of hair at her neck. That same scent of toast and cinnamon Tom had carried that day at Oakbridge tickled her senses. His manner of assistance today couldn't be more different. In fact, after their last encounters, his attentiveness almost seemed strange.

"Your horse is uncommon. What breed is he?"

Tom dragged in a breath. "A Trakehner. Horatio's sire was a Prussian cavalry mount and his dam a variant of the same breed used for farm work."

Vicky raised her brows. Prussian cavalry horses were rare in England. Nor, if she remembered her geography, was Prussia particularly close to the Swiss Confederation.

"How did you acquire him?"

"My uncle bought him for my seventeenth birthday. He traveled to Prussia himself to purchase him. We've been through a lot, Horatio and I." Tom glanced back at the horse with a boyish grin.

Vicky smiled at his obvious affection for the animal. "I take it you were close to your uncle. Did you enjoy living in Solothurn? I know how worried your mother was for you, especially when no correspondence was crossing the Channel."

"I see our mothers remained friends even after I left," he said, arching a brow.

When he said nothing more, Vicky turned her head away. She pursed her lips. She should have known better than to speak of the war after the way he'd acted at the ball.

Tom cleared his throat. "I *was* happy in my uncle's home." His words sounded clipped, but his eyes focused on something out in the distance.

"What was it like?" she asked, wondering if he'd answer.

His gaze remained forward. "Cozy. Busy. It was the first time I lived with people who actually enjoyed each other's company."

She nodded. From a young age, Vicky had understood the unspoken truth about Tom's parents. The Earl and Countess of Halworth had the opposite of a happy marriage. When they were small children, Tom barely spoke of his father. By the time Tom had reached adolescence, if he spoke of him, it was with anger in his voice.

"I wonder that you returned at all." She'd meant it genuinely, but she frowned at the thought of him never returning to England. She immediately shook her head at herself. He was kind to escort her home, but it wasn't as though his return had meant they'd regained their friendship as she'd once hoped.

"Were it not for my mother's pleadings, I would be there still."

Vicky's brows scrunched together. Poor Tom. He'd been exiled from his home at fourteen, only to be pulled back by duty to his family. *Duty* alone had forced him to leave the one place he'd been happy.

She couldn't read Tom's expression, but as he stared into the distance, she felt certain he was thinking of the past. Perhaps they were more alike than she'd thought after their last few encounters. She, too, was leaving contentment behind to attend to her familial duty.

Tom cleared his throat. "Victoria, I feel there is something I should say."

She met his gaze. His light brown eyes shot away and then back again. "Charles tells me Mr. Carmichael is spreading a rumor that I imposed myself on you at the duchess's ball." He made a frustrated noise in his throat.

"But why would he—" She broke off, remembering how Mr. Carmichael had condemned Tom to her the other day in his carriage. But she hadn't agreed with him.

"He has taken a dislike to me. He tried to goad me into challenging him to a boxing match, and when I refused, he told his companions I took advantage of your good nature."

"Oh dear." Vicky bit her lip. She looked up at him. "Do you box?"

"By no means! But he nearly killed Charles's friend the other day."

"He did what?"

Tom hesitated. Then he described the events of the boxing match, although she suspected he glossed over the gruesome details.

"Has Mr. Kirkham recovered?" she asked.

"His face resembles raw beefsteak, according to Charles, but he will recover. I imagine his inebriated state might have relaxed his muscles somewhat."

Vicky frowned. "And you say it was all sanctioned in the rules?"

Tom exhaled. "So it seems. Yet . . ." He swallowed. "In any event, I wish to apologize for my conduct at the ball. Despite what Carmichael and society are saying, I had no wish to"—he searched her face—"impose. I apologize."

She looked down, away from those brown eyes she'd once known so well. "That is kind of you. Thank you."

She heard Tom exhale.

Then she frowned. "I don't understand why Mr. Carmichael would behave in such a manner. He is a close friend of my father's."

Tom's brow furrowed. "Is he?"

Vicky nodded. "And my father has never been one for pugilism. I do not know Mr. Carmichael well, but my father trusts him." Of course, her father had trusted Dain enough to allow him to marry Althea. As much as it pained her to admit it, his judgment wasn't infallible. "There must be an explanation," she mumbled.

"I daresay," said Tom, clearly unconvinced. "Just take care."

He sounded concerned for her. Maybe she'd wronged him. Maybe a small part of him did still wish to be friends. She smiled. "Thank you. I shall."

Tom nodded. Then he said, "Did you really think Silby's grays so well-matched?"

She tilted her head up to catch his eye. "In speed."

He made a strangled sound in his throat, and she hoped he was choking on a laugh. She suspected he didn't laugh often anymore.

"I would concur on that point."

"But they were overly powerful to draw the weight of that curricle," she pronounced.

"They were rather too spirited as well," Tom said. "Did you see what spooked them?"

Vicky sighed and shook her head.

"When did you see the pole had cracked?"

"When I leaned over the front. I assumed it must have happened when the horse reared. But then when I told Mr. Silby of it, I had a better look and it seemed like almost too much damage from just one rearing horse." She frowned. "Did you think it odd?"

He puffed out a breath. "Him not seeing such obvious splintering was unpardonable."

"You all but called him out," she said, rolling her eyes.

He cut a sharp glance at her. "I would never do that."

She raised a brow.

"Silby strikes me as the sort who leaves such matters up to a groomsman. And curricles have never been the safest of vehicles—although one would think that would make Silby more aware of the dangers, not less," he grumbled in a low voice.

"And to that end, I shan't be going anywhere with Mr. Silby again."

Tom's lips pitched upward at one corner. "He seems to be a great friend of Carmichael's."

Vicky shook her head. "Not according to Mr. Carmichael. Apparently, Mr. Silby was quite close with Mr. Carmichael's late cousin."

Tom frowned. "Silby was Carmichael's second at the boxing match. Why would he entrust a second's duty to a mere acquaintance?"

Vicky thought for a moment. "Perhaps Mr. Silby is well versed in the rules."

Tom raised his brows but said nothing. Then he seemed to consider something. "You know, there is every possibility that Silby will tell Carmichael you asked me to escort you home."

Vicky tilted her head. True, that would seem forward of her. Still, Mr. Carmichael himself had said she would dislike Silby. "If anyone blames me for wishing to be rid of Mr. Silby, I don't much care," she pronounced with a decided nod.

Again she thought Tom started to smile, but it disappeared a moment later. Then she looked up and realized they had arrived at Aston House.

Sarah informed Vicky she would begin preparing her a bath. Vicky thanked her, and Sarah bobbed a curtsy to Tom before starting up the front steps. Vicky had quite forgotten her unruly state, but as she looked down, she saw the mud on her clothes was dry and now beginning to crack. They must have made a curious sight walking down the streets of Mayfair.

"I'm surprised we didn't get more stares," she murmured.

"We did get a few," Tom replied. He appeared more amused than anything.

She smiled. "Thank you. For *all* your help."

He shook his head. "I must help you up the stairs before I accept any thanks."

She let out a surprised breath, though she didn't know why she'd expected anything less. "Very well."

He tied Horatio's reins to a railing. Then he offered his hand as he had in the park. She gripped it with hers and pushed downward. One by one, they climbed the steps as he supported her weight.

"I could carry you again if you'd prefer," he said.

She rather thought he must be teasing, but she shot him a glare. "Lord Halworth, if you do that again, I will . . ."

He raised his brows.

"Well, I don't know what I'll do, but it shall not be pleasant."

That slow smile washed over his face as it had when they'd danced at the ball, and she bit her lower lip to keep from smiling back.

"I have been warned, Lady Victoria," he said as they reached the last step.

Was he teasing now? He must be. At the door's threshold, she turned to face him.

He angled his head, and his steady gaze seeped into her. "Do take care of yourself."

Unable to speak, Vicky nodded and released his hand to step inside. In her peripheral vision, she glimpsed Sheldon holding the door open as always. Suddenly feeling she should say more, she turned back to Tom. "Would you care to come in and have some refreshment before you depart?"

He glanced over his shoulder. "I would like to, but I must get Horatio home. It's been a long ride," he said, giving his horse a worried look.

It was her fault if Horatio was fatigued. "I am sorry. We can have the stable boy give him a rubdown if you wish."

Again Tom shook his head. "Thank you, but I always attend to Horatio myself. We should be going."

She nodded. "Of course."

After descending the steps and pulling Horatio's reins to turn him around, Tom gave her one more look. "I am relieved you were not too badly injured."

She offered him a smile. "Thank you." It had been so heartening to have a normal conversation with him. She gazed into his brown eyes and for the first time, she no longer resented that he wasn't the same boy she'd known. "Will you be attending the Chadwick musicale on Sunday?"

For a long moment, Tom made no reply. Then, he said, "I shall see you there."

Vicky's eyes widened. She gave a quick nod and took a few steps farther inside.

At least he'd agreed to be social. She peeked at Sheldon and thought she spied a hint of a smile on his wrinkled face. A moment later, whatever she'd seen had gone, leaving her to wonder if it had been a mere flight of fancy on her part—she'd never known Sheldon to smile at anything.

She turned back to Tom and waved. Tom raised his free hand and started down the street with Horatio in tow.

Vicky watched him turn the corner, then exhaled. Despite today's excitement, she felt more content than she had in a long time.

After a physician had come and pronounced she would be well after a few days' rest, Vicky settled into a lavender-scented bath. As the warm water washed away the grime from the park and dulled the throbbing around her knees and elbows, the enormity of what had happened finally sank in. She could have been seriously hurt today—even killed. If she hadn't jumped or if Tom hadn't tried to intervene, everything could have ended in far worse a fashion.

She sank deeper into the bathwater, until her head was almost submerged, and smiled. Once when she was about ten, she'd talked Tom into a contest to see who could climb the highest hay bale without tumbling down. She'd won, but only because she'd nearly slipped and Tom had lost his footing while keeping her from sliding down onto the dry field. She'd emerged unscathed, but Tom had gotten a nasty lump on his head for his trouble. Poor Tom. He was still trying to keep her from breaking her neck.

But he'd been so sweet today, supporting her on his arm all the way home and apologizing for his actions at the ball. She couldn't begin to understand all he'd endured since he'd left England, so she wouldn't delude herself into thinking he wouldn't return to his stoic demeanor the next time they met. Still, it would be good to see him again under less dire circumstances.

Vicky hummed a tune as she stretched out her legs and splashed her feet around in the water.

Later, after she'd dressed and propped herself and her legs up on the bed with a mountain of pillows, she heard a scratch at the door. Vicky glanced up.

Althea closed the door behind her.

Vicky blinked, unsure what her sister's appearance meant. "Thea, come in."

Althea approached the bed with slow steps. A single crease between her brows marred her ivory face. "Vicky, I thought I should come. Mama told me about the accident."

Vicky nodded and gestured at her knees. "They ache, but I should be better soon."

Althea nodded. "Can I—that is, can I get you something?"

Vicky smiled, but shook her head. "Thank you, though. It was kind of you to ask."

"Or I could ring the bell for Sarah?"

"No, Sarah deserves some rest as well. But perhaps you could hand me my book?" She pointed at the dressing table behind Althea.

Her sister fetched the volume and opened the cover. "Good heavens, *Pride and Prejudice* again?"

Vicky exhaled. "I read it when I want to escape," she said, hoping the statement neutral enough not to lead to another argument. Though she'd actually picked it up again to see if Mr. Carmichael's assessment of Mr. Darcy held any merit.

Althea handed it to her. "I still contend it is not *Mansfield Park*'s equal."

"Lord Axley said the very same thing at the ball. Of course, that pantheon of moral correctness Fanny Price cannot compare to the prejudiced Lizzy Bennet," she said with a smile. They'd debated the subject so often, Vicky knew all Althea's arguments by rote. "I will never understand how you can like poor Fanny. She sits about watching everyone else, doing little to change her own position at Mansfield."

Althea shook her head. "What *could* Fanny do? She has little power within the household. She does what she is able and still manages to marry the man she loves."

"But not by her own actions," Vicky replied, realizing this was the first time in weeks she and Althea had held a normal conversation. "One day Edmund realizes he loves her and she benefits from that lucky happenstance. You know, the other day Mr. Carmichael said he has no patience for the Edmund Bertrams of the world."

Althea raised an eyebrow. "I cannot say I'm entirely surprised. What is your opinion?"

Vicky shrugged. "I've never *disliked* Edmund Bertram. Although, I have sometimes thought that if Fanny Price had tried reforming Henry Crawford, she could've changed his ways. They do say reformed rakes make the best husbands."

Althea turned away. "Men cannot be changed."

Vicky fell quiet. They were no longer discussing fictional gentlemen. "Still," she began, attempting to lighten the mood, "I agree that the way Fanny's character was written, she and Edmund were well-matched."

"Vicky," Althea said, turning back to face her, "I came to apologize."

Vicky closed her lips. She held her breath so as not to say anything wrong.

"I've acted very badly." Althea looked down at her hands.

When she did not continue, Vicky spoke quietly. "You're suffering. But you must know I feel terrible about everything you endured."

Althea sat at the foot of the bed and rubbed her eyes. "I fear I'll never be free of him."

Vicky's chest constricted. "But the separation—"

Althea cut her off. "I'll still have the memories. Even if the separation succeeds, he will keep haunting me."

Vicky grimaced. "One day, the memories will fade. You'll find some happiness again." She reached across her legs for Althea's hand. It felt cold and slight.

"But I cannot remarry."

Vicky bit her lip. "Wasn't there a scandal when we were young? Lord and Lady Boringdon's divorce? Didn't she remarry?"

Althea frowned. "A Sir Arthur Paget. But they were already . . . involved before her divorce. That's why her husband could obtain a Parliamentary divorce."

Vicky nodded, now recalling Parliament had dissolved Lord and Lady Boringdon's marriage on the grounds of adultery. The scandal had appeared in every London newspaper and had been the source of local Hampshire gossip for quite some time. Vicky hadn't attended to the legalities of it all, but she'd remembered it because not only was Lady Boringdon the daughter of the Earl of Westmorland, but she and her second husband had married in a village church not too far north of Oakbridge.

"Where are they now?" Vicky asked.

Althea threw her a glance. "Who knows?"

Vicky bit the inside of her cheek. "I suppose you'd miss society if you had to retire to the country."

Althea sighed, confirming the statement.

Vicky had thought as much. If *she'd* had to leave society, she'd dance a jig to celebrate.

Althea was different.

Althea put her free hand on top of Vicky's and squeezed. "I am sorry about your knees. I blame myself."

Vicky rested her other hand on top of the two on the bed. "That's ridiculous. It was an accident."

"But if not for me, you wouldn't be looking so hard for a husband, and you *certainly* wouldn't have been out with Mr. Silby."

"By your reasoning, Dain is at fault. If he hadn't been so monstrous, you wouldn't have had to leave him." For the first time, it occurred to Vicky that Althea had always loved children, but now, with the future uncertain, who could say if she'd have any. "Are you certain you don't, er—care to commit adultery with someone? Then Dain would *want* a Parliamentary divorce and you could eventually remarry," she said in a rush.

Her sister's eyes widened. "You would have me besmirch my reputation further?"

Vicky shook her head. "I only thought that if it gave you the option to have a family of your own one day, it might be worth considering."

Althea pursed her lips and looked at the floor. "I'd best let you recover." She stood, turned, and whispered something Vicky couldn't make out, immediately followed by the words "when I was imprisoned in his house."

"Thea, what about when you were imprisoned?"

But Althea hastened to the door.

"Althea!"

Her sister did not stop. Vicky swung her legs over the side of the bed to catch her. But her right knee buckled as she stepped forward; she gasped at the pain.

"Blast!" Vicky collapsed back onto the bed. She rubbed her knees with a whimper. For now, she'd have to preoccupy herself with Mr. Darcy.

CHAPTER THE ELEVENTH

*He was suffering from disappointment and regret, grieving
over what was, and wishing for what could never be.*
—Jane Austen, *Mansfield Park*

Tom took a swig of his whisky. The peat of the malt coupled with the pungent odor of pipe tobacco and cigars permeating the club started to turn his stomach. He set his glass on the round oak table. He shouldn't have let Charles talk him into coming to White's.

Today after they'd left the horses at Tattersall's (Tom couldn't bear to watch Horatio's actual sale), Charles had proposed they come in for a drink to ease their sorrows. Tom had agreed under the condition that Charles help him meet possible hotel backers, but Tom soon discovered that the men Charles knew were either young and dissolute, or over fifty and spoke of his father with fond remembrances.

Tom had no intention of entrusting his livelihood to anyone remotely connected with his father, so in the mode of a man who'd accepted the day would bring him nothing but misery, he'd consented to remain as his brother's guest while he mentally berated himself for becoming someone who needed a drink to feel ordinary.

The longer he drank, the tighter Tom's shoulder muscles grew. It couldn't be wholly due to this illicit whisky from Scotland he never could have afforded the excise taxes on, were he to attempt to buy a bottle himself. His father had put Tom's name down on the club's membership waitlist when he was a boy, but had switched his name for Charles's while Tom was abroad. If Tom had needed further evidence proclaiming his father would never have understood him, he'd have gained it today. The club's leather wing chairs were slick and uncomfortable; the air was thick with smoke. In this particular room, men sat drinking or eating slabs of roasted meat. The club supplied the sort of food his father had loved to eat, and the members exuded the bland, aristocratic pomposity his father had proudly projected. The only pastime Tom might've enjoyed was the billiards table, but two gentlemen from Bath currently monopolized it.

Yes, the membership would've been well wasted on him. Tom swallowed another sip of whisky and set the glass down with a clunk.

Charles looked up from his own glass and gave Tom a boorish scowl. "Do you have to make such a bloody racket? You're disturbing my perfectly good sulk."

Tom shook his head. "Damn your sulk. Today I had to sell the best horse I ever had because of your penchant for fine foods."

"It wasn't all mine," Charles replied, looking down at his drink.

"I'm sure most of it was Father's," Tom allowed, "but *you* kept making purchases even though you knew our financial state." He dragged in a ragged breath.

Charles was silent a moment. "Someone had to keep up appearances. I couldn't allow all of London to think we have no money."

"But we *have no money*," Tom grumbled under his breath.

Charles picked up his glass and brought it halfway to his lips. "Well, that's hardly common knowledge," he said, sipping his drink.

Tom's back teeth clenched until his jaw hurt. "I blame you."

"I don't care. You're not the only one who lost a horse today."

Tom sat forward to launch into a tirade enumerating all the reasons Charles was at fault when Geoffrey Murton entered through the carved wooden doorway. Tom clamped his mouth shut and looked down into his glass. He eyed Murton, or Dain as Tom now remembered was his title, in his peripheral vision.

He nearly groaned aloud when Dain walked toward their table. Why in hell would he seek Tom out? They'd never liked each other. When they were at Eton, Dain had been nothing better than a bully. He'd forced the smallest boys to do his bidding and take the blame whenever he landed in trouble. Although Tom had been two years younger than Dain, he'd often been obliged to interfere; through subtle subversion, he'd saved more than one student from a beating they would've suffered at one of the Master's hands thanks to Dain's scheming.

Eventually, Dain had discovered what Tom was doing. Unlike the rest of Dain's prey, Tom had experience with bullies, and Dain soon learned Tom was immune to intimidation. Throughout their school days, they'd maintained a silent enmity.

"Gentlemen." Dain nodded at them both.

Tom nodded in return. "Dain."

"Mr. Sherborne," Dain said, nodding at Charles.

"Lord Dain," Charles said.

"How are you acquainted?" Tom asked.

"Mr. Sherborne attended my wedding," Dain replied.

Charles nodded.

For a few moments, none of them spoke, and Tom hoped Dain would simply walk away now that they'd said their hellos. Unfortunately, he lowered himself into the empty chair opposite Tom. Tom took another sip of his drink, bracing himself.

"I cannot help but notice neither of you seem inclined toward conversation," Dain commented.

Tom regarded him with cold eyes.

"Yes, as you can see, we required fortification." Charles lifted his glass as proof. "The events of the day have been rather trying."

"That is unfortunate," Dain said, not taking the hint. "Let me order you another round."

Tom swallowed uncomfortably at the thought of more peaty heat burning down his throat, but he remained silent, waiting for Dain to get to the point.

Charles shook his head. "Thank you, Lord Dain, but that won't be necessary."

Tom raised a brow. It wasn't like Charles to refuse a drink. Maybe he'd caught on to Tom's disapproval of Dain.

"I insist," Dain said with a smile. "You see, I have cause for celebration."

Tom didn't know how much more small talk he could endure. "Why does your good humor extend to our table?"

Dain, apparently unaffected by Tom's hostile tone, answered jovially. "I have just acquired two beautiful stallions at Tattersall's. One is a Thoroughbred—"

"A fine breed, Thoroughbreds," Charles interrupted, swirling the remaining amber liquid in his glass in a distracted manner.

Nodding, Dain continued, "And the other is rather unique. I admit I was surprised to see its kind at the auction. They are only bred in Prussia."

Tom's jaw threatened to crack.

"Some breed called Trakehner."

The rat had bought Horatio. Tom's knuckles itched to knock the innocent smile off Dain's face. He forced himself to stay silent, reveal nothing, but Charles shifted in his chair.

"The odd thing was, the previous owner of the horses wished to remain anonymous. I had to go to quite a bit of trouble, and surrender quite a few sovereigns, to discover who had sold them."

Tom tilted his chin downward and looked Dain squarely in the eye. "And what did you achieve by obtaining this information?"

Dain returned Tom's stare. "Leverage."

Tom's gaze flicked to Charles, who held his glass loosely; he seemed unmoved.

"What could we possibly have that you want, Dain?" Tom asked, keeping his tone neutral.

"It seems fairly obvious to me that the Sherbornes have fallen into dire straits. If not, why sell two such fine animals anonymously? The Halworth name alone would've raised the minimum asking price."

Tom could not deny it. Dain smiled.

"Of course the integrity of the Halworth name would be significantly damaged if someone made your financial situation known. Since I have always considered myself a benevolent fellow, I offer you a proposition to ease your economic burden."

Tom leaned forward in his chair. "I do not make bargains with extortioners. As far as I'm concerned, my father tarnished his title and the Sherborne name far more than you ever could. So I suggest you leave."

"Tom," Charles interjected, "let's not be hasty. We can at least listen to Lord Dain's offer."

Tom glared at his brother.

"What is it you want?" Charles asked.

Dain's smile widened. "I want Halworth."

Tom wasn't sure he'd heard Dain correctly. "Halworth? You want the estate?" he asked, incredulous. He looked at Charles. His brother's frown proclaimed him as puzzled as he. "Halworth is entailed to the legitimate male heirs of the Sherborne family. I could not sell it to you any more than I could breed a flying hedgehog."

Charles snorted.

"I am no imbecile," Dain said, his tone icy. "I am fully aware of the entailment. However, there must be large portions of your estate that can be sold."

"Isn't your primary residence in the north?" Tom asked.

"One can always have more, Halworth," Dain replied with an arched brow.

Dain was greedy as the devil—as he'd always been. "Your wife will likely inherit Oakbridge. Why do you need our land?"

"Because it is ripe for the taking."

Tom grunted, annoyed he'd let the conversation go on this long. "Thank you for your offer. Halworth is not for sale. I couldn't care less if you shout our situation from every rooftop in Mayfair." He was bluffing—anything Dain spouted about their finances would hurt Tom's chances of finding support for the hotel. Still, he stood and gave Dain a condescending smirk worthy of his father. "Take your wagging tongue to the devil."

He looked to Charles, but his brother made no move to follow. "Are you coming?"

"When I've finished my drink. I shall see you later."

Tom glared at Charles in disbelief, but his brother did not rise. He didn't even blink.

Tom's hand clenched into a fist. Dain had nearly pushed him beyond his stores of self-control, and now Charles—

For a full quarter minute, he forgot to breathe. He was sick. Sick in the mind and on the verge of causing a scene. Without sparing either man another glance, he pivoted and stalked out of the club. It took every ounce of control he had to tamp his rage back down as he stepped out onto the street and turned toward home.

He dragged in an unsteady breath. He *could* control his anger—stop the fury from exploding to the surface. Yet the one thing he could not stop was the relentless thrumming of his pulse in his ears and the nauseating feeling that he was merely deluding himself.

CHAPTER THE TWELFTH

She has great discernment.
—Jane Austen, *Mansfield Park*

Frustration was not an emotion Susie often indulged. As she saw it, there'd been many disappointments in her sixteen years—most notably the early death of her mother—and if she were to dwell on them all, she'd be a very unhappy person.

And yet, even as Susie reminded herself of her luck—a half brother who loved her and had saved her from a life on the streets—she couldn't suppress the frustration that'd been bubbling inside her ever since Tom had refused to let her help with their financial problems. After selling Horatio yesterday, Tom had been moping about the house, looking at turns either angry or forlorn.

If only he would allow her to find some employment!

When she'd kept house at Tom's uncle's hotel, she'd always had something to do. She'd grown so accustomed to working that she still hadn't gotten used to living the idle life of a proper English girl.

It didn't help that there was little to do in the Halworth town house other than read, and Tom wouldn't let her leave the house unaccompanied. He claimed he feared for her reputation if someone recognized her out on her own. Since no one on the fashionable side of London even knew she existed, his argument made little sense, but she attributed it to his overprotective nature.

She shook her head and smiled as she left her bedchamber and walked toward the staircase. If anyone had come to her a year and a half ago as she was folding bed linens and told her she'd soon be living in a grand London town house, reading at all hours of the day, she would've thought them mad. Were it not for Tom's insistence that she learn to read, write, and make basic calculations, and her reluctant acquiescence to sit through his daily lessons, Susie would never have been able to sign her name, let alone finish the massive *A Comprehensive History of the Norman Conquest* currently tucked under her arm.

She grinned as she started down the stairs. Soon she'd know more about English and French history than Tom and Charles combined. If, with the aid of other books in the library, she expanded her body of knowledge further, perhaps Tom would allow her to become a governess. As their financial situation grew steadily worse, she didn't think it would be long before Tom accepted her help.

Her spirits buoyed by that thought, Susie opened the library door with a spring in her step. As she entered the room, a large book slammed shut. She turned in the direction of the noise; Charles stood at the desk, his stance rigid. At the sight of her, his posture relaxed.

"Ah, Susan. To what do I owe the pleasure?"

Susie looked down at the closed book. Judging by its shape and size, it was one of the estate ledgers. Her gaze flicked up at Charles. His wavy, light brown hair fell over his forehead in a dashing style that complemented his square brow and aristocratic features. Within days of their first meeting, Susie had assessed him as the type of young man who liked to project a roguish air to perpetuate a rakish reputation. Whether he deserved his reputation or not, Susie had not yet determined.

When he and Susie were alone, he was always polite, but she knew he wasn't at ease with her. She did not blame him, however. She must be a constant reminder of his father's adultery. But, at this precise moment, Charles's green eyes peered at her innocently.

She took the book from the crook of her arm. "I was just going to look for a new book."

Charles walked over to her and held out his hand.

She gave him the volume.

"*A Comprehensive History of the Norman Conquest.* Good God, you *must* be bored to take this thing on," he laughed.

She shrugged and smiled a little. "It *was* a bit dry. What about you? Why aren't you at the club?" she asked, taking the book from him.

"I grew tired of it," he said, turning to examine the shelves. "One meets such bothersome characters at White's these days."

Susie frowned, unsure of his flippant tone. Charles wasn't often home at this hour. Had he truly tired of the club? And why had he been looking through the ledgers? Of course, he had every right to do so, but ever since she and Tom had come to England, Charles hadn't shown the slightest interest in any estate business.

She wondered where Tom was now. She remembered him mentioning something about trying to find hotel backers, but she couldn't remember if it was supposed to be today. He was usually here in the early afternoon, poring over ledgers and drawing up his hotel plans until it came time to dress for supper. This recent development would certainly intrigue him.

Susie walked behind the desk and opened the ledger to the middle. "What were you looking for?" she asked, her tone neutral.

Charles turned. "What do you mean?" he asked, looking down at the hand she held on the page.

"When I came in," she elaborated, "you closed the ledger. Weren't you reading it?"

For a moment, Charles said nothing. Then, he shook his head. "Not at all. It was lying open on the desk, so I closed it. Father didn't like having important matters lying about for all the servants to see."

Susie nodded and made an understanding noise. She didn't know why Charles would be reading the ledgers, but she also didn't know what reason he would have to lie about reading them. Perhaps, as he'd said, he'd simply closed the book. Susie looked at it again and shut it herself. She smiled at Charles.

"Where's Tom?"

Charles shrugged. "I haven't the faintest." He took a book off one of the shelves and opened the front cover. "As the saying goes, I am not my brother's keeper." Closing the book, he turned and smiled enigmatically. "Nor, perhaps, should *you* be, Susan. You may be disappointed in the end." Book in hand, Charles headed for the door.

Susie watched him go, wondering if he'd meant she'd be disappointed in him or in Tom. Whatever he'd meant, she had no other living family besides the two of them. She took a deep breath and straightened to her full height. Charles may not know her very well yet, but of one thing she was certain: she wasn't about to let his surly behavior keep her from looking out for her brothers as much as she could.

Vicky's eyes flew open, a strangled sound emanating from her throat. She rolled over to the other side of the bed. Images from her nightmare replayed in her mind. She slowed her breathing to calm herself. The dream had been a grotesque revision of that day she'd gone to Halworth Hall to find Tom all those years ago. The day she'd walked in on Tom's father knocking him to the ground with his meaty fist. A maid had been crying in the corner of the drawing room, her face still blotchy with tears. But Tom's father had greeted Vicky cordially—he'd said only, "Boys will be boys," and strode from the room with a smile. Vicky hadn't known what to think.

The maid had scurried off, and when Tom had pulled himself off the parquet floor, he wouldn't answer any of her questions. They'd never had another conversation. She'd visited Halworth Hall every day until Tom had disappeared, but the butler had always turned her away. Then when her mother told her Tom wouldn't be returning, she'd sent letters to him through his mother, but he'd never replied. In truth, she didn't know how many he'd received.

Perhaps it was natural to dream of that day after seeing Tom so often in the last few weeks. She had slept fitfully the previous night, so she'd retired to her room to relax before it came time to dress for the Chadwick musicale. So much for a peaceful nap. She would have done better to stay awake.

She squinted at the clock on the mantel. Her snooze had extended far longer than she'd intended. She rubbed her knee to gauge its healing progress. Thankfully, it felt much better, so she went to ring the bell for Sarah. Settling in at her dressing table, she brushed her hair and wondered why Sarah hadn't awoken her earlier.

Vicky dabbed lilac-scented water on the insides of her wrists. Perhaps Sarah was helping Althea dress. At breakfast, their father had told them that Mr. Barnes had managed to secure a proctor to begin the suit for Althea's separation in the ecclesiastical court. They could begin proceedings very soon.

In the wake of that happy news, their mother had insisted Althea attend the musicale tonight. If Althea continued to absent herself from social events, she would soon incite curiosity. Their father agreed, and Althea had admitted Dain hated musicales and was unlikely to make an appearance.

Vicky knew her parents were being practical, but she secretly believed Althea unprepared to mingle at a social gathering. Althea had completely ignored Vicky's attempts to draw her out at breakfast, and Vicky had given up for the day.

Whether Althea wished for her help or not, Vicky would be her shadow tonight. She narrowed her eyes into the mirror. Woe betide anyone who pained Althea while Vicky stood by her side.

CHAPTER THE THIRTEENTH

Even now her self-command is invariable.
—Jane Austen, *Sense and Sensibility*

Vicky stood close to Althea's arm as they entered Lord and Lady Chadwick's music room. Numerous sconces holding beeswax candles lined the walls and bathed the room in a yellow glow. Her sister had shown surprising composure in the carriage and as they'd entered the house, but as they walked farther into the room, Althea's hands started to shake. In *Sense and Sensibility,* when Marianne first saw Mr. Willoughby in London after weeks of separation, she'd made a spectacle of herself and Elinor had to take her home.

Vicky knew her sister had always been far more circumspect than Marianne Dashwood, but Althea hadn't spent one minute in public since she'd escaped Dain. Vicky didn't know how she'd behave if her fear got the better of her. Their parents seemed ignorant of Althea's discomfort and allowed some old friends to whisk them away. Vicky hooked her arm into her sister's to support her.

"Let's find some seats," Vicky said.

Her sister made no protest, and they started toward the rows of gilded chairs facing the front of the room. Vicky stopped short as she spotted Mr. Silby in the corner, conversing with a gentleman she didn't know. His evening clothes were again fashionably understated; tonight's dark blue coat was a far cry from that nearly violet day coat he'd worn to the park.

"What is it?" Althea asked.

"Mr. *Silby*," Vicky murmured. "Let's keep moving," she whispered, but by then he had caught her eye.

Mr. Silby excused himself from his companion and moved toward them.

"Too late," Althea said.

Vicky pressed her lips together. Of all the unhappy outings she'd endured thus far, Mr. Silby's had been the worst. Pain stitched through her right knee, reminding her to never again allow a gentleman to dissuade her from riding her own mount or walking on her own feet.

Mr. Silby looked on the brink of nodding at her, but then something or someone else caught his attention. He changed course, heading for the hall beyond the music room. Vicky let out a breath and hastened to an empty row of seats.

"How odd of him not to greet us," Althea said as Vicky pointed at the pair of chairs near the aisle.

Having spent an afternoon observing some of the workings of Mr. Silby's erratic mind, Vicky wasn't much surprised by his behavior. "Perhaps he sensed my displeasure the other day." Of course, *that* might be giving his powers of observation too much credit.

"All the more reason for him to inquire after your health or offer his apologies."

"I don't disagree," Vicky replied, casting her gaze toward the instruments at the front of the room.

The Chadwicks thought their four daughters highly accomplished, so every year they staged a musicale. Vicky thought the older girls only moderately talented, but the youngest daughter, Emily, was one of the best amateur players of the glass armonica Vicky had ever heard. The instrument looked much like a square pianoforte on the outside, but where the keys would have been were a series of glass bowls of descending sizes attached through the middle with cork and an iron rod. As the player touched the bowls with dampened fingers, and moved them with a foot pedal, music lighter than air transported the listener to an enchanted glade.

Assuming the musician knew what they were doing. No one, after seeing Emily Chadwick perform, would dare debate that fact. Sadly, Vicky had heard that Emily's health had been deteriorating.

Vicky shifted in her seat, thankful she was relatively fit, save for her aches. She hated to admit it, but most of her body was sore from Thursday's curricle vault. Bruises had formed around both knees and one elbow, which she'd been obliged to cover with a shawl. Still, Vicky hadn't even considered allowing such trifling injuries to keep her in bed when Althea had to attend. And, as her mother had told her, Mr. Carmichael would also be present, which would perhaps give her another chance to speak with him and ask him to explain his behavior toward Tom.

Vicky felt a light tap on her left shoulder. She turned. Mr. Carmichael smiled down at her. Speak of the devil.

"Are you surprised to see me?" Carmichael asked with an amused expression. The coffee-brown flecks she'd noticed in his eyes the day they'd gone to Gunter's, though nearly invisible by candlelight, drew her in nonetheless.

"Not at all. In fact, I was just thinking about you."

Carmichael grinned and inclined his head toward her. "Indeed? Nothing unflattering, I hope."

Vicky shrugged, offering a small smile. If only he wasn't so likable. Then she'd have no compunction questioning him about his conduct.

Carmichael turned to Althea. "I'm glad to see you accompanying your sister, Lady Dain."

"Thank you, Mr. Carmichael," Althea replied.

"May I join you?" Carmichael asked.

Vicky motioned for Althea to move down a seat. They both stood and moved down, leaving Mr. Carmichael the aisle. He lowered himself into the chair.

"How did you enjoy your outing with Silby?"

Vicky nearly snorted at the question. "It was memorable, I assure you."

He raised his eyebrows. "In what respect?"

Vicky related what had transpired in the park the other day. Carmichael's expression transformed from amusement to incredulity and finally, to anger.

"What the devil did Silby think he was doing?" He stopped and murmured an apology for his coarse language.

Vicky waved off his apology. "I am sure it was an accident."

"He should've let you alight from the vehicle before fiddling with anything." Mr. Carmichael twisted in his chair as though scanning the room for Silby.

Vicky exhaled. "What's done is done, I suppose."

"Were you hurt?" he asked, turning back to look her up and down.

She cleared her throat, unsure how much she should reveal. After all, she didn't want to be responsible for Mr. Carmichael doing Silby an injury. She glanced at Althea, who merely raised her eyebrows. Vicky had no idea what that meant, so she said, "Only a little."

He frowned. "How little?"

"I am well enough to be attending a musicale, Mr. Carmichael, so let us leave it at that."

"If you'll excuse me, ladies," he said, inclining his head.

"Where are you going?" Vicky asked, though she thought she knew.

"You will forgive me, but such idiocy is not to be borne." He started to stand.

Vicky's eyes widened. "Mr. Carmichael, I shall *not* forgive you if you take one step in that direction." He stared down at her. She stared back to show him she was in earnest.

"Mr. Carmichael," Althea said calmly, "this is hardly the time or place."

He muttered something under his breath and settled in his chair, but his brow remained furrowed. "Did you return in that clod's vehicle? Or was it too damaged?"

Vicky let out a breath. "The pole had cracked, and I feared for the horses. But Lord Halworth happened to be in the park, and he was kind enough to escort me home."

Mr. Carmichael sat silent for a moment. "Lord Halworth?"

Vicky nodded.

"I did not believe you were at all desirous of his company after the duchess's ball."

Vicky pursed her lips, knowing she had given him that impression. "At that moment, I would have preferred anyone's company to Mr. Silby's," she replied in a lowered voice. "I was fortunate Lord Halworth was there."

Mr. Carmichael said nothing. A muscle flexed in his jaw. Vicky had told her father Tom's concerns about Carmichael, but he'd shrugged them off, assuring her that Mr. Carmichael's boxing prowess was well-known. Her father had even hinted that *he* might have told Tom to leave her be if he'd attended the ball with them. He didn't believe Mr. Carmichael would spread rumors about Tom, and in short, saw no misconduct in Carmichael's behavior.

Vicky wasn't wholly convinced. His vehement reaction to her glossy version of Mr. Silby's behavior at the park didn't instill her with confidence either. Like Colonel Brandon looking for his missing ward, she needed to probe to reach the truth. She looked behind them to see if anyone listened to their conversation, but the guests around them spoke to each other animatedly. She looked to Mr. Carmichael.

"Do you . . . that is, did you . . ." She paused, wishing this didn't feel so awkward. "Do you dislike Lord Halworth?"

She felt Althea's gaze penetrate the side of her head.

Mr. Carmichael turned toward her. "Why should I? I barely know the man."

Vicky shook her head, trying to make sense of his expression. He'd arranged his features to look perfectly innocent, but something belied his words.

"I heard you and Mr. Silby were quite rude to him at the ball and at a particular boxing match."

Carmichael tilted his head, considering her. Finally he spoke. "I was rude at the ball because I could see how pained he made you. I've known your family a good while, so I take exception to anyone who would take advantage of your good nature."

Vicky bit her lip. "I see." So he *had* noticed her discomfort that night.

"And as for the boxing match . . ." He paused and gave her what appeared to be a rueful grin. "What can I say except"—he stopped and then shrugged—"men will be men."

He wasn't excusing his behavior. Yet something worrisome nagged at the back of her mind. Then it hit her. Tom's father had used that phrase when he'd struck Tom all those years ago. *Boys will be boys.*

She frowned. "Do *men* publicly besmirch another man's reputation by mentioning a lady's name? A lady who told you she had no quarrel with that particular gentleman?"

A single crease appeared between Mr. Carmichael's brows. "Perhaps if that particular gentleman deserved it."

Vicky sighed and tilted her head away from him.

Carmichael exhaled. "You are quite right. It was beneath me. I have little patience for those who foist themselves on others, but . . ." He swallowed. "I should not have involved you. I do hope you can forgive me."

Vicky peeked up at his face. His dark eyes had clouded with regret. Another crease marred his brow. She glanced at Althea, whose look echoed her own thought that his distress seemed genuine.

"I shall, if you promise not to speak another word about this to anyone else," Vicky said, raising her chin.

He nodded slowly. "Of course."

Vicky offered him a smile. "Then you are forgiven."

Carmichael's lips canted up at one corner. "Thank you."

Althea leaned across Vicky and asked Mr. Carmichael if he'd ever seen Emily Chadwick play the glass armonica.

Carmichael leaned over to look at Althea. "No, but I've been told her playing is quite remarkable." Vicky glanced at her sister, silently thanking her for changing the topic.

"Do you play an instrument yourself?" Althea asked Mr. Carmichael.

He gave a regretful smile. "With little proficiency, I'm afraid."

Vicky raised her brows. "Really? What do you play?"

"My mother wished me to play the pianoforte. She even employed a music master to teach me when I was young."

Vicky couldn't quite imagine him as a child. She looked down. His large, long-fingered hands looked far more suited to boxing than creating beautiful music on the small keys of a pianoforte.

"Do you still play?" Althea asked.

"As I grew older, my father did not approve."

"He did not approve of music?" asked Vicky.

He paused for a moment. "He did not approve of me," Carmichael replied flatly.

Vicky closed her mouth. She hadn't expected such an admission.

"He must be prodigiously proud of you now," said Althea. "How could he not be?"

Carmichael's jaw shifted. "He is long dead."

"Oh, I'm sorry," Vicky and Althea said simultaneously.

He shook his head as though it meant nothing, but Vicky could see from the way his dark eyes blackened that it did. She bit her lip. What made some people so cruel to their children?

"Well . . . ," Vicky said, trying to change the subject, "then you should definitely play again."

Althea clicked her tongue, as though to reproach Vicky for telling him to defy his dead father, but Mr. Carmichael laughed.

"I believe you're right, Lady Victoria." The planes of his face softened as he looked down at her. His black eyes warmed until she saw the brown flecks again, making her smile.

The Chadwick girls chose that moment to enter the room and sit at their instruments. The guests quieted as a beaming Lady Chadwick walked to the front to introduce each of her daughters.

Vicky dragged her gaze from Mr. Carmichael's, but she felt his linger on her. After the girls curtsied at their introductions, they took their places and began to play. Vicky detected a few wrong notes from the sisters playing the flute and the violin, but fifteen-year-old

Emily and her glass armonica were impeccable. Lilting tones tinkled through the air as her fingers touched the edges of the glass bowls at exactly the right times.

Vicky rather wished she'd bothered to learn too. She'd never had much talent at the pianoforte, but it couldn't be too late to learn a new accomplishment. Perhaps she'd find the glass armonica easier.

Out of the corner of her eye, she saw Carmichael's foot wave back and forth to the rhythm of the piece.

Althea caught her glance and leaned closer. "What were you thinking?" she whispered in her ear.

"What do you mean?" Vicky mouthed.

"Confronting Mr. Carmichael about Tom that way," she said even more quietly.

"I *thought* I would get a satisfying answer to my worries."

"Now he knows you speak to Tom about him."

Vicky frowned at her sister. "So?"

"You don't want to arouse his jealousy. He may not like it."

"If he grows jealous over something so inconsequential as me speaking to other men, I don't know that I want *him*."

Althea sat back in her chair and inhaled, looking down into her hands. Then, as though she felt eyes boring into her back, her head whipped toward the rear of the room. She sighed and the tension in her neck and torso melted away as she turned back to face the musicians.

Her sister must have thought Dain had appeared. Vicky sneaked a quick glimpse behind them and saw Tom stepping into the room. His gaze drifted around for a spare seat and landed on her. She gave him a small smile. He nodded and started toward the empty chair in the row behind them.

Carmichael craned his neck around at the movement. When he saw Tom, his jaw stiffened, and his foot stopped waving. As he turned back to face the musicians, Vicky had no doubt of his displeasure with Tom's arrival.

Again, Vicky worried what that might mean. She didn't understand why Carmichael should dislike Tom.

True, even Tom believed he'd acted badly at the ball—he wouldn't have apologized otherwise. Yet Mr. Carmichael hadn't actually explained his behavior. She exhaled. Should she ask him again?

As the music ended, the audience gave the girls a hearty round of applause. Their duty dispensed with, most guests made their way to the refreshment table, or moved to congratulate the Chadwick girls.

Mr. Carmichael stood and offered Victoria his arm. "Would you care for something? It appears they have chocolate ices," he said with a grin. "And," he continued, craning his neck to see above the crowd, "there's not a pistachio in sight."

Despite her worries, Vicky let out a short laugh. "In that event, I would be delighted, Mr. Carmichael."

Carmichael quirked an eyebrow, then turned to Althea. "Lady Dain, would you accompany us as well?" he asked.

Althea did not answer. Vicky looked at her sister. Her eyes were wide against her pale skin, her shoulders tight with tension. She stood frozen in terror.

Vicky followed her sister's gaze. Dain stood in the doorway of the music room.

Vicky swallowed against the sudden dryness in her throat. What could he be doing here?

Carmichael must have seen their expressions because he said, "Ladies, are you well?"

Vicky didn't know what to tell him. Should *she* take the liberty of telling him about Dain—which would be inadvisable here—or should she pretend nothing was amiss? She turned to her sister for guidance, but Althea trembled where she stood.

Vicky glanced at Dain. He spoke to a middle-aged gentleman with a beard, but Dain's eyes fixed on Althea. Why Althea couldn't hide her emotions tonight when she must have done so for months, Vicky couldn't tell, but it didn't matter. This was precisely what she'd worried about. *She* had to act quicker than Elinor Dashwood had with her sister and spare Althea whatever disaster was to come. "Mr. Carmichael, I must ask a favor of you."

"Of course, Lady Victoria," he said, concern etched on his brow.

"Would you keep Lord Dain away from my sister and me for the rest of the evening?"

Carmichael observed her steadily for a few moments. Then he looked to Althea. Vicky could see his mind working out what to say. Finally: "May I ask why?"

"I'm afraid I cannot explain." She glanced back at Dain. "I know how strange this must sound, but we would be so grateful. Truly."

Mr. Carmichael glanced at Althea again, but she would not meet his gaze. He frowned but said nothing.

Vicky bit her lip. He would refuse and Dain would be free to stride over and take Althea from her. Vicky would have no way to stop him. Then she remembered Tom sat behind them. "Very well. I shall ask Lord Halworth." She turned around and said, "Tom?"

Mr. Carmichael blanched at her use of Tom's Christian name.

Tom turned from the older gentleman he was speaking to. "Yes, Lady Victoria?"

Before she could ask him to get rid of Dain, Carmichael interrupted.

"No, I am at your service," he said firmly.

Ignoring Tom, he gave Vicky and Althea a half bow and walked toward Dain. Vicky exhaled.

Tom excused himself to the old gentleman and stepped closer to her. "What was that about?" he asked.

"Mr. Carmichael has something pressing to attend to."

Tom raised his brows, encouraging her to elaborate.

"Well . . ." She caught his gaze and realized she couldn't tell him anything more. "We are in need of refreshment," she said abruptly, her eyes flitting to the food table.

"I could fetch ices, if you'd like. Is chocolate still your favorite?"

She nodded, her lips spreading into a grin. He'd remembered. "And Althea likes lemon."

As Tom neared the refreshment table, he noticed Mr. Carmichael now stood with Lord Dain. He wondered again what Vicky had sent Carmichael to do. Was Dain part of that duty?

Tom redirected his path to take him as close to the two men as he dared, his steps silenced by the Turkish rug covering the floor. The men stood just beyond the doorway to the music room. Tom positioned himself against the wall next to the doorjamb, but due to the noise the other guests were making, he could only hear snippets of conversation.

"You shouldn't have come," Carmichael said.

"What can you mean, Carmichael?" Dain replied.

A gentleman walking past Tom coughed, rendering Carmichael's response inaudible. Tom moved closer to the doorway.

"Don't get in my way, Carmichael. You know how much is at stake."

"This is not about business. It is about you making the Astons uncomfortable, and I cannot have that. Not now."

What were Carmichael and Dain involved in? Tom shifted his weight. Should he make his presence known, or wait to see what else they would reveal?

"Just leave. Now," Carmichael ordered.

"I refuse," Dain said flatly.

Tom threw a quick glance over his shoulder to see what Carmichael would say to that. Carmichael leaned close to Dain's ear and whispered something. Dain looked outraged, and he stared at Carmichael for a moment. Tom pivoted to the side to get a better look. Carmichael grabbed Dain by the arm and dragged him toward the front of the house.

Tom watched them go, then stepped into the hall to see if anyone else had seen. The hall stood empty. Should he follow? His gaze flew back into the room to see if he'd be missed. Vicky caught his eye. Damn. He had forgotten the ices.

Mulling over the possible ramifications of the conversation he had just witnessed, he moved to the refreshment table. After obtaining the ices, he returned to Vicky and Althea.

"What happened to you?" Vicky asked as she took her chocolate ice and a spoon.

"I was unexpectedly detained." He gave Althea the other bowl, and she took it with a quiet murmur of thanks.

"It is lovely to see you after so many years, Althea." Tom winced, realizing he shouldn't be so informal in public. "I should say 'Lady Dain' now, of course."

"You needn't bother," she said. Then she looked up and caught his eye. "That is, we needn't stand on ceremony after all these years." Althea gave him a small smile, but it didn't reach her eyes.

He nodded, but for the first time, he noticed the pallor of her cheeks. He frowned inwardly. Althea had always been a good few inches taller than Victoria, and slimmer by the sheer virtue of her height, but now she looked almost bony. She had to be thinner than he remembered her being at any time in their childhood. She could not be well. "I saw your husband and Mr. Carmichael—"

"We are in your debt for helping Vicky the other day," she interjected. "And for that day at Oakbridge. It seems you are making a habit of rescuing my sister from dire straits."

He shook his head and shot Vicky a glance. She studied her ice and spooned more into her mouth. "Not at all," he said. It seemed they had no wish to speak of whatever had just occurred between

Carmichael and Dain. For Althea's sake, Tom hoped Dain had softened with age, but he would never like the man.

Vicky interrupted Tom's thoughts. "Have you saved any more damsels in distress today?"

"Sadly, the driver of the runaway carriage I halted *today* was foolish enough to actually stay inside it," he said with a hint of a smile.

"Your heroic timing seems to be improving."

He inclined his head. "It does every day, I daresay."

Vicky giggled. The green flecks in her eyes sparkled as her laughter filled the air.

He'd forgotten how the sound of her giggles always made him smile—how her glee lit up her face. Memories of the old days rammed him in the chest. "Do you recall the time we went fishing and you insisted on trying your luck in the middle of the brook?"

"The time I got my foot stuck in the mud hole?"

He nodded. "I had to wade in, help you yank your foot out, and then we both fell in."

Vicky laughed again. "Oh dear, I believe you're right." Vicky looked at Althea. "I never did recover that boot."

Althea smiled. "Did you limp all the way back to the house?"

Vicky considered. "No. I discarded my other boot by the stream for the fairies."

Althea scoffed. "The fairies, indeed."

Tom shook his head. "Ah yes—you were particularly interested in fairy stories that summer, as I recall."

Vicky lifted her chin. "I beg your pardon, but I was *eight*. You two simply do not have the inclination to believe in the fantastic. I must say I pity your lack of imagination."

"Have you ever *seen* anything fantastic?" Althea asked her.

Vicky wobbled her head. "Not as yet. That doesn't mean I won't. According to Mr. Carmichael, there was a pig at Vauxhall Gardens that tells time."

"Nonsense," Althea said.

"Almost certainly," Vicky agreed. "But wouldn't it be lovely if it could?"

Ah, Vicky. It really was remarkable how little she'd changed.

As if echoing his thoughts, Althea made a frustrated noise.

"It would be quite a feat," Tom said, "but what would be the point?"

"Precisely." Althea nodded.

Vicky wrinkled her nose. "Why must there be a point? Cannot something be lovely merely for the sake of being lovely?"

Did she have any idea how fanciful she sounded? How naive? How would she ever survive in the cruel world with such notions? But the world had not been cruel to *her*. Perhaps she could afford to maintain her pretty philosophy. Or perhaps she'd be hurt all the worse for it.

He'd have to tell her what he'd heard from Carmichael and Dain. Let her do with the information as she would, but at least she'd have the knowledge. "May I call on you tomorrow?"

She raised her eyebrows, but her frown disappeared. "If you can drag yourself away from your cynicism," she said.

"I fear *that* may be impossible."

She sighed. "Then leave it at home for the day." She brought a spoonful of ice to her mouth.

Tom blinked, trying not to stare as the tip of her tongue shot out to lick chocolate from the corner of her lips. He cleared his throat. "I shall do my best."

CHAPTER THE FOURTEENTH

I can recall nothing worse.
—Jane Austen, *Pride and Prejudice*

Through the carriage window, Vicky stared into the dark London streets. How pleasant Tom had been this evening. He'd even gotten Althea to converse. The old Tom may be gone, but at least he was no longer the cold stranger who'd only helped her out of duty. He'd even surprised her by asking if he could call tomorrow. She hummed one of the melodies from the musicale.

Her mama glanced at her across the carriage. Vicky brought her hand to her face, covered her mouth with her palm, and pretended to scratch her cheek. She had no real reason to be so pleased. Tom was simply paying a social call. For all she knew, he would forget to come.

She lowered her hand from her face and glanced at her sister's profile. Althea looked out of the opposite window. Dain hadn't returned to the music room, but then neither had Mr. Carmichael.

Vicky wished he hadn't disappeared, but perhaps he'd been obliged to escort Dain somewhere more suitable.

Mr. Silby had approached her and Althea after Tom had departed, offering useless apologies and his assurances that he'd had his curricle thoroughly inspected after the other day. He'd even asked her to take another drive. She'd had to put him off with fake excuses; nothing could induce her to get in a carriage with that man again.

Had Mr. Carmichael been present during the exchange, he might very well have said—or done—something rash. Yes, he'd been far better employed effectively ridding them of Dain.

Vicky brushed Althea's upper arm. "Well, Thea, you confronted your greatest fear. You should be proud."

Althea continued to stare out the carriage window. "Meeting him is not my greatest fear."

"Perhaps not," their mother said. "But you did comport yourself well. We must thank Mr. Carmichael for convincing Dain to leave."

"Carmichael is a fine man," their father said, looking at Vicky pointedly.

Vicky nodded. "I agree. I like him very much," she admitted.

Her mother gave her father a meaningful glance.

Vicky tried not to roll her eyes. "That does not mean, however, that I have made a decision." She needed more time. She still didn't know Mr. Carmichael well. What if someone else came along? "Papa, you really should tell Mr. Carmichael about—"

A loud explosion sounded, and Vicky's body jerked. Pistol fire! The horses whinnied and the carriage came to an abrupt halt. Vicky looked at her parents in the seat opposite her. Her father held the carriage door handle with one hand and her mother's arm with the other while her mother clung to him. She'd almost flown off the seat at the sudden stop.

"Papa?" Vicky asked hesitantly.

He shook his head and raised a finger to his lips. Vicky turned to Althea. She was pale as a sheet. Vicky entwined her arm with Althea's. Yelling erupted outside the carriage doors. The four of them sat tensely, straining to make out the words.

Both carriage doors flew open. A man stood on each side. The one near Vicky was so large, his form filled the doorway. His fraying clothes hugged his huge frame. Vicky wrinkled her nose as the stench of the unwashed emanated from where he stood. The man's severely pockmarked face twisted in a sneer. He trained his pistol on Vicky's father.

"Milord," the man said with thick sarcasm. The brute had a thick East London accent.

Vicky tried to see past the man, hoping the footman or driver wasn't lying dead in the road. The Aston footmen always carried pistols to protect the family—the frequency with which the wealthy found themselves at the mercy of highwaymen seemed to increase every year.

"What is it you gentlemen want?" Vicky's father asked in a steady voice.

The man near Vicky said nothing. He motioned to his accomplice standing on the other side of the carriage. The other man was shorter, but just as pungent. His clothes, nothing more than rags, hung from his gaunt figure.

He seized Althea's arm. Althea screamed. Vicky held tight to her sister's other arm. She wouldn't let them take her without a fight.

"Damnit," the one near Vicky said, "not 'er. Get the other one. *This* one." He pointed at Vicky.

"Gentlemen," Vicky's father said louder, "perhaps we can come to some arrangement. You must know I could give you any amount of money you desire. Leave my daughter."

The pockmarked man moved the gun closer to her father's head. "Shut yer gob. Yer not long for this world, and wer takin' 'er." He turned to his partner, who still pulled Althea's arm.

Althea shook her arm, trying to break the thin one's grip.

"I told you," the big one barked. "It's this one." He grabbed Vicky's arm.

His grip squeezed her upper arm through her cape, and Vicky winced at the pain.

The other man shook his head, revealing a deformed ear. "This one," he said, yanking Althea's arm again.

"Get over 'ere and take this one 'fore I shoot *you*," the pockmarked man said.

The accomplice made a face, but he let go of Althea's arm and abandoned the door, presumably to walk around to the other side of the carriage.

When he disappeared, Vicky's father hit the other one's gun hand, forcing it upward. The pistol exploded into the roof of the carriage. Her mother screamed. The man let go of Vicky's arm in the confusion, and Vicky gaped in horror as her father lunged at him, knocking him onto the street. Her father landed on top of him and pummeled him before the fellow could get his bearings.

By then, the thin man had reached them both. He kicked Vicky's father in the side as Vicky's mother shrieked. Vicky looked around for a weapon, but the only thing she'd carried to the musicale was her reticule. Although she doubted it could do much damage, it was all she had. Reticule at the ready, she jumped from the carriage and hit the thin man in the head. He turned and grabbed her arm, crushing it in a punishing vise.

"Unhand her!"

Vicky looked up.

Her sister stood at the foot of the carriage, gray-faced but angry. The man sneered. Still gripping Vicky's arm, he lunged for Althea. She blanched.

At that moment, something within Vicky snapped. She brought her knee up into the man's groin with as much force as she could muster. The grin left his face as he released her and stumbled backward, holding his breeches.

Vicky looked at her sister.

Her torso wavered as though she would faint.

"Blast it, Thea, get back in the carriage!" Vicky helped her climb inside and shut the door.

She threw a glance at her father over her shoulder. The pock-faced man had somehow pushed her father away and had gotten to his feet. They circled each other. Though the ruffian's pistol no longer held powder, he wielded it by the barrel, trying to hit her father with the butt of the gun.

Vicky saw a few people watching from the sidewalk. "Help!" she yelled.

No one moved. What was wrong with them? She screamed

again, cursed at the bystanders, and looked for the carriage driver and footman. The footman lay unconscious on the ground, bleeding from the leg, but the driver had disappeared. Meanwhile, her father took a punch to the gut. He crumpled forward and the brute started bashing him in the face.

Vicky threw her arms in the air to hail a hackney cab coming down the road in the opposite direction. The cab carried on despite her shouts and the wailing of her mother and sister within the carriage. The other scoundrel—the one she'd struck—raised himself onto his knees, but his eyes were squeezed shut. Hopefully he was too dazed to help his partner.

The villain continued to thrash her father. She jumped on his back, throwing all her weight on top of the huge man. Grabbing a handful of his hair, she yanked it as hard as she could. He grunted and threw her off, sending her flying backward. The dull pain in her joints, left over from Thursday's fall, flashed to life as she landed on the packed dirt. An even harder object poked into her side. She reached behind herself and felt cold metal. The footman's pistol.

She examined it. Still loaded. She stood and aimed it at the attacker.

"Stop or I'll shoot!" Vicky yelled.

The gigantic brute landed one last punch to her father's side before turning to face Vicky. Her father fell to the ground, no longer moving; his battered frame lay prostrate on the street.

Her throat swelled; tears threatened behind her eyes.

"Come on, luv, give us the gun," the man growled, taking a step toward her.

Her gaze flew back to the animal who may have killed her

father. He was staring at her with the same sneer he'd worn when he'd shoved open the carriage door. Her jaw clenched so hard, she thought it might crack.

His lips turned up at one corner. He didn't think she'd do it. He wasn't afraid of her at all.

Acid burned in her throat. "Don't try it unless you want a ball in your chest." She cocked the pistol. The sound reverberated in the still night air.

He froze.

The other man now inched toward her.

She swung the pistol his way, and he stopped in midstep.

"Both of you get out of here before I kill you."

"You've got one shot," the pockmarked one said. "Even if you hit one of us, whoever lives can still take yeh."

She hurled him a hate-filled glare. "Do you want to take the chance you'll be the one I kill? Then by all means, stay."

The men exchanged glances. It seemed neither of them wanted to die.

"This ain't over, luv," the pock-faced man said.

"Leave!" Vicky shouted. She aimed the barrel of the gun at his head, her finger on the trigger.

He spat in her direction. Then he motioned to his partner. They ran off, disappearing into the shadows.

CHAPTER THE FIFTEENTH

"But what," said she, after a pause,
"can have been his motive?"
—Jane Austen, *Pride and Prejudice*

As Tom strode down the street toward Vicky's town house, he resisted the urge to walk faster. He couldn't shake the feeling that he was actually looking forward to seeing her again. Last night at the musicale, he'd thought he only wanted to call on her to tell her what Dain and Carmichael had said. Now he wondered.

She was still so like the girl he remembered from their childhood—the Vicky who always urged her horse to jump ridiculously tall hedges or snuck into the Oakbridge kitchens to pilfer enough strawberry tarts to make herself ill.

He'd done his best to forget such images. They only caused a dull ache somewhere in his chest. But yesterday when they'd reminisced about the day she'd lost her boot in the stream, he'd felt—comforted.

Before he'd left for Eton as a boy, he and Vicky had rarely been out of each other's company. When they were even younger, Charles and Althea had often tried to tag along, but they'd always given up. He and Vicky had never paid them much attention. They should have been kinder, especially since he and Charles had been forced apart for so many years.

His regrets returned, and with them, his hatred for his father. Tom's mind swirled with images: playing soldiers on the staircase with Charles and the old man's angry glare as he caught them, walloped Tom in the head, and left his ears ringing for the rest of the day; his father yanking his mother's arm and throwing her against an armoire as he shouted at her over an imagined slight; Charles's trembling hands and wide eyes blinking up at Tom as Tom pulled him up the stairs to hide in the nursery while their mother's muffled screams echoed in his ears. Tom inhaled to dispel the memory of that sound, to drown the shame of never having done enough, and to quiet the rage that always built within him when he remembered.

That rage only brought him closer to becoming his father when all he wanted was to forget him.

When his mother's letter telling him of his father's death had reached him, Tom hadn't shed a tear. To this day, he never had. Instead, he'd let the old tyrant's demise turn him into a shell of his former self. To some degree, he knew he shouldn't have let it happen. Yet, the numbness was far preferable to . . . feeling.

Tom rubbed his left temple as he turned the corner onto Kingsford Square. The Astons' town house stood across the way. A hackney cab waited in front. Tom had erred on the side of propriety and made certain to come during accepted calling hours. He inspected his pocket watch. Four o'clock. Perhaps Vicky was otherwise engaged.

He crossed through the small grassy park in the center of the square and peered into the ground floor windows as he strolled to the front door. People moved quickly through the house. Too quickly.

Something was wrong. He stepped up to the door and knocked. When Vicky's maid greeted him instead of the butler, Tom's concern grew.

"Good afternoon, Sarah. Is Lady Victoria in?" Tom asked.

"She is, Lord Halworth, but she's with her father."

"Shall I wait?" Tom asked, but as Sarah started to answer, Vicky descended the staircase. Her eyes widened at the sight of him.

"Tom! You're here."

He looked her up and down, but other than a dark bruise on her arm that she must have covered with a shawl the night before, nothing looked out of the ordinary. "If I have come at an inopportune moment, I can return lat—"

"No, please, come in," she said as she reached him. Sarah moved out of the way.

Vicky lowered her voice. "I *must* speak with you."

With a frown, Tom nodded and stepped over the threshold into the entry. Vicky motioned with her head that he should follow her. Now that he stood closer, he saw scrapes on her hands and wrists he didn't remember from the night before. She started down a hallway. He lengthened his strides until he was by her side.

"Are you well?" He gestured to her arms.

She looked down at the scratches. "Oh, I'm fine. It's Papa we're worried about. He was knocked unconscious. A physician is with him now."

Unconscious. Christ. That explained the hackney outside. "What happened?"

Vicky pointed to a room overlooking the street. Tom followed her through the doorway into a sitting room with blue paneled walls. Vicky lowered herself onto the settee and waved at Tom to take the chair opposite. When they were both seated, she told him how they'd been attacked the night before.

Tom didn't know what to say. How could one person attract such ill fortune so often?

When Vicky related that one of the attackers had said *it wasn't over*, a muscle under his left eye jumped.

"Tom, do you think it's possible that these accidents of the last few days are not accidents at all?" she asked. "I cannot help thinking that there was too much damage to that pole on Mr. Silby's curricle."

Tom tapped his fingers against the armrest. Silby hardly seemed clever enough to facilitate such an "accident." Added to that, runaway carriages were fairly common, and curricles, in particular, were not the safest of vehicles. Tom shook his head. He wanted to believe the incidents were unrelated.

Yet, what about the man at Oakbridge? He *had* wanted to harm her.

"Could that fellow at Oakbridge have been behind it?" Tom thought aloud.

"These were dirty men with cockney accents," she said with a decided shake of her head.

"We never heard him speak," he reminded her.

She frowned. "True. But that greatcoat he wore . . . The men last night barely looked as though they could afford the ragged shirts on their backs, let alone a greatcoat."

Tom nodded. "So perhaps someone paid them. But who?" The man who'd first attacked her? Or someone who'd paid for both attempts?

Vicky's eyes widened, then looked up at him with certainty. "Dain."

Tom's brows knit together. "You think Althea's husband did this to you?"

Vicky nodded. Then she exhaled. "I suppose I might as well tell you. I hope Althea doesn't hate me for this, but—" She licked her lips. "You must promise not to reveal it to a soul."

Apprehension knotted his stomach. "Of course. I give you my word."

She sighed and offered him a small smile. "Althea is seeking a legal separation from Lord Dain. He has been abusive toward her. She returned home the day the bandit attacked me. She escaped from their house in the middle of the night."

Tom sat back in his seat. "Dear God."

Bile rose in the back of his throat. He'd hoped for Althea's sake that Dain had changed, but he was the same selfish persecutor he'd been at school. Worse.

He choked down his disgust, but his own culpability slapped

him in the face. "Had I been here during their courtship, I could have told you of his character."

Vicky's eyes darkened. "What do you mean?"

"When we were at Eton, he bullied the smaller boys—forced them to do things or take things he wanted. They also took the Masters' punishments in his stead. He enjoyed having power over people."

Vicky looked down into her hands. "When you came upon us at the ball, he was trying to intimidate me. When I weakened, he seemed to enjoy my suffering."

Tom clenched his fist until it ached. "I could have spared you all this pain." If only he'd been home when they'd announced Althea's betrothal. He didn't remember ever receiving a letter from his mother or Charles about Althea's intended. They'd mentioned she'd married, but even if they *had* told Tom his name, it would've been too late to help. Of course, mail from his family had been infrequent in those days, thanks to Bonaparte's armies.

"I don't know if you could have changed Althea's mind about him," Vicky said quietly. She lowered her head. "I should have realized what he was from the first."

Tom let out a breath. Poor Vicky. Poor Althea. "You mustn't blame yourself. How could you have known?"

Vicky shook her head. Her gaze remained focused on her lap. "None of us saw through his charming veneer. And Thea never said anything . . ." She trailed off. "Indeed, she says very little to me at present."

His shoulders tensed. "There is a rift between you?"

Vicky looked away. "She will tell me nothing of what Dain did.

And our conversations are strained."

Tom knew the feeling. His interactions with Charles hadn't improved since they'd sold the horses. Not that he'd expected them to—

"'Tis silly, I know, but after you . . ." She looked up and caught his eye. "After you left, Althea and I grew very close. We had no one else. Now I have—"

She broke off, but Tom mentally supplied the rest of the sentence: *nobody*. And yet she had her parents, both of whom cared for her well-being, which was more than he'd had after his banishment. Until he'd met Susan and moved to his uncle's home, he'd truly been alone.

"It can be difficult for victims of . . . a man such as Dain to speak of what they've endured."

Vicky looked up, blinking rapidly.

He cleared his throat. "Have patience. She may recover in time." The words came easily enough, but he didn't know if he believed them. Perhaps she shared his thoughts, for tears welled in her eyes. The point of her heart-shaped face rounded out as her chin trembled. The urge to take her in his arms struck him like a blow. The force of it slammed him back, rooting his body to the chair.

He swallowed hard. He was damned tired of behaving this way.

As though it had a life of its own, his hand shot forth and gripped hers. Her tear-filled eyes flew up to meet his gaze. For a moment, the tears stopped. Her eyes widened a fraction. The contours of her cheeks relaxed. Time stood still.

Then she blinked. "Have *you* recovered?"

He held his breath. He could only shake his head.

More of her tears leaked out, and she swiped them away with her free hand. "I'm so sorry."

"There's nothing you need apologize for."

"I feel so sickened by what she went through—what *you* went through."

He froze, remembering her hazel eyes filled with shock as his father knocked him to the floor. His resentment as his father laughed and put on a civilized veneer for Vicky. His hopelessness as the maid ran from the room. And finally, his shame as Vicky crouched to the floor to help him stand.

Tom gulped, hating the thickness in his throat.

Vicky looked down at his hand enfolding hers. "I tried so many times to speak with you after that day, but you would not see me. Did you ever receive my letters?"

Tom closed his eyes. He'd been so worried for her safety. He couldn't have her dropping by at a moment's notice. Not when he had a father who did what his did. The image of his father pressing that maid into a wall as she writhed to get away rushed into his head. The sound of her desperate wails for help as his father yanked her skirts upward—Tom shut his mind to the rest.

All he had thought of in the ensuing hours was what could happen if Vicky came back and his father caught her alone. The idea had turned Tom's stomach. The odds that the old man would touch an earl's daughter were slimmer, but if he did, prosecuting him would be nearly impossible, and Vicky's reputation would be destroyed. She'd be infamous in the eyes of society with no respectable future. Tom couldn't let any of it happen to her.

His eyes opened, and he dropped Vicky's hand. He stood and walked to the window to avoid seeing the hurt he knew would be there. "I received a few. I didn't know what to say."

He heard her inhale.

"You could have said . . . *anything*. We always could before."

He shut his eyes again. Perhaps now was the time to tell her everything. She wanted to know. But as he turned to her, carefully avoiding her face, the words choked him. He couldn't force them out. He could barely think them. How could he possibly say them aloud? Instead, he said what he truly felt. "I'm sorry."

He allowed his gaze to drop to her face. She nodded once, but he couldn't read her expression.

"I can't—"

"No, Tom." She looked up at him, now with shielded eyes.

He clamped his jaw shut.

"The past is done. We must learn to accept that." She spoke to herself in that moment, and he knew she didn't understand what he'd meant with his apology. She thought he'd apologized for offering no explanation. But he was sorry for all that had happened since that day five years ago—losing their friendship, Althea's marriage, everything that had come to pass when he'd fought against his father's cruelty.

"At any rate," Vicky said, clearly attempting to change the subject, "Dain must have hired those ruffians to attack us. No one else has a reason."

Tom inhaled and stretched his shoulders back. He sat in the chair again. "I see why he'd imagine himself entitled to take his wife back, but what would he gain by kidnapping you? Leverage over Althea or your father?"

Vicky frowned. "Those men seemed confused. I believe they grabbed me by mistake."

"But that man at Oakbridge was intent on harming *you*, not Althea. How would anyone have known she'd arrived there? It's probable you were the target all along."

Vicky's eyebrows scrunched together.

A new idea crept into Tom's head. He knew who might be behind the attack, and it wasn't Dain. "If Dain were behind it, his problems would be solved by kidnapping Althea—not you."

Vicky nodded.

"Therefore it stands to reason that it *wasn't* Dain who orchestrated the attack."

"But then who—"

Tom interrupted before she could finish the question. "Carmichael."

As Susie took a quick step backward, retreating behind the facade of the long row of houses outlining the massive square, she realized the folly of this endeavor. She shook her head. She was not at all pleased with herself or her judgment. Unfortunately, that day she'd seen Charles going through the ledgers had piqued her curiosity.

He'd been acting strangely ever since. Although the town house was large, Susie couldn't be deaf to the servants' gossip. With the ovens working, the kitchen was the warmest room in the house, so Susie often took a seat out of the cook's way and went about her reading. In the last few days, Cook had observed Charles was no longer making luncheon his first meal. He was actually eating breakfast in his room and leaving the town house every day before noon.

This odd behavior, coupled with their encounter in the library, had prompted Susie to follow him. But, as she now recognized, her actions had probably been due to boredom and loneliness.

She certainly hadn't bargained on how hard it would be to follow someone in this part of London. In Mayfair, the few trees and decided lack of people milling about provided little to hide behind. Added to that, the majority of houses were connected, leaving little to no room for small alleyways. If only she'd had to follow Charles into the part of London she'd grown up in, where alleys, nooks, and crannies abounded. It would've made her task much simpler. With so few people and spaces to blend into, it couldn't be long before Charles saw her skulking behind a corner.

She glanced out from behind the side of a house. Charles pulled out his pocket watch, looking anything but suspicious. For all she knew, he was walking to his club. As usual, his hair was impeccably coiffed and his brown coat and trousers gave him a look of effortless style. His walking stick swung in perfect rhythm to his footsteps.

Oh dear. This was folly indeed. What had she hoped to accomplish? Even if she did see Charles doing something odd, what could she say to him—or to Tom?

Susie sighed and looked at Charles again. She shook her head. It was no small wonder he found it hard to speak to her. She couldn't even give him the benefit of the doubt or leave him to his privacy.

Resolving to turn home, she gave Charles one last look, expecting him to turn the corner and disappear from view. But, instead, he paused at a large mansion at the end of the square. Charles looked up at the door, leaning lightly on his walking stick, one leg in front of the other, in a pose Susie imagined the royal dukes affected often. He seemed to be pondering whether to climb the steps of the town house.

Charles turned his head to the left and right. Was he trying to see if anyone had noticed him there? After another moment's hesitation, he climbed the stairs and used the knocker. An unpleasant-looking butler answered, and after they exchanged words, he showed Charles in.

Susie frowned. Why had Charles looked to see if anyone was watching him? Had he suspected her presence? Or, perhaps more to the point, who had Charles gone inside to meet?

As precisely as he could, Tom related the conversation he'd witnessed between Dain and Carmichael last night, but when he'd finished, Vicky shook her head.

"Tom, my father trusts Mr. Carmichael completely. They are business partners. What reason would Mr. Carmichael have to harm him?"

Tom stretched his palm open. "Who's to say that Carmichael intended *anyone* harm? Perhaps the plan was simply to abduct you and those men took matters into their own hands. Unless Carmichael would benefit financially by your father's death. You say they're business partners?"

Vicky twisted her hands in her lap. "I don't know the particulars of their arrangement. I can ask."

Tom nodded. "Of course, if Carmichael marries you and Althea is granted a separation, he will, in effect, control Oakbridge when your father dies."

"But what reason could Mr. Carmichael have for wanting Oakbridge? He is extremely wealthy. He owns at least three large properties in various parts of the country."

"Why stop at three when he can obtain another?" The more Tom thought about it, the more it made sense. Carmichael had been trying to keep Tom from Vicky since nearly the first moment he'd met the man. If Tom's theory were correct, it would also explain why Carmichael had attempted to discredit him to society.

"But why resort to these so-called accidents, then?" Vicky asked. "I cannot imagine Mr. Carmichael would want to marry me if I were maimed or irrevocably injured."

"Whether Carmichael meant actual harm to come to you or not, perhaps he's orchestrated these accidents to make *you* more inclined to marry quickly."

Vicky rubbed her throat. "If he did—and I'm *not* conceding that," she emphasized, meeting his eye, "then it has worked."

Tom frowned. "How so?"

Vicky shifted in her seat. For a moment, she was silent. Then as if deciding something, she met his gaze. "I must marry someone, Tom. If I wish to stop Oakbridge from eventually going to Dain, I have no choice. My parents gave me until the end of the season, but now, with everything that has happened, I'm certain they'll say it would be foolish to wait much longer to decide."

Tom's jaw went slack. That was why she was defending Carmichael? Because her parents were forcing her to marry? "Why him?"

She shifted again. "At the moment, Mr. Carmichael is my best option."

"I see," he said, though he didn't really see at all. "But if Althea is seeking a legal separation, then why must you marry?"

She fiddled with a piece of lace on the skirt of her dress. "It is not certain they will win the case. And it may take years. I must marry as soon as possible so my father can petition the prince regent to make me the legal heir."

Tom sat back in his chair. It was all much more complicated than he'd realized. And all because Althea had married Dain. He squashed his guilt and looked at Vicky. She was worrying at her lower lip. Her hooded eyes would not meet his. He couldn't blame her. It must have sapped a fair amount of her pride to tell him this.

He shouldn't interfere with her plans. She needed to marry and try to be happy with her decision. Yet the thought of letting her walk into Carmichael's arms when the man was likely involved in some nefarious scheme sat like a stone in his stomach.

"Without Dain and Althea's separation you would have no reason to marry—unless you wanted to."

She nodded slowly.

Carmichael's reasoning flashed through him like lightning. "Then perhaps Carmichael orchestrated the whole affair to get you into a position where you would have to marry him."

Vicky's lips parted.

"Does he know about Althea and Dain?" Tom asked.

She shook her head. "He acted as though he didn't. I was going to ask my father to tell him just before we were attacked. Papa's been too unwell for me to broach the subject again."

"Last night, Dain said something was at stake, and Carmichael said that was precisely why he wouldn't allow Dain to upset your family. 'Not now,' he said. I remember it distinctly." He raised his brows. "It sounds to me that Carmichael must know of the separation proceedings. Did he show you any interest before?" If he hadn't, it seemed all the more likely that he'd planned everything after hearing of Althea's intentions.

Vicky shrugged. "He was very amiable when I met him in the winter, but he was at Oakbridge conducting his business with my father. He wasn't there to see me."

"And he paid you no special attention."

Her brow furrowed. "Not as such."

"And now?" he prompted.

Vicky looked away, not meeting his gaze. "I believe he likes me."

The sentiment was no more than Tom suspected, but it irked him nonetheless. "And you are interested in him," he stated, modulating his tone to sound neutral.

She opened her mouth as if to speak, but instead she let out a sigh.

Tom stood and paced to the window so he could unclench his jaw without her noticing. "What if by marrying him you're putting your family in more danger?"

"The whole idea is all rather far-fetched, Tom," she said.

He turned back to her.

"The idea that Mr. Carmichael would pay ruffians to kidnap Althea—or even me—to frighten me into marrying him? All so he can gain control of Oakbridge? Why would he even attempt such a thing?"

"Dain recently propositioned me to sell him pieces of Halworth. I refused of course, but he and Carmichael are clearly affiliated in some way. Perhaps the land connecting Oakbridge to Halworth has some value we don't yet realize?"

Vicky worried at her lower lip again. "It all sounds like something out of one of Mrs. Radcliffe's romances, not what occurs in the real world."

He exhaled, trying to ignore the strange burning sensation in his chest. "The whole scenario is fantastic, yes. But why should that preclude it from reality? Do you truly believe abductions and schemes only belong in the realm of fiction, even now?"

"This just doesn't—those kinds of novels are simply not true to life."

He ran a hand through his hair. "Just because sensational events happen in novels, that doesn't mean they cannot *happen*. And just because ordinary events occur during the majority of one's life, that doesn't stop the unexpected from happening at a moment's notice."

She lifted her chin.

"I daresay we both know that to be true by now," he muttered.

For a long moment she did not answer. The silence stretched. Then she sighed. "You are rather insufferable when you're right."

He huffed out a breath.

"But I do think you should read Miss Austen's novels anyway."

"I will happily do so if you promise to take care."

She nodded and offered a small smile. "I will concede that if Mr.

Silby's curricle had been tampered with, Mr. Carmichael's friendship with him could have given him access to the vehicle."

"I agree."

"Yet last night when I told him of the accident, Mr. Carmichael seemed genuinely angry at Mr. Silby's carelessness."

Tom raised an eyebrow. "He couldn't very well act pleased, could he?"

"I suppose not."

Tom nodded. "Just don't trust him until you know more. Dain may be a scoundrel, but he's not particularly clever. I don't believe he could have planned all this."

"What about the bandit at Oakbridge? And the . . ." She trailed off, looking past him.

"The what?" Was there another incident she hadn't told him yet?

She exhaled and nibbled at a cuticle. "The other day, I saw a strange man in a black greatcoat staring at me from a street corner."

Tom's jaw tightened.

"I was in a carriage—with Mr. Carmichael." She looked up at him with worry in her eyes. "That must absolve him, mustn't it?"

He considered carefully before answering. "It might, but it could mean he was having you watched."

This time her cheeks lost their color.

"Did Carmichael see him?"

She shook her head. "I was about to point the man out, but he disappeared. I told Mr. Carmichael afterward."

"Did you get a good look at him?"

She nodded. "Black hair. Nondescript face. He was familiar, but I couldn't place him."

"The man at Oakbridge had black hair." It was his only distinguishing characteristic thanks to that mask.

She caught Tom's gaze. "You're right." She took a deep breath. "It could have been him."

He gave a shallow nod. "Is your family taking extra precautions?"

Vicky's brow furrowed. "I will speak with my parents." She looked up at him. "I do appreciate you discussing this with me. It's good to know I'm not going mad—that someone else agrees these accidents have been far too coincidental. Even if we don't wholly see eye to eye."

Surprised, Tom didn't speak for a moment. "As always, I am happy to help."

Her smile faded.

"I could not bear the thought of anything happening to you." The words escaped before he could stop them. Before he could think. But they were true. Then her smile returned, and he didn't care how they might have sounded. He peered into her hazel eyes. Flecks of green glittered at him, and as one moment turned into many, he realized he was staring.

Vicky looked away first. "Thank you, Tom."

He closed his eyes and wished to God he were imagining the ridiculous urge to loosen his cravat. "I'll call again soon to see you're all right."

Vicky smiled from beneath her lashes. "That would be lovely."

He nodded. "Please give my regards to your family." He stood, anxious now to be away from her captivating eyes. "And please take care," he said sincerely.

She rose from her chair, and the warmth in her smile almost undid him, so much did it remind him of happier times. She offered him her small hand. He hesitated before grasping it.

"You may depend upon it," she said with a nod. The green flecks twinkled at him without mercy.

CHAPTER THE SIXTEENTH

It was a wretched business, indeed!
—Jane Austen, *Emma*

An hour after Tom's departure, Vicky left the comfort of her bedchamber and started down the hallway toward her father's room for her turn to sit with him. The doctor had departed shortly after Tom, ordering the earl to rest, so now Vicky's father lay in bed while his wife and daughters took turns trying to entertain him. According to the doctor, in addition to the various cuts and bruises on his face and body, her father had two broken ribs and a sprained wrist. His face looked awful, but Vicky was grateful he was alive and would recover.

Vicky tapped the third volume of Mr. Godwin's *Fleetwood* against her thigh. It wasn't one of her favorites—she found the title character wholly unlikable, though his exploits were somewhat more believable than those in Mrs. Radcliffe's novels—but her father had recently finished the second volume, so she hoped the ending would divert him. She frowned, remembering Tom's unexpected thoughts on sensational novels, and almost ran into Althea in the hall. Vicky stepped to the side to keep from colliding with her.

Althea gripped both ends of her floral shawl with tight fists. "I was looking for you. Papa says it's your turn."

"Are you well?" Vicky asked. She hoped her father hadn't said anything to distress her sister. The earl hated to be bedridden and his pain could have caused him to be short with her.

"I'm tired."

"You should rest." None of them had slept more than a few hours. The house had been in uproar ever since they'd returned home. Their carriage driver had run back to the town house for help and had returned with most of the male staff and a number of pistols. In addition to tending her father, the doctor had removed the bullet from their injured footman's leg. He would recover—if his wound didn't fester.

Althea nodded.

"How is Papa?" Vicky asked.

"He seems well enough. He was dictating his correspondence to me. I heard Tom came and went."

"Yes, he expressed his concern for us all. He also told me he overheard some of Mr. Carmichael and Dain's conversation before they disappeared last night. Apparently, one of them mentioned business dealings with the other. Would you know anything about that?"

Althea shook her head. "I was never privy to Dain's plans."

"I told Tom I thought Dain was behind the attack last night, but Tom believes Mr. Carmichael and Dain must be working together.

After speaking with Tom, I'm not certain myself that Mr. Carmichael isn't involved."

Althea drew in a breath. "Did Tom ask why you thought it was Dain?"

Vicky bit the inside of her cheek. She hadn't meant to tell Althea this way. "Do not be angry, Thea. When he told me what he overheard, I had to tell him. But I told him just enough to get his perspective."

"No." Althea glared daggers. "You had no right."

"He swore he would be silent. He won't break his word."

"How do you know?" Althea cast her gaze at the ceiling. "You don't even know him anymore!"

"I know he would not betray a confidence. He may not be the same boy he was when he left, but—"

"You always take his part. You always did. Even after what he did to you," Althea said with another hard look. "Meanwhile, you let your own sister . . ."

"Let you what?" Vicky asked.

"When I tried to tell you of *my* circumstances, you chose to ignore me."

Vicky shook her head. "When did you tell me? We've barely spoken of—"

"Those last months I was in London. When I was all but a prisoner in my own house." Althea's dull brown eyes met hers. "You never once replied to my pleas for help. I worded everything vaguely in my letters, but I believed you, of all people, would understand me. Had Tom *ever* written you, you would have boarded the next boat crossing the Channel to aid him."

Vicky inhaled, ignoring her comment about Tom. "I never received any letters from you."

Althea spoke over her. "Every week, I waited for your assurances that Papa would come to help or that you would at least try to visit, at which time I could tell you what was happening in person, but you were too busy or too dense to understand."

Vicky swallowed twice. "I sent letters to you weekly. Your replies never reached Oakbridge, and I thought I had done something to offend you. At the very least, I thought you too busy to write."

Althea folded her arms across her chest. "Every week I received letters from Mama and Papa, but never once from you."

"Did it not occur to you that Dain might be intercepting them?"

Althea's lips parted. "It makes no sense. Why would he allow me our parents' letters, but not yours?"

"I cannot guess his motives, but I *know* I sent you many, many letters. Can you sincerely believe me capable of leaving you to suffer if I knew what he was doing to you?"

Althea looked away, clutching the edges of her shawl as if to keep her balance.

Vicky exhaled. "Hate me if you must, but if you care to know the truth, Poole will verify my statements." Their butler at Oakbridge always supervised incoming and outgoing post so nothing was ever mislaid.

"Very well, I shall."

"In the meantime, I must attend to Papa." Vicky sighed and dropped her chin. "I'm sorry I told Tom without your permission. It's been a trying few days for us all. Thank you for assisting me last night."

Althea wouldn't catch her eye. "I didn't *do* anything."

"If you hadn't distracted him, I wouldn't have thought to kick him."

"*I* nearly fainted. *You* saved Papa's life." Her voice held a petulant note.

Was she jealous? Vicky frowned. "I couldn't have done it without your aid."

"I rather doubt that. Excuse me." Althea brushed past her and disappeared down the hall.

Vicky let out a sigh. She wished she could comfort her sister, but she didn't know what else to say. Her gut twisted with remorse. No wonder Althea couldn't confide in her. She thought Vicky had betrayed her. Maybe when Althea heard the truth from Poole, she wouldn't think so badly of her.

As Vicky started again toward her father's chamber, Althea's comment about how Vicky would have done anything to see Tom came back to her. Well, her sister wasn't wrong. To see Tom, Vicky *would* have braved the dangers of war. But to spare Althea from what Dain had done, she would have swum the Channel wearing little more than a smile.

A while later, Vicky was wishing she'd picked a different novel—or at least left this one for her father to read on his own.

"*'For one moment, perhaps for the last moment so long as we both shall live, I will believe her innocent!' I stole a balmy kiss from the ripest lips that nature ever formed. She stretched out her arms toward me. I kissed her again. I felt one flash of the joys of heaven, on the verge of the abyss. I drank in madness as I stood."*

Vicky cleared her throat. She'd forgotten the way Fleetwood spoke of his wife and his former mistresses on the Continent. Every time she had to read such an intimate passage, she glanced at her father out of the corner of her eye. He was lying on his back, keeping his gaze trained firmly at the ceiling. He didn't stop her.

She kept reading to hide her embarrassment. Fleetwood had allowed his friend to persuade him that his wife had been unfaithful.

"'Perhaps, indeed, you were never told how frequently they met.'

"Thus did this damnable calumniator lead me on, with half words, with broken sentences, and 'ambiguous givings-out,' to the most horrible conclusions."

Someone scratched at the door and Vicky swallowed, thankful for the interruption.

"Come in," Vicky's father said.

Sheldon bowed his balding, white head. "Mr. Carmichael is downstairs, my lord."

Vicky's eyebrows lifted. "Did you send for him?" she asked her father.

"No, although I'm glad he's here."

Vicky wondered if he was as glad as she to have an excuse not to continue the book together.

"I have something to ask him. Go down and explain what happened so he isn't too surprised when he sees me."

Vicky smiled. "Of course, Papa." She rose from her chair. But as she left the chamber and walked down the corridor, she wondered at Carmichael's unannounced appearance. Was he here to explain why he'd not returned to the musicale after disappearing with Dain? Whatever his business, she'd have to be cautious with him.

Vicky descended the stairs. Mr. Carmichael stood in the entry, garbed in an immaculate black coat and trousers. His torso faced away from her, but his foot tapped against the floor in an agitated pattern.

She cleared her throat.

He started and turned toward her. "Lady Victoria, thank God you are well." As she reached the bottom stair, he took hold of both her arms and looked her up and down, concern stamped across his features. When his gaze narrowed in on her scraped arms, his jaw tightened.

Startled, by both his display of emotion and that he seemed to know about last night's attack, Vicky stepped back.

"Did my mother send for you, Mr. Carmichael?"

Carmichael blinked. He lowered his hands from her arms. "No. I heard what happened, and I came straight away."

How could he possibly have heard? Could Tom be right—was Mr. Carmichael behind the attack? And was she imagining it, or did he look slightly guilty?

No. Vicky brushed away such ridiculous thoughts. There had to be a perfectly logical explanation why he knew.

"How did you find out?" she asked.

"An acquaintance of mine who works at *The Weekly Tattler* knows of my partnership with your father. He told me this afternoon."

It certainly was a logical explanation.

"I had to . . . persuade him not to print the incident."

"That was good of you." If Mr. Carmichael hadn't, it would have been the talk of the town. She wondered how much he'd had to pay to keep his acquaintance silent.

"How are your parents and sister?" Carmichael asked, interrupting her thoughts.

"My father was the only one hurt. He has two broken ribs and is badly bruised, but a physician has seen to him. He is resting now."

Mr. Carmichael let out a breath. "May I see him?"

Vicky hesitated a moment. She didn't want to give Tom's theory credence, but she also couldn't ignore the possibility that Mr. Carmichael might somehow be involved with Dain. She still hadn't asked her father what would happen to his share of the revenue from his agreement with Mr. Carmichael in the event of his death—she'd wanted to wait until he was slightly more recovered. Whether Mr. Carmichael had planned the attack or not, perhaps it would be unwise to let him alone with her father. Unfortunately, her father had asked to see him.

She briefly entertained the idea of asking Mr. Carmichael to leave and creating an excuse to tell her father, but it would involve deceiving them both, something Vicky couldn't bring herself to do. And Tom's theory was still just that—a theory.

"I'm sure Papa would welcome a *friendly* face." She looked at him pointedly, trying to gauge his reaction, but he merely nodded. Vicky led him up the stairs and knocked quietly on her father's door. She entered with Mr. Carmichael in her wake.

Her father had propped himself up with pillows and now sat up in bed.

"Lord Oakbridge. How are you feeling?" Mr. Carmichael asked.

Vicky studied his face. Carmichael's brows were knit, and although his voice betrayed nothing, he seemed genuinely concerned.

"Lady Victoria told me of your condition," Carmichael continued.

"I am as well as may be expected. Please sit. I would welcome the chance to turn my mind from the events of last evening." Her father's voice sounded strained. He must be in pain.

Worried, Vicky interjected. "Papa, you shouldn't speak too much. It cannot be conducive to healing."

"Victoria, you cannot begrudge me a little conversation with Mr. Carmichael. We shall not be long."

It was a dismissal. Vicky wanted to protest further, but when her father decided something, there was no changing his mind.

"As you wish, Papa," she said doubtfully. She turned and walked to the door.

Carmichael bowed as she left.

Vicky grabbed the handle and looked back at her father. He motioned for Carmichael to sit in the chair she'd abandoned next to the bed. She closed the door behind her, wishing she could stay. What could her father want to ask Carmichael that was so private?

Of course, it might be possible to hear what they were saying if she bent close enough to the keyhole. Listening at keyholes was, perhaps, less than ladylike, but desperate times called for . . .

She crouched and put her ear to the opening. The door was rather thick, but she could still hear parts of the conversation.

"It was good of you to come," her father said.

"How could I do less?" Carmichael responded.

Vicky raised her eyebrows. Had her father asked him to visit after all? Why would he deceive her about such a trivial matter? And when would he have asked Mr. Carmichael? She hadn't even seen them speak at the musicale. Lost in thought as she was, Vicky missed the next few things said. Annoyed with herself, she concentrated on their words.

"I'm glad you remembered," her father said. "I am concerned about our solicitor Mr. Barnes."

"Has something happened to him?" Carmichael asked.

Vicky frowned, thinking it suspicious that that had been Carmichael's first assumption.

"He hasn't responded to any of my summonses. I wanted to keep this matter within the family, but circumstances have made that impossible. I wouldn't ask this of you, but of course, Mr. Barnes is your solicitor as well."

Carmichael didn't respond, but Vicky thought she heard him shift in his chair, perhaps leaning in. She pressed her ear closer to the keyhole.

"As you know, we are suing Lord Dain for a legal separation from Lady Althea in the ecclesiastical court."

Vicky gasped and forced her ear even closer. Tom was right— Mr. Carmichael *had* known about Dain. So why had Carmichael questioned her when she'd asked him to keep Dain away from them last night?

Her father continued, "But such things take time, so in the interim, Barnes was applying for a writ from the Court of Chancery that would keep Dain from having power over her."

"I shall speak with Mr. Barnes myself to see what's happening," Carmichael responded.

"Thank you," her father said. "I was hoping you would, but I also recall you mentioning having a friend in the Court of Chancery. Was he a clerk?"

Carmichael didn't respond immediately. "He is indeed. Shall I ask him if the papers have been reviewed?"

"I should greatly appreciate it," Vicky's father said.

Vicky frowned. Carmichael had hesitated to offer his services to her father. Why? Her frown disappeared when she heard footsteps coming toward the door. As quietly as she could, Vicky tiptoed down the hall and ducked into the nearest room—an empty guest chamber. She closed the door, but kept it slightly ajar.

The door to her father's room creaked as Mr. Carmichael opened it, wished her father good health, and walked down the hall toward the stairs. Vicky cracked the door a touch wider and peeked at Mr. Carmichael's retreating form. As much as she hated to lend credence to Tom's ideas, she had to admit Carmichael's actions last night and his responses to her father's questions did appear rather suspicious. Coupled with the strange conversation Tom had witnessed, it seemed possible Mr. Carmichael was tangled in some strange dealings with the man Vicky loathed most in the world!

Vicky stared at Mr. Carmichael's broad, dark form as he descended the staircase. He wasn't a Mr. Darcy, or a Mr. Knightley, or even a Colonel Brandon, really. But he—

Just before disappearing from view, he turned around. Vicky ducked back inside the room, unsure if he'd seen her. She listened for anything that might betray what he was doing.

Finally, the thud of his footsteps grew farther away.

Vicky inhaled, trying to calm herself. What a goose she was. It shouldn't have mattered if Mr. Carmichael saw her standing in the doorway. After all, eavesdropping was no crime. Someone like Elizabeth Bennet might even have waved and said hello.

But as Vicky recalled the speed with which he'd turned around, almost as though he expected to do battle with whoever watched him, she was happy she'd hid. Lizzy Bennet, heroine though she was, had never had to contend with the events of the last few weeks.

Tom's words played in Vicky's mind: *Just because sensational events happen in novels, that doesn't mean they cannot* happen. Though it pained her, he'd been right. Her life was looking less and less like one of Miss Austen's novels and more and more like an utter mess.

CHAPTER THE SEVENTEENTH

She would keep the peace if possible.
—Jane Austen, *Emma*

Susie's eyes widened as Charles strode into the kitchen. It was still some time before the evening meal. She sat near the hearth, trying to focus on reading. In a desperate bid to distract herself from worrying about what Charles had been up to this morning, she'd been trying to finish *Pride and Prejudice*, the first novel she'd allowed herself in months.

A few minutes after Charles had disappeared inside that town house, she'd hurried home, only to find another pair of bailiffs demanding payment. When she'd inspected the bill, she'd seen it was for various game birds and two large hams from Fortnum & Mason. It was dated within the last week.

Charles.

There could be no doubt. Still, she wondered when he'd eaten them—she'd definitely seen no evidence of them at their meals.

And now, Charles stood rummaging through the larder, shaking off Cook's questions about whether she could make him something. Susie thought of Tom and all the sacrifices he had made for his mother and brother. He'd uprooted himself from Solothurn and the contentedness he had found with his uncle's family; he'd returned to a home that had caused him nothing but pain and sold his cherished horse to cover Charles's debts.

And was Charles even grateful? He'd done as little as possible to help Tom find backers for his hotel—the one hope they all had to survive and keep the estate intact.

Susie stared at Charles as he sliced a block of cheese and arranged the pieces on a wedge of bread. He truly did not understand what Tom was trying to do for them all. Perhaps he didn't even care. The thought made her pulse quicken and her fingers tingle.

She had to confront him. Tom didn't deserve such shabby treatment—especially not from his own brother.

"Charles?"

His head swiveled over his shoulder.

"Susan, I didn't see you there." He crunched into his bread and turned to face her.

Susie doubted that. He knew this was one of only two rooms she could frequent in the afternoon because of the house's lack of heating.

"I knew you couldn't maintain your schedule of dry history for much longer," he said with a snort and a gesture toward her book.

Susie ignored his comment. "How was your outing?" she asked.

"Tolerable," he said, turning back to rummage through the larder.

"Did you go to your club?"

He grunted in the affirmative. "You know, it's warmer than this old pile of stones."

Susie pursed her lips. "I wouldn't know, actually."

When Charles said nothing, Susie got to her feet and said, "Charles, would you accompany me upstairs?"

His head turned, and seeing her determined stare, he furrowed his brow. He looked at Cook and the scullery maid, seeming to understand that Susie had something to say to him privately. He grabbed another chunk of bread and motioned for her to precede him as they exited the kitchen.

Susie took him up the servants' stairs until they had reached an empty hall. Tom only employed two footmen in the town house, and she knew neither of them were likely to be skulking around this semidark hallway at this time of day. Still, she peered in both directions before looking Charles straight in the eye.

"Charles, more bailiffs were here today. They had a bill signed *by you* from Fortnum & Mason."

If Charles knew what she meant to ask, he showed no sign of it. "Well, what of it?"

"The bill showed you had bought various meat and game products, including two hams."

Charles said nothing.

"Charles," she asked gently, "what did you do with the food?"

"It was delivered here, of course."

Susie sighed. "We haven't eaten ham since before we left Halworth Hall. And I've reviewed Cook's ledger of food received.

Fortnum & Mason hasn't delivered anything to the town house since we took residence. What happened to it? I'm sure if you tell Tom he will understand—telling him must be better than having him furious when he sees the bill and isn't given a reason."

Charles shrugged one shoulder. "Why should it matter to you?"

"I worry about you. We *are* family."

He crunched another bite of bread. "Would it trouble you so much if your personal welfare didn't depend on Tom?"

Susie ignored the barb. "Perhaps you gave the food to whoever lives in that house you visited today."

Charles's eyes narrowed. He graced her with a cold stare. "What house?"

"I, well," she faltered. "I followed you," she finished, meeting his gaze with an equally determined expression of her own.

"You *followed* me?" he repeated, incredulity etched on his face.

"You went into a house in Harborough Square, and before you entered, you looked both ways down the street as though wondering if anyone saw you. Who lives there, Charles?"

"Who the bloody hell do you think you are?" he exploded.

Susie stepped back at the vehemence in his voice. Still, she raised her chin. "You've been behaving strangely ever since that day I saw you poring over the estate ledgers. The servants told me you started leaving the house earlier. I was simply making certain you were all right."

He paced toward her. "Let us make one thing clear, shall we? What I do is none of your affair. I don't care if you are related to me by blood. You do not know me. In future, keep your concern to yourself. And if you ever follow me again, you will regret it."

With that, Charles pivoted on his heel and disappeared down the servants' staircase.

As Susie watched his rapidly retreating form, she inhaled deeply. *If you expect me to give up on you so easily, brother, then you don't know me either.*

CHAPTER THE EIGHTEENTH

He had not a temper to bear the sort of
competition in which we stood—the sort of preference
which was often given me.
—Jane Austen, *Pride and Prejudice*

After he'd left the Astons', Tom took a hackney cab to Covent Garden. At the musicale, he'd overheard Lord Axley speak of attending the theater Wednesday evening. As Lord Axley and his acquaintances were currently the only prospective backers Tom had met, he planned to propose his hotel to Lord Axley there—or, at the very least, set an appropriate time and place to discuss it with him.

Tom's spirits lightened as he considered the possibilities and returned to the town house. As he climbed the steps, Tom noted the tasteful exterior and only slightly damaged roof. Maybe he could still sell the place He sighed. They shouldn't be forced to live in the place that had been the setting of his father's shameful affairs. He'd completely forgotten his plan to rent new accommodations, but maybe now with the leftover money from the sale of the horses he could manage it. He'd have to consult the books.

As he closed the front door behind him, Susie came down the hall in a dull brown frock. He suppressed a frown at the dress.

"Did your visit with Lady Victoria go well?"

He decided not to tell Susie about the attack on the Astons. There was no need to worry her. "It did."

"I'm glad." She paused and then glanced behind herself. "I don't like being the bearer of bad news, Tom, but more collectors were here today."

He groaned.

"It seems word is getting around that the Sherbornes can no longer pay their bills."

Tom swore under his breath. This had to be Dain's doing. By now, he must have told Carmichael about the horses and Tom's financial problems. At this very moment they could be formulating ways to ruin him. His mind reeled at how easily they could squash his hotel before he even lined up the necessary backers. He'd have to accelerate his plans.

He looked at Susie and debated telling her his troubles. Especially what had happened to the Astons and how Carmichael was likely playing a dangerous game to win Victoria. But with one glance at the creases between her brows, he decided against it. Susie had enough to worry about handling the bailiffs.

"I suppose we don't have enough to cover what they claim we owe?" he muttered, placing his hat on an entry table.

"We still have enough left from the sale of the horses, but I believe the problem will get worse long before it gets better."

Tom pinched the bridge of his nose. Once the money from the

horses' sale went to the bailiffs, Tom wouldn't be able to afford to rent other accommodations. So much for selling this cursed town house. It would take far too long anyway, and with Dain and Carmichael aware of their situation, attempting to do so would only make the severity of their financial problems more evident.

"I think we should have a talk with Charles," she continued.

"What good would it do?" Tom said, running his hand through his hair. "You know he won't stop his spending."

"Perhaps we need to do something more serious, then."

Tom looked at the ceiling. "You mean visit his creditors? Cut off his lines of credit? That really would proclaim to all London that we are near poverty."

Susie stared at Tom with her large brown eyes, entreating him to be reasonable.

He sighed. "Very well, I shall meet you in the library. Have one of the servants fetch Charles."

"No need for that." Charles's voice rang clearly down the hallway. He'd emerged from the corridor leading down to the kitchens. He was chewing a chicken leg. "Well? What do you want?"

Tom shook his head. "Come with me."

Tom walked toward the library with Susie following close behind. Charles brought up the rear. In the library, Tom gravitated toward the warmth of the fire, although he knew his contentment would be short-lived. With a deep breath, he sat in the chair closest to the hearth. Susie slipped into a red armchair opposite him. He grimaced as Charles scraped the parquet floor while turning a chair to face them both.

"Doesn't this look jolly," Charles said, taking another bite of his chicken leg.

Tom let out a breath. "I'm glad you're in good humor. It should make this more pleasant."

Charles raised his eyebrows.

Susie gave Tom a sharp look. Tom sighed and got to the point. "I'm cutting off your lines of credit."

Charles studied his chicken leg. Tom suspected he was weighing his options. After a few moments' silence, he caught Tom's eye. "And just what will that solve?"

Tom barely suppressed a grim laugh. "It will solve having to pay for your frivolous expenses, and it will keep you from contributing further to the stress on this family and the estate."

Charles shook his head slowly. Tom waited for a response, but when Charles said nothing, he continued.

"You must come to grips with our situation and stop being a source of the problem."

Charles stood and walked to the far side of the library. His voice was flat when he spoke. "Do you think *I* am the only one contributing to this family's problems?"

"You certainly aren't helping," Tom replied.

Susie started to speak. "I think what Tom meant—"

"Don't!" Charles interrupted her. "Don't presume to tell me what my brother was trying to say. His words were quite clear." He turned to Tom, pointing his finger at Susie. "I suppose *she* helps in some way? She is contributing financially to this family?"

"You know very well the daughter of an earl cannot work. But apart from that, she doesn't *buy* anything. How do you think Susan feels when you go out every night, spending to your heart's content, and I can't afford to buy her clothing that doesn't resemble rags?"

"Pfft," Charles said. "I couldn't care less how she feels. You would rather side with some bastard half sister you found on the streets than a brother you've had all your life. So why should I care what either of you think of me?"

Tom stood. "You shut your damn mouth."

Charles eyes went wide with fury. "And what am I? Some peasant you can order about? Let me ask you this, brother: What are you doing to save this glorious family?"

"You know what I'm doing. I've been trying to get backers for my hotel—a task I've asked you to aid me in numerous times, if you recall—so this family will have enough to live on for a good many years."

Charles scowled. "And I suppose you're doing everything in your power to do so?"

Tom felt his jaw clench so hard his teeth might have cracked. He ground out, "What in hell is that supposed to mean? Of course I am, you idiot."

"Then why didn't you make a deal with Lord Dain? We could have solved all our monetary problems in one blow. But you're too bloody proud to deal with a former rival. You're too proud to accept that you can't run the estate—that you're a failure!"

Tom blanched. "Didn't you ever learn to have opinions of your own? You sound just like Father."

Charles's face turned beet red. "I am no man's puppet! All those years I faced him *alone* while you lived comfortably in your little Swiss paradise. You couldn't stand up to Father. So you left Mother and me to pick up the pieces of your departure. And then when he died, you came back and stole what Father wanted to give me. Well, I'm through with trying to be polite. I'm through with you!" He turned toward the door.

Blood pounded in Tom's ears. Didn't Charles know why he'd left? For all those years of their childhood, Tom had endured their father's beatings, watched him bully and control his mother and his brother, and he'd been powerless to stop him. Not until he'd walked in on his father actually forcing himself on one of the housemaids had he truly understood the extent of the old man's depravity.

In the wake of that discovery, and Victoria accidentally witnessing the aftermath, Tom finally told his father he wouldn't stand for it any longer. The old man simply instructed two of their burliest footmen to drag Tom from his bed and throw him out into the cold. Thankfully, one of them had been human enough to grab him a change of clothes.

Tom hadn't stood up to their father until it was too late, but he *had* tried. For what little good it had done.

Could Charles not know Tom had only inherited the estate through their father's neglect? Tom hadn't expected or wanted the blasted place. The earl could have gone before Parliament to disinherit Tom, but he hadn't. There was no way of knowing what had prevented the old man from doing it, but nothing could change his lack of action now.

"Charles—" Tom stepped forward and grabbed his brother by the arm.

Charles spun around and punched Tom in the stomach. The force knocked him two steps back, the pain sending shock waves through his midsection. He struggled for breath.

Susie jumped out of her chair with a cry.

Charles tore open the library door, stepped through, and whipped it closed with equal force. Four books on the shelf closest to the door thudded to the ground. Charles's steps echoed on the marble as he stomped to the front door. He slammed it as he left.

Tom knelt on the floor and tried to breathe through the lightning-quick zigzags of pain.

"Are you all right?" Susie asked, bending over him.

He nodded.

"You could have handled that a bit better," she said, offering him a rueful smile.

"I know," he grunted, taking a deep breath and holding it.

"Should we go after him?"

He shook his head and exhaled. "Let him calm down. He has to come back sometime."

Susie stood and started pacing the room.

"Tom, I should have told you days ago, but I couldn't be sure anything was truly amiss. He was only acting strangely—"

Tom shook his head. "Start from the beginning." He inched his way back to his chair and hauled himself up to sit.

Susie sat opposite him. She explained how Charles had been looking through the ledgers the day after they'd sold their horses and how he'd started leaving earlier than normal. "Please don't be angry, Tom, but today I decided to follow him."

He closed his eyes and tried to breathe normally. His first

impulse was to lecture her about her safety, but she'd only argue, and he didn't have the strength for another disagreement. "Tell me what you saw."

"Not much, actually—only Charles going into a house. I wasn't going to say anything to him, but when I came home, and saw the bill from Fortnum & Mason that Charles had signed, I couldn't help myself. I confronted him about the bill and the house, and he completely lost his temper. I don't know what it could be, but I think there's something very wrong with Charles. Have you ever seen him act as he did today?"

Tom shook his head. "Not in the past year. He never had a temper when we were young. He must have developed it . . ." The change in his brother could not be wholly attributed to their father's influence. Tom was just as much at fault. Charles had been right about one thing—Tom's exile had been relatively comfortable compared to Charles's years under their father's power. Was it any wonder Charles was behaving erratically?

Tom let out a deep sigh. Guilt crept up on him again, and he didn't know how much he could take in one day. He felt his self-control cracking, and he didn't have a bloody idea what to do about it. "You were right to tell me what you saw, but there is no need for you to trouble yourself further. Whatever Charles might be doing, he'll find it difficult once I cut off his lines of credit."

"Tom, if there's one thing I do know about Charles, it's that very few things will stop him from getting his way."

Tom exhaled again and tried to relax into the back of the chair as he contemplated that sentiment.

Susie walked over to one of the bookshelves and retrieved a volume. "This may not be the right time, but I just finished this, and perhaps it might afford you some measure of escape." She handed him the book.

He opened the front cover. The title page read:

PRIDE AND PREJUDICE:
A NOVEL.
IN THREE VOLUMES.
BY THE
AUTHOR OF "SENSE AND SENSIBILITY."

Wasn't this the author Vicky and Carmichael had spoken of at the ball? The same one Vicky had asked him to read?

"There's a certain Mr. Darcy character who reminds me very much of you."

He raised a brow at her. "Susan, I really haven't the time . . ."

"Yes, I imagine that is precisely what Mr. Darcy would say," she said with a smile. "This just might illuminate some peculiar truths about your nature."

Tom stood with a harrumph he only half meant and walked to the desk with *Pride and Prejudice* gripped in his hand.

CHAPTER THE NINETEENTH

It was folly to be disturbed by it.
—Jane Austen, *Emma*

"Victoria, listen to this!" her mother exclaimed from her writing desk.

From the corner of the blue parlor, Vicky looked up from her embroidery. Her mother twisted around in her chair, waving a letter above her head in triumph.

She brought it to eye level. "*Mrs. Jacoba Carmichael and her son Mr. Simon Carmichael are pleased to invite the Earl and Countess of Oakbridge, Lady Dain, and Lady Victoria Aston to join them in their box at the Covent Garden Theatre to see* The Conquest of Taranto *on Wednesday at five in the evening.*" Her mother looked up from the card. "How *perfect.*"

Going to the theater might be amusing, but Vicky wouldn't call it "perfect." She looked at Althea, who had glanced up from a book to hear their mother's news, but her sister wouldn't meet her gaze.

"It's very kind of Mrs. Carmichael to invite us," Vicky said.

"Kind, indeed. And opportune," her mother added, turning back to her desk to write their reply.

Vicky frowned. "How so? Papa cannot go to the theater in his condition. And those kidnappers are still on the loose—"

"Pish, my dear. Althea and your father will stay at home, and you and I will attend the theater with two of the guards your father hired. Mr. and Mrs. Carmichael won't mind."

Vicky glanced at Althea, but she'd turned her attention back to her book. "But, Mama, do you think we'll be safe in a crowded theater? Even with the guards—"

"Mr. Carmichael will be as good as a third."

Vicky scrunched her brows together. "How so?"

Her mother turned in her seat and fixed her gaze on Vicky. "You must have noticed how he dotes on you, my dear."

"Hardly *dotes*, Mama. We get on well together, perhaps, but he hasn't shown me any particular favor."

Her mother and Althea gave identical, ladylike sniffs of disbelief.

Vicky bit the inside of her cheek and rose from her chair. A few days ago, she would've been pleased if Mr. Carmichael showed her favor over other ladies, but now, after Tom's assertions and the conversation between Mr. Carmichael and her father, she didn't know what to think.

Someone rapped at the door, and Vicky's mother called for them to enter.

Sheldon bowed. "My lady, Mr. Silby has come to call on Lady

Victoria." He sent a glance at Vicky.

Her eyes widened. "Please tell him we are not at home, Sheldon."

He nodded, but Vicky's mother spoke her name in an exasperated tone.

"I'm sorry, Mama, but I have no intention of marrying Mr. Silby. Had Tom not been at the park that day, Mr. Silby would have insisted on driving Sarah and me back in his damaged curricle. He is reckless and a bore besides."

"It is rather early to be calling," Althea said with a look at their mother.

"Oh, very well." The countess waved a hand in the air. "Sheldon, you may do as Lady Victoria says."

"At once, my lady." He gave a solemn nod.

"Feel at liberty to make that a standing order for Mr. Silby," Vicky cut in.

Sheldon inclined his head, and Vicky smiled as he caught her eye and left the room.

"And what of Mr. Fothergill, Mr. Shore, and Lord Blankenship?" her mother asked.

Vicky eyed her, wondering if she knew Vicky had given similar orders regarding those three. She very likely did. "Had you been present, Mama, you would have felt the same as I."

Her mother hummed in her throat. "Thus we are left with Mr. Carmichael."

"Even Mr. Carmichael predicted I wouldn't like Mr. Silby," Vicky pointed out.

Her mother raised a delicate brow. "Victoria, have you seen Mr. Carmichael bestow half so much attention on any other lady?"

"I am hardly in his company all of the time," she replied, heading for the door.

"Hmm . . . I see."

Vicky turned, unable to help herself. "*What* do you see, Mama?"

"You mistrust him," her mother said.

"What? Well, yes. That is, no, I—" She snapped her mouth shut. She didn't know how many of Tom's suspicions she should tell her mother. She'd told Althea, but her sister hadn't mentioned it since. Vicky caught Althea's eye. Her sister dipped her chin but said nothing. It seemed she didn't intend to repeat Tom's doubts. Which was just as well. Vicky wanted to question Mr. Carmichael herself. Tom's concerns could still prove unfounded, and she didn't want her parents to think badly of him if that were the case.

"But do you *like* Mr. Carmichael?" Althea asked.

Vicky inhaled. "I . . . well, I . . ."

"That *is* the material point," her mother confirmed.

Vicky closed her lips. Did she like Mr. Carmichael? An image of his dark eyes gazing deep into hers as though he could read her thoughts—and liked what he read—brought a tiny smile to her lips. She *had* liked him. Until Tom had planted doubts in her mind. Yet she had no evidence to condemn Mr. Carmichael. And she *had* enjoyed his company.

Of course she liked him. What remained to be seen, however, was whether she could trust him.

"Lady Oakbridge, Lady Victoria, what a pleasure." Mr. Carmichael's mother greeted them with a smile as she rose from her seat and dipped into a polite curtsy. At the edge of the box, Mr. Carmichael turned and bowed. Their box was well appointed with red velvet chairs and curtains. Gold-plated candle sconces adorned the plush walls. As it was just off the center of the theater, the box afforded a perfect view of the stage.

Vicky smiled and curtsied.

Mrs. Carmichael kissed Vicky's mother, and then Vicky, on both cheeks. Mr. Carmichael's mother should have been an imposing figure with her glossy black hair, still untouched by gray, and her height allowing her to tower over both Vicky and her mother, but her demeanor was so warm and inviting that Vicky couldn't help but like her. "I know that Lady Dain is residing with you. I am sorry she and the Lord Oakbridge couldn't accompany you, but"—Mrs. Carmichael lowered her voice—"Simon apprised me of the accident. Is the earl recovering well?"

Vicky's mother nodded. "Very well. He'll be as good as new in a week, I'd wager."

"Days, with his strong constitution," Mr. Carmichael interjected. He stepped forward. "Lady Oakbridge, thank you for joining us." Then he stepped to Vicky and smiled.

Vicky smiled back, despite her reservations. He looked into her eyes in that same way he always did. Yet, this time her stomach fluttered and she didn't know what to think. She cast her gaze to the floor. Their mothers moved to the front of the box as Mrs. Carmichael pointed out a shared acquaintance in a box across the theater.

Vicky licked her lips. "Do you know the play, Mr. Carmichael?"

His mouth tilted up at one corner. "I cannot say I know much about it, other than that it's a sort of romance."

She raised her eyebrows. "*The* Conquest *of Taranto*? What

could be romantic about a conquest?"

He laughed, and she recognized what she'd said.

She exhaled. "Unless, of course, Taranto were a person," she said, shaking her head at herself.

He cleared his throat. "But then the play would hardly be suitable for ladies," he said, gazing into her eyes.

She felt color rise in her cheeks. "You're quite right, of course." She narrowed her eyes at him. "Although, I'm sure it would be perfect for the sort of men who frequent boxing clubs."

A slow grin spread across his face.

Her stomach flipped again. What was wrong with her? Surely she'd insulted him, but he didn't seem to mind one bit. And she, it seemed, was growing more susceptible to his charms.

She ventured a glance at their mothers, but they still talked near the edge of the box. Vicky turned and saw their two guards standing awkwardly at the door. Then she realized the box contained only four seats. The poor men couldn't stand for hours.

She leaned closer to Mr. Carmichael. "Would you be so good as to speak to someone about securing more seats for our . . . companions?"

He seemed to notice the guards for the first time, even though he must have known they were coming. Her mother had written as much in her reply to the invitation.

"Ah, an oversight, I assure you," he said, and left the box to procure the chairs.

Vicky smiled at the guards and wandered over to her mother and Mrs. Carmichael.

"Oh, Victoria," her mother said as she came near. "I was just telling Mrs. Carmichael how thoughtful Mr. Carmichael was in visiting your father so soon after the accident."

Vicky groaned inwardly, remembering how strange his visit had seemed.

"No, no, Lady Oakbridge, it was the least he could do. Indeed, he should have done more."

"But what more could he have done?" Vicky's mother asked.

Mrs. Carmichael flourished her fan in the air. "A number of things! Ferret out the villains, perhaps?"

"Surely that would be a job more suited to a Bow Street Runner than Mr. Carmichael," Vicky's mother protested. "Indeed, one is currently on the case."

Actually, the runner had not yet found anything to report. But when Vicky opened her mouth to say so, her mother looked at her, urging her with her eyes to let the matter lie.

"Indeed, Mrs. Carmichael," Vicky said instead, "would you not prefer to keep your son safe at home? If only so he might be available to accompany you to the shops? To be sure, that must be preferable to worrying what trouble he's getting into elsewhere?" she said with a smile.

"Oh, bless you, my dear. Simon hasn't the patience to accompany me to the shops."

Vicky gaped at her for a moment. "But, the day we went to Gunter's, he said he was going with you."

Mrs. Carmichael laughed. "To the shops? Dear me, no. The poor boy would be less than useless."

"Oh—oh, dear. Then I suppose I must have misunderstood."

She thought back. Only a few days later, Tom had told her about the boxing match. Was *that* why Mr. Carmichael had left her that day?

"Think nothing of it, my dear." She inclined her head. "My son tells me you are fond of horses."

Vicky nodded.

Mrs. Carmichael's easy smile deepened. "Simon has such a lovely stable of Thoroughbreds at our house in East Anglia. And it's so near Newmarket—very convenient for racing. Has he told you of it?"

"I don't recall him mentioning it."

Mrs. Carmichael shook her head fondly. "The poor boy has so much on his mind. But I shall see he tells you all about it."

Vicky nodded and started to reply, but Mrs. Carmichael continued in her unaffected way. "Your mama tells me you enjoy learning estate management."

"Oh . . . " Vicky glanced at her mother uncertainly. She didn't usually tell people outside the family about Vicky's odd interests. But her mama beamed at her with encouragement. "Indeed, yes. I help at Oakbridge as much as I can. With all aspects of the estate."

"How extraordinary. My mind could not grasp the minutiae of running such a large estate as Oakbridge." She touched Vicky's mother's arm. "Countess, how fortunate you are to have an enterprising young woman for a daughter."

Vicky's mother nodded.

Mrs. Carmichael faced Vicky again. "Did you know Simon recently purchased a property in southern Hampshire?"

Vicky started at the news. "No, I—"

"Well, as I say, it was a recent acquisition. He's having the most dreadful time trying to find a land steward in the area. Of course, he's having to do it all by post, which can be a challenge—oh, there he is. He will tell you of it himself."

Vicky turned. Mr. Carmichael had returned with two chairs. The guards thanked him but did not yet sit. He waved off their gratitude and joined the ladies.

"Simon," his mother said, "do tell our guests of the Hampshire property."

"Yes," Vicky's mother said, casting a sly glance in Vicky's direction, "I had no notion you were looking for anything in the neighborhood."

Vicky eyed her, wondering if that were true. She was becoming acutely aware that the possible match between her and Simon Carmichael seemed to be the only matter preoccupying the thoughts of both their mothers. It was the same as when Fanny Price's relations at Mansfield Park tried to convince her to marry Henry Crawford. Vicky furrowed her brow and looked at the carpet. She didn't wish to think of Mr. Carmichael as someone as faithless as Henry Crawford, even if Tom already did.

"It is hardly in the neighborhood, Lady Oakbridge," Mr. Carmichael said. "The house is a converted abbey on the edge of the New Forest. There is some surrounding parkland, however. I believe it is situated some twenty-five miles from Oakbridge."

Only half a day's journey by carriage if the roads were good. Vicky's throat went dry. Had he bought the house to appeal to her? It must be ideally situated if it sat on the edge of the New Forest.

Her parents had taken her and Althea there various times in their childhood, and Vicky had loved the little forest hamlets and the wild ponies roaming free in the woods and villages. She'd asked her father if they could take one home to graze at Oakbridge, but he'd told her only the king had the power to do such a thing. And now Mr. Carmichael owned a house there.

"Tell Lady Victoria your woes in finding a steward," his mother urged.

Before he could begin, the orchestra finished tuning their instruments, signifying the play would soon begin. Mrs. Carmichael and Vicky's mother took the pair of seats at the front of the box, leaving Vicky to sit behind her mother and beside the last empty chair while Mr. Carmichael closed the door to the box.

She took a deep breath. The entire evening had been one great maneuver to facilitate the match. Why couldn't their parents let well enough alone? If he wanted to propose, he would do so. And she—well, she didn't know what she wanted. She wondered if Mr. Carmichael's mother had persuaded him to buy the Hampshire property or if it'd been his own doing. Tom's contention that Mr. Carmichael already owning multiple estates wouldn't keep him from acquiring more had proved correct. But surely he wouldn't have bought an abbey in Hampshire if he thought he'd one day gain control of Oakbridge?

"I'm sorry."

She turned to him. She'd been so preoccupied she hadn't noticed him sit. "What for?"

He gave her a sideways glance. "About my mother insisting I

bore you with the details of finding a steward."

She frowned. "Why should that bore me?"

He raised a brow. "Simply because we are at the theater."

She stared at him. "And what should that matter?"

He leaned closer. "Most young ladies have no interest in such affairs."

She pursed her lips. "Indeed." She should've known. He thought—as so many men did—a woman's role was strictly ornamental.

"Have I offended you?"

She let out a breath. "If you'll recall, I'm not completely out of my depth on the subject of estate management."

Mr. Carmichael raised his brows, then winced. "Of course. It slipped my mind."

"Just as it slipped your mind to tell your mother you cut our afternoon at Gunter's short to take her to the shops."

He exhaled. "I apologize. I had another engagement I could not miss."

"Yes, I know. Your boxing match." She narrowed her eyes. "I don't care for being lied to."

He caught her gaze. For a few moments, he said nothing. "No more do I." He chuckled without humor and looked away. "Unfortunately, one cannot always voice everything one thinks."

"Perhaps not, but one needn't obfuscate the truth either."

"Sometimes, needs must. For propriety's sake, or safety's sake, or even to gain an advantage over an opponent."

Vicky frowned. "For safety I can understand, but I'm afraid we do not agree on the other matters."

He eyed her. "You do not cease to surprise me."

Realizing more from his gaze than his words that he was complimenting her, her lips parted.

"Thank you," she said after a pause.

She angled her body to face him. When they were sitting, his face was not so uncomfortably above hers. "Why did you buy that abbey in Hampshire?"

His unguarded expression became enigmatic. "I did not own a house in Hampshire."

"And owning estates everywhere else does not content you?" she said, fishing for an answer.

"Evidently not," he said with an exasperating grin.

She sighed at his evasiveness and faced forward, turning her attention to the people taking their seats in the box opposite theirs. How could she ever get to know him if he wouldn't answer direct questions with direct answers? How could a union between them ever work under such circumstances? He'd admitted he was *often* evasive. And then there was the fact that he'd apparently known about their situation with Dain at the musicale and had *still* questioned her when she'd asked him to make the scoundrel leave.

"Is something vexing you?"

Vicky started at the words whispered so close to her ear. He'd leaned closer. "Yes, I—" She considered what she should admit. Then she realized she had to make him understand. Otherwise, she'd have to concentrate her efforts on someone more forthright. "Forgive my bluntness, but let me be so clear as to say *I* would always prefer the truth in future. If you do not feel you can accommodate this request, I cannot see the wisdom of us continuing in this way."

She ventured a furtive glance at their mothers. They were chatting away, seemingly oblivious to the conversation behind them. Vicky continued, "I was most grateful for how you removed Lord Dain from the musicale, but why did you not say you knew the truth about him and my sister?"

He blinked—uncertainly, she thought. "Your father told me sometime after we went to Gunter's. I do not recall the precise date."

"I'd deduced as much. Yet, at the musicale, you acted as though you did not know."

"I did nothing of the kind," he argued.

She shook her head. "Mr. Carmichael, I am no shrinking violet who swoons at the mere mention of violence—"

"Victoria!" Her mother turned and whispered, "Lower your voice."

Vicky glowered at her but closed her mouth. Her mother faced forward, doubtlessly to expound to Mrs. Carmichael on Vicky's myriad virtues. Mr. Carmichael smirked. Vicky harrumphed and folded her hands in her lap. She watched the sceneshifters finish placing various small trees in front of the curtain, ostensibly to approximate the greenery of the Spanish seacoast.

"I do apologize," Mr. Carmichael said after a moment had passed. He sounded in earnest, though a trace of a smile played upon his lips. "You would be unmistakable for a shrinking violet."

She nodded.

"And you have my vow I will tell you no more falsehoods in future."

She looked at him askance.

"My vow as a gentleman."

Finally, she allowed her frown to subside.

"And, so," he said, leaning close with a contrite smile, "am I forgiven?"

She tilted her head as the brown flecks danced in his dark eyes. His charm troubled her; Henry Crawford came to mind again. She couldn't let herself be persuaded so easily. "Not until you fully explain why you hesitated when I asked you to remove Dain."

He sat back. "God's teeth, woman! Is a man not allowed some hesitation? I had no wish to air your family's dirty laundry in public."

Mr. Carmichael's mother turned around and graced him with an icy stare. He said no more. Vicky had never heard such an outburst cross his lips, and for a moment she sat in stunned silence. But as she replayed his mother's comical glare, and his obedient compliance, Vicky let out a short giggle. Then another. She looked at Mr. Carmichael. He eyed her warily. She nearly burst out laughing on the spot.

He began to chuckle. She giggled again. "God's teeth!" she imitated. Then, he, who was usually so controlled in his actions, let out an unregulated hoot. And very inconveniently too, because at that moment, the theater had just grown very silent as trumpets declared the hero's arrival onstage to begin his first speech.

At Carmichael's laugh, all heads in the upper boxes craned their way. The actor whose opening lines had just been trod upon looked up as well, regarding them with an indignant expression. Vicky sat stock-still with embarrassment, horrified as another round of giggles threatened to burst free. One glance at Mr. Carmichael told her he was similarly afflicted. So, the pair of them did the only thing possible. They simultaneously bent over their laps, clapped their hands over their mouths, and gasped with muffled laughter.

As Tom turned the corner into the upstairs lobby of the theater, hoping to utilize the intermission to obtain something better than the gin many were swilling in the pit, he fairly skidded to a stop. Victoria stood in the lobby in a curve-hugging, yellow satin dress, arm in arm with Carmichael. The pleasure on her face was unmistakable as they strolled; she spoke with animation. Tom's gut tightened as Carmichael leaned close to her ear and whispered something. She gave him a wry grin, but he looked very pleased with himself.

Tom took three strides toward them before realizing that breaking up their little tête-à-tête would only cause a scene. He ground his back teeth together. Why were they suddenly so intimate when only days before, Vicky had agreed to be cautious with the man who could have ordered the attack on her family? Tom glared at them both.

He took a steadying breath. What could Carmichael do in such a public place? Without doubt, Vicky had a chaperone present. And if Carmichael wished to marry Vicky, he had no reason to harm her until he'd wed her. Frowning, Tom sidled back the other way. After all, he hadn't come to the theater to enjoy the play, to have another altercation with Carmichael, or even to help Victoria. Still . . .

He looked back at them. He should greet her anyway. If only to let Carmichael know someone else was watching him. As Tom turned, a large, broad-shouldered man emerged from the crowd to tower over Victoria's back. He shadowed her gait. Carmichael ignored the fellow, but Vicky glanced back and smiled at him. The man watched the crowd as he followed her. He must be some sort of guard. Occasionally, dukes from Austrian principalities had visited Solothurn, and men of similar aspect and bearing had often guarded them. It seemed the Astons were taking extra precautions as he'd hoped.

Tom exhaled. He couldn't help Vicky more than a guard could. As he descended the stairs to the ground floor, the trying thought that Vicky still felt Carmichael was her best chance for marriage gnawed at him. He rubbed at a strange, sudden tightness in his chest, then decided to ignore it. He dropped his hand to his side. He would call on her tomorrow and find out what she'd learned about Carmichael, if anything.

And in the meantime, he'd have to content himself with extolling the merits of his hotel scheme. Lord Axley had offered him a cigar down in the pit, and Tom had no intention of letting the man's proximity go to waste.

CHAPTER THE TWENTIETH

She hoped they might now become friends again.
—Jane Austen, *Emma*

Vicky leaned closer to her looking glass and played with the curls framing her face, trying to improve the effect in any small way. In the morning, Tom had sent a note saying he'd be calling around teatime.

"You look lovely."

Vicky turned over her shoulder and saw Althea in the doorway. Vicky bit her lower lip to hide her astonishment that her sister had paid her a compliment.

Althea herself looked better than she had in quite a while. She was still very thin, but her peony-pink day dress brought out a blush in her cheeks. Vicky smiled at her and turned back to the mirror. She pinched some color into her own cheeks.

"Thank you. Do you think Cook will serve strawberry tarts today?" she asked, believing it safer to keep to mundane topics.

"I think you're going to quite a bit of trouble for a boy who broke your heart long ago."

Vicky's hand froze at her temple. Thea was right. This was simply tea. Tom's presence shouldn't influence her state of mind. However, she did want to look pretty, if only for herself. She glanced at her cornflower-blue dress with its delicate cap sleeves and nodded. The dress showed her figure to its best advantage.

Still, why did it follow that the only purpose of looking well was to attract a gentleman's attention? She didn't seriously believe Tom could ever be interested in her in that way. He never had been. And she wasn't so arrogant as to believe her appearance could sway him to such thoughts.

"Tom didn't break my heart. He broke our friendship," she said into the mirror.

Her sister's reflection stared back at her from where she stood, just inside the door. Her chin tilted downward, and her eyes widened slightly. "There was little difference at the time."

Vicky had snapped at everyone who'd approached her in those first weeks after he'd left. Then she'd wept on her mother's shoulder when she finally realized Tom was abroad for good and would probably never reply to her letters.

She took a deep breath. Things were actually starting to feel familiar between them again. He was concerned for *her*, and not just out of gentlemanly conduct. She was certain he was coming today to keep an eye on her. So to some degree, he must wish to be friends again. Which was quite gratifying, really, after missing him for so many years.

She smoothed down the hair at her temple. "Don't worry, Thea. No doubt Tom is just calling to see we are well."

Her mind flitted to Mr. Carmichael. They'd had a lovely evening at the theater, and she liked him even more. He'd answered all her questions about his strange behavior to her satisfaction. For the first time in days, she felt sure all would turn out well. Perhaps her life had become a sensational novel for a few weeks, but surely it would end like *Pride and Prejudice* and leave her happy and in a position to help her dear family.

She faced Althea. "I'm charged with finding a husband, and I will not shirk my duty," she said with a decisive nod. She'd sounded a bit too much like an army officer, but Althea bobbed her head. Her pursed lips pointed down at the corners.

Vicky opened her mouth to placate her further, but Sarah poked her head through the doorway.

"Excuse me, Lady Dain, Lady Victoria, but Lord Halworth has arrived."

Tea had gone much better than Vicky had anticipated. She'd worried her parents might take Tom to task for what had happened all those years ago, but as her father was still recovering, he'd remained in his bedchamber, and her mother, though not precisely friendly, had been behaving herself admirably. Tom seemed to be in good humor as he regaled them with stories of Swiss customs, especially their affection for their cows.

Althea had even spoken up to ask Tom to describe the countryside. As Tom talked of the great snow-topped Alps that stretched into the sky and of waterfalls that trickled down their slopes to create cracks and crevices in their sides, Vicky wished she could have seen what he had.

"It must be a magical place," Vicky said with a sigh.

Tom took a bite of his cake. "I wouldn't say that, exactly."

"Why?" Althea asked.

Tom tilted his head. "Like anywhere else, there is poverty—although the poor there do not live in anything so vile as some of the conditions I've seen here in London."

Vicky's eyebrows shot upward. "Really? What have you s—"

"Where is Charles today, Lord Halworth?" Vicky's mother interrupted.

Vicky's gaze flew to her mother. She gave Vicky a pointed look.

Tom cleared his throat and took a gulp of his tea. Vicky rolled her eyes. Leave it to her mama to force conversation away from "unladylike" topics.

"He had an engagement, I'm afraid," Tom said. "He did send his compliments to you all." Tom cleared his throat again and caught Vicky's eye. With a barely perceptible snap, he tilted his head toward the door.

Vicky frowned. Did he want to leave?

"I had thought he might accompany me here," Tom went on, "but his schedule is a constant mystery. Sometimes he frequents the club, but like as not, he is somewhere *outside*." He emphasized the last word and made another motion with his head.

This time Vicky understood. She set her teacup and saucer on the table.

"Mama," she asked with a smile, "would you mind my showing Tom the garden? I don't believe he's ever seen it, and the sun has just come out." She nodded toward the window as proof.

Her mother glanced outside. "I don't see why not. Perhaps Althea would care for some sun as well."

All eyes slid to Althea, who shifted in her seat.

"Thank you, no," she said into her teacup.

Vicky could have kissed her.

Tom set down his plate of cake. Vicky stood and Tom did the same, murmuring his thanks to her mother. He gestured for Vicky to lead the way.

"Don't be gone long, Victoria," her mother said.

Vicky sighed inwardly. "Of course, Mama."

Her mother gave her a look that betrayed her unhappiness at the prospect of Vicky and Tom being alone together, but Vicky ignored her. They stepped out of the parlor into the hall, which led them out to a brick-lined pathway to the garden. Compared to the grounds at Oakbridge, the garden here was minute, but there was a multitiered ornamental fountain running across half its width, beds of roses on either side, and a lovely old bench in the very back corner shaded by a mature elder bush. Vicky took the left path around the roses.

Tom's footsteps thudded on the grass as he caught up to her.

Vicky glanced at him over her shoulder. "I'm sorry. Sometimes Mama can be a bit overbearing."

Tom shrugged, but a smile played upon his lips.

"I take it you wished to speak privately," she said, raising her brows.

He nodded. "I'm glad you understood. I'm not certain what I could've tried next, short of angering your mother further by asking to see the garden myself."

Vicky smiled. "That would have been amusing, at least." She skirted the rose bed until they reached the fountain.

Vicky looked at Tom, but he was gazing into the water.

"Truthfully, ever since that day I nearly carried you through the front door of Oakbridge, I've been waiting for her to scold me as though I were still a boy."

Vicky raised her brows. "Why?"

He threw her a sidelong glance. "For acting the way I did back then. For driving you away."

Vicky's head pivoted toward him slowly. Had he actually spoken those words? Her lips parted. "Why did you?" she asked quietly.

His brow creased as he stared into the water. "To protect you."

Her head gave a little shake. "Protect me? From whom?"

"From *him*," he murmured.

Vicky frowned. Whom could he mean? Then her mind flew back to that day at Halworth Hall and the way his father had knocked him to the ground. "Your father?"

He nodded. "He was—not a good man."

Vicky pressed her lips together. Of course, she'd known the Earl and Countess of Halworth did not have a happy marriage. Tom had never spoken of his father in a flattering light. When she was still a young girl, Vicky's own father had cautioned her to stay out of the earl's way when she visited Tom at the Hall. "But surely he would not have hurt me," she whispered.

Tom's gaze centered on the flow of the fountain. "I couldn't take that chance." He paused. "He never much cared whom he hurt."

Vicky heaved in a great breath. As she exhaled, the weight that had settled on her soul since the day Tom had stopped speaking to her seemed to ease. She hadn't done anything to make him hate her. In truth, he'd never hated her at all. She wanted nothing more than to take his hand in hers and squeeze it tight.

"Tom," she began with a shake of her head, "I never should have doubted—"

"No," Tom cut her off, turning toward her. "I don't blame you. I could not speak of it. It was too painful. I still cannot." He turned from the fountain and motioned to the bench at the end of the garden.

Vicky nodded, and they slowly continued on. She didn't know what to say. She was lucky in so many ways—in all the ways he was not. He deserved better.

"Althea seems improved in her spirits," Tom said.

Vicky made an affirmative noise. "Today is the first time I've seen her so well. I've tried to take your advice and be as patient as possible, but we had a row the other day. She's been so different lately."

"That's no surprise."

Vicky glanced up at him.

His jaw looked tight. "What she must have endured with Dain would change anyone."

Vicky frowned. "I'm ashamed to admit I still don't really understand."

His gaze cut sideways to meet hers. "The world is not the fairy tale you believe it to be. Though Oakbridge and your family were as close to perfect as I ever thought I'd know."

Vicky's lips parted. Was that why he'd always spent so much time with them?

"You and your family have caught a glimpse of what mine has suffered. All one can do is consign such things to the past and attempt to move on."

Vicky's chest tightened.

"Althea was fortunate to escape him when she did. Now she may have some chance of returning to her old self," Tom said.

Vicky swallowed to quell the burning in her throat. If only she knew what to say to help. But perhaps there was nothing she *could* say. And that in itself was a sobering thought.

They reached the bench beneath the elder bush, and Tom waited for Vicky to sit before lowering himself next to her. The sweet scent of cake and fresh roses wafted toward him and the effect was profound enough to make him sit a good half foot closer than he knew he should. Her head tilted up to look at him, a tentative smile upon her lips. Unnerved, he leaned back into the bench, feeling like a damn fool.

He should get to the point of his visit. "I saw you and Carmichael at the theater last night," he said, letting his gaze rest on a small daisy poking its head out of the grass.

Vicky's head swiveled toward him, but he refused to meet her eyes.

"Why didn't you say hello?"

He swallowed. "You were enjoying yourself. My presence would've spoiled Carmichael's manners."

She scoffed, and he threw her a knowing look.

"Did you ask about his dealings with Dain?"

She pursed her lips for a split second. "Apparently, my father told Mr. Carmichael about Althea's situation. I asked why he hesitated to remove Dain, and he said he was trying not to make a scene for my family's sake."

Tom shook his head. "That doesn't explain what he said to Dain at the musicale."

"He could have meant he didn't want Dain disturbing us because of Althea. And I don't believe he'd want Oakbridge. He's just purchased an abbey a half day's ride away."

Tom resisted the urge to make a face. Carmichael was no fool. Owning a house so close to Oakbridge could only make his pursuit of Victoria easier. "Another reason for you to marry him."

Vicky frowned. "I found his explanations perfectly satisfactory."

Tom angled toward her. "His explanations sound vague at best."

She lifted her chin. "He's not the only gentleman I know who does not relish explaining his actions."

He made an involuntary noise of protest, but said nothing. She had him there.

Her eyes softened. "Why must you find him so objectionable?"

He exhaled. "He and Dain are involved in *something*. I just don't know what."

"It could be anything under the sun, as far as you know.

Something not necessarily sinister," she said with a small smile and a tilt of her head.

He shook his head. They'd mentioned great stakes and not in the way one discussed games of chance or a day at the races. But there was no way to make her believe him. Carmichael was Vicky's best marital option, and she'd made up her mind to trust him.

"What did your father say about his business arrangement with Carmichael?"

She hesitated. "I haven't asked him yet. I was waiting until Papa was less out of sorts."

Tom thought it a rather important matter to not broach immediately, but he didn't think she'd take kindly to him belaboring the point. "I wrote to my mother about the Halworth land Dain was trying to buy. I haven't hired a new steward yet, but I hope she'll find someone qualified to assess the land's value while I remain here. You might have your father's steward do the same at Oakbridge—especially at the border of the two properties."

Vicky wet her lips. "I shall speak with Papa today. It would indeed be best to possess all the facts before I must...make a choice."

Tom let out a great breath and turned so he faced her fully. "Just please don't rush into anything. I don't want *you* to wake up and find yourself shackled to a man you don't know."

She dropped her gaze. "I have to marry someone."

He frowned. "I know." No one knew the anvil's weight of responsibility better than he. Marriage to Carmichael would mean saving her family and the home she cherished, a prominent position in society, wealth, a country house an easy distance to Oakbridge, and an honorable life. Yet if Carmichael and Dain had an arrangement concerning Oakbridge land as Tom suspected, her marriage would be for naught. And she would be trapped. No family's reputation could withstand two divorces, even if they could acquire them.

She stared out at the fountain. He dragged his eyes from the errant tendril of hair curling at the nape of her neck to the water sloshing down the stones in a calming rhythm.

He wished he could help her, but he simply didn't know anyone worthy of her. Perhaps Charles knew somebody, but from what he'd seen of Charles's friends, none of them would suit.

There had to be some solution, yet it evaded him.

He couldn't let her be bound to Carmichael. He refused! Even if he had to marry her himself.

Tom felt a wave of heat rush over him. As soon as the thought materialized, he shoved it down and away. It was a poisoned thought born of his complete lack of trust in Carmichael's intentions. Tom had nothing to offer Vicky—not money, not security, not even love—only a shared childhood and a useless title. It would be reckless. It would be the opposite of protecting her. It would be saddling her to a bloodline tainted by the basest traits and appetites—to someone wholly undeserving of her.

He sighed and rubbed his brow.

"I began reading *Pride and Prejudice*," he said to keep himself from continuing down that path.

Her face lit up. "Did you?"

He nodded. "Elizabeth Bennet. I see why you are so fond of her. She is charming."

Vicky's smile widened as she angled her torso toward him. "I'm so glad you think so. She is my particular favorite of Miss Austen's heroines."

He cast his gaze away from the green flecks in her eyes. "I cannot say I care much for this Mr. Darcy thus far," he confessed, thinking of what Susie had said about the character's resemblance to him.

Vicky hummed in her throat. "Mr. Carmichael told me he doesn't care for him either. I wonder if you will think alike when you've finished it."

Tom didn't much like the idea of agreeing with Carmichael on anything, but he held his tongue.

"I know you have a responsibility to your family," Tom said, "but you don't have to do anything yet. See if you meet someone at the next ball. I'll even assist you if I can." Assist in binding her to a stranger. This could not end well.

Vicky tilted her head. "That might be helpful, actually. You'd be something like a brother."

A brother? He supposed when they were children, he was the closest thing she'd had to a brother. But for some reason the idea rankled. He cleared his throat. "Yes. Something like that."

His stomach churned. No. This could not end well. Not well at all.

CHAPTER THE TWENTY-FIRST

*The power of doing any thing with quickness is always
much prized by the possessor, and often without any
attention to the imperfection of the performance.*
—Jane Austen, *Pride and Prejudice*

With a light heart, Vicky walked into the parlor with Tom at her heels. She stopped short as Mr. Carmichael rose from a chair opposite Althea. For a moment, she felt Tom's body close at her back. Her gaze flicked to Mr. Carmichael's face, and she immediately lost the reassuring feeling of Tom's presence as he stepped to her side. Carmichael had been smiling to greet her, but as he saw Tom, his features froze. He bowed formally.

"Victoria," her mother said from the armchair next to Mr. Carmichael, "look who's come to call."

Vicky curtsied. "Mr. Carmichael. What a pleasant surprise. I was just showing Lord Halworth the garden."

Tom nodded. He eyed Carmichael with a cold stare, but somehow managed to plaster a polite smile on his face. That was more than she could say for Mr. Carmichael, whose jaw looked etched in marble.

"Good day, Mr. Carmichael," Tom said.

"Lord Halworth," Carmichael replied shortly, as though he wished he could say nothing at all.

Vicky pressed her lips together. Tom was right. Carmichael's manners were nearly nonexistent in Tom's presence.

"The garden was charming, Lady Oakbridge," Tom said to her mother. "I have merely come in to take my leave and thank you for the tea."

"It was good of you to come, Lord Halworth," Vicky's mother said with a smile more polite than genuine.

"Do come again, Lord Halworth," Althea said from her chair, surprising Vicky.

Tom's mouth curved into one of his rare smiles. "Thank you, Lady Dain. I believe I shall." He bowed, gave Vicky another quick glance, and exited.

Vicky watched him go. She couldn't question his decision to leave after witnessing Mr. Carmichael's discourtesy. Conversation would've been awkward at best with both men in the room.

Vicky faced Mr. Carmichael. He'd been watching her with a furrowed brow.

She tilted her chin upward. She didn't care if he *was* angry. They were not tied to one another. Not yet. Her actions were none of his concern.

"And how are you today, Mr. Carmichael? No worse for wear after our foray last night?" she asked, giving him a direct look.

His face relaxed a fraction. "How could I be after having the pleasure of your company?"

That was a pretty compliment and he knew it. Not that she

was immune to it—she'd had a lovely time with him. Tom's worries aside, that was the plain truth of the matter. She smiled, and he smiled back.

"Perhaps, if Lady Oakbridge doesn't object, you might show me the garden as well. I don't recall ever having seen it."

"Oh," Vicky said, surprised, "of course." She glanced at her mother.

Her mother practically shooed them out the door.

Once outside, Vicky led Mr. Carmichael to the fountain and gestured expansively at the rippling water. "Well?"

"Cleverly designed. It's reminiscent of the one at Chatsworth, albeit on a much smaller scale."

Vicky tilted her head. "Then you're acquainted with the bachelor duke?"

The Duke of Devonshire was one of the most powerful peers in England, and very possibly *the* wealthiest. Vicky had seen him at various occasions last season, but he was too old for her taste. He had to be nearing thirty and still seemed disinclined to marry, which had earned him his alias—much to every society mama's chagrin.

Carmichael nodded. "Mildly acquainted. I was only invited to Chatsworth once."

"That's once more than I. Why only the one time?"

"It's rather indelicate."

She looked up at him with a disbelieving glare.

His lips twitched. "But you are no shrinking violet, I believe."

She nodded.

"One of the other guests may have mentioned something about

my fortune rivaling the duke's. So far as I know, neither I nor that person have been asked to return," he finished with an embarrassed laugh.

Vicky shook her head. "So silly are the ways of men. You all pretend to be so civilized, yet you take offense at the slightest ill word and then take violent action. Like your boxing match. In the end, you can hardly call yourselves superior to women. Indeed, you are far worse."

He snorted and turned to look at her. "Is that so?"

She raised her chin and met his gaze. "Yes. Because of your violent impulses. Beyond that, we are the same."

"I have known women to have violent impulses."

She frowned. "Have you?"

He nodded. "And history is riddled with examples. Cleopatra tried to murder her brother, Eleanor of Aquitaine her husband and son, and the Tudor Queen Mary killed hundreds."

"You're right." She bit her lip and saw his gaze slide to her mouth. "Then I suppose we are no different after all."

He took a step closer. She had to tilt her neck back to meet his eyes. The sunlight warmed them further. "In many ways we are practically the same person."

Her brow furrowed. What did that mean? He'd somehow moved even closer, and now towered over her by so much that she had to drop her chin, which meant she was staring into his white cravat.

"We're both clever . . ." He took her hand in his and she looked down at his ungloved palm cradling her small hand in his larger one.

"We're both perceptive . . ." He rested his free hand on top of the one he had captured. His strong fingers warmed her cool hand. "And we both know what we want in life." He punctuated the last word by squeezing her hand.

She tilted her neck back to see his face. "I don't know that I *do* know what I want."

She knew what her parents expected of her, however, and he was right before her, smiling in a most beguiling way.

He took his top hand from hers and touched her chin gently. "Perhaps I can help with that." His dark eyes fixed her to the spot as he bent and brushed his lips against hers. The softness of them surprised her, and she stiffened for a moment, realizing she had no idea what to do. He smelled of sandalwood and the strawberry tarts Cook had sent in with tea. It was not at all bad, really, for such a little kiss, and when he raised his head, she must have looked more pleased than she felt because his lips quirked up at one side.

A moment later, his hand moved to her waist while the other remained under her chin as he pulled her close and lowered his head once more.

This time when their lips connected, Vicky closed her eyes to be spared the strangeness of looking at his features so closely. His lips slanted against hers and her mind grew cloudy. The fingers cupping her chin slid up and caressed her cheek. She could melt into him if she let herself.

When he pulled back, his chest rose and fell roughly. She drew in a deep breath, and stared at his cravat. She couldn't bring herself to meet his gaze. Her first kiss. It had been pleasant. She'd even like to try it again, but it hadn't helped make up her mind.

Did she want Carmichael? Forever?

His thumb brushed her cheek and she tilted her gaze up to see his expression. He was smiling down at her with the first real tenderness she'd seen from him. He'd looked at her with humor and with friendship in his eyes, but never with tenderness. She felt her jaw slacken and her eyes grow wide.

"Victoria," he said quietly, "will you marry me?"

Her lips parted and she let out a tiny, breathy, "Oh!"

"I know it seems sudden," he said with a lopsided grin, "but after last night I had nearly made up my mind." She must have frowned because he said, "You must admit we get on well together." He paused and searched her eyes for an answer.

"Yes. Of course we do," she said.

"Few ladies of my acquaintance have ever made me laugh. Let alone in public."

She smiled at that, and he enclosed her hand in both of his.

"I'll safeguard you. And your family." He squeezed her hand.

Her family. This was the moment they'd worked for. Mr. Carmichael wanted to marry her. If she said yes, Oakbridge would be safe from Dain. She would be the future mistress of her childhood home. She would have the resources to help her sister—perhaps even be able to provide her a property of her own. All she had to do was say yes.

Yet was *this* the way she should feel? It certainly wasn't how she'd felt when Elizabeth Bennet and Mr. Darcy finally expressed their feelings—or the happiness she'd experienced when Edward

Ferrars finally told Elinor Dashwood they were free to be together.

The memory of Tom's pleas for her to wait until the next ball flashed through her mind. She'd all but promised him not to do anything in haste. The "yes" Mr. Carmichael wanted stuck in her throat. She didn't owe it to Tom to wait—after all, it wasn't as though he knew any real alternatives—but perhaps, just possibly, she owed it to herself.

She didn't think she was in love with Mr. Carmichael. She did *like* him—very much. She even liked the way he'd kissed her, but was she completely convinced she wanted to marry him? No. Not yet. How could she tell him that?

She licked her lips, which only reminded her of their kiss, so she took a deep breath. Raising her free hand, she rested it on top of his. "Would you . . ." She peered up at him through her eyelashes. "Would you give me a few days to contemplate your lovely proposal?"

His smile faded. Two lines materialized between his brows. She bit her lower lip, silently pleading with him not to be angry.

"Of course." His tone was guarded.

"I just"—she paused and tried to formulate the right words—"I have to think on a few matters." She pressed his hand.

His jaw shifted. "Would any of those 'matters' have to do with Lord Halworth?"

She relaxed the pressure on his hand, and his arms dropped to his sides. She frowned. "Why do you dislike him so?" She lifted her chin to stare him in the eye.

"Why do you *like* him so?" he shot back, his voice rising in volume.

"He is my friend," she said, matching his loudness.

"Friend, indeed," he repeated, shaking his head.

"Yes. He has been for a very long time—longer than I've known you."

He scowled at that. "People change."

"Of course they do. I'll fully acknowledge Tom has changed. And *I* have changed. But that still does not explain why *you* have any reason to dislike him."

He shook his head at her and turned, pacing away from the fountain, only to wheel around and stride back. "Your father told me what happened at Oakbridge with the bandit."

Vicky gave a little shrug. "Yes?"

"Did it not seem peculiar that Halworth appeared *just in time* to see it happen and then managed to lose the scoundrel?"

"That was my fault. I got in the way—"

"Then," he interrupted, "he made another miraculous appearance just as Silby's horses ran away with you. And if I'm not mistaken, he failed to help you on that occasion as well." He raised his brows on the last word, daring her to argue.

"I jumped from the curricle. He couldn't have prevented it."

"You shouldn't have felt the need to jump. If he knew what he was doing, you wouldn't have had to."

Vicky furrowed her brow. "So you object to the way he tried, yet failed, to help me? Or are you accusing him of something else?"

For a moment he made no answer. "Do you recall the day we went to Gunter's? The man you saw lurking in the alley? What was his height and build? Could it possibly have been Halworth?"

Vicky's mouth dropped open. "Mr. Carmichael! That is preposterous. That man had black hair. And, why would Tom watch us from an alley in such a manner?"

"Halworth was watching us last night at the theater. I saw him during the intermission."

"Apparently, he didn't greet us because he didn't want to put you in an ill humor," she said with a sniff.

Carmichael rolled his eyes. "Such considerations have not bothered him thus far."

Vicky glowered at him. "I really don't think you're being fair—"

"All I know is that his finances are not what they should be. From what I understand, the late earl put the Halworth estate deeply into debt. Meanwhile, Halworth and his brother are here in London taking part in the season. A season that just happens to be Lord Halworth's first time ever making appearances in society. From what I've observed, he pays no lady any special attention except for you." He paused, and Vicky held her breath. "There could be no better way out of his considerable financial difficulty than to marry you: the girl he grew up knowing, whose estate abuts his own, and who just so happens to have a considerable dowry."

Vicky felt the color drain from her cheeks. The old earl had been a profligate spender—that was common knowledge. Tom could easily have financial troubles. That would certainly explain his wardrobe, which was, she now realized, just the tiniest bit shabby. His coat today had been fraying at one elbow, but she'd assumed he had an unobservant valet.

But Carmichael couldn't be correct in his thinking. Tom had

no wish to marry *her*. He'd made that abundantly clear today when he'd offered to help find her a husband. Specifically a husband other than Mr. Carmichael.

"But he doesn't want me," she said to fill the growing silence.

Carmichael gave her a penetrating look.

"He's all but said so," she said, but it sounded silly even to her.

Carmichael shook his head. "His presence at the aforementioned events and his subsequent actions strike me as highly suspicious. It's clear to me, at least, that he wants your dowry for his own and he's willing to do a great deal to get it."

Vicky narrowed her gaze. "That's ridiculous, Mr. Carmichael. Tom is incapable of such scheming."

"We shall see."

She exhaled and turned her gaze to the sky. Both Carmichael and Tom were being utterly absurd. Tom doubted Carmichael's loyalty and Carmichael doubted Tom's goodness. Yet even as she repeated to herself how silly both men were being, a pinprick of doubt slipped past her defenses. Tom's presence that day at Oakbridge and in Hyde Park had been dreadfully coincidental.

"I shall leave you," Carmichael said, interrupting her whirling thoughts. "Just know that *I* know you for the kind, generous person you are. The lady I wish to marry. I would hate to see you bound to a man who wanted only your money. You are worth far more than that." He took her hand and kissed it.

Vicky's chest swelled at his sweet words, and she couldn't help a small smile from escaping. He released her hand with a smile of his own. As she watched him nod and stride from the garden—a tall, broad-shouldered man who wished to marry her—she wondered how a girl could possibly feel so confused.

When Vicky reentered the drawing room, her father was reclining on the sofa next to her sister.

"What are you doing out of bed, Papa?" she asked with a frown.

"I am well enough to sit down here," he replied. "I saw Mr. Carmichael take his leave. What did you say to him?"

Vicky took a deep breath. "I told him I needed time to consider his proposal."

"So he proposed!" her mother said at the exact moment her father said, "Time?"

Vicky favored both her parents with her most determined gaze. She nodded.

Her father spoke first. "What is there to consider? Carmichael is prosperous, handsome, influential; you seem to like him well enough. He would make a fine husband, especially considering the situation," he said with a look in Althea's direction.

Vicky threw a glance at Althea. Her complexion was paler than a blanched almond. Vicky shook her head, annoyed at her father's inattention to her sister's feelings, and indeed, her own. It seemed his injuries were bringing his practicality to the fore.

"Have you set your sights on another gentleman who could be brought to the question?" her mother asked.

Vicky hesitated, her mind flitting to her outings with some of the most trying men in England, and then to Tom and his promises to help her. "Not as such."

Her father uttered an exasperated sigh. He put one hand on the sofa cushion as though he planned to jump up and pace across the room, but then he clutched his side and slowly sat back. After taking a number of shallow breaths and adjusting his legs into a different position, he said, "Unfortunately, time is now of the essence. Before he joined you here, Mr. Carmichael apprised me of some distressing news. The day after we encountered those men"—he gestured to his wounds—"I asked Mr. Carmichael to do something for me. I'd not heard from Mr. Barnes for some time, so I asked Carmichael to find him and discover if there'd been any development in the proceedings for Althea's separation." He readjusted his left leg again. "It seems Mr. Barnes is missing."

Vicky frowned and looked at Althea, whose head had flown upward. Of course, Vicky had already been aware of Mr. Carmichael's errand, but this news came as a surprise.

"What do you mean 'missing,' James?" Vicky's mother asked.

"Carmichael did not find him at his offices, nor at his home. His family also seemed unaware of his whereabouts. Carmichael then went to the Court of Chancery and learned the papers for the writ of *supplicavit* had also gone missing. They were received, but they'd been taken from the clerk's office."

"How is that possible?" Vicky asked. She peered at Althea. She was looking more ghostlike by the second.

"It seems someone within the court must have acted to remove them," her father said.

"Dain," Althea stated.

"Has he influence over someone there?" Vicky asked.

"It wouldn't be difficult to obtain. Some men have no scruples when it comes to money," her father said.

Her mother nodded in agreement.

Vicky inhaled, remembering Mr. Carmichael had said he had a friend at the Court of Chancery. Her mind flew wildly to Tom's theory about Mr. Carmichael's intentions. What if Carmichael *was* behind the papers going missing? And could he also be responsible for Mr. Barnes's disappearance? Vicky shook her head, trying to rid it of such thoughts. Why would he do such a thing when he could marry her without stooping to nefarious schemes? Still, Tom's suspicions, her feelings, the truth—they all whirled about her, clouding her judgment to such a degree that she knew not how to proceed.

"What about the measures in the ecclesiastical court?" Vicky asked.

"The proctor has been in contact with me, and he shall be registering the citation to summon Dain to the court in the next few days," her father said.

Vicky smiled at Althea. At least that was good news. The writ of *supplicavit* would only protect her for a year, after all, whereas if the ecclesiastical court granted Althea's separation, it would be permanent.

"However, there have been other incidents at Oakbridge, similar to the one you encountered," her father continued.

Vicky started. "What kinds of incidents?"

"The tenants have reported strange men on the estate. The bridge to the village is on the verge of collapse, despite the extensive repairs we did last year, and one of our prized Thoroughbreds took ill and may not recover. I had a letter from the steward today."

Vicky grew cold. Sabotage! Who would do such things? Now she regretted more than ever getting in the way of Tom catching that ruffian. He could have led them to whoever was behind all this. "What do you think is happening, Papa?"

He raised his brows. "Dain seems the most likely candidate, but I don't know why he would bother. I'll tell the steward to take further precautions, but there is no way to watch every acre of the estate every hour of the day."

Vicky bit the inside of her cheek. "Tom overheard Mr. Carmichael and Dain talking at the musicale." She shot a glance at Althea.

Her sister nodded for her to continue.

"He heard them say something was at stake. And Mr. Carmichael said something about Dain not upsetting us."

Her father frowned.

"Dain offered to buy portions of Halworth land from Tom. Tom refused, but he's having the land evaluated to see why Dain would want it. Tom thinks Mr. Carmichael and Dain may have an agreement to gain control of Oakbridge or the land bordering the estates."

"Ridiculous," her father stated. "That land is primarily fields and trees—on its own it hasn't any extraordinary value. And Carmichael has no need of Oakbridge. Nor does Dain, for that matter."

"Perhaps," Vicky said doubtfully, "but it does seem awfully coincidental that I came across that bandit on the border of the estates." Then she remembered how Mr. Carmichael had tried to keep Dain from her at the ball. "Mr. Carmichael and Dain did speak of 'business' at the duchess's ball. Do you know what they could have meant, Papa?"

He frowned again and shook his head.

Vicky decided to appeal to his pragmatism. "I do believe it would be prudent to have the steward inspect our side of the border between Halworth and Oakbridge, even if it only yields us some peace of mind."

Her father seemed to consider it. "I shall include it in my letter to him this evening."

Vicky smiled. "Thank you, Papa. I'm starting to believe all these accidents befalling us aren't accidents at all."

"What can you mean, Victoria?" her mother asked.

She caught her mother's eye. "I think Mr. Silby's curricle was tampered with before our drive, and as much as it pains me, Mr. Carmichael could have gained access to it."

Her mother gaped. "Victoria, how can you—"

"Mama, I do like Mr. Carmichael. But . . ." She exhaled. Wasn't it reasonable to want to be sure of his innocence before agreeing to marry him? She turned to her father. "May I ask what will happen to the land you and he bought by the canal if something should happen to you?"

"Your mother would inherit my half, including any revenues, in perpetuity," he answered with a level gaze.

Vicky let out a relieved breath. At least now she knew Mr. Carmichael wouldn't benefit in that way from her father's death. "I'm glad."

Her father and mother exchanged a glance. "Vicky," her father began, "you cannot let Tom's imagination get the better of you. He may have motives of his own."

"What do you mean, Papa?"

"He's not the same boy who left. And his estate is in ruin."

Vicky's brows knit.

"You cannot put your faith in every word he says," her mother added.

Vicky frowned. "Will you at least ask Mr. Carmichael what his business is with Dain?"

"As you're bound to see him before I do, you may ask him yourself," her father said. "But I shall make more . . . *indirect* inquiries."

Vicky nodded.

"My dear," her mother said, "we shall do what we can, but you must make a decision soon."

Vicky glanced at Althea. Her eyes were sad, but she met Vicky's gaze with a surprisingly encouraging expression. "I understand."

Despite herself, she couldn't stop a shiver from running down her spine.

Vicky left the parlor, anxious to escape her parents' uneasy glances. She needed to be alone so she could digest the events of the day in a rational manner.

As Vicky reached the foot of the stairs, Althea called her name. Vicky turned and waited for her sister to catch up before she started climbing. "I'm sorry about the papers, Thea, but you must not give up hope."

Althea shrugged. "He may never let me go."

"He will have no choice if the ecclesiastical court says he must. You'll see. Papa will not rest until you are free of him."

At her sister's resigned look, Vicky forgot her own troubles. She linked her arm around Althea's elbow.

"And nor will I for that matter. I can marry Mr. Carmichael and persuade him to use his enormous fortune to buy the favor of every ecclesiastical and Chancery judge."

Althea turned her head and gave Vicky a pointed stare. Such a breach of morality clearly didn't sit well with her.

"If there were no other options," Vicky mumbled.

"And if there *are* no options other than Mr. Carmichael?" Althea asked.

Vicky shrugged as though the question had not been the very one plaguing her. "As Mama and Papa say, he's a fine man."

"He is, indeed."

Vicky nodded.

"But is he the man you want?"

Vicky stopped in midstep. She turned and eyed her sister warily. Althea looked sincere—like her confidant again.

Vicky exhaled. She recalled how Tom had shared so many of his private thoughts with her today—how he'd offered to help her find a husband just as a true friend would. Then her mind strayed to Mr. Carmichael and the way he'd kissed her and looked at her with such tenderness. He seemed to truly care for her. But he didn't *love* her. At least he'd *said* nothing of love.

"I don't know."

Althea's brown eyes bored into hers. "Then you must follow your instincts. Regardless of the consequences. Or rather," she amended, "you must accept there may be consequences to your decision."

Vicky hesitated. "But you—"

"There were signs early on—even during our courtship, but I believe I chose to ignore them. To ignore my instincts." She turned her head away as she spoke, resuming the climb.

Vicky followed in mute astonishment until they reached the top of the stairs. "What signs were there, Thea?"

Althea shook her head. "They are irrelevant now."

"No, please," Vicky said, thinking of Tom's theory.

Althea sighed. "He always wanted to know where I'd be on a given day and would be jealous of any man he thought was enamored of me. It began as telling me their faults, but eventually, I believe he warned them off or threatened them. Of course, I only learned such things after we married."

Vicky's heart thundered in her chest. Mr. Carmichael had told her of Mr. Silby's faults before her outing with him—of course, he'd been completely correct in that respect. Yet, today he'd done the same regarding Tom. Then there was his lack of candor, which still concerned her. "Did he . . . keep things from you?"

Althea nodded. "He spoke in half-truths, and in this way I rarely knew reality from what he'd fabricated." She opened her mouth as though she would say more, but quickly closed it. Then she pivoted and headed down the hall to her bedroom.

Vicky followed. "Thea, why tell me this now?"

Her sister turned, her hand on the knob to her room. "I wrote Poole."

Vicky nodded for her to continue.

"He confirmed he put your letters to me in the post regularly. Dain must have . . ." Althea turned away, tears glistening in the corners of her eyes.

Vicky put her hand on Althea's arm, twisting her around so she could pull her into a tight embrace. Althea rested her head on Vicky's shoulder.

"I've been a fool." Althea's voice trembled. "How could I have thought such things of you?"

Vicky shook her head. Dain had made Althea so mistrustful. "We *will* bring things to right. I wish with all my heart I could have spared you everything."

Althea sobbed once into Vicky's shoulder. "And I you this marriage business. But certainly, you will choose more wisely than I did."

Vicky rubbed her sister's back. The doubts Vicky had banished about Carmichael were returning. "Do you think Mama and Papa are correct about Tom?"

Althea wiped her eyes. "I don't know. Perhaps they still harbor ill feelings toward him because of how he treated you before he left."

"Thea, he explained it all today. He apologized."

Althea raised her brows.

"Tom's father was a monster not unlike Dain. Tom thought the earl would harm me if I kept returning to Halworth. The last day I went there and saw Tom, his father struck him so hard it knocked him to the floor. The earl laughed it away—blamed Tom. I didn't know what to think. But I don't think Tom was at fault."

Althea shook her head. "Nor I."

Vicky grimaced. "What should I do, Thea?"

Althea looked at Vicky through puffy, red eyes. "You must not marry a man you cannot trust."

"But how can I know whom to trust?"

Althea exhaled. "I cannot say. And I'm sorry. You deserve better than a rushed courtship of necessity."

Vicky smiled. "Thank you. But I also must find a husband for Oakbridge's sake."

Althea's face fell.

For the first time, Vicky thought to ask her, "Did *you* wish to be mistress of Oakbridge? To have the title and control the estate?"

Althea raised her chin. "Of course. It is our home. But you shall run the estate far better than I could have. Drainage and crop yields hold little interest for me."

Vicky sighed. "So you won't despise me for inheriting it?"

Althea eyed her. "How could I? Oh, Vicky, your life is still ahead of you."

"Yours is too, Thea."

Althea worried her lip. "What did Tom say in the garden?"

Vicky told her how Tom had asked her to wait until the next ball before making any decisions—how he'd help however he could.

Althea raised her brows, then nodded. "Very considerate of him. I agree. We shall both help you. That will give you time to think on your feelings for Mr. Carmichael, and perhaps we can introduce you to someone new."

Vicky's heart lightened. With both Tom and Althea helping her, she'd have a much better chance. Of course, the odds of someone she'd never met being a better prospect than Mr. Carmichael were slim at best, but that was not the point. She pulled her sister into a hug. Tom had been right. Her patience had paid off. Her sister was recovering, she and Tom were friends again, and Mr. Carmichael wanted to marry her. The world looked bright once more. Perhaps everything would end like one of Miss Austen's novels after all. Vicky held in a breath as she smiled into Althea's hair.

CHAPTER THE TWENTY-SECOND

*To be fond of dancing was a certain step
towards falling in love . . .*
—Jane Austen, *Pride and Prejudice*

Tom strode into Lord and Lady Branbury's ballroom with a spring in his step. He was still walking on air from his successful meeting with his new financiers. Lord Axley and his business partners, Mr. Parker and Mr. Risdale, had signed the preliminary contracts today, and tomorrow, Tom would start proceedings to buy the parcel of land he'd found just outside of Mayfair. The site of London's soon-to-be first luxury hotel. Tom grinned, causing a group of debutantes standing in a semicircle to giggle behind their fluttering fans. Even they didn't bother him. Everything he'd planned was finally coming together. Now he could spend the evening helping Victoria.

Tom scanned the room.

Unlike the themed decor at the Duchess of Rutherfurd's ball, the Branburys had bedecked the room in a decidedly more traditional style. Large golden candelabrums and hundreds of beeswax tapers illuminated it from all sides, producing a soft flickering light. Chairs positioned along the walls provided seating for weary dancers and gossiping matrons. But he didn't see Vicky or her family.

Registering his strange disappointment, Tom walked to the refreshment table, hoping to see someone he'd met at the Rutherfurd ball. As he skirted the edge of the dance floor, he spotted Mr. Silby. Tom winced. Silby also moved toward the refreshments. Before Tom could turn to avoid him, Silby made eye contact. Tom nodded to be polite and tried to continue past him, but Silby closed the distance between them, effectively stopping Tom in his tracks.

"Lord Halworth," Silby said.

"Mr. Silby."

Tom felt it only proper that Silby continue, but the fool simply stared at him. Tom wondered if he could step around him and move away. But then, the man clearly had something to say. Better to get it over with. Tom stared back and, at length, Silby spoke.

"I never had the chance to thank you for the other day."

Tom nodded, though he didn't believe him sincere. "It was no trouble. I couldn't stand idly by."

"Nonetheless, I don't know what I'd have done if I'd lost one of my grays. Lady Victoria was quite correct—I would have to go to considerable trouble to replace them."

Tom frowned. "That would've been a tragic loss. Made more so by the potential damage to the lady *inside* the curricle," Tom countered.

Silby didn't speak for another moment. "Oh yes. How fortunate you were there to help her."

Tom clenched his jaw. What was wrong with the fellow? Was he feebleminded or just tactless? Tom inhaled. Perhaps both.

"If you'll excuse me." Tom inclined his head and turned before the man could utter another word.

Finally achieving his goal to reach the refreshment table, Tom picked up a glass of champagne and glanced around the room looking for someone to talk to. As his gaze alighted near the entry, he saw Vicky standing behind Althea and their mother. The earl must still be recovering from his injuries.

With grace Tom hadn't realized she'd possessed, Vicky glided into the room in a light blue gown accented with white lace. Her chestnut-and-copper tresses sat aloft in an intricate style, and the few curls framing the sides of her face emphasized her high, delicate cheekbones. A tentative smile played upon her lips.

Tom blinked, realizing he'd been holding his glass of champagne halfway between his chest and his mouth. He lowered his arm and watched Vicky step farther into the ballroom.

The countess moved to greet people. But Althea held back and waited until Vicky stood beside her. Althea wore a deep red gown, looking considerably better than she had recently, but anyone who'd noted the Astons' appearance would be unable to keep from admiring Victoria first and foremost.

Tom grabbed two more flutes and moved along the edge of the ballroom toward Vicky and Althea. He wound his way through families and groups of gentlemen until he finally came within ten feet of them.

Vicky looked as though she were scanning the ballroom. He

took another step toward her, and their eyes met. They smiled in unison, and he moved closer.

"Lady Dain, Lady Victoria," he said, handing the women their glasses. "You both look stunning this evening."

Althea nodded at the compliment and smiled, but he was almost sure Vicky's cheeks turned a shade pinker. "Thank you, Lord Halworth," Althea said. "You're looking well."

"Thank you. I feel well," he said, realizing for the first time in a long while that he did. He scanned the room behind them. "No guards tonight?"

"We didn't know how to explain their presence in the ballroom," Vicky said. "But they came with us in the coach."

Glad to hear it, Tom nodded. "What's on the agenda for this evening?"

Vicky looked at Althea. "Well, I believe dancing was mentioned—and meeting new people. As my acting brother for this evening, you promised some assistance on that front," she said with a smile.

She was absolutely correct, but at the word "brother," a sinking feeling washed over him.

"Of course." He paused, thinking with some apprehension he had no more acquaintances today than he did yesterday. Unless he included Lord Axley's business partners—or rather, *his* new business partners—but he believed Mr. Parker and Mr. Risdale were married. Nor did he know if they'd be in attendance.

"Are you quite well, Tom?" Vicky asked, peering at him.

He nodded and tried not to look at the way the candlelight

danced over the copper strands of her hair. "I was thinking the only gentleman I've seen tonight whom I actually know is Mr. Silby."

Althea made a strangled sound in her throat.

Vicky rolled her eyes. "There's no escaping him!"

Tom laughed. He looked to Althea. "Do you see anyone *worthwhile* whom Vicky could meet?"

Althea surveyed the room. She frowned. "I'm afraid not."

"Hmmm . . . ," Vicky said. "What about that man talking with Helen Chadwick?"

Tom turned and saw the oldest Chadwick girl standing with a tall, blond-headed gentleman next to a potted tree. The fellow looked ordinary enough, but still Tom heard himself say, "Him?" before he could stop himself.

Vicky gave him an imperious look as Althea said, "George Harcourt. He's an anti-abolitionist whose family still owns a plantation in the West Indies."

Vicky's face fell.

Tom angled his head to look sympathetic, but felt peculiarly satisfied that his first impression had been correct. "How unfortunate."

Vicky's eyes narrowed. "Is this your idea of being helpful?"

"If it is, I am clearly failing."

"What do you propose to *do*, then?" she asked with a mock glare.

Tom spotted a lanky man standing across the room. "What of that fellow pulling out his snuff box? He looks somewhat familiar."

Vicky's eyes widened. "Where?"

He gestured toward the man. Vicky and Althea saw him just as he sniffed the tobacco up his nose.

Vicky made a face and angled her stance so she faced away from the man. "Lord, I hope he doesn't ask me for a dance."

"Who is he?" Tom asked.

"Arthur Fothergill," Althea said. "He came to Oakbridge when we were children."

"The Viscount Lindsley's son?" The pale, lanky fellow wiping his nose had certainly changed from the short, ruddy-faced boy he recalled. "Why don't you wish to dance with him?" he asked Vicky.

"She had an unhappy outing with him at the British Museum," Althea supplied.

"He's a boor, and he nearly spilled snuff on me twice," Vicky said, keeping herself angled away from Fothergill.

Tom moved so they needn't speak so awkwardly, and Althea followed. "More boorish than Silby?"

"No one's as boorish as Mr. Silby," Vicky whispered with a hint of a smile. "But Mr. Fothergill runs a close second."

Tom caught himself grinning at her, but looked away as musicians struck the first chords of the opening dance from a balcony above them.

Tom glanced back at her. "As they are both here this evening, the least I can do is ask you to dance before they claim the honor. It may even help our cause, as nothing intrigues men more than a lady in demand."

He placed his half-empty champagne glass on a tray one of the footmen was carrying; Vicky did the same. He offered Vicky his arm. "Do you mind, Lady Dain?"

Althea shook her head. "Of course not. I shall keep a wary eye out for potential suitors as you dance. Enjoy yourselves."

"Mama is just over there, Thea," Vicky said, pointing to the left side of the room. Clearly, she worried about leaving her sister alone.

"Shall we escort you—" he began.

"No, no. I'll be fine," Althea said. She walked toward Lady Oakbridge with a small wave in their direction.

Vicky took his arm, and they started toward the dance floor.

"Oh, bother," she said, stopping him midstride.

"What is it?" he asked with some alarm.

"I was hoping it would be a waltz," she confided as they reached the other couples.

"I see." It was not a sentiment he shared. "But then we would both be disappointed."

She looked up at him questioningly.

"I do not know the waltz."

She blinked. "What do you mean you don't know the waltz?"

"In the Swiss Confederation, it was banned for its lewdness. The first time I witnessed it was at the Duchess of Rutherfurd's ball."

"Oh," Vicky said as he placed her across from him in the line of couples. "Then you must learn."

He raised his brows.

"No acting brother of mine would be so woefully uneducated," she said with a nod. She jested, of course, but the comment irked him.

The gentleman in the couple to his right gave him a brief glance, then must have shared a look with his partner, for Tom caught her giving him an odd look a moment later. He inclined his head to the lady, a young, thin blonde with ringlets who looked as though she had more beauty than sense. She glanced away quickly.

Annoyed, he bowed to Victoria as the minuet dictated and took her gloved hand. The first steps of the dance brought them closer together, still holding hands. As quietly as possible, he said, "You may care to refrain from calling me 'brother' if you wish our little ruse to work."

Her brows knit as they stepped apart.

When they stepped together again, she whispered, "What ruse?"

They turned sideways and he mouthed, "That you are so in demand."

She half turned toward him even though she was supposed to remain facing forward as they danced down the line of couples. "Pardon?"

He tried not to raise his voice to meet hers. "You heard."

They parted and danced around the left-hand couple only to meet again in the middle.

"It just so happens, Lord Halworth," she said, emphasizing the formality of address, "I am not so unwanted as you think me."

He frowned at her tone.

"I'll have you know Mr. Carmichael has asked for my hand," she said loud enough for the couples next to them to hear.

Tom's gut clenched at the words even as the other couples cast interested gazes at them. He stammered out a few strangled syllables before he caught himself, regained his composure, and said stupidly, "In marriage?"

She nodded. She was guarding her expression; he couldn't read her at all.

"And what was your reply?" he whispered.

"I told him I'd have to consider it," she admitted, again perfectly audible.

He didn't know what he'd expected. Carmichael's actions had made his intentions clear. But blast it all, Vicky could *not* marry him! They parted again and danced in mirrored circles.

"But what of his strange behavior?" he asked when they were face-to-face.

"That is part of the reason why I said I had to think about it," she said.

His mind rushed back to their conversation the other day. "You said you would wait before making any decisions about Carmichael."

"And I have waited," she said, looking him in the eye.

He swallowed. The image of her smiling up at Carmichael as they strolled through the theater arm in arm the other night flashed through his mind, and he felt ill. He held his breath for a moment, then tried to inhale deeply.

She looked up at him. Her hazel eyes locked with his. "I must find someone else tonight or not at all." This time, she *did* bother to whisper.

There was some emotion etched on her face, but Tom couldn't identify it.

He breathed gravely. "What—what if he tried to murder your father?" he asked, looking around to make sure no one overheard as the music swelled and they stepped around each other to trade places.

She shook her head. "I cannot believe that of him. Besides, my mother would inherit my father's portion of the partnership—Mr. Carmichael wouldn't benefit."

Mercifully, the dance ended and Tom hid his annoyance with a bow. How could she even think of shackling herself to that . . . *clod*? Even if he wouldn't benefit financially from the earl's death, he could still be using all the so-called accidents to persuade Vicky to marry him quickly. Tom still had yet to hear if his mother had found someone to appraise the land Dain had wanted—which meant they wouldn't know its value until after Vicky had made a decision.

Damn it all, how was Tom going to find her someone other than Carmichael in one night? He didn't know any more gentlemen now than he did earlier.

He offered her his arm and felt her small hand rest lightly on his coat. Contentment—so utterly foreign a feeling—washed over him. The sensation came upon him so suddenly, he looked down at her in surprise, and the smile she smiled as she caught his eye nearly undid him with its brilliance. He could see why Carmichael wanted her. She was guileless and kind, beautiful and courageous. He couldn't fault Carmichael his taste in this instance. Victoria would be a credit to any husband. In fact, he could hardly believe she had no other marital prospects. Were the gentlemen of London complete fools?

He grimaced. For the most part, they seemed to be just that. Which left her to Carmichael. Tom would simply have to accept it. Yet the very thought caused bile to rise in his throat.

He led her to the side of the ballroom as slowly as he could. One option remained, and amazingly, the thought of it didn't leave him cold. Only slightly queasy.

They reached the edge of the ballroom, and he turned her to face him.

She released his arm. Her eyes widened slightly, but one corner of her mouth curved upward. "Are you quite well?"

He nodded. He swallowed. Perhaps he'd lost his wits for the evening, or perhaps the satisfaction of finally accomplishing something was making him think things he wouldn't otherwise, but it didn't matter. He had to say something to stop her from making an abominable mistake. "What if I had found someone else for you? To marry," he finished as though the thought needed clarification.

Her eyebrows flew up. "Have you? Is he here?" She tried to peer around him.

He paused. He cleared his throat. "What if . . ." He exhaled. "What if it were me?"

Her eyes darted to his. Her mouth opened and closed. Then she said quietly, "*Is it* you?"

He stared down at her. Was she giving him a way out? Or did she not believe him to be serious? He'd rather see her married to nearly anyone but Carmichael. And who better than *he*, who knew her and actually cared for her well-being.

He nodded solemnly. "Marry me?"

Her eyes searched his. "Are you . . . certain you wish me to?"

"I don't want to see you make a mistake. He's not the man for you."

She frowned. For a moment she said nothing. Then she spoke softly. "But, do you care for me?"

He looked into Victoria's eyes. The green flecks within them seemed to gleam with the fire of rare emeralds. The urge to take her hand or to brush his thumb over the smooth curve of her cheek yanked at him, but propriety forced him to do neither. "Vicky, you must *know* I do."

"Perhaps you more than care?" she almost whispered.

The hope in her voice caused a startling pang in his chest. Then a moment later, it left him numb. She wanted more than the marriage of convenience he had meant—she wanted more than a way out of her family's mess. More than *he* could offer her. He was damaged in his bloody soul; his father's actions and example had seen to that. He was too flawed to love her as she wanted or deserved.

"Vicky," he began, and as her eyes caught his, he knew whatever he said next had to be nothing less than the truth, even if it hurt her. "I will always care for you—but I am marred beyond repair, I fear. Ever since my father's death, I've not been able to—" He took a breath. "Rather, my feelings are not as they once were." He closed his eyes and ran his hand through his hair. "I don't know how to explain except to say I am cold . . . inside. Indifferent. Most of the time, actually." He lifted his eyelids to look at her. Her eyes widened with pity.

"Except *you* make me remember who I once was. And, for a time, when we're together, I feel ordinary again." He searched her face, but he couldn't read her. "I don't know if that is enough. I know it is far less than you deserve." He paused. "But I swear I'll keep you safe as long as I am able."

She let out a long breath. "I know you would, Tom."

He nodded in thanks.

"But . . ." She dropped her gaze. "I don't know if that is enough."

His chest tightened. "Do you—are you in—" he stammered, then caught himself. "Will Carmichael give you what you want?"

She looked up, meeting his stare with unflinching candor. "As much as you would, I daresay. Perhaps more," she finished almost to herself.

"Then he did not speak of love?" he asked, though he knew the answer.

She glanced up at him, and he thought he could read the conflict in her eyes. "Not so explicitly."

Thank heaven for that.

"Tom, I—I know you don't believe in fairy stories. But I do still wish to have my Austen ending if I can."

"And you deserve one." Yet fate had dealt her undesirable cards, and she had little choice but to accept them. He cleared his throat. "Though, wishing for something does not make it so. In such a situation, it might be better to choose the least of two—er . . . evils." He winced. Had anyone *ever* proposed in a less tempting way?

Vicky said nothing for a long moment. "Tom, might you fetch me a drink? I believe I have some thinking to do."

He nodded, uncertain. "Of course. I'll return shortly." He just hoped that, for once, fate would deal in his favor.

CHAPTER THE TWENTY-THIRD

My good opinion once lost is lost forever.
—Jane Austen, *Pride and Prejudice*

Vicky sank into a nearby chair and snapped open the fan hanging from her wrist. She hoped the fan would cool the beat of her pounding pulse, but it did nothing but unnerve her further. She opened it fully, shielded her face, and took three deep breaths.

Tom had proposed.

Actually proposed marriage!

Something she'd thought impossible had truly just occurred. She'd never have believed it, except she'd just witnessed it. As a girl, she might've harbored fanciful dreams that they'd one day fall in love and Tom would propose like some great chivalric knight, but the years following his exile had dashed all such hopes. The reality of his unexpected proposal in no way equaled what she'd once imagined in her childish heart.

His valiant intentions were ever present, but Tom didn't love her. He didn't know if he ever could. She'd have everything she'd always wanted if she accepted him—everything but the thing she'd wanted most.

And what of Mr. Carmichael? He hadn't said he'd loved her either, but he'd implied it would be possible in the future. If love would be possible with Mr. Carmichael, wasn't that more than Tom had offered? It was certainly more than Tom thought himself capable of. Her heart had nearly broken for him when he told her of his melancholy. She didn't understand why he felt such apathy, but it certainly explained many of his actions.

"That fan does you little justice."

Vicky started at the deep voice. Mr. Carmichael's broad-shouldered frame towered over her. He smiled, and she lowered her fan instinctively. "Good evening, Mr. Carmichael."

"I apologize for startling you."

She smiled. "It's quite all right. I was just woolgathering, I suppose."

He gestured to a nearby chair. "May I?"

"Of course." Though she didn't know what to say to him, or even how she felt at the moment.

He picked up the chair back with one hand and moved it closer to hers before sitting.

"Are you enjoying the evening?" he asked.

"It is lovely, yes." Vicky turned to look at the dancers. "And how has your evening progressed?"

"It has been rather uneventful thus far—and, might I add, rather empty until I saw you."

With a pleased laugh, she pivoted to meet his gaze. He was smiling at her, his eyes crinkling a bit at the corners. She remembered the way he'd kissed her. How sweet he'd been. How she'd liked it. Then she wondered how Tom might kiss her and immediately felt her cheeks redden.

Carmichael's smile widened. "Were you able to give any more thought to my proposal?"

"I—" She sucked in a breath. "I did, yes."

"And?"

Her throat suddenly went dry. "I admit I am still considering it, Mr. Carmichael."

His smile faded. "I see."

"May I ask you a question?" she said, peering up at him through her lashes.

"Anything."

"Do you—that is, do you think you might one day—" She broke off and he raised an eyebrow. She looked away. "You never spoke of love," she finished, embarrassed down to her toes.

"Ah." He took her hand in his. "Victoria, I have great feeling for you."

She searched his eyes. He seemed sincere.

"I would not have proposed otherwise. As you know, I have no need of your dowry."

She bit her lip. He would be marrying her for herself alone.

"Good evening, Carmichael."

Vicky's neck snapped up. Her gaze collided with Tom's. He stood in a relaxed stance, holding her glass of claret with one hand.

His features betrayed nothing, but she recognized the ice beneath his cordial greeting. His eyes dropped to her hand captured in Carmichael's. She felt her color rise.

"Halworth," Carmichael replied with no cordiality at all.

Tom held out the glass of claret to her.

She pulled her hand from Carmichael's grasp and took it. "Thank you."

She quickly took a sip, but when she looked up, they were both staring at her. She suppressed the inclination to fidget in her seat. "It is a lovely evening, is it not?" she said to fill the growing silence.

"It would be lovelier still if you would consent to dance the next with me," Carmichael replied with a smile for her.

"Oh, I—"

"I'm afraid Lady Victoria has promised the next to me," Tom said over her.

Her gaze shot to his face—he hadn't so much as mentioned the next dance, although perhaps his proposal had impeded whatever progress he'd planned on that front.

Tom wouldn't meet her eyes. He was observing Carmichael with an odd expression.

"You have anticipated me, Halworth," Carmichael said as a muscle flexed in his cheek. He turned to Vicky. "Are you engaged for the quadrille as well?"

"No—"

"Yes," Tom interrupted.

Vicky gaped at Tom. She knew he didn't like Mr. Carmichael, but he couldn't possibly think he could monopolize her. The society gossips would count them engaged by the end of the ball if he persisted. Was that his aim?

"Lord Halworth," she said as calmly as she could, "you cannot claim all my dances for yourself."

He stared down at her with the expression he'd worn at Oakbridge just as he'd lifted her and tried to carry her to her front door. "Is that not a fiancé's prerogative?"

Her mouth nearly dropped open. She shot to her feet. "You—you are not my fiancé!"

Heads turned in their direction. She'd said it a bit too loudly. She pressed her lips together before her anger got the better of her.

"You didn't say no," he pointed out.

Her eyes widened. "I didn't say yes," she whispered back. She turned to Mr. Carmichael. "Mr. Carmichael, I must apologize. I—"

"There is nothing you need apologize for, Lady Victoria," he said, rising to his feet and using his full height to tower over them both. "Lord Halworth was once again attempting to take advantage of your good nature. Just as I suspected he would. Did you tell him of my proposal?"

"Yes, I—"

"So he knew tonight would be his last chance to prostrate himself at your feet—to convince you to lend your dowry to rebuilding his crumbling finances. All while preying on the fact you would be so near Oakbridge as to make the change in your circumstances negligible. What a shabby device." He turned to face Tom head-on. "You, Lord Halworth, are shabby in every sense of the word."

Tom stepped forward. "My financial affairs are none of your concern, Carmichael."

"But, Tom," Vicky cut in, realizing she needed to know, "are you in financial trouble?"

He turned to her. "No. I will soon be building London's first luxury hotel. I have just lined up all the necessary backers. I will gladly tell you all you care to know."

A hotel? Like his uncle's? She hoped that would make him happy.

"Convenient that he offers to tell you now that there is an audience to contend with."

"And what of your secrets, Carmichael?" Tom rejoined, facing Carmichael again. "I saw you with Dain at the Chadwick musicale. I heard you speak of your *mutual dealings*. Perhaps you can explain once and for all how you can involve yourself with someone who has acted so despicably and how you can then presume to marry a daughter of the very family he has wronged."

Vicky looked at Carmichael.

He glared daggers at Tom as his fist clenched at his side. "Business is business," he ground out.

"Pardon me as I scoff at your dull platitude. I am certain it eased Lady Victoria's mind."

"See here, Halworth," Carmichael growled, closing the distance between them. "If you believe for one damn moment that I will allow you to touch Lady Victoria—"

"And if you think for a bloody second that I will allow her to say yes to you, you arrogant clod—"

"Gentlemen!" Vicky snapped.

Their heads pivoted down to look at her.

"Not that you deserve that title! How dare *either* of you presume to tell me who I will be *allowed* to marry. This is *my* life." She scowled at them. "I don't know how I thought I could marry either of you. You don't care a fig for my opinion."

She pointed at Mr. Carmichael. "You still haven't explained what 'business' you have with Dain." He opened his mouth, but she raised her hand. "I am tired of your evasions."

Then she turned to Tom. "And *you*." He pivoted to face her fully. "Proposing just to keep me from *him* is no grounds for marriage. I shall not be another burden on your shoulders. Nor shall I assent because you feel the need to save me as though I were still a child." She felt tears threatening behind her eyes. She held her breath to dam them back.

Tom's eyes softened. "Vicky, I—"

"No," she pronounced with a lift of her chin. "Leave me alone."

She looked at Mr. Carmichael. His lips parted as he started to speak, but she was too angry to care. "Both of you."

Tom watched as Vicky all but ran away from him into the bustling crowd. He truly was a louse. The urge to follow her and apologize swept over him, but as he started after her, Carmichael's iron grip closed over his forearm. He turned and stared at Carmichael until he let go.

"Do not lay your hand on me again, Carmichael," he said in a low voice as he tried to bury the outrage building in his chest.

Carmichael had the audacity to tilt his head. "What could you possibly do to stop me?"

Tom's whole body tensed. The man's demeanor and thinly

veiled threats, which Tom had now been on the receiving end of on two separate occasions, were so reminiscent of his own father's that his stomach churned. He fixed Carmichael with an inflexible glare. "You disgust me."

Carmichael's eyes narrowed. "I assure you the feeling is mutual."

Tom clenched his back teeth and, with a backward scowl at Carmichael, he stepped away in search of Vicky. She'd been right. He'd acted abominably. He must apologize.

After a few paces, he thought he glimpsed her blue dress. Her delicate, shapely form maneuvered through the crowd as she left the ballroom. Could she be going to the retiring room? If so, she'd be out of reach. He followed her to the hallway adjoining the ballroom and looked both ways. To the right was the ladies' retiring room; to the left, the foyer and front door. He couldn't see her, but he turned left to be sure she hadn't been so angry as to attempt leaving the ball completely. As he turned, he heard footsteps clack on the marble floor behind him. He spun around. Carmichael marched close at his heels. Tom swallowed his frustration and stopped to face him.

"What do you *want*, Carmichael?"

"Just making sure you leave, Halworth. Lady Victoria has been distressed enough for one evening."

Tom shook his head and continued down the hall to the front entry. "I have no intention of leaving."

"I say you are," Carmichael rejoined.

Tom clenched his jaw harder but ignored the barb. He'd reached the foyer, but it stood empty. The front door was shut and not one footman waited about. It seemed everyone had arrived and the servants were occupied elsewhere. He went to the door and opened it, again looking both ways for Victoria. It would have been foolish for her to stand outside alone, even if waiting for her carriage, but he wouldn't have thought it beyond her, especially in her agitated state.

Carriages lined the sidewalk. A few coachmen talking in a group threw glances at him. The guard who had shadowed Vicky at the theater stood among them facing the door.

Tom caught his eye. "Did Lady Victoria leave the house?"

The man shook his head.

"Thank God for that," Tom whispered under his breath. She must have gone to the retiring room after all. He'd wait outside it until she came out.

He closed the door to the night air and turned. Carmichael stood mere inches away.

"And where," Carmichael said, "do you think you are going?"

"Get out of my way, Carmichael," Tom managed through his teeth.

"Not a chance." He leaned even closer.

A hammering commenced in Tom's left temple. "I need to see that Lady Victoria is well," he said, deliberately emphasizing each syllable, partly in an attempt to keep his temper and partly to make his intentions clear.

"The best way to keep her well is to keep her away from *you*."

"We were *both* told to leave her alone, as I recall," Tom returned as the hammering increased. "But she has a habit of acting foolishly when she is angry."

Carmichael's gaze narrowed. "The only foolish thing she's ever done was allow you to insinuate yourself into her regard. You with your debts and your knack for showing up whenever she happens to be in danger."

Tom opened his mouth to reply, but Carmichael continued.

"Yet you never seem to actually *help* her when you arrive so propitiously. Somehow she is always injured." Carmichael leaned closer.

Tom's hand balled into a fist at his side. The pounding had expanded to behind his eye now. "What exactly are you saying, Carmichael?" He wanted to hear the lout say it aloud.

"That you have manufactured scenarios so she may feel indebted to you. That you have weaseled your way into her affections. All so you may profit from her sizable dowry and save your pathetic excuse for an estate."

Tom's neck was afire now and the flames were traveling up to his ears. The pounding distorted into a roar rolling through his head. That anyone—even such a coarse brute as Carmichael—would believe him capable (and accuse him to his face!) of such deplorable behavior was all but inconceivable.

"I say, Lord Halworth," Carmichael continued, "that whatever claim to honor you purport to have is lower than the dust beneath my feet."

The fire licking Tom's neck raged over the back of his head until it engulfed his face. Though he doubted his ability to speak with any efficiency, he spat, "Whereas your continued association with Dain is so honorable, it is incomprehensible, even to her. She would have no need to marry anyone if not for Dain's behavior. Convenient that Dain's friend just so happens to want to make her his wife."

Carmichael stepped forward, closing the minuscule distance that remained between them. He spoke through clenched teeth. "Understand this: You. Will. Not. Have her."

Tom's entire body ignited. Even had he wished to, he could not have stopped his hand from flying forward and shoving Carmichael back. Carmichael's eyes widened as he stumbled. Then his lips curved into a mocking grin so similar to Tom's father's that for a moment, Tom thought the devil had brought him back to life.

"So there is nerve in you after all. A duel then, Halworth. Unless your honor truly is as weak as your fist."

This time, Tom wasn't imagining the red that clouded his vision as outrage thundered through his ears. "I accept."

CHAPTER THE TWENTY-FOURTH

How she could have been so deceived!
—Jane Austen, *Emma*

Vicky flopped over onto her side, burying her head deep into her feather pillow. She yanked the coverlet over her head and squeezed her eyes shut, which did nothing to dispel the images of Tom and Carmichael ceaselessly churning in her mind.

When she thought of what they had said last night, she wanted to throw things at the wall and stamp her foot like a child. But she refused to sink to their level of immaturity. She was a lady, after all.

Her lower lip jutted out and she pressed her body deeper into the bed, throwing her fist into the pillow until feathers swirled in the air. Those horrible, loathsome, boorish . . . *troglodytes*! She was sick to death of them both: sick of their rudeness, their inability to listen, and their egotistical, high-handed behavior.

This must have been how Marianne Dashwood felt after Willoughby had broken with her or Fanny Price had after Henry

Crawford ran off with her married cousin, Maria. Even in Miss Austen's books, men were undeserving scoundrels. Marianne and Fanny had been well rid of them!

Vicky flipped onto her back and glared at the ceiling. She'd spent the remainder of the ball in the ladies' retiring room just to avoid Tom and Mr. Carmichael. Which had not been particularly easy. Or pleasant. Eventually, her mother and Althea had found her. Vicky had refused to return to the ballroom, so they'd gone home early. She hadn't been able to explain what had happened—had she tried, she would have broken into tears.

Her eyes started to prickle even now. Damn both Mr. Carmichael and Tom! She absolutely could *not* marry a Mr. Willoughby or a Henry Crawford. There had to be another way. Yet she'd humored that argument many a time before, and no solution had presented itself. Her stomach clenched; she knew the truth; she was in an impossible situation with appalling choices as her only solutions. She grabbed her nearly ruined pillow and thumped it onto the bed three times. Tears clouded her vision as she clouted the pillow one more time for good measure. Then she buried her face in it and sobbed.

Tom flinched awake as a hand shook his shoulder. His eyes flew open. Charles held a walking stick in one hand, his hat in the other, and was still wearing his greatcoat over his evening clothes. He must have just returned home.

"I heard about your little escapade last night," he said, giving Tom a pointed look.

Confused, Tom shook his head.

Charles raised an eyebrow. "Perhaps if I mention a certain appointment you will understand my meaning?"

"Christ." Tom swallowed. So Carmichael's challenge hadn't been a nightmare as he'd hoped. He scrubbed his hand over his face, then swung his legs out of bed. "How did you hear?" He went to the armoire to dress.

"Word gets around."

Tom clenched his teeth as he retrieved a pair of trousers.

"You'll be in need of a second—unless you secured one last night."

"I did not."

"Very well. I shall make the necessary arrangements. I suggest you do the same."

"Thank you for your concern, but you needn't bother," Tom replied, tugging a shirt over his head. He turned and faced his brother. "I shall apologize."

For a moment Charles's mouth gaped open. He stepped forward. "You cannot be in earnest," he pronounced.

"I am very much in earnest." Tom fastened the buttons of his waistcoat. "I lost my temper, but I am not above admitting my mistake. Carmichael is"—he broke off as his pulse jumped the way it had the night before. He took a deep breath—"the worst of brigands. But I do not think either of us should die for that."

"You seriously believe he will accept an apology?"

Tom shook his head. "I caused the offense. Therefore I have the right to apologize. He cannot argue with the rules of conduct. Had I challenged him he'd have the same right."

Charles turned away. "This is madness. What of your honor? What of the family honor?"

"I am secure in my own honor. And the family's is already tarnished, as I believe you know."

Charles strode to the door. "This will damage it beyond repair. And you'll have only yourself to blame this time." He left without another word.

Tom threw his cravat around his neck and yanked it tight. "So be it."

Tom stood in the foyer of Brooks's Club, holding his body rigid as he stared at the man behind the desk with what he hoped was the air of an earl who knew his own worth. The man ignored him as he wrote in some kind of ledger. Another man had gone to fetch Carmichael from the bowels of the club. The men at the front desk had informed Tom that club policy stated all visiting nonmembers wait for an escort before entering.

Tom hoped his irritation wasn't obvious. He wouldn't have ventured into Brooks's at all, except he'd already called at Carmichael's town house, where the man's mother—a surprisingly charming woman—had said Carmichael would not return until later that evening. Tom couldn't wait so long. He had to conclude this business before he ended up with a pistol in his hand.

Resisting the urge to tap his boot against the floorboards, he glanced up the wide staircase for any sign of Carmichael or the man who'd gone to fetch him. Large portraits of gentlemen garbed in the ornate fashions of the last century stared down at him from the wall behind the stairs, mocking him and his situation. He set his jaw and turned halfway toward the door.

How had he let Carmichael bring him to this? He knew the man's tactics well enough by now. Regardless of how Carmichael had baited him, he should have walked away. Recalling Carmichael's insults, Tom glanced at the lacquered door. He willed his legs to stand steady, ignoring how his feet itched to take him home. Apologizing to that clodpoll was the last thing he thought he'd ever do. He could still leave. Leaving would calm the firestorm of righteous fury already pooling in his gut.

But to leave now would mean failing himself. It would mean every battle he'd ever waged to avoid becoming his father would've been for naught. If he didn't stop this duel, he would truly be his father's son—and how could he go on, knowing what he'd become?

Tom clenched a fist. The entire situation was his own doing. He'd told Vicky he was broken and then he'd proven it. Even Carmichael, for all his threats, had done no more than lay a hand on him.

Pride could not be Tom's foremost concern now. He had plans for the future and people to care for—things far more important than damage to his ego.

"Our appointment is tomorrow, Halworth. Or were you hoping to postpone the matter? In truth, I'd expect nothing less," Carmichael stated, descending the stairs from the first floor of the club.

Tom glanced up to meet Carmichael's sneer and willed himself not to respond in kind. It was just what the oaf wanted. "I need to speak with you, Carmichael."

"So I gathered."

Tom gestured to an area farther away from the man at the desk and the fellow trailing behind Carmichael. The door to the club was closed, and if they stepped nearer to it, their conversation might be out of earshot.

Carmichael came to the bottom of the stairs but made no move to go where Tom had pointed.

Tom stared at him, then walked toward the door, not looking back. In moments, Carmichael's footsteps echoed on the parquet. When Tom neared the doorway, he turned and faced him. Carmichael inclined his head with sarcastic civility.

"I shall come to the point," Tom began. "I wish to apologize for my conduct last night. I was at fault." Tom paused, his stomach swirling at the words. It had to be done.

Carmichael's expression remained unreadable. He watched Tom with a face so devoid of emotion, Tom felt his patience slipping.

Fire licked its way up into his chest. "Do you understand me?"

Carmichael nodded slowly, and the corner of his mouth quirked upward. "Only too well, Halworth. I understand you are the most illustrious coward I have ever met."

He said the last so loudly, the men at the desk looked up from their work. Tom threw them a scowl and their gazes shot down.

"Call it what you will," Tom replied with what he thought to be amazing restraint, considering the blaze still spreading through his torso. "You challenged me. I have apologized. Consequently our business is at an end."

Carmichael stepped closer. "I'm afraid it's your business that's at an end, Halworth. No woman in her right mind would marry you now, let alone Lady Victoria."

The fire swirled faster. "What are you saying?"

"Lord Axley has chilled to your hotel scheme. I think you'll find it is dead in the water."

Flames clawed their way up toward his neck. "*What* did you say to him?"

"To him? Nothing. To his partners? To the rest of my many financial contacts? There is a great deal to say about your sad situation. A brother with debts, an estate with larger ones, death duties still to be paid: in short, the worst of financial risks."

Carmichael smirked, and Tom's stomach plummeted. Carmichael had summed up his entire financial situation. How could the man know everything in such detail? Then Tom remembered what Charles and Vicky had said about Carmichael's extensive connections, and his pulse started a military tattoo he could feel in his brain.

"And a coward to boot, let's not overlook that," Carmichael finished.

The heat under Tom's cravat intensified, burning through his ears. "You do not simply play with my living. Did it occur to you that my family and hundreds of tenants will suffer?" he ground out.

Carmichael shrugged. "Someone will eventually take on the estate when you lose it. Someone far more capable than you'll ever be, I daresay. I'm doing your tenants a favor in the long run."

Tom refrained from pointing out how ridiculous a notion that was. Tenants always suffered when ownership changed hands. "Would that someone be you? Or one of your partners, perhaps?"

Carmichael raised an eyebrow as though the thought hadn't occurred to him. Tom didn't believe it for a second.

"Come to think of it, that might be a proposition worth considering."

Tom shook his head. "You mean to ruin me. And you imagine Victoria will thank you for it."

"You needn't worry about Victoria. Before long, she'll be none of your affair."

Unable to hear more, Tom wheeled around to leave. Charles stood in the doorway with a face as cold as stone. "Charles, what are you—"

"I followed you. I had planned to talk some sense into your thick skull, but there's no need now. This scum has uttered his last insult. I'll see to that."

Tom moved to crowd Charles out through the door.

Charles sidestepped him and faced Carmichael with an unyielding glare. "Carmichael, I challenge—"

Tom grabbed his brother's arm and yanked him backward. "No!"

Charles's eyes widened with loathing. "You bloody—"

Tom shouted over him, "Hold your damned tongue!"

Charles glowered at him with a look of disgust identical to the one on Carmichael's face.

The cravat around Tom's neck threatened to choke him as he boiled. Every impulse his father had thought lacking in him roared to life with appalling force.

"I shall see you at dawn, Carmichael," he spat. Then he pushed past his brother and stormed out of the club in a euphoric haze.

CHAPTER THE TWENTY-FIFTH

How can they suit each other?
—Jane Austen, *Pride and Prejudice*

When Vicky's mother knocked on her door later that afternoon, Vicky was so fatigued with her own thoughts, she welcomed her mother's presence.

"It's nearly three o'clock," her mother stated, stepping into the room. "Are you ill?"

Vicky cringed as she realized she'd have to answer her mother's questions. Vicky put the third volume of *Pride and Prejudice* down on the coverlet, wondering how much she should reveal. "My head aches."

"Then perhaps you should stop reading."

Vicky sighed.

"Were you too tired from last night to have luncheon with us?" her mother asked.

The untouched tray of food Sarah had delivered sat at the foot of the bed where Vicky had banished it. She nodded, resolved not to explain further. The mere thought of recounting how Tom and Mr. Carmichael had humiliated her . . . Blast them! She looked at her hands.

"You're awake now, so you might as well go downstairs. Mr. Carmichael has come calling, and you mustn't keep him waiting."

Vicky huffed out a breath. What was he doing here? Hadn't she said she had no wish to see him?

"Mama, I cannot speak with him. My head is throbbing. I must stay in bed."

Her mother eyed her. "What happened last night?"

Vicky shrank farther into bed. She had to tell her something.

She took a deep breath. "Mama, I simply do not wish to speak with him. Can't you tell him I'm indisposed?"

Her mother crossed the room and sat on the side of the bed. "Victoria, are you still considering his proposal?"

How could she tell her mother she couldn't marry him because he'd treated her like an infant who didn't know her own mind? He'd been her one and only real prospect. Unless she counted Tom. Which she didn't!

When she didn't answer, her mother pursed her lips and dropped her chin. Finally, her inquisitive stare forced Vicky to speak.

"I cannot marry him, Mama. If you'd heard how they spoke to me last night you could not ask it of me—"

"They?" her mother interrupted.

Vicky blinked. "Tom and Mr. Carmichael."

Her mother raised an eyebrow. "What did they say?"

Vicky looked at her lap. "I cannot repeat it." Her throat choked up and she swallowed to hold back the tears. She swiped angrily at the few that leaked out, inhaled, and looked at her mother. "They are the most heavy-handed tyrannical brutes on this side of the Thames, and I cannot shackle myself to either of them. I will not end like Althea. I cannot—"

"Are you saying Tom proposed to you?" She'd never seen her mama so wide-eyed.

Vicky nodded. "I know nothing has changed. I know I must marry. But not either of *them*." She exhaled, waiting for her mother's arguments.

For a moment, her mother didn't speak. "Victoria, you were perfectly well-disposed toward Mr. Carmichael until Tom spoke against him. Now Tom inexplicably asks for your hand and you won't even see Mr. Carmichael?"

Vicky frowned. "No, Mama, they both—"

"Forgive me, my dear, but have you forgotten what is at stake?"

Vicky swallowed at the lump in her throat. She shook her head. Still she said, "You would see me trapped with a man who doesn't love me?"

"I would not see you come to harm, Victoria. And if Dain becomes master of Oakbridge, that is precisely what will happen. To all of us."

Vicky looked down, knowing the statement to be true.

"Marry Tom if you must. Or Mr. Carmichael. Either way we can negotiate for the estate to stay intact."

Vicky's stomach wavered. She loved Oakbridge—she couldn't

bear to see anything change it for the worse. Yet she was trading her future for *property*. When she viewed it in that light, it didn't feel heroic. It felt like she was selling herself. "Mama, you and Papa said I could choose my husband."

"And so you shall. There is no longer time to dither. You heard what's been happening on the estate and in the Court of Chancery."

"I am aware, but—"

Her mother stood. "I'm sorry, Victoria. I wish it could be otherwise, but you marrying for love is no longer a luxury we can afford. Regardless of your decision, you must speak to Mr. Carmichael. He deserves nothing less."

Vicky set her jaw and looked down at her hands. She should have known her mother wouldn't be sympathetic. Yet, not one of the heroines in Miss Austen's novels had been forced to marry a man she couldn't trust! Elizabeth Bennet's father's estate had been entailed away to her cousin Mr. Collins, but she'd still refused his offer of marriage. Her father had even *encouraged* her to refuse him. Of course, Mr. Collins was nothing like Mr. Carmichael.

Vicky's head started to throb. She *would* have to face Mr. Carmichael eventually. She still didn't know what to say to him. How could she be expected to choose between two men she didn't even like at the moment?

"Will you ring the bell for Sarah, Mama?" She still needed to dress. "You may tell Mr. Carmichael I shall be down presently."

Her mother nodded and stood to ring the bell pull. She turned to leave, then seemed to reconsider. She walked over to the side of the bed and pulled Vicky into a tight embrace. "All will be well, my love. You'll see."

Vicky hugged her back, surprised at her mother's display of affection, but savoring it nonetheless. After a few moments, Vicky pulled away.

"I'd best get ready."

Her mother smiled.

A quarter hour later, Vicky descended the stairs as she tried to ignore the fluttering in the pit of her stomach. After asking a footman where Mr. Carmichael was waiting, and being directed to the back garden, she took a fortifying breath. She knew she didn't look her best; she'd been abed all day and had dressed hastily, but then again she wasn't sure why that should matter. She didn't feel like making a good impression. If anything, he should be the one trying to regain *her* favor.

A crisp breeze rippled across her skirts and played over her face as she stepped outside. The clouds sat thick in a gray sky.

She soon spotted Mr. Carmichael in a well-cut, fashionable slate coat and trousers, in the middle of the garden beside a stone bench. He and the bench stood inside a semicircle of knee-high boxwood hedges. He faced away from her staring out over the garden, perhaps looking at the cascading fountain where he'd proposed—where he'd kissed her.

She started, realizing that had only been a few days ago. She'd been hopeful then; no doubt he had been as well. What a difference a few days could make.

He must have heard her footfalls, for he turned as she approached. "Good afternoon, Victoria."

Vicky didn't attempt to smile, though she noted the way his dark eyes brightened at the sight of her. "Good day."

"As you did not reappear last night, I thought I should call." He looked her up and down. "How are you?"

Vicky almost scowled. She must look worse than she thought. "Well enough."

A line appeared between his brows. "I must apologize for last night. You should not have been obliged to witness that exchange. I—"

"That exchange shouldn't have happened at all. You both acted like children squabbling over a toy," she pronounced, her anger returning. "I thought I made myself perfectly clear, Mr. Carmichael."

He regarded her with uncertainty. "I do not think of you as a toy. Halworth on the other hand—"

She held up a finger. "Enough. You said more than enough last night. I will not hear any more on the subject." She turned her head away and looked beyond him at a yellow rosebush swaying in the wind.

In her peripheral vision, he nodded slowly. "Will you at least accept my sincere apology?"

She caught his gaze. His brows knit together, but his eyes were clear. He did look sincere.

"Why must you always do things you need apologize for?"

He exhaled and glanced away. Then he met her eye with a self-deprecating smile. "You're the only person I know to whom I regularly feel the need to apologize."

She bit the inside of her cheek, not knowing what that said about him. Or her.

"Yet I would gladly continue to do so, if you'll have me."

Vicky inhaled. "Mr. Carmichael, I was honored by your proposal. I still am. But you cannot ask me to decide now."

Carmichael's eyes bored into hers. She didn't know what he was thinking, but the longer he stared, the more uncomfortable the silence grew.

"Forgive me, but I must ask you to decide now."

She gaped at him. "You must excuse me, but I *cannot*."

He stepped toward her. "Because of Halworth."

"Partially," she admitted. "But also because despite your apology, I am still angry. With you both."

His mouth opened and closed. He shook his head. "What else would you have me say?"

She sighed. "Nothing. I want a husband I can trust. Someone who asks my opinion and actually listens. Not someone who will humiliate me in a ballroom full of people by treating me like a witless child."

"*I* humiliated you?" His eyes grew wide with indignation. "*I* was protecting you."

"You *both* humiliated me. And I was in no need of protection."

"I say you were."

She threw up her hands. "And who are you to decide?"

He stared at her. "Someone who cares for your well-being."

Her gaze softened. "I thank you. Sincerely. But caring does not mean making my decisions."

He let out an exasperated breath. "You don't wish your husband to protect you from harm?"

"Of course I do, but only when needed."

He scoffed and looked away.

She pursed her lips. "I'll have you know I faced down our attackers with a single pistol."

He gawked at her. "Are you mad? You could have been beaten, or killed. Or worse."

"I saved my papa. Had I done nothing—" She took a deep breath, still unable to think about what could have occurred. "I would do it again." She raised her chin. "That's what one does to save the people one loves."

"I quite agree. But as a woman you mustn't—"

Her eyes widened. "Yes. Even as a woman."

He exhaled, then tilted his head down. "When Elizabeth Bennet heard Wickham had run off with her sister, did she go to London herself to ferret them out?"

"No, but she had no idea where they were. *I* was witnessing my father being beat to death!" A lump rose in her throat at the words, and she paused to swallow. "The situations do not equate."

"Perhaps not, but there is no reason for you to be so reckless in future."

"Reckless?" She bit her lip. Perhaps she did act rashly—even more so than Elizabeth Bennet—but she *wasn't* Elizabeth Bennet. As much as she'd wanted to model herself after her heroine, she was only herself.

He shook his head. "This conversation is utterly ridiculous."

She wrinkled her nose. She didn't think it ridiculous in the slightest.

"You'll think differently when you have a household to run and responsibilities," he continued.

She blinked. Was that why he wanted her? For her housekeeping abilities? Certainly that was what many gentlemen expected of a wife, but she'd somehow thought he'd cared for her as more than the steward of his house. She shook her head. "I don't believe I shall."

He looked up and scoffed. "That is why you're considering Halworth. You imagine he will let you do whatever you wish."

Vicky frowned. It was true, Tom knew her well enough that he might not try to control her.

"Well, how very convenient that would be for you," he continued. "To go on acting like a child forever with a sorry excuse for a husband who cannot even keep his estate in working order." He paused. "Perhaps you have forgotten his debts? Debts your dowry would only partially cover. And what will happen to your pretty arrangement when he's run through your money?"

She shook her head. "He has his hotel."

Carmichael looked her in the eye. "I think you will find he has nothing of the kind."

Vicky's mouth went dry. "What do you know?"

"More than enough."

She glared at him. "If you think I act like a child, I wonder at your desire to marry me."

He exhaled and looked away. "Eventually we must all put away our childish ideals."

Her lips parted. Was that what *he* was doing? Or what he wanted her to do? Either way, she'd thought he genuinely liked her as she was. But he didn't *really* know her. "You may be right, Mr. Carmichael, but I have no idea of changing my behavior at present."

"You will have little choice when you marry."

Dain had certainly forced Althea to change drastically. That would *not* be her lot in life. "One always has a choice," Vicky said, holding his gaze.

He did not speak.

"Perhaps you should leave for today, Mr. Carmichael," she said with more bravado than she felt. She didn't like this imperious side of him any more than the way he'd acted last night.

He inclined his head. "Very well. Think on what I've said."

He bowed and walked around her. His arm brushed hers as he passed. The contact threw her off-balance, and he caught her arm to steady her. Half-turned toward her, he looked down into her eyes. Despite everything he'd said, her pulse quickened. His dark eyes slid over her face down to her lips. Her breath caught. "When you've come to your senses, I will return," he said.

Come to her senses? Now he thought her irrational? Her lips parted to give him a piece of her mind, but he continued, "Which is more than anyone can say for Halworth."

She pulled her arm out of his grip.

Her cheeks burned. Another of his prevarications—how fatigued she was of hearing them.

She opened her mouth to berate him, but before she could utter a syllable, he strode from the garden without even a fleeting glance back at her.

CHAPTER THE TWENTY-SIXTH

I have thought only of you.
—Jane Austen, *Emma*

Tom paced the Astons' foyer, waiting for Vicky to walk down the marble staircase. He rubbed the back of his neck to relieve his knotted muscles. He'd finished most of the necessary business of the day. First he'd gone to Lord Axley, who'd confirmed Mr. Parker and Mr. Risdale had withdrawn their backing. Axley could not fund the hotel alone. Carmichael had indeed done all he could to ruin him. Which seemed somewhat ironic considering Carmichael had all but stated he intended to kill Tom on the morrow.

He grimaced. What in hell was wrong with him? He'd allowed Carmichael to goad him into a duel not once, but twice. Well, Carmichael and Charles. Still, he'd fight Carmichael himself twenty times rather than watch his brother duel that bully for *his* sake.

Yet the feeling he was nothing but a miserable failure whipped at his shoulders. If he died tomorrow, he would fail his family. Even if he lived, he'd fail to help them thanks to Carmichael's interference.

He stopped in midstep and scrubbed a hand across his forehead. The most sickening thought of all was that regardless of tomorrow's outcome, his father had won. For years, Tom had fought to keep himself from turning into his father's ideal son. But last night and today, he'd failed to quell the abominable urge to fight, failed to ignore his monstrous craving to silence the man who'd impugned his honor, and failed to reason with him.

At those crucial moments, the gentleman Tom had always striven to be (a sensible, logical, upright fellow cast in the mold of his uncle) had disappeared behind the shadow of an uncontrolled, violent cretin.

Tom swallowed down his nausea. If he lived, he'd have enough regrets to last him the rest of his days.

He wouldn't allow his behavior toward Victoria to be another. His sole remaining occupation for the day was to apologize to her. Tom threw a glance up the staircase, inhaling to calm his impatience.

He forced himself to adopt a relaxed stance near the circular table in the center of the foyer. Even as he'd drafted his will with a solicitor and written letters of farewell to his mother and to his uncle's family, he'd tried to assure himself that his fits of temper (twice in as many days) would not cost him his life. Tom was a decent shot, but from what Charles had told him, Carmichael was better than decent. Actually, "unrivaled marksman" was the phrase Charles had used.

Of course, a duel often hinged on luck as well as skill. As for luck: well, Tom's luck had never been in high supply. But he would *not* leave Victoria to Carmichael's machinations, nor could he leave the family that depended on him.

So make your own *luck, you bloody fool.* He'd repeated the sentiment in his head as the day wore on—even as he'd walked to Vicky's house. Of course, when he realized he'd also been telling himself all he wanted was to see Vicky one last time—to apologize to her before it was too late—he'd nearly turned back. Such thinking should not grace the brain of a fellow about to make his own fate.

Tom took a deep breath and glanced up at the empty staircase again, wondering for the first time if she'd even see him. Then he wondered what he'd do if she wouldn't.

As soon as Mr. Carmichael left, Vicky ran back into the house. She didn't stop until safely in her room. She locked the door behind her, threw herself on the bed, and buried her head in the coverlet, pounding her fists into the soft feather mattress.

Her situation was intolerable. Mr. Carmichael didn't want *her*. He said he cared for her, but his idea of caring for a wife seemed to mean directing her every thought and action. She couldn't deny her attraction to him, but how could she marry someone who wouldn't accept her for who she was? Perhaps she *would* change eventually, but she wouldn't do so because her husband wished it. For all his good qualities, Mr. Carmichael would trap her.

Which left Tom. Surely he'd grown accustomed to her by now. Surely he wouldn't try to change her? Then she remembered why he'd proposed: to keep her from marrying Mr. Carmichael.

If she refused Carmichael, Tom's reasons for marrying her disappeared. Yet, it wouldn't be in his character to withdraw his proposal. He'd consider himself bound to her. And she'd trap *him* just as surely as Mr. Carmichael would trap her.

She held her forehead in her hands. How could she do it to him, knowing how it would feel? She couldn't. Tom deserved better too.

Vicky stood and flopped into a chair near the fire. There, she found herself staring at the intricately patterned wallpaper, as if the answer might emerge from its whorls. A knock at the door startled her out of her mental tirade.

"Who's there?"

"It's Thea. May I come in?"

Vicky sighed, but pushed herself up to go to the door.

As she opened it, her sister gasped.

"Vicky, are you well?"

Vicky touched her hair self-consciously and felt how disheveled it was. Then she dropped her hand and turned back to the bed. What did it matter?

For a moment, Vicky considered pretending nothing had happened, that all her hopes hadn't been shattered, but she couldn't bring herself to do it. She walked back to the bed and sat. She looked at her sister. Althea's brows knit together.

"Thea, I don't know what to do."

Althea nodded slowly. She closed the door behind her and walked to a chair. "Mama told me Tom proposed. Does Mr. Carmichael know?"

Vicky bobbed her head.

"What did you say to him?"

So many things she didn't care to relive at the moment. "I told him I wanted a husband I could trust."

"What said he?"

Vicky swallowed. "He said I should banish my childhood ideals."

Althea raised her brows. "There have been recent times where I would have agreed with him," she stated.

Vicky looked away.

"And what of Tom?"

"I cannot trap Tom into marriage."

Althea frowned. "He proposed. How would you trap *him*?"

Vicky couldn't meet her gaze. "He could not speak of love. Only duty."

"Perhaps, as Papa implied, Tom has other considerations."

Vicky eyed her sister, not liking where she was headed. "Such as?"

Althea said nothing. They both knew she'd meant Vicky's dowry. If Mr. Carmichael was right, Tom could have more need of it than he'd let on last night.

"If," Althea said, "Tom has more pecuniary concerns, you would hardly be trapping him. Instead, you could see it as—a partnership."

Vicky's head started to swirl. She'd go mad if she continued in this vein. She needed rest.

Vicky looked at her hands and stilled as she realized she was wringing them together. Then she raised her head as someone scratched at the door.

"Who's there?" she asked, trying to keep her voice from breaking.

"It is Sheldon, Lady Victoria."

Vicky uttered a relieved sigh at the butler's voice. The last thing she wanted was to attempt to explain her feelings to yet another person.

"Yes?"

"Lord Halworth is here, my lady. Shall I tell him you will receive him?"

Althea raised an eyebrow.

Vicky couldn't see him now—not like this. She needed to prepare herself. And she was sick of men turning up without notice, telling her what she thought. "Tell Lord Halworth he may come back tomorrow if he pleases, but I will not see him today," she called through the door.

"As you wish, my lady," the butler intoned from behind the door.

Althea frowned. "At least hear what he will say."

Vicky shook her head. She looked out the window onto the square but barely registered the bustling people below.

"Not all men are like Dain," Althea said, her voice more steady and sure than she'd sounded in weeks. "I cannot speak for Mr. Carmichael, but we have known Tom since he was born. If anyone had reason to lose his generosity, it was he—especially after his father threw him out. Yet, he rose above it. Even had we not known him all our lives, his goodness would be unmistakable."

Vicky turned back and looked at her sister. She sat in the upholstered chair, her spine straight, her face composed and assured. Her delicate hands lay still in her lap, and her cheeks held the slightest bloom. It was almost as though her true sister, and not the fragile imitation of recent weeks, had returned.

But Althea's serenity could not reach Vicky. "What if he does need my dowry?"

"Even if it were so, that would not change who he is. And now he is here, you may put the question to him directly. Ask him if he needs your dowry. At least then you will know the truth."

She couldn't bear to listen to him say the words. Her chest constricted at the thought. "Tom is the last person I wish to see at the moment. I cannot hear another argument to the contrary!" She wheeled around to face the window as her tears burst free. Hating her weakness, she swiped them away. Then she felt her sister's presence close at her back. Althea's light touch on her arm brought more tears forth until Vicky gave an involuntary sob.

Her sister turned her away from the window and wordlessly folded Vicky into her arms. It had been so long since she'd cried into Althea's shoulder. Gripping her sister's willowy torso, she wept with all the bitter frustration and misery in her heart.

Tom studied the massive vase overflowing with blue and purple blooms on the entry table. He hadn't yet decided whether to tell Vicky about the duel. A part of him wanted to explain everything. Yet he couldn't hurt her again by revealing she was part of the reason he'd accepted Carmichael's challenge.

Hearing footsteps, Tom looked up. The butler descended the staircase. Vicky was not with him.

"Lord Halworth," the man began formally, "Lady Victoria will not see you."

Tom took a step backward. Could the man be serious? Yet he'd wager Sheldon had never made a jest in his two hundred years of life.

"Is she unwell?"

"I cannot say, my lord," Sheldon replied. "She did say you might return on the morrow if it pleased you."

Tomorrow might be too late. "I must see her today."

"I'm afraid she will not see you, my lord," the butler said, his expression unwavering.

"Then you may tell *her* I refuse to leave," Tom stated.

The man blinked once, turned, and ambled slowly back toward the stairs.

Tom rubbed his neck. He couldn't wait another ten minutes for Sheldon to return. He closed his eyes and took a breath, willing himself to have patience. When his eyes opened, the butler had only reached the foot of the stairs. Whatever patience Tom had gained in the last few moments evaporated.

In a series of quick strides, he reached the staircase, ascended the bottom steps before Sheldon could, and yelled, "Victoria! Victoria, I must speak with you."

"Lord Halworth," the butler sputtered.

No doubt he'd never seen such a display in his life, but Tom didn't care. "Vicky!"

Two men appeared as if from nowhere. A moment later, hands gripped Tom's arms with vise-like strength. One of the men Tom recognized as the guard he'd spoken to last night.

"Unhand me, damn you!" Tom tried, rather unsuccessfully, to sound superior, hoping it would be enough to make the burly guards take pause. He called Vicky's name, louder this time.

The men started dragging him down the stairs.

Tom did his best to hold his ground, and managed to grab the railing on the staircase, but their combined strength overpowered him. They yanked at his arms until his hands began to lose their grip.

"I don't believe that will be necessary," a commanding voice intoned.

Still holding the railing, Tom craned his neck. Vicky's father stood in the foyer. He held his side with one hand as though the effort to speak loudly had pained him. Then again, maybe the scene he'd just witnessed had pained him.

The guards released their grip on Tom's arms, and the earl motioned for Tom to follow him. Tom straightened to his full height. He threw a glance at Sheldon and the men, who eyed him warily. It seemed his brief theatrical display was over.

With a swift downward yank, he pulled his waistcoat back to its original position and strode down the stairs with more dignity than he felt. He followed Vicky's father down a hall until they reached a room not far from the entry. The earl walked around a large desk and sat behind it, gesturing for Tom to sit.

Tom took a walnut armchair. He hadn't seen the earl since before the attack on their carriage. A dark bruise marred his cheek. Various cuts on his brows and lips had yet to heal. His light brown hair seemed grayer than Tom remembered.

For moments, neither of them spoke. As the silence lengthened, a muscle in Tom's neck screamed at him to stretch it. He didn't have time for this. All he wanted was to see Vicky and be on his not-so-merry way. He was grown now, and he wasn't going to stand being treated like an errant child, even by Lord Oakbridge. Not today.

Resolved to break the silence, Tom opened his mouth to speak. Lord Oakbridge cut him off.

"Let us come to the point, shall we?"

Tom nodded. They could have done so moments earlier.

"I know quite well how Vicky once felt about you. I daresay when you were young, she cared for you and your opinions more than her own sister's. But you must now be aware that Vicky changed after you left England. A part of her disappeared and has never quite returned."

Tom frowned. It had taken him some time to see it, but of course she'd changed. Yet he wouldn't say it had been for the worse.

"Sir, why are you telling me this?"

The earl sat back in his chair. "Victoria told her mother you proposed marriage last night."

Tom nodded. "I did." Was Lord Oakbridge irritated he hadn't asked his permission first?

"I take that to mean you gave some thought to the offer," he prompted, watching Tom closely.

Tom hesitated for a split second. "I did."

Lord Oakbridge nodded almost imperceptibly. "For a moment, let us pretend I am not Vicky's father and that I'm not fiercely protective of her. Now imagine yourself in my position—on one side there is a man who has expressed interest in Vicky who is wealthy and known to be honorable. On the other is a boy she has cared for in the past, in dire financial straits—albeit with a title of significance— but who also has the distinction of breaking her heart once before. Whose suit would you promote, I wonder?"

"I am no longer a boy, sir," Tom said evenly.

Lord Oakbridge inclined his head. "Perhaps not. Yet at nineteen I would hardly call you a man of experience."

Tom said nothing. When viewed in such stark contrast, he was clearly the lesser suitor. But as for breaking Vicky's heart, he was at a loss. She'd essentially still been a child when he'd left England. They'd been friends—the best of friends, even—but nothing more.

The earl cleared his throat, and Tom focused. He knew what the earl wanted him to say, but he'd never agree Vicky should marry Carmichael. Just the thought had his pulse thrumming in his ears again. The hand lying on his knee clenched into a fist. He *would not* let it happen.

"I do not know if Victoria has told you, but we both have suspicions about Mr. Carmichael—"

The earl put up his hand. "I will not hear any more nonsense about Mr. Carmichael. He has done a great deal for this family and is a man of unimpeachable moral character."

Tom exhaled and sat back in his chair, appalled by the ridiculous statement. *Unimpeachable moral character?* How could everyone be blind to Carmichael's true nature? He looked over the earl's battered face—the only man he'd ever respected as a boy. "Did you think the same about Dain?"

The earl got to his feet. "That's quite enough. It may not have been your intention, but you have been a black cloud over Victoria's life for the last five years. Now it is time to stop causing her pain. Allow her to move on."

Tom shook his head. "Sir, you mistake me—"

"I do not," the earl snapped. "Let her go."

CHAPTER THE TWENTY-SEVENTH

He cannot much longer deceive himself.
—Jane Austen, *Mansfield Park*

Shortly after five o'clock, Tom arrived home, still stinging from Victoria's refusal to see him. He felt such a fool. He'd practically yelled down Aston House to see her, and all he'd received was her father's lecture.

Entering the library, Tom rang the bell and asked for Susie when the butler came in. The man bowed and left.

Tom sat behind the desk. He pulled a piece of paper from the drawer and inked his pen. His hand hovered over the paper as he struggled with what to say. The devil knew what she thought of him.

A small drop of ink clung to the tip of the pen. Too tired to react, Tom let it fall to the page. After a moment, he put the tip of the pen to the dot and drew a line, which he then made into the letter *M*.

My Dear V—

"Tom?"

He looked up. Susie stood just inside the door. He motioned for her to come in. As he looked at her strawberry-blond curls and dimpled cheeks, he realized today might be the last day he spent with her. No, blast it all, he *would* make his own luck on the morrow.

"Are you all right?" Susie asked.

Tom sighed and put his pen back in the stand. "I want to ask a favor."

"Of course. You know I'd do anything you asked," Susie said, sitting in one of the armchairs.

He took a deep breath. "If I don't return tomorrow—"

"Tom, don't say such things."

He swallowed. "We must prepare for whatever may occur. If the worst should happen, which I do *not* anticipate, will you deliver a letter to Lady Victoria for me?"

Susie's eyes widened.

"I know I haven't had the opportunity to introduce you to her, but make Charles take you. If I leave it to him, I worry he'd wait too long or even forget. And I would like you to be acquainted. You think similarly on many points. She could use a friend. So could you," he finished with a weak smile.

He should have introduced them before, but it was too late now.

He shook his head. When was it ever appropriate to discuss one's father's infidelities? He'd been shielding Vicky from his father's secrets for so long, he hadn't known how to stop.

Despite the hardship his request might impose, he knew Susan wouldn't refuse him. But the silence stretched and still she did not answer.

"Does she know about me?" she finally asked.

Tom looked down at his letter. "Not as such."

In his peripheral vision, Susie narrowed her eyes.

He met her gaze. "I'm sorry."

"Did you ever tell her what Father was doing to you—and the others?"

"She saw what he did to me; she now knows it was a regular occurrence. As to the other—" He cleared his throat and cast his eyes at the paper. He'd only spoken the truth once. After months of Susie asking him to tell her stories about their father, one day in Solothurn, Tom had lost his temper and blurted out his ugliest memory of the old man. She'd stopped asking for remembrances after that day.

"So you just let her wonder all these years? That is why you stopped speaking to her in the first place. Doesn't she deserve to know the entire truth? Especially if, as you say, the worst should happen," Susie said matter-of-factly.

"I told Victoria I was protecting her from him. That is all she ever need know."

"Why?"

"Susie," Tom muttered, "it's of no consequence now."

"Because of your pride? Your likeness to Mr. Darcy defies belief."

"I beg your pardon?"

"I know you hate what our father's profligacy did to the family, yet you can barely speak of how it affected you, or Charles, or me. Or her."

He ran his hand through his hair; he certainly thought of it enough. "What good could come from rehashing it?"

She shook her head. "Does it not occur to you that you injure others besides yourself by never speaking of these things?"

"I do try—" He had tried the other day with Vicky, but it hadn't made him feel better. She had at least seemed to understand why he'd had to cease their friendship.

Susie tilted her head when he didn't continue. "Mr. Darcy doesn't speak of his sister's attempted elopement with Wickham to keep her reputation intact, but if he had, Wickham wouldn't have been able to run off with Elizabeth Bennet's sister. You do harm others by keeping these secrets, Tom. You harm yourself by remaining such a mystery to those around you."

Tom shook his head. "Father is gone. He cannot hurt anyone else."

She sighed. "Yet he has brought you to this." She gestured to the paper in front of him.

Tom winced. Could all this have been avoided? He cast his gaze at the ceiling. Devil take it, he'd go mad if he continued this way.

"Perhaps I should have told her. But it wasn't because of my pride. It was—" *Shame.*

"Then again, why would you tell her the truth just because you're in love with her?"

Tom's eyes snapped up. "What?"

Susie regarded him with raised brows.

After a few seconds, Tom broke the silence. "I simply cannot see her marry Carmichael."

"Why might that be?" she asked with a tip of her head.

"For too many reasons to count! The man is a lout. An arrogant, swaggering, self-serving—" He felt heat rising under his cravat, so he shut his mouth and took a deep breath. "I would pity any woman he married."

Susie folded her hands in her lap. "Would you fight a duel for *any* woman?"

He caught her gaze. She stared back with a delicately arched brow. "Very well, I care for her." He'd spoken louder than he'd intended. In a more regulated voice, he said, "Is that what you wanted to hear?"

She angled her chin down. "That's evident. Since you've been spending time with her, you've been happier than I've seen you since we returned to England. *Clearly*, you care for her. The question is, how *much* do you care?"

Tom raked his hand through his hair and held it there. Damned if he knew. Enough to feel physical revulsion at the idea of her marrying Carmichael—or any other man of their acquaintance, he knew that. But Vicky knew her own mind, and the type of marriage he'd offered wasn't enough for her. It shouldn't have to be.

"Tom, Father is dead. You are free to live as you please. What reason do you have to keep hiding your emotions?"

He met her penetrating look. "They do me little good. They never have." They'd only ever caused him or those he loved pain.

Susie shook her head. "That's not true. They led you to me. They led you back here to your family."

"That was duty, Susan. My honor. Not some elusive sentiment."

She scoffed. "If you really believe that, you are a fool. You would risk your life tomorrow because of *duty*?"

He made no answer. "I *am* a bloody fool, Susan. You'd best make your peace with that." He took his pen from the stand.

She stood and walked to the door. "You better not give up, Tom Sherborne," she said with another shake of her head. "I will not allow that." She exited the room, leaving Tom staring down at his barely begun letter.

The image of his body lying bloodied in the park assailed him again, and with it, a picture of Vicky in Carmichael's arms.

Tom made a fist, cracking the pen and breaking off the tip. His hand shook as he forced it open. He peered down at the pen's remains, then slammed the pieces onto the desk. He cradled his head with both hands. He couldn't give up—not if he wanted to keep Vicky safe.

CHAPTER THE TWENTY-EIGHTH

She was overpowered by shame and vexation.
—Jane Austen, *Pride and Prejudice*

Vicky awoke with a start, gasping in huge breaths. Her heart thrummed in her chest. A thin line of moonlight streamed through a crack in the curtains and tiny embers glowed in the grate. Her crumpled sheets lay in a heap at the foot of the bed, the work of yet another nightmare. She pushed herself up to recover them, then turned onto her side and tucked them around her.

With an exhale, she closed her eyes and tried to sleep. But her mind returned to the sound of her name echoing through the house as Tom called for her today. What a coward she was, unable to face him. What if he'd wanted to say something important? He would hardly have behaved in such a way for anything trivial. She knew him better than that.

Today Tom had called for her, and she hadn't come. Then she'd had a dream where she'd needed him, and he didn't appear.

She rubbed a hand over her forehead. The image of his clear gaze staring down at her as he proposed flashed through her mind. For one moment, he'd made her feel as though the world existed for them alone. As though the hopes she'd treasured when they were children could finally be set free. As though their futures lay together. A tear rolled down her cheek.

She shook her head and let out a short, frustrated grunt. She could no longer think of Tom in that way. Those dreams had been the fancies of a naive little girl.

A scratching at her door interrupted her thoughts. She sat up slowly. "Who's there?" The door opened a crack, and she saw Sheldon's white head illuminated by candlelight in the doorjamb.

He did not come in or even peer inside the room, but whispered from the doorway, "My lady, a girl is at the servants' door asking to see you."

Vicky frowned. "What is the hour?"

"A quarter to four, Lady Victoria."

"What could she possibly want?"

Sheldon cleared his throat. "She requests an audience. She says Lord Halworth's life is at stake."

Vicky's breath caught. What could this mean? "Tell her to wait. I'll be down at once."

She waited for Sheldon to close the door, then jumped out of bed. She threw a thick shawl over her shift and collected a candle from her dresser. After lighting it in the fire's embers, she hurried downstairs.

Sheldon stood at the foot of the back stairs waiting, looking remarkably well-groomed and awake despite the hour and being obliged to do his duty in a dressing gown. As Vicky approached, he escorted her to the kitchen. He motioned to the door leading to the mews, then opened it and stood aside.

Vicky stepped to the threshold to stand face-to-face with a young woman in a dark cloak. As the girl saw Vicky, she pushed the hood of her cloak all the way back until it fell around her shoulders. Strawberry-blond ringlets framed her oval-shaped face.

"Lady Victoria?" the girl asked.

"Yes," Vicky said cautiously.

The girl frowned. "Forgive me for calling at such a strange hour. My name is Susan Naseby—"

The girl paused. Vicky stared at her. "Yes?" Vicky prompted. "How are you acquainted with Lord Halworth?"

The girl took a breath and lifted her chin. "Lady Victoria, I am Tom's sister."

Vicky gaped at the girl for countless seconds before regaining her composure enough to shake her head. "That's absurd. Tom has no sister."

"We did not even know of each other until our father forced him to leave Halworth Hall."

Vicky stepped backward. "Are you quite certain?"

Miss Naseby nodded.

"Good heavens." Vicky spotted a chair near the doorway and plopped into it. "So you met him when?"

Miss Naseby took a tentative step inside the doorway. "Five years ago, just after Tom left Halworth Hall, he came to London.

He found his old nurse who was in service there. She let him stay with her. Mrs. Robbins also knew my mother, and she'd persuaded her mistress to employ Mama as a seamstress. When my mother grew ill, I delivered the pieces between Mrs. Robbins's lodgings and ours. One day when I went to Mrs. Robbins's, Tom was there. He must have thought me too young or too small, because he insisted on walking me home.

"When he saw my mother, he recognized her as having worked as a maid at Halworth Hall when he was a boy. He asked Mama where my father was. She told him my father was a gentleman from Hampshire."

Vicky's eyes widened.

"I'd never known anything about my father. Mama would say no more, but Tom encouraged Mrs. Robbins to speak. She told him my father was, in fact, Lord Halworth himself. Tom offered to take care of me if Mama needed help."

Vicky closed her eyes, imagining the fourteen-year-old Tom discovering he had a sister he'd never heard of. He wouldn't have hesitated to help her. Miss Naseby spoke with conviction; the girl believed the story she'd told to be true.

Vicky stood, telling Sheldon he could retire. She faced Miss Naseby with what she hoped was a clear head. "Miss Naseby, I do apologize if I was rude earlier. Please come inside and tell me how I may be of help."

The girl smiled. "Please call me Susie. I feel I know you so well from listening to Tom's stories of you."

Vicky smiled. What *had* Tom told his sister about her?

"Do come upstairs, where it's warmer." She ushered Susie through the kitchen and led her upstairs to her bedroom.

Once safely behind closed doors, Vicky asked Susie to sit while she stoked the dying embers to provide them with more light. "Do you still live with your mother?" she asked over her shoulder.

For a moment, she didn't answer. "Mama died some time ago."

Vicky swallowed the lump in her throat and moved to sit on the bed beside her. "I'm so sorry."

Susie looked into her lap. "Tom took me to Mrs. Robbins's. We stayed there for a fortnight. Then Tom got word from his mother saying his uncle would take him in, and with the money his mother sent, Tom brought me to Solothurn, hoping his uncle would be charitable enough to take me as well. He did, but we both had to work in the family hotel: I was a maid, and Tom worked at the desk."

Vicky felt her eyes welling with tears despite herself. She looked down at her hands and folded them together.

Susie tried to reassure her. "I needed to tell you this so you could understand. Tom always wants so badly to do what is right, but he feels thwarted at every turn. And because he feels all his efforts fail, I think he doesn't believe he deserves happiness."

Vicky pressed her lips together. She could well believe it.

"This business with Mr. Carmichael hasn't helped things."

Vicky stiffened at the mention of Mr. Carmichael. How much had Tom told Susie? "It was all very unpleasant the other night," Vicky admitted.

Susan nodded. "That's why I came here. In the space of a day,

Mr. Carmichael has put a stop to Tom's hotel and has ruined his credit. It appears to me that Mr. Carmichael has been trying to goad Tom into a duel since they met, and now he's finally succeeded. You must help me stop it."

The blood rushed from Vicky's cheeks. "A duel?"

"At St. James's Park this very morning."

Vicky shook her head. "But why would they fight a duel?" Her throat went dry as she remembered Mr. Carmichael's words in the garden. *I will return. Which is more than anyone can say for Halworth.* "Not . . . over me?" she whispered.

"I believe so," Susie said softly.

"Why would Tom do such a thing? It's so unlike him." She looked into Susan's eyes. "Isn't it?"

She nodded. "Yes. But he loves you."

Vicky's breath hitched in her throat. "Loves me?"

Susan nodded again.

"How do you know?"

A dimple deepened in Susan's cheek as she smiled. "It is quite plain to anyone who knows him well." Then she sobered. "He would not do this otherwise. Though he cannot realize it himself," she said, rolling her eyes.

Vicky looked down at her hands. "He told me he couldn't love me. That he felt cold inside."

Susie shook her head. "Everything he endured with his father and the aftereffects of his death have kept Tom from realizing what he wants. He said he told you he was protecting you from the earl."

Vicky looked up and nodded.

"Did he tell you anything else?"

Vicky shook her head

Susie sighed. "My mother was not the first the old earl seduced. Nor was she the last."

Vicky's stomach lurched.

Susie eyed her. "The day you saw his father beat him, Tom was trying to save a maid from his father's attentions. Tom gave her money so she could leave before . . . before the worst could happen. Whenever the earl realized the women he'd violated were with child, he dismissed them without references."

Vicky's gut churned with disgust. "Like your mother?"

Susan nodded. "The earl recognized what Tom was doing and dismissed the maid anyway. That was when he put Tom out."

Vicky swallowed, remembering Tom's face as Lord Halworth had knocked him to the floor when she'd entered the room that day. How she hadn't known what to think, but still knew Tom couldn't have done anything to that girl. Vicky shut her eyes, imagining what Tom must have witnessed and endured all those years. Her nightmares were the reality of Tom's past.

Tom had been trying to help that poor girl. But despite his efforts, he hadn't succeeded.

After that day, he'd stopped speaking to *Vicky* as well. All so he could protect her. She didn't really know if the earl would have threatened her had she continued to go to Halworth. She'd been far more sheltered and protected than any servant in his employ, but clearly Tom had thought he might. Tom had been protecting her then, and he was protecting her now. But who was going to protect him?

"When is the duel?"

Susie frowned. "At dawn."

Vicky sprang to her feet. She glanced at the clock above the mantelpiece. It was a quarter past four. The sun would be up in less than half an hour.

Vicky scratched at Althea's door, and, at hearing her sister's voice, she entered. Althea sat up in bed, looking bleary-eyed but concerned.

"You were right about Tom. I should've listened to you and spoken with him when he came here today."

Behind her, Susie coughed politely.

"I cannot delay. I'm going to St. James's Park to stop Carmichael and Tom from killing each other."

"What do you mean?" Althea asked.

"They're dueling at dawn."

Althea blanched. "You shouldn't go alone." She threw her legs out of bed.

"Susie—Miss Naseby"—Vicky gestured at Susie, who bobbed a curtsy to Althea—"is accompanying me. She's Tom's sister."

Althea frowned, then looked at Susan, then inclined her head. "Hello, Miss Naseby."

"I'm sorry we haven't time for introductions," Vicky said. "We must go."

"Of course," Althea said. "I'll call for a guard to accompany you."

"There's no time to wake anybody," Vicky said, casting a glance down the hall. "With any luck, we'll be back soon."

Althea shook her head, but Vicky dashed through the door with Susie following at her heels.

CHAPTER THE TWENTY-NINTH

This was the end of it.
—Jane Austen, *Mansfield Park*

The sun had not yet risen, but the darkness had waned enough for the first vestiges of dawn to illuminate the thin layer of fog blanketing St. James's Park and its early morning inhabitants. The mist would probably burn off in a few hours, but Tom couldn't help thinking it might be an ominous portent of what was to come.

Near him, Silby and Charles, acting as Carmichael's and Tom's seconds, loaded and examined the pistols. Dressed in a black coat and trousers, Carmichael stood beside Silby, watching the process. His stance was relaxed, but his jaw clenched and unclenched. The requisite doctor stood farther off, rummaging through his medicine bag, presumably ensuring he possessed all the necessary instruments to treat a bullet wound.

Tom turned from the scene, half of him unable to grasp that he actually waited to live or die. Despite the heaviness of his greatcoat, the chill of the morning air seeped into his chest.

He'd spent the previous evening thinking about what a mess he'd made. Susie was right. He should have told Vicky everything—about his father, about Susan, about how it had all affected his family. He'd also managed to make a mess of things with Charles. Tom should have cared for him better.

Had Tom continued thinking, he barely would have slept an hour, so he'd finished reading *Pride and Prejudice*. It had taken his mind off his troubles temporarily, but he'd again concluded that Susie was right. Like Mr. Darcy, Tom had caused countless people pain by not saying anything about his father's behavior and shouldering his family's secrets alone. He didn't know whom he could have told, but the fact remained that he had done little and people had suffered for it, which was something he'd have to live with for the rest of his days.

Tom closed his mind to the imaginary laughter of his father echoing in his ears. If the rest of Miss Austen's novels were anything like this one—where the well intentioned were redeemed and the villains revealed by their own actions—he couldn't blame Vicky for preferring the world of her books over reality. Reality was never so simple.

"Everything is prepared," Charles said.

Tom's stomach dropped. He turned and faced his brother. He looked impeccably well put together in a matching brown coat and trousers and a green, striped waistcoat. They hadn't spoken since the debacle at Carmichael's club yesterday, but Charles's features were composed and somewhat unconcerned—as though today were any other day.

It was an unalterable fact that they'd spent years in different worlds. And they'd grown into very different men, but Tom couldn't walk into this with the thought that Charles hated him for leaving him to contend with their father's cruelties alone. "Charles, I—" Tom gestured for Charles to move with him out of earshot of the others. Still holding Tom's dueling pistol, Charles followed.

When they were a safe distance away, Tom cleared his throat. "I wish to apologize. For yesterday; for the other evening. For it all, really."

Charles frowned.

"You didn't deserve to be left with Father. You were right. I should have . . . done *something*."

Charles's jaw clenched and unclenched. "Why didn't you?"

"I had no means of doing so. God knows I would have taken your place with Father if you could have been safe elsewhere."

Something in Charles's face shifted.

"I don't know what you endured with him, but you damn well didn't deserve it. None of us did."

"Lord Halworth, we are ready," Silby interrupted loudly from where he stood by the doctor.

Tom nodded once at the other men, then extended his hand to Charles.

His brother stared at it for a few moments. Then he grasped Tom's hand and shook it once. Tom exhaled.

Charles handed Tom the pistol he'd loaded. Tom gripped it in his right hand, feeling the weight. Ornate etched swirling patterns covered the silver-plated barrel, and the smooth wood of the handle felt cool to the touch. Since Carmichael was the challenger, Charles had brought their father's dueling pistols.

Tom swallowed. "If Carmichael's as good a shot as you say, Halworth might be yours after all," he said, trying to lighten the mood.

Charles didn't even crack a smile.

"Gentlemen, take your places," Silby called out.

Charles walked to Silby.

"I will count ten paces, give the signal, and then you shall both turn and fire," Silby pronounced.

Tom and Carmichael moved to the center of the lawn. Tom glanced at Carmichael's face, but the man wouldn't meet his gaze. Carmichael's eyes were hooded, his jaw still working visibly. He turned to face away, and Tom did the same. They stood back-to-back, pistols aimed at the sky.

Tom had expected something more than silence from Carmichael, but apparently, he'd decided not to indulge in any last-moment taunts or gloating. Perhaps the gravity of the occasion was affecting him. Regardless, the sooner this was over the better.

Silby began to count.

"One."

Tom gritted his teeth and took a step forward. He would make his own luck. The frost on the grass crunched under his boots.

"Two."

Tom stepped forward again, feeling somewhat unsteady. He took a deep breath and the strength began to return to his limbs. He thought of Vicky and the letter he'd given Susie to deliver in the event of his death. He wondered if Vicky would even mourn him.

"Four."

Of course she would mourn him. They'd been friends.

"Five," Silby called.

The blood drained from Tom's face. If he died, there'd be no one to stop Charles from challenging Carmichael to another duel. And if he were dead at Carmichael's hand, Charles would certainly want revenge. Tom gripped the pistol handle tighter. The chill in his torso stretched into his extremities. Maybe it wasn't too late to stop this insanity. Even if he or Carmichael didn't deliver a fatal shot, a wound could fester, causing either of them to be ill for months before dying a painful death. He assumed Carmichael didn't care to die any more than he did.

"Seven."

Carmichael and Charles had goaded him into this, and he'd foolishly believed agreeing to fight would put an end to the matter. He'd thought this duel could keep Carmichael away from Victoria. He knew now he'd been deceiving himself.

Vicky would decide for herself. All Tom could do was support her decision. That was the only claim he could make on her . . . the only claim he ever should have tried to make.

This was absurd. He could stop this. Apologize again. Swear not to interfere. That was something his father never would have done.

"Nine." Silby's voice seemed distant.

"Wait!" Tom yelled. He turned to address Carmichael, throwing his empty hand out to the side while still pointing his pistol straight in the air. Carmichael looked over his shoulder before turning to face Tom.

"Ten. Fire!"

Carmichael leveled his gun at Tom. Not moving his gun hand, Tom looked Carmichael straight in the eyes and put his other hand up in an allaying gesture.

"Fire!" Silby shouted again.

Carmichael's brows furrowed, but he waited. Tom exhaled.

Tom opened his mouth to speak. "Mr. Carmichael, I—"

A shot rang out.

Tom's eyes closed instinctively. His body tensed in anticipation of the bullet piercing his flesh. Seconds passed.

He felt nothing.

Slowly, he opened his eyes. Carmichael lay on the ground. Movement in the corner of Tom's eye turned his attention to Silby, who was wreathed in smoke. Silby struck the doctor's shocked face with the butt of a pistol.

Tom flinched at the thud it made against the man's skull. Tom's pulse jumped in his neck, but he pivoted and raised his pistol to bear on Silby, just as Charles reached for something under his coat.

Another pistol. Though he was within arm's length of Silby, Charles turned and leveled it at Tom's chest.

Time slowed to a crawl. Tom gaped at his brother and the gun in his hand. His gaze dropped to the pistol, then flew up to meet Charles's eyes. His brother stared back with a cold, unyielding glare.

"Shoot him!" Silby yelled at Charles.

Tom took a slow breath, though his pulse thrummed out of control and heat clawed its way out of his stomach into his chest.

Charles stood stock-still, his finger on the trigger. Then the corner of his mouth slanted upward. Tom blinked. Silby moved to grab the gun.

Charles turned, held Silby off with his left arm, and clubbed him in the head with the butt of the pistol. As the gun made contact, the pistol fired up into the air. Silby dropped to the ground with a thump.

Throwing his pistol aside, Charles turned back to face Tom.

Tom lowered his gun. He let go of the breath he'd been holding. "God's blood," he whispered. He released the gun's hammer and ran his left hand over the back of his neck. He took a tentative step toward his brother. "Charles, what—why . . ."

Charles produced a length of thin braided leather from his coat pocket, rolled Silby onto his stomach, and set about binding his limbs. "After you rebuffed Dain at the club that day, he decided to apprise me of what he termed 'a very lucrative proposition.' He recognized you and I were at odds, and he wanted the pieces of Halworth that adjoin Oakbridge. I decided to humor him and discover his intentions. See to Carmichael and the doctor."

Both men lay on the grass, seemingly out cold. Still eyeing Charles, Tom crossed the field and knelt by Carmichael. Blood seeped from his arm into the blades of grass. "Carmichael's shot in the arm. See if the doctor has something we can use to staunch the blood."

Charles finished binding Silby's ankles and inspected the doctor's head. "I think he'll be all right once he awakens." He brought the doctor's bag to Tom and pulled out a handful of rolled bandages. Charles knelt and started rolling one around Carmichael's wound.

"After I'd met Dain a few times, he hinted that if I were to dispatch you, I would have control of Halworth and power beyond my wildest dreams—if I allied myself with him."

Tom shook his head as the angry heat in his chest flared back to life. "Dain wanted me dead?" He'd known Dain had no honor, but he hadn't thought him capable of this. Thank God Charles had thought to see what he'd wanted. "And Silby?"

Charles continued wrapping Carmichael's arm. The blood slowly soaked through the cloth. "Dain paid him well, I take it. As for Carmichael, I gleaned that Dain wanted him eliminated because of a land deal they were partners in. As you know, I couldn't be less interested than I already am in matters of business, but it seemed to me that if Carmichael were to perish, Dain would reap all the monetary gains from their partnership. Dain had Silby pour poison into Carmichael's ear about you, primarily that our accounts were so far in arrears that you needed Victoria's dowry to survive. Knowing Carmichael, Dain believed this would lead to a confrontation. Silby and I were to ensure a duel occurred, and that neither you nor Carmichael left the field alive." He secured the last bandage with a double knot.

Tom swallowed to keep from gawking. That explained why Charles had forced his hand yesterday. "It is reassuring to hear you never planned to shoot me."

Charles smirked. "When I learned Dain wanted you dead, I played along until I was in a position to stop it." He paused and frowned down at the red splotch on Carmichael's bandage. "That's not to say I didn't consider doing it"—he looked up and caught

Tom's eye—"but only for a moment." He shrugged. "You are my brother, after all."

Tom frowned, not quite sure what that meant. He decided he didn't need immediate clarification.

Carmichael groaned. He opened his eyes and they narrowed. Whether from the pain or from the sight of Tom, Tom couldn't guess.

Carmichael's gaze appeared unfocused. "What the blazes just happened?"

"Silby shot you," Tom said.

Carmichael raised his neck. "Silby?" He looked at his arm and laid his head back upon the grass. "Why in hell would Silby shoot me?"

"He was acting under Dain's orders," Tom said. "Dain meant for us to kill each other. Charles and Silby were supposed to ensure we didn't botch the job." Which meant Carmichael had never been behind any of the incidents involving Vicky's family. Tom ran his hand through his hair.

Carmichael blinked. "Dain? I thought he might be holding a grudge when we fell out after the musicale, but . . ." He trailed off as though loath to imagine Dain's state of mind. He lifted his head again and tried to sit upright. "Where's Silby now?"

Charles took Carmichael's good arm and supported his weight so he could sit. "I have taken the pleasure of incapacitating him," Charles replied.

Carmichael tilted his head at Charles. "I take it you had a change of heart?"

Charles nodded. "Something to that effect."

"I owe you an apology, Carmichael," Tom said.

Carmichael winced as he crossed his good arm across his body to cradle his wounded one. "You've tried that twice already, Halworth."

But he meant to finish it this time. "I thought you capable of everything Dain has orchestrated. My"—*feelings for Vicky*—"my lack of control brought us to this."

Carmichael shifted. "I'll concede I thought none too kindly of you. Though I now understand your animosity. Now, where's the bloody doctor?"

Tom supposed that was the best he'd ever get by way of apology from Carmichael. He looked over his shoulder to where the doctor still lay unconscious. "Silby knocked him out." Trying to think where he could find another doctor at this hour, Tom rose to his feet. They'd deal with Dain later.

"Tom!"

Tom twisted toward the voice. Susie ran through the park toward them. When she reached them, she doubled over with exertion. He took her arm to steady her as she caught her breath.

"Thank goodness you're unhurt," she gasped. "Lady Victoria's been taken."

All Tom's breath seized in his throat.

"What do you mean?" Carmichael demanded from the ground, echoing his own thoughts.

Susan glanced down at Carmichael and then met Tom's gaze. "We were coming here to stop the duel. She was in front of me." She paused to take a breath, and Tom heard rather than felt his pulse begin that familiar tattoo. "As we neared the park entrance, a man with light brown hair jumped from a coach and grabbed her. When I tried to stop him, he knocked me to the ground. He threw Victoria into the carriage, and I pretended to be unconscious. They drove off."

All feeling drained from Tom's limbs just as wrath sparked back to life in his torso. He looked past Susie across the park, replaying the scenario in his mind's eye.

"Dain," Charles said grimly.

That sick whoreson—

Tom blinked to clear his head. They had no time to waste. The devil knew what Dain planned, but judging by what had happened to Vicky over the last few weeks, Tom had no doubt of its malevolence. "Are you all right?" he asked Susan.

She nodded. "You mustn't worry about me now."

He looked his sister up and down. She appeared well enough. He could leave her with Charles. "Which way did the carriage go?"

"Toward Green Park. Then it turned toward Piccadilly."

Tom turned to Charles. "He could be leaving town. Did he tell you of his plans?"

Charles furrowed his brow. He shook his head. "I knew nothing of this."

Tom swallowed. "Perhaps I can catch up before the carriage disappears." Frenzied worry swirled through his brain. How could he find them?

"He's going to his cottage near Richmond," Carmichael said.

Tom looked down at Carmichael, who tried to push himself up from the grass.

"How do you know?" Tom asked.

Charles supported Carmichael's good arm and managed to heft the man's bulk into a standing position.

"He mentioned the cottage to me once. He spoke of the women he had occasion to take there. I shall not elaborate in deference to this young lady's tender ears."

Tom looked at Susie. "Carmichael, this is Susan Naseby. Our sister."

Carmichael looked to Tom. "Take my horse." He briefly described the way to the cottage.

Tom nodded. "Thank you."

Carmichael's jaw worked. "Just bring Victoria back safely."

Tom set his own jaw. He'd bring Vicky back. But not for Carmichael's sake. Tom no longer held his fury at bay. It spread through him like wildfire, only to pool in his mind and obscure every thought save two. One: Dain would pay for this. Two: Vicky must know how he truly felt.

CHAPTER THE THIRTIETH

No man of common humanity, no man who had any value
for his character, could be capable of it.
—Jane Austen, *Pride and Prejudice*

er thumping heart echoed in Vicky's ears as she pulled at the cords around her wrists. Dain had tied her hands with long strips of leather so that her hands were crossed. Her arm still throbbed where Dain had grabbed her and shoved her into the carriage.

Dain sat across from her in the carriage, eyeing her with a perverse grin, a pistol in his right hand.

Vicky wriggled her wrists and sneered at him. "Just what do you hope to achieve by this?"

Dain smirked and looked out the carriage window. "Come, dear sister, I thought you more intelligent than that. Surely you can guess what I'm after."

Vicky's stomach plummeted just as her fingers itched to scratch Dain's eyes out. For all she knew, Tom could be lying dead in St.

James's Park at this very moment. All because Dain wanted to play at being a kidnapper.

"Since *I* am in the carriage and not your wife, I can only assume you wish to bargain with my father to cease Althea's separation suit." Surely the ecclesiastical court had summoned him by now. Why else would he resort to this?

Dain snorted with laughter. "That might make sense had I not a more permanent solution in mind."

Vicky frowned. What did he mean by that?

"*My* reputation shall not be sullied."

"Is that what this is about? Your reputation in society?" She sucked in a breath. "What of my sister's reputation? What about what you did to her?"

Dain leveled her with a glare. "Your sister's reputation will not be sullied if she returns to her husband."

"You have *kidnapped* your own sister-in-law! If anyone should hear of this—"

"I do not intend that anyone shall, *dear* sister. *You* are the last obstacle between me and the estate that was promised me."

Vicky's breath caught. So Dain had wanted Oakbridge all along. But the only definite way to ensure Vicky didn't inherit was to get rid of her completely. Her hands started to shake; she grasped them together to keep him from noticing.

Dain couldn't truly be a murderer. As Tom had said, he was a bully who gained what he wanted by intimidation.

Vicky raised her chin. She wouldn't let him intimidate her. "Oakbridge was never *promised* to you."

He smiled then. "Your father certainly didn't expect *you* to inherit the estate. With your bookish ways, what man of consequence and title would marry you?"

Vicky's cheeks burned with embarrassment. But Dain continued, "No, as Althea's husband, Oakbridge was meant for me. And it shall be mine. I shall have access to the two foremost jewels in the crown of the land in North Hampshire. As soon as you are gone."

Vicky's throat went dry. Dain truly thought her the last obstacle in his way.

After being injured, her father hadn't attended any social functions. Perhaps the condition of his health was still widely unknown. Dain must believe her father close to death. The only explanation for him to possibly think that would be if *he'd* been behind the attack on their coach. The attackers could have reported to Dain the severity with which they'd beat the earl.

"You said you would have two jewels?" Vicky said, trying to grasp his reasoning.

A smirk tilted his lips. "The current Lord Halworth will no longer be problematic after today, and I happen to be on close terms with his successor."

"Charles?" Vicky swallowed, disgusted at his casual attitude as he discussed Tom's demise.

"Putting Halworth into a situation where his life was in danger, however, took a little planning. Charles proved a willing pawn, and as so often happens, a solution presented itself when Carmichael made the mistake of removing me from the Chadwick musicale. Despite our business dealings, Carmichael actually threatened me to stay away from you all," Dain continued. "And how could I let *him*, a commoner with delusions of grandeur, tell me to stop seeing my own dear family?" He laughed as though Carmichael were the biggest fool in England. "Your face betrays your disdain, Victoria. I'm gratified to see your mettle has not gone astray. It makes telling you my accomplishments all the more satisfying."

Vicky scowled daggers at him. He was mad. How had they never noticed? How had he hidden it so well?

He snickered again at her expression, and explained how he'd played Carmichael's and Tom's dislike for each other against them. How he'd used Charles and Silby to ensure it came to a duel.

Silby, too, was part of Dain's horrible scheme? No wonder she couldn't seem to be rid of him. "How did you convince Mr. Silby to join you?"

He looked disappointed she hadn't guessed. "How guileless you are. Money, my dear. His father stopped paying his debts long ago, and the old man is the hearty sort—it will be many years before Silby inherits the title. I offered to pay him generously for any services rendered. The demands of Silby's pocketbook were more pressing than any scruples." He paused and regarded her with narrowed eyes. "He is, regrettably, not particularly capable. He drew more attention than I'd wished with his clumsy curricle."

Vicky's skin crawled. The runaway curricle had been a ruse. The confirmation that Silby had actually tried to kill her that day left her cold. She remembered how put out he'd acted when she'd had Tom escort her home. What might Silby have tried if she hadn't insisted?

Dain smiled, his amber eyes now as inexpressive as stone.

"At least I will have the pleasure of punishing *you* for your impudence personally. One should never let one's lackeys have all the fun."

Her stomach dropped. She sat back, though her heart threatened to burst from her chest. She needed to gauge his sincerity. "Come now, you might as well stop the pretense. You're no killer," she said, trying to sound confident.

"Am I not? You should tell that to your solicitor, Mr. Barnes."

Her palms grew clammy with sweat, and she struggled to control the trembling in her legs. He could be lying to scare her. But Carmichael had told her father Mr. Barnes had gone missing.

She looked into Dain's eyes. His eyebrows arched up, and he stared back with a slimy grin.

Then he reached into his coat pocket and retrieved a pocket watch. He held it by the chain and let it dangle in front of her nose.

Bile rose in her throat as she saw the rust-red blood encrusted on the chain. Then she saw the engraved initials on the silver surface: *EB*. Edward Barnes. Nausea rolled over her. She couldn't now doubt what Dain was capable of. And if he could do something so terrible to a man he barely knew, what would he do to her?

Still, she couldn't help glaring at him. "Why do this? You need neither money nor land."

He tucked the watch back in his pocket. "Oakbridge was promised me, and I shall have it. Halworth is but a bonus, yet one well worth it to exact my revenge on that self-righteous fool Tom Sherborne. I would have done it long ago had he not disappeared to the Continent."

Vicky recalled Tom telling her how he'd thwarted Dain when they were at Eton.

A small muscle jumped in Dain's cheek. "No one wounds *my* reputation without paying the price." Then his eyes raked her from the top of her head to the tips of her ankle boots. "A lesson you will learn well today."

Her stomach lurched. "You may have blocked the writ of *supplicavit*, but the case for the separation in the ecclesiastical court still stands."

He cut a sharp glance her way. "I can still bargain with Althea to drop the suit. When she knows I have you, she won't hesitate. That doesn't mean I need actually return you."

She swallowed hard.

His leer settled on her torso. "What a shame I didn't meet you before Althea. You would have made a deplorable wife, but I gather I would have much preferred your company in my bed."

The blood rushed from her face as another swell of bile surged upward. She coughed, trying to choke it down.

"I'm certain you'll have more vigor than that dullard I married," he said, glancing out the window.

"She had enough courage to flee from you," Vicky hissed.

He shrugged. "Courage, you call it? More of an instinct for survival, which I've seen mongrels display."

"You're repulsive! How dare you speak that way?!"

He laughed.

The sound made her limbs shake. Evil like Dain's didn't exist in the novels she'd so long escaped to—those same novels she'd insisted her own life emulate. Tom and Althea and even Mr. Carmichael had been right. She'd been so absurdly naive. And now her punishment would be death and—she knew not what else—at the hands of a madman.

"Such spirit." His eyes roved over her body.

She struggled against her bonds to keep from being sick all over the carriage.

"We'll see how much spirit you have when I'm through with you."

CHAPTER THE THIRTY-FIRST

What he means to do, I am sure I know not . . .
—Jane Austen, *Pride and Prejudice*

Tom kicked the flanks of Carmichael's horse, urging it to gallop faster. He'd just received more detailed directions from a local innkeeper and now hurtled down a country lane toward Dain's cottage. Trees grew densely on both sides of the road. He hadn't passed another building since he'd left the inn.

The early morning mist had dissipated as he'd left London and though dark clouds loomed in the distance, the weather was holding. Wet roads would've put him even farther behind Dain's carriage, so perhaps, for once, luck was on his side. He must be getting close now.

He'd been thinking of how he'd make Dain pay for every sick scheme in his sick brain. Those thoughts alone had kept Tom sane amidst the onslaught of fury, anxiety, concern, and the fifty other emotions he hadn't felt with such intensity in years. The rage inside him still blazed, crowding out rationality and reason, but he didn't care.

What good could levelheadedness do him now when Vicky was in danger? The day after the Astons' carriage was attacked, she'd told him Dain was behind it, but in jealousy he'd turned her attention to Carmichael. Yet Dain was a monster far more akin to his father than any of Henry Halworth's children had turned out to be.

Tom's fists tightened on the reins.

He shook his head, allowing the molten anger to obscure all other thoughts besides getting to Vicky. He had to be close.

Then, beyond tall trees, on the right side of the lane, a gabled Tudor cottage with dark wooden beams showing through the white plaster appeared. It was small, but well-kept, and exactly as the innkeeper had described. Relief swelled through him. Tom slowed Carmichael's horse and dismounted a good distance from the cottage.

He led the horse between the trees on the left side of the road and tied the reins to a low branch. With steady hands, he took his dueling pistol from inside his greatcoat and examined the powder in the pan.

The pan still appeared full. Yet the gun had been bouncing around in his coat during the entire ride from London. He clenched his jaw. All he could do was hope that when it came time to use it, it would fire correctly.

Tom inched his way toward the cottage through the trees, watching for any movement. A large coach sat in front of the cottage, but he saw no coachman. Tom stopped behind a hedge near the house and crouched down, listening. When he heard nothing but rustling leaves, he crept to the door on the side of the cottage. Pressing himself against the wall, he peered through the closest window, looking for any sign of Vicky. A kitchen lay beyond the door. The room stood empty save for a wooden table in the center of the room.

The handle gave under Tom's hand. The door's hinges squeaked minimally as he eased it open. He stepped past the threshold and slowly closed the door behind him.

At the far side of the kitchen, a narrow stairwell led up to another floor. Beside it stood a door leading to what he presumed was the rest of the ground floor. Tom snuck across the kitchen and put his ear to the door. No sounds of movement.

Then, from above him, a thump echoed. The blistering wrath within him flashed to life. Moving to the stairs, he mounted the steps as rapidly and quietly as possible.

Vicky cringed as Dain dropped his heavy black greatcoat to the floor. Her stomach still churned, and she squeezed her eyes shut, hoping she could keep the nausea under control.

Dain walked to the foot of the bed.

Vicky opened her eyes and gave him a defiant glare, even though she felt anything but daring. He stared at her with a depraved look in his eye. A moment later, his waistcoat fell to the ground. Vicky forced herself to breathe. Her head swam.

She couldn't believe this was happening. She was alone with a madman in a deserted cottage without hope that anyone could save her. Of course, Susie knew someone had abducted her, but Susie had been lying unconscious on the ground when they'd driven away.

And now Tom or Mr. Carmichael or both might very well be dead because of her foolhardiness. She tried to suppress the image of Tom lying on a grassy field in a pool of blood, but nothing she did could keep it from invading her mind.

When they'd arrived at the cottage, Dain had dragged her up the stairs and into this small room. Although she'd kicked and screamed and scratched at him with all her strength, she'd been no match for his crushing grip. He'd dealt two blows to the side of her head, and she'd been so dizzy with pain he'd been able to gag her, throw her on the bed, and bind her to the posts by her hands and feet with little resistance.

She tried to shut out the panic threatening to engulf her. She squashed her eyelids together to block Dain's terrible face looming over her. Her life couldn't have turned out more dissimilar from one of Miss Austen's novels. Yet even after Dain's cutthroats had nearly beaten her father to death, Vicky had continued to think all would end well with some handsome gentleman who loved her proposing marriage. She had to be the foremost imbecile in England!

Dain had ruined so many lives— Althea's, Tom's, Carmichael's, her own, and, if Dain did kill her, everyone in her family and on the estate would suffer when he gained control of Oakbridge.

If only she hadn't let Tom and Carmichael rile her. If she'd accepted one of their proposals instead of acting like a child, none of this would have happened. Dain wouldn't have had a chance to abduct her unseen in the predawn hours.

She and Tom could have been happy. He might have come to love her eventually. Susie thought he already did. But now he would be lost to her forever.

She gasped for air beneath the gag, wishing for a way out of the room—out of this nightmare—but she knew there was no escape. It was all she could do to hold back a scream. She wouldn't give him that satisfaction.

Perhaps sensing her despair, Dain grinned his sadistic smile and started to laugh.

When Tom reached the second level, he peered around the corner of the stairs. Three doors led off the hall, two on the right side of the corridor and one on the left.

Dain's voice emitted a repulsive laugh from behind the nearest door on the right. Tom pulled the hammer of his pistol back until it was fully cocked.

He rushed the door.

Wood splintered and flew as the door crashed back on its hinges.

The scene before him made the hairs on the back of his neck stand on end. Vicky lay on a bed in the center of the room, her mouth gagged and her hands and feet tied to the bedposts. Dain, down to his shirtsleeves and trousers, his outer garments lying on the floor, hovered over her.

Vicky screamed beneath the gag.

Dain turned, and Tom saw the disturbed glare of a madman.

The blaze roared in his head. He leveled his pistol at Dain's heart. "Step away from her."

"It would seem Silby and your brother have failed me. I can only hope Carmichael is lying dead in the park," Dain said with a half smile, half sneer.

As he spoke, he inched toward a table near the bed. A pistol lay on its surface.

Tom stepped forward. "I will shoot if you take one more step," he said through clenched teeth.

Dain stopped. "Somehow I doubt that. You were always one to shy away from a fight."

Tom gripped the pistol tighter as an image of his father's cruel smile flashed before him. The vile old man: Tom's unrelenting reason for never fighting. But this time, he refused to close his mind to his father's memory. Despite this scorching wrath within him, he could never be like that man. Or like the man in front of him. He knew it now as he knew his own name. As he knew he would protect Vicky and those he loved with his last breath. The inferno in his brain subsided and he felt a great weight fly off his shoulders.

The corner of Dain's mouth curved into a smirk. "As I thought. All censorious bluster and no ballocks." He stepped toward the table.

"Not today." Tom pulled the trigger. The powder in the pan flashed, exploding with a deafening boom.

Vicky squeezed her eyes shut as the blast echoed through the room. For a moment after it ended, she lay motionless on the bed. Then, she inched her eyes open.

Dain still stood. The pistol had misfired. Dain laughed, and Vicky watched in horror as Tom charged him. Their bodies collided with a thud, followed by a crash as Tom slammed Dain against the wall. But Tom was alive. Alive!

Vicky worked her right hand back and forth, trying to loosen the leather around her wrist. She cringed at each impact of fist against flesh, but she continued to struggle with the cord. Finally, the bond relaxed. She wriggled and pulled until her hand came free.

She untied her other hand, and then her feet, tore off her gag, and swung her legs over the bed.

In another moment, she'd snatched up the gun from the side table. She pulled back the hammer, swinging the weapon toward Dain, but he and Tom still struggled on the floor. She didn't dare shoot while they were so close together. Then with one quick move, Dain struck Tom in the head and pinned him to the ground.

"Stop!" she screeched, aiming the gun at Dain's back.

Despite the command, Dain didn't turn until he'd punched Tom again, this time squarely in the jaw. Still holding Tom to the floor, he turned his torso and looked at her newly liberated wrists and ankles with that same twisted sneer, his face bloodied and swollen from the fight.

"Get up," Vicky ordered. "Get off him or I'll shoot."

Dain stood slowly, and the sneer disappeared. "You couldn't possibly shoot me, Victoria." He clucked his tongue against the roof of his mouth. "I'm afraid you're too kindhearted."

He stepped closer to her, his hands raised in a placating gesture. Her arm steady, Vicky raised the gun higher.

Dain stopped moving. "Besides," he continued, "what would everyone say when it became known that you killed your own brother-in-law?"

Vicky glanced at Tom out of the corner of her eye. Blood covered his face, but he stood and took a slow step away from Dain—moving so she could shoot the fiend. Vicky almost smiled.

Tom had come after her. Just as he always did. But he trusted her to do what she must—to save them both.

And she loved him for it.

She forced her attention back to Dain. During her silence, he'd crept even closer.

"Come now, dear sister, I don't think you could live with yourself knowing you'd taken a life."

Sister? How *dare* he call her that now? She thought of how he'd broken Althea into a frail, nervous creature. She thought of poor Mr. Barnes and the family that would never see him again. She thought of her father after the attack, lying bloodied on the road. And finally, she thought of what might have happened to Tom at the duel.

All because this man before her thought himself entitled to more land and more power.

Blood roared in her ears. The world would be well rid of him. But could she really do it? Could she kill him where he stood?

"Put the gun down, and I promise I'll be gentle," he said with a confident smile.

Monster.

Vicky pulled the trigger. She smelled the acrid tang of the

smoke, felt the gun recoil in her arm, and watched Dain's face as his eyes went wide with shock. She held his gaze as he registered he'd been shot. His body crumpled to the floor.

Vicky dropped the pistol.

A moment later, Tom's strong arms surrounded her. "It's over."

She buried her head in his chest as relief washed over her.

"Are you hurt?" he asked, pushing her away from him so he could look her up and down.

"I'm fine now that you're here," she replied, wishing to be back in the safety of his arms.

His eyes lingered on something at the side of her face, and she saw the muscles in his jaw harden.

"He hit you," he said in a cold tone. His eyes flashed with anger, but he raised a gentle hand to her cheek and lightly touched the edges of the bruise.

Vicky pulled her handkerchief from her pocket to wipe the blood from his face. "Are you all right?" she asked.

The side of his mouth quirked upward as she dabbed at his split lip and battered chin. "It's nothing some rest won't mend."

Vicky lowered her hand and caught Tom's gaze. His rich brown eyes stared into hers and something fluttered in her stomach. Her heart still raced, so she took a few deep breaths. He rubbed his hands over her arms, which were cold despite the long sleeves of her dress. How had he known that?

"It seems you can no longer fault my heroic timing," he said with a smile that reached his eyes.

Her breath caught in her throat as she glimpsed the old Tom

grinning down at her. She scoffed for effect and tilted her head to the side. "I do believe *I* delivered the final blow." She couldn't help but smile back at him. "I suppose without each other, we might not have succeeded."

Tom brushed a piece of hair away from her eye. "You truly are extraordinary, Victoria Aston. You always have been."

Her heart beat so fast, she thought he must be able to hear it. She felt her cheeks flush and her breath caught again, so she looked down, away from his gaze.

"Let's go outside," he said.

She nodded.

The cold air sank into her as they left the cottage. Tom walked her toward a wood across the road, where he'd tethered a horse. She shivered and in a moment, he'd shrugged out of his greatcoat. He draped it around her shoulders and held out the sleeves for her to put her arms through. The coat still held the warmth from his body, and she relaxed into the heat. He looked down at her with a smile and buttoned the coat around her. Vicky held her breath at the intimacy of it.

As he pulled the last button at her neck through the opening, his fingers grazed her chin. A small, involuntary sound escaped her.

Gently, Tom pulled her chin up with his index finger and thumb. "So much of this trouble started because I couldn't imagine you with Carmichael. I couldn't fathom it. I thought him guilty of everything you rightly attributed to Dain. I was a bloody fool."

Vicky exhaled. "You needn't apologize—"

He shook his head. "Please, I must tell you."

She nodded for him to continue.

He moved his hand to hold hers. "When Susie told me I was like your Mr. Darcy, I didn't want to believe her. But now, I recognize that I have acted very like him: saying the wrong thing, saying nothing at all. Or waiting to say the right thing until it seems too late."

"You're not like Mr. Darcy. And I wouldn't have you be. You're *you*. And I wouldn't trade you for a dozen perfect gentlemen. The reality of you is far better than any fiction." The words came out all at once, before she could think, and as he started to smile, she realized she meant every word.

He squeezed her hand. "I've been a fool about so many things."

She exhaled. She'd been just as much a fool as he.

"All I've wanted to do is help you. To keep you safe . . . I still do. I doubt I'll ever stop."

She must have frowned, because he lifted his hand and ran his thumb along the edge of her jaw. "But not because you can't protect yourself. It's because I want you by my side every single day. Because I cannot envision a future where I can't be near you."

She shook her head in disbelief just as her heart, still beating so fast, swelled in her chest.

A crease appeared above the bridge of his nose. "I know I don't deserve you, but I want to give you all the love I know you deserve. I will try, Victoria. If you'll have me."

Vicky held her breath. For so long, she'd tried to forget him, their friendship, and her girlish hopes for the future, but she'd only been deceiving herself. She must have always loved him. And now

Tom loved her. *Loved her!* His hair, in more disarray than usual, stuck up at strange angles and his brown eyes shone down at her with hope. Vicky blinked as she felt the back of her eyes tickle with tears of utter happiness.

She was half giggling and half crying when she threw her arms about his neck and hugged him close. He stumbled forward and pulled her tight against him. She laughed as her tears fell onto his shoulder. He smelled of the morning air and faintly of toast and cinnamon, just as he had that day at Oakbridge.

After a few moments, he eased his head back to look at her face, perhaps curious to see if she was in earnest, but when their gazes locked, he grinned and crushed her back against him. "Thank God for you," he said into her ear. "All this time I thought you needed saving, but really it was me."

He took a slow step backward and she relaxed her hold on his neck, tilting her head up to see his expression. His smile was gone, replaced by a very serious look. She raised her eyebrows, wondering what had gone wrong. As she continued to gaze at him, he moved closer, angling his head until his lips hovered over hers.

She breathed but couldn't look away—didn't want to look away. He brushed her lips with his, and she sighed. His eyes crinkled at the corners, and he pulled her into him until their bodies touched. He deepened the kiss. Her lips parted as her arms tightened around his neck. The world beyond them vanished.

She lifted herself up onto her toes to get even closer. His arms encircled her, and he lifted her off the ground. Vicky melted into him, knowing she'd never felt as safe as she did now that she was in

Tom's arms. She tilted her head back and beamed at him. "You'll be hard-pressed to get rid of me now, Tom Sherborne."

Horses' hooves thundered up through the ground. Tom pulled Vicky behind him.

Charles, Althea, and one of the guards who'd tried to haul Tom down the stairs of Aston House reined in their horses. Charles and the guard both held pistols.

Tom let out a long breath. Vicky moved to his side.

Charles vaulted from the saddle. "What's the verdict?"

Tom made a grim face. "Dead."

Charles glanced at Althea and offered his hand to help her dismount.

Althea nodded once. "I don't imagine many will miss him."

Vicky's eyes sliced toward Charles. "Dain told me Charles was working with him to kill you," she whispered.

"He was only pretending so he could understand Dain's plan. If he hadn't, Carmichael and I would be dead."

Vicky exhaled. "What has become of Mr. Carmichael?"

"He is quite well, I assure you," Charles answered as he set Althea on her feet. Althea pulled Vicky into a tight embrace. "It was a clean shot through the arm." He looked at Tom. "The doctor awoke shortly after you left. He seemed well enough to do his duty. And Susan was with them. Lady Dain came to the park with Mr. Jones." Charles gestured to the guard. "I felt I owed it to you both to come along." Charles met Vicky's gaze. "I swear I had no notion he would abduct you. I must apologize."

Vicky nodded, then looked at Althea. "He planned to bargain my life to get you to drop the suit."

"Did he hurt you?" Althea asked. She glanced at Tom.

"You needn't worry over Dain again," Tom cut in.

"Was there a carriage driver?" Charles asked.

"Yes, but I never saw him," Vicky replied.

"Perhaps you could survey the perimeter of the house for him, Mr. Jones?" Charles asked the guard. The man nodded and moved toward Dain's carriage.

Tom gave Charles a pointed look, then pulled him aside. "Dain's body is upstairs. Should we alert the local authorities?"

Charles made a face. "You've killed a peer—even though he perpetrated a conspiracy to murder you, it will not go well for you."

"Actually," Vicky cut in, "I—"

"Tom did nothing of the kind," Althea stated.

They all looked at her.

"Lord Dain and I were beset by robbers," Althea continued. "Lord Halworth ran them off, but arrived too late to save my husband from his fate."

Tom stared at Althea.

Charles cleared his throat. "Are you quite certain—"

"I will not have Tom or Victoria or any of us suffer any more than we have for Dain's crimes. This is our only option."

Tom glanced at Vicky. Her lips parted as she regarded her sister. "Thea, you needn't do this for me. I did what I had to, but—"

"No 'buts,' Vicky," Althea said, raising her chin. She looked at Charles and Tom. "I am determined, gentlemen."

Tom held her gaze. Hers did not waver.

Charles nodded. "Your guard. Can we rely on his discretion?"

"Oh, I think so," Althea said, glancing toward the man with the hint of a smile.

Tom raised his brows. Jones seemed devoted to his job—or was he devoted to his employer?

Charles grinned. "Very well. I shall take care of appearances in the house. I'll leave Mr. Jones to you, Lady Dain."

Althea shook her head and pressed Vicky's hand. "Feel at liberty to call me Althea again. I am no longer Lady Dain—in name, perhaps. But never, ever again."

CHAPTER THE LAST

Let other pens dwell on guilt and misery.
—Jane Austen, *Mansfield Park*

Two and a half months later, after the scandal of Lord Dain's death had disappeared from the pages of the society papers and the immediate memories of the gossipmongers, the Astons, the Sherbornes, and the Carmichaels gathered at Oakbridge to celebrate Althea's freedom. It was an informal affair held in the early afternoon under two large white tents on one of Oakbridge's lawns. Bowls overflowing with flowers, tiered trays of petit fours, and artfully arranged pyramids of fruit adorned two round tables. The hosts and guests sat at a long rectangular table under the other tent, dining on cold roasted venison, sea asparagus, Stilton, and pigeon pie.

Vicky caught Tom's eye. He tilted his head toward her and smiled. She beamed back, then looked out beyond the tent to the gardens, now blooming with color under the summer sun. How good it was to be home. And Oakbridge seemed all the more cheerful now that the unpleasantness with Dain had ended. Oakbridge was safe once more.

"How did you manage to get your horses back?" Carmichael prompted Tom from across the table. He sat near the head of the table next to Althea, who sat between him and Vicky's father. "Lady Dain tells me it was something of a coup."

"It was Althea's idea, actually," Vicky said with a smile at her sister.

Althea shrugged.

"Modest as usual," Tom said. "Charles and I mentioned to Vicky and Althea that Dain had purchased our horses at Tattersall's. As nearly all Dain's property would go to the next viscount, Althea, Mr. Jones, and I went to Dain's town house to see if he'd stabled them there."

Vicky cast an eye at the broad-shouldered, ginger-haired Mr. Jones standing at the edge of the tent. At Althea's request, he'd decided to stay on as her personal guard. After Dain's death, Althea no longer looked over her shoulder in fear, but Mr. Jones's quiet presence seemed to offer her an extra measure of serenity.

"Dain's stable master was the one person who ever helped me in that house," Althea said. "So I thought he might help again."

Tom nodded. "When she told him Dain was dead—it was not yet widely known—he expressed concern that the new Lord Dain would not keep him on. I offered him the same position at Halworth Hall. After that, we spirited the horses out of Dain's stables. She rode one and I the other," Tom admitted.

Vicky grinned at her sister. How wonderful it was to see her nearly back to her old self.

Carmichael inclined his head to Althea. "Well done, madam." Then he said to Tom, "It certainly sounds more interesting than resting in bed for weeks without the use of your arm."

Unlikely as it seemed, Charles's efforts to uncover Dain's intentions had actually managed to win Mr. Carmichael's respect. To make amends for the damage he'd done with Tom's backers, Carmichael had decided to partner with Lord Axley to fund Tom's hotel. He, Tom, and Charles could now have proper conversations without resentment. Carmichael also seemed genuinely fond of Susie, as did his mother.

After everything, Vicky had visited Mr. Carmichael in London. She'd expressed her gratitude to him and told him marriage was no longer in her immediate purview. He hadn't been happy, but he'd seemed to grasp something had happened between her and Tom at the cottage. Although she and Tom hadn't yet decided anything, with Dain gone, she was in no rush.

Vicky hoped Mr. Carmichael would eventually move on. He hadn't ever truly understood her. Besides, a man like him was sure to find more than his share of women vying to marry him.

Vicky's father chimed in. "At least your dear mother was kind enough to care for you, Carmichael," he said, nodding at Mrs. Carmichael across the table.

Mrs. Carmichael laughed gaily. "It was no holiday, I assure you, Lord Oakbridge."

The table broke into laughter.

Vicky's father continued, "*My* family left me all alone while they went to the theater and balls and—"

Vicky, her mother, and Althea protested loudly at his exaggeration, while the men laughed.

"Well, Lord Oakbridge, I fear the ladies of your family treated you poorly," Carmichael remarked in a tone that meant he was playing along. "I was lucky, for not only was my mother by my side, but Miss Naseby took it upon herself to care for me."

"I had no choice after Charles left the park to help Tom rescue Lady Victoria," Susie said a little farther down the table.

Charles rolled his eyes. "It's not as though we left him wounded without *any* help," he protested. "The doctor was awake by then. Between the three of them, the situation was well in hand."

Susie raised her brows. "I nearly went to get a magistrate to listen to Mr. Carmichael explain what had happened."

"Thankfully, I had the presence of mind to emphasize to Miss Naseby that dueling was illegal," said Mr. Carmichael. "When Silby woke, I told him he had better disappear if he didn't want me prosecuting him for attempted murder."

Vicky exhaled. It was a good thing Mr. Carmichael had, or Silby's involvement with Dain might have called their story about Dain's death into question. Thankfully, they hadn't heard from Silby since that day. According to their acquaintances in London, he seemed to have vanished entirely.

Charles, meanwhile, was keeping busy now that Tom had split the responsibilities of running the estate between the two of them. They were also planning to start a horse-breeding program—with

Vicky's help, of course—using Horatio as the first stud. After Horatio's brief showing at Tattersall's, various lords and horse enthusiasts had expressed interest in breeding him with their English Thoroughbred mares. Even Mr. Carmichael was planning to breed one of his mares with Horatio.

Vicky looked around the table at the smiling faces of the people she loved. She relaxed as their laughter rang out beyond the confines of the tent. She glanced at Tom, and his slow grin warmed her from the inside out. Unbidden, the thought that her life had finally taken on the guise of one of Miss Austen's novels popped into her head. Perhaps it would continue to do so for some time, but Vicky would not worry over when circumstances might once again change. She would always love Miss Austen's stories, but after all that had transpired, Vicky no longer believed life could be summed up by one author's perspective of the world. For why else would so many books exist if not to impart different truths about life and all its complexities? Indeed, as much as Vicky had always wanted to emulate Elizabeth Bennet, she now realized she was more than content to simply be herself.

Later, when everyone had eaten their fill and the party dispersed—some moving indoors to escape the humid afternoon warmth, some starting a croquet game on the lawn next to the tents, and some disappearing into the grotto to see the trickling fountains—Tom offered Vicky his arm.

"Could I persuade you to join me for a walk?"

She peered at him through her lashes. "I believe I could be persuaded."

They strolled through the gardens until Tom stopped at the base of a hill crowned with mature oaks. Tom grinned as he tilted his head toward the ancient oak tree they'd often climbed as children.

"What had you in mind?" she asked with a laugh.

"A race, of course," he replied with mock seriousness.

"Indeed?" She glanced down at her daffodil-yellow dress. "I'm hardly appropriately attired."

"When has that ever stopped you?" he asked, his eyes crinkling with amusement.

She raised her chin. "Quite right." Then she took off, sprinting toward the top. She giggled at his surprised shout and ran harder. The hill sloped steeply enough to take her breath. Tom's boots thumped on the grass behind her. They'd almost reached the tree.

He passed her as they reached the hillcrest, and she laughed again with a mixture of happiness and indignation as he pretended to stumble. Her hand shot out and touched the tree seconds before his.

"So unjust," she said, catching her breath.

"I believe you're the one who got a head start," he said, taking a step closer.

She lifted her chin and smiled. "To you, I meant."

He raised his brows as he took her hand. "You won fair and square."

She swallowed. How didn't he need great gulps of air as she did? "You always used to *let* me win," she said. Her cheeks, still warm from the race, heated even more as his gaze locked with hers.

He stepped closer and covered her hand with his other palm. She dragged in another breath, unable to look away from his earnest brown eyes.

"Then, you were not the strong, capable lady who saved my life."

Her breath caught. "What has that to do with anything?"

"You're far too determined for me to give you an advantage you didn't ask for—or take, in this case."

Though she thought him rather wonderful for saying so, she narrowed her eyes. "You know me too well." She wet her lips, wishing he would kiss her. With everything that had happened since the day at Dain's cottage, they'd rarely been alone together.

Then he laughed. "It occurs to me that our situation is far more similar to Emma and Mr. Knightley than Elizabeth and Mr. Darcy." He'd just finished *Emma*, after completing the other three of Miss Austen's novels. "I live on the neighboring estate, we grew up together—"

"I believe I told you my stance on fictional gentlemen, Tom Sherborne."

"That they're what every lady truly desires?" he teased.

She gave a short laugh. "That." She bobbed her head. "And I wouldn't exchange you for the best of them."

That devastating smile of his that came on by degrees warmed his eyes until she couldn't look away.

"You never actually gave me an answer, you know," he said.

Her lips parted. His proposal. She never had answered it. But he hadn't broached it again either. "I wasn't certain you still wanted to—"

He cut her off with a kiss that stole her arguments, stole her doubts, and stole her heart all over again.

He squeezed her hand. "Will you despise me if we wait until I have more than debts to offer you?"

"Never, but with your new partners for your hotel, I cannot imagine it will be long."

He winced. "It could be years."

She shrugged and clutched his hand tighter. "I think you under-estimate yourself, but I am quite content to stay here until we are both ready." Her gaze flicked below them to the house and the ver-dant fields and dells stretching out as far as they could see. "And until then, I'll only be a few miles away."

He smirked at her obvious delight. "What will your parents say?"

She inclined her head. "These are *our* lives, are they not?"

He nodded solemnly and brushed a stray lock of hair away from her cheek with gentle fingers. "Very well. From this day on, we make our own future."

Vicky raised herself up on her toes and kissed him. She lifted her chin and beamed at the boy she knew and loved so well. "Together."

HISTORICAL NOTE

As I was creating the story for this novel and began researching marriages and divorces in Georgian and Regency England, I discovered that, despite what I'd almost always read in historical novels, it *was* actually possible for a woman to divorce her husband in this era. In fact, there's even a divorce in *Sense and Sensibility*. The woman Colonel Brandon loves as a young man is forced to marry his elder brother. Due to the brother's neglect, she commits adultery and he divorces her, a fact notably absent from many TV and film adaptations.

In the eighteenth and first half of the nineteenth century, the word "divorce" was used interchangeably for the Parliament-granted divorce and for (what I've termed) a legal separation that was granted by the ecclesiastical (church-controlled) courts. The Parliamentary divorce was the kind of divorce we know of today; the legal separation meant the couple would be legally unbound in every way, except they didn't have permission to remarry. For clarity's sake, I opted not to use the word "divorce" as they did then, and have used the term "legal separation" to delineate between the two types.

In a case like Althea and Dain's, two easier courses of action actually existed: you could simply walk away from your marriage (abandonment), or you could draw up a mutually agreed-upon private separation agreement. It's likely that most unhappy couples used these options rather than involving the courts. If a wife abandoned her husband, however, she would have lost all her personal property. Of course, as I mentioned, Dain had no interest in giving Althea (or her eventual inheritance) up willingly by agreeing to a private separation agreement.

As you might expect, far more options existed for a man to be rid of his wife than for a wife to be rid of a bad husband. However, the courts *did* make a distinction between a couple who couldn't get along (generally because of adultery) and abusive husbands (recorded abuse was almost exclusively by men). By the early 1800s, one or two physical confrontations or even just threats of violence would be enough grounds for a separation.* A number of documented cases exist where wives divorced their husbands for cruel behavior.

In one such case (*Turst v. Turst*), the husband beat his wife to force her to give him sole control of her property. When she refused, he hid their children from her, then threatened to throw her in a madhouse where she'd never be found. She escaped and lived under

*Lawerence Stone, *Road to Divorce*, 205

a different name, visited only by her brother. Then, after nine years, her husband found her again, kidnapped her, locked her in a room, and beat her—again to force her to sign her property over to him. After at least four days of this treatment, a maidservant saved her. In 1738, the wife sued her husband for divorce and the ecclesiastical court ruled in her favor. She was entitled to alimony from her husband, but unfortunately, she never achieved contact with her children. This is only one example of a real case of marital cruelty. There are many far more graphic and sad.

As I mentioned, the only way for a couple to be able to remarry was to petition Parliament to grant a divorce (which was the equivalent of what we think of as a divorce today). However, Parliament only gave men these divorces, the logic being that men shouldn't be forced to have heirs who weren't their actual children. And in the days of no DNA or paternity testing, a man could never be certain a child was his if he suspected his wife was committing adultery. The divorce of Lord and Lady Boringdon that Althea and Vicky discuss in Chapter Ten is one such case. Lady Boringdon took up with Sir Arthur Paget (a diplomat, Member of Parliament, and Privy Councillor) after her husband had taken a mistress. Lord Boringdon then sued for divorce, Parliament dissolved their marriage in February 1809, and two days later, Lady Boringdon and Sir Arthur Paget married in Heckfield, Hampshire. They then moved to Sir Arthur's estate in Southampton, where they lived by all accounts happily until his death in 1840. They had nine children.

Women *could* sue for separations on the grounds of a husband's adultery, but they only won rarely and usually with extenuating circumstances. As they generally have throughout history, ladies definitely held the short straw, but they did have *some* legal options. If you care to learn more on the subject of marriages and divorces during this period, Lawrence Stone's *Road to Divorce* and *Uncertain Unions and Broken Lives* have been invaluable to me. I have tried to be as accurate as possible regarding all divorce/separation proceedings that would've taken place during 1817, but I've made some deliberate omissions, and I hope I'll be forgiven if there are any slight inaccuracies in this work of fiction.

Hotels did exist in London in small numbers during this period. They were generally places where gentlemen stayed if they didn't have a house in the city or for travelers who needed to buy time while they looked for lodgings to rent. The luxurious, grand hotel Tom envisions—emphasizing customer comfort, cleanliness, and all manner of amenities—existed in other European cities but had not yet made its way to London.

The glass armonica Emily Chadwick plays was an instrument invented by Benjamin Franklin in the 1760s after watching performers creating music with water glasses. The glass armonica's lilting sounds briefly appear in the 1999 film version of *Mansfield Park*. Mozart and Beethoven both composed music for the glass armonica. Though the music the instrument made sounded beautiful, the bowls were made with lead glass. In the following decades, rumors surfaced that the instruments were making those who played them ill. To this day, it's unclear whether there was enough lead in the glasses to cause lead poisoning. Lead was present in many materials during the eighteenth and nineteenth centuries, so lead poisoning was extremely common. Benjamin Franklin himself lived a long life. Regardless of the truth, the instrument fell out of favor in the nineteenth century.

"Gifted" animals made interesting attractions in Britain, starting in the seventeenth century. Toby the "sapient pig" was possibly the most well-known of these animals in the early 1800s. Toby toured the country with his owner (who turned out to be a skilled illusionist) and made a sensation whenever he appeared at fairs, shows, and pleasure gardens. Toby was renowned for his many abilities, which included reading, playing cards, telling time, and guessing people's ages and even their thoughts. In 1817, he even published his own "autobiography"! Vicky's hope of meeting an oracular pig was my little nod to Hen Wen in Lloyd Alexander's The Chronicles of Prydain.

The novels of Ann Radcliffe that Vicky thinks are sensational nonsense are what is now referred to as Gothic literature. At the time, Mrs. Radcliffe's books were called romances, so I've refrained from using the term "Gothic" in the book. Critics of the time generally thought of Gothic novels as cheap entertainment, but Radcliffe's novels were usually considered the exception. Her books were wildly successful (so much so that Radcliffe became the highest-paid professional writer of the 1790s), so I imagine even someone like Tom who'd been living in Switzerland would have read her novels. Jane Austen pokes gentle fun at Radcliffe's novels in *Northanger Abbey*, which, along with *Persuasion*, was published in December 1817, after the events of *Dangerous Alliance* take place.

William Godwin, the author of the novel *Fleetwood* (published 1805), that Vicky finds so uncomfortable to read to her father is now perhaps better remembered for being the father of Mary Shelley and the husband of Mary Wollstonecraft than for his own political and philosophical works and novels. His novels also contain some Gothic influences. His book *The Adventures of Caleb Williams* (1794) was one of the first mystery novels ever written and became a great success. *Fleetwood*, however, was a commercial failure, possibly due to its violent content.

Jane Austen was known to have many fans in her lifetime, and by the time *Emma* was published in 1815, she was receiving letters from members of the aristocracy telling her how much they enjoyed her stories. Apparently, the prince regent, who became the de facto king of England after King George III went mad, kept a set of her novels in all of his lodgings. Though during her life, her books were published only under the guise of "a lady," near Austen's home in Chawton, Hampshire (where she revised *Sense and Sensibility* and *Pride and Prejudice* and wrote *Mansfield Park*, *Emma*, and *Persuasion*), her family didn't make an effort to hide her identity. Jane Austen died on July 18, 1817, very soon after the events of *Dangerous Alliance* come to an end. Today, two centuries after the anniversary of her death, she has fans the world over. She is, as Virginia Woolf wrote in 1932, "the writer whose books are immortal."

One reason I love to read and write about this era is that by the end of the eighteenth century, even the English upper classes thought affection on both sides should be a prerequisite for marriage. Before then, advantageous—and often affectionless—marriages were the norm. By this period, the demands of the heart were finally taking priority over parents' agendas when it came to making a match. Nevertheless, if you were really lucky, you could secure both! I hope you have enjoyed reading about the Astons and the Sherbornes and their small slice of life in late Georgian England.

ACKNOWLEDGMENTS

Dangerous Alliance's journey from story idea to the book you're reading now is a long one—fourteen years in total. There were long stretches where I'd set it aside, but something would always compel me to come back. As the culmination of a goal I've had for so long, I have many wonderful people to thank who have helped and supported me over the years. To all my relatives and friends who've encouraged me and been so excited for me on this odyssey, I can't possibly name you all, but you know who you are, and you have my love and gratitude.

One of my initial readers was my thesis advisor at the U.S.C., Gina Nahai. Thank you, Gina, for being one of the first people outside my family to give me the confidence to believe I could be an author. My lovely writer friends, Kate Abbott, Rebecca Chastain, Delilah Marvelle, Tara Creel, and Lana Pattinson, read various versions of *Dangerous Alliance* out of the goodness of their hearts, gave me feedback on what I could do better, and steeled my resolve to keep revising and querying. Ladies, I salute you with hugs and a golden quill. To all my friends in the Novel Nineteens, thank you for your support and enthusiasm as we've gone through this exciting and sometimes daunting debut year together.

Thank you so much to Jessica Cluess, Alexa Donne, Shelley Sackier, Samantha Hastings, and Tobie Easton for your wonderful blurbs and generosity. I appreciate it more than I can say.

Many thanks to Brenda Drake and everyone involved in Pitch Wars 2016, including my fellow Pitch Warriors for the community, the information sharing, and the happy squealing over Twitter and Facebook. Of course, I can never speak of Pitch Wars without professing my gratitude to Tobie Easton, who picked *Dangerous Alliance* to mentor despite having an embarrassment of choices, helped me see all the issues I could no longer recognize after revising the book through so many iterations, and ended up being one of the greatest friends I could ask for. Thank you, Tobie, for talking me through difficulties and complications (both real and imagined) more times than I can count, for your selflessness, for your innate ability to cut to the root of a problem in both writing and in life, and for always being there. In my humble opinion, you're simply the best.

A million and one thanks must go to my editor Kristen Pettit for falling in love with *Dangerous Alliance*, for helping me strengthen it further, and for making it possible for my manuscript to become an actual, physical book. Thank you to Kasi Turpin for creating the gorgeous font on the cover and to Jessie Gang for designing such a beautiful book jacket and interior that evokes the tone and feel of the story so perfectly. Thank you also to Clare Vaughn, Jessica Berg, Gwen Morton, Alison Klapthor, Meghan Pettit, Shannon Cox, Kristopher Kam, and everyone at HarperCollins who worked on *Dangerous Alliance*. And of course, thank you so very much to my amazing, indomitable agent Jennifer Unter for your professionalism, your experience, your guidance, and everything else you've done to help make this dream of mine come true.

Finally, I must thank my family who has loved and supported me and truly made me feel like I could make my goals become reality. Cheryl and Manouch, thank you for taking me into your family and for all your aid and encouragement over the years. I love you guys. Shaida, thank you for reading *Dangerous Alliance* so many times, for going to writing events with me, and for all the rest of it.

Big hugs and thanks to my brother, Aaron, for always providing me with a different perspective and always having my back. To my sister, Mariella, thank you for listening when I've needed to vent, for cheering me on, for loving my characters as much as I do, and for continually being the best sister ever.

My parents brought me up with a shining example of what love should be, instilled a love of reading and books in me from the time I was a toddler, gave me the confidence to believe I could make my dreams come true, and buoyed me in so many ways while I pursued this dream. Mom, thanks for all the long nights you stayed up reading me library books when I was a kid and for unapologetically introducing me to great romance novels at the right time.

To my dad, Jonathan Cohen, whose love of books was boundless, who couldn't have been more encouraging when I decided I wanted to be a writer, and who was always excited to read another version of *Dangerous Alliance*, I wish you could have seen this day. I can imagine your face and what you'd say and do, though, and I know you'd be as thrilled as I am. Thank you for always inspiring me, Dad. I love you always.

And to Nasson: you deserve infinite thank yous for being my best friend, my biggest fan, and my staunchest advocate. I love you for everything you've done and everything you continue to do, and I feel lucky every single day to have you as my original YA hero.